What others have said about John O'Hara:

"O'Hara's stories as a whole provide the best conversation in America. O'Hara was evidently in love with life itself, and his esthetic purposes were a direct extension of this attitude."
—Frank McShane, *The New York Times Book Review*

"It was in a proud loneliness that John O'Hara spent his prodigiously productive lifetime, creating a body of work of magnificent dimensions. He wrote fearlessly and bravely . . . No writer in this country in this century has tried harder to achieve the excellence he claimed.

" 'It isn't bragging if the guy does what he says he's going to do.' "

—George V. Higgins, *Harper's*

"More than any other American novelist, O'Hara has both reflected his times and captured the unique individual for generations to come. . . . Deserves the Nobel Prize."
—*The Los Angeles Times*

"Few writers have a better ear, a crisper style, a swifter punch."
—*The New York Times*

Other books by John O'Hara available from Carroll & Graf Publishers

From the Terrace
Hope of Heaven
Sermons and Soda Water
Ten North Frederick
A Rage to Live

John O'Hara

The Lockwood Concern

Carroll & Graf Publishers, inc.
New York

To Barklie McKee Henry
who many times has
proven himself
a friend

Reprinted by arrangement with Random House, Inc.

First Carroll & Graf edition 1986

Carroll & Graf Publishers, Inc.
260 Fifth Avenue
New York, NY 10001

ISBN: 0-88184-217-6

Manufactured in the United States of America

BOOK 1

□

ON Sunday afternoons people would drive out to have a look at George Lockwood's wall, and sometimes they would see, from a distance, George Lockwood doing the same thing they were doing. He was there every day, had not missed a day since the first pick had cut into the ground.

He never spoke directly to the workmen, never complained at the slowness of their work, never praised them, never addressed them individually, although he knew most of them. Some days when he visited the place he would look at the wall for a few minutes, then turn away and go back to his car, and the workmen would know that he was disgusted with their lack of progress. Other days he would come out in the morning, stay till noon, be driven home for lunch, and return to stay all afternoon. When this occurred every man was handed a dollar bill at quitting time, with no explanation given and none needed; George Lockwood was pleased. Sometimes the dollar bonus was distributed for six days running; other times a week would pass with no bonus at all.

The wall was being built of brick, two feet thick and eight feet high above ground. It was to have a two-inch concrete top, in which would be embedded iron spikes at intervals of twelve inches. The wall was a sizable project: it surrounded thirty acres of land.

The land had been farmed continually since the early Eighteenth Century. It was land that sloped gently, the high land of the Oscar Dietrich farm, which was now owned by George Lockwood. Earlier Dietrichs had cleared about twenty acres of the land, leaving timber above, which was to the south, and more timber to the east and west. It had not been the best land on the Dietrich farm, and in recent decades it had been used as pasture for the Dietrich Holsteins. George Lockwood was building his wall on a strip that had been cut out of the timber to the south, east and west, so that there would be a stand of trees on both sides of the wall. Thus the property would be surrounded by trees as well as by brick and mortar, since George Lockwood planned to plant trees on both sides of the front, or north, wall.

The thirty acres was not all that George Lockwood owned. He had bought the entire two hundred acres of the Dietrich farm and the parcels of timberland to the south. People who wondered what he was going to do with the Dietrich farm had their answer when the wall was half finished: George Lockwood sold the Holsteins and the farm equipment, and razed the Dietrich farmhouse, barns and outbuildings. In a month's time the Dietrich farm was no more; an establishment that had existed for more than a hundred years vanished in a few weeks. Some said it was a sin and a shame, some said it was a crime; but others said that Oscar Dietrich must have got a good price; Oscar always knew what he was doing. He moved to the Lebanon Valley and bought another farm.

Pretty soon a second gang of workmen were being employed by George Lockwood in a project that was the opposite of the wall-building: the new men were engaged in removing the Dietrich fences; stone, post-and-rail, snake, and wire. As time went on the Sunday visitors to George Lockwood's wall could see that all traces of previous ownership were being systematically obliterated. Then, one Sunday in the middle of May, they saw that the wall was complete, that a tall temporary board gate was in place.

A door, with Yale lock, had been cut out of the board gate. On the door was painted the order: Keep Out. All through the summer the people continued to visit the Lockwood place, but the gate was always closed, and they could not see what they knew to be going on behind the wall: George Lockwood was building a house.

In the town of Swedish Haven, two miles to the east, no one had been surprised by George Lockwood's decision to build a high brick wall with spikes on the top. The unusual, they said, was usual for George, and it was correctly guessed that he had first built his wall so that as few people as possible would be able to see what kind of house he was building. The contract for the wall had been given to a Swedish Haven man; the main contractor for the house was from Hagerstown, Maryland, and he brought with him his own carpenters and bricklayers. The plumbing contract was given to a Reading firm; the electrical work was being done by a Philadelphia firm; the interior woodwork was assigned to some Italians in New York; the painting, plastering, and paper-hanging were being done by a Fort Penn outfit, the roofing by a gang from Gibbsville. The landscaping was in the hands of a man from Westbury, Long Island; the driveways were being built by a Port Johnson company. Workmen who lived within fifty miles of the Lockwood house came and went each day by truck; the contractors, foremen, and workmen who lived at a greater distance were put up in Gibbsville and Swedish Haven hotels and boarding houses. At the outset the main contractor would say to each sub-contractor: "What I want you to understand is that Mr. Lockwood minds his own business and wants people to mind theirs. When this house is finished he doesn't want any local people to know their way around it. That's what he's paying good money for. First-class work, and his privacy. And you've got to admit, he doesn't haggle over money. When I think of that overtime . . ." The subcontractors and workmen who arrived after the wall was completed made quick estimates of the cost of the wall, and there were those among them who wished they had put a higher price on their own work. A man who would spend twenty thousand, thirty thousand dollars on a wall was not likely to quibble over a few hundred. But there were others among the sub-contractors who had dealt with rich men before, and who had learned that a rich man might spend a lot of money to do something unusual, but he would know what he wanted and would see that he got it.

These latter sub-contractors were soon congratulating themselves on their guesses about George Lockwood. He came to the a-building house every day, rain or shine or stifling heat, wearing a floppy Panama, dressed in a crash-linen suit, and carrying a cane, which was unusual for a man in his early fifties. He would stroll about in the grounds, nodding but never speaking to the foremen and workmen except to say "Excuse me" when he got in the way. He would climb ladders and walk precariously placed planks. On the very hottest days he would sometimes help himself to a dipperful of water from the workmen's pail and fan himself with his Panama and wipe under his collar with a fancy silk handkerchief, but he stayed on, never lingering too long over any particular job, but visiting each job several times a day. And he seemed to miss nothing. The workmen early realized that when he visited a particular job several times a day, he was noticing something; for the next day the foreman on that job would make some changes in the work already done. The orders to the foremen came down from the sub-contractor, who got his instructions from the main contractor, who was the only man on the job with whom George Lockwood would have conversation.

The main contractor, Robert Brackenridge, had a shanty on the grounds. In it he had an unfinished table, some camp chairs, dozens of tubes containing blueprints, fire extinguishers, first aid kit, a telephone, an army cot, a 16-gauge shotgun, several kerosene lamps, a small oaken filing cabinet, a Pennsylvania Railroad and a Prudential Insurance calendar, a water cooler, a board on which hung numerous tabbed keys, and a two-burner kerosene stove. In this shanty, and nowhere else, was George Lockwood seen to sit down, and workmen in the vicinity could overhear conversations through the screened windows. They learned little except that Lockwood called the contractor Robert, and that he was thoroughly acquainted with the blueprints and the details of the specifications. When a sub-contractor was called to the shanty for a conference, Robert Brackenridge would do all the talking, while George Lockwood, smoking pipe or cigarette, nodded in approval.

For shelter from the summer showers the foremen and workmen had an army mess tent, sides removed, and there they would gather to eat their lunch, sitting on stacks of building materials that also needed protection from the rain. The workmen were from so many different places that the electricians tended to keep with electricians, carpenters with carpenters, but they were united in their baffled curiosity about the man who was footing the bills. These were men with special skills; well paid, independent, quietly proud American artisans, who could do things that George Lockwood could buy but could not do himself. They respected his understanding of their work, and they agreed among themselves that it was better to work for him than for a man who would waste their time in friendly conversation and picky suggestions. They quickly—and accurately—surmised that George Lockwood had made a study of the art of building a good house, and it did not matter to them that they did not like him. In a few months the house would be finished, and they would be off on other jobs, and they would remember him as a man who had treated them right without patronizing them. They would remember the day he killed two copperheads with his cane, the cane that they had thought was only the sign of a dude; and they would remember how he had taken charge when one of the bricklayers had a sunstroke and fell off a scaffolding. He had the bricklayer carried to the shade of the tent, showed the other bricklayers how to rub the man's wrists and ankles, and got some turpentine from the painters and applied it to the back of the man's neck. When the man came to, Lockwood made him stay where he was until the doctor arrived from Swedish Haven to examine him for concussion and broken bones. On that occasion there never had been any question as to who was giving orders. "Turpentine. I never heard of that before," said one of the men. "Where would he find out a thing like that?"

"Where does he find out a lot of things?" said another. "He don't need Bob Brackenridge. Bob Brackenridge needs him."

Two days later, when the bricklayer returned to work, George Lockwood looked at him as though he had never seen him before, and quickly turned away as the man came forward to thank him.

In mid-October the house was finished except for certain interior woodwork that was being done by the Italians from New York. The lighting and the plumbing were functioning, and the furnace had been tested and proven satisfactory. The house was ready for occupancy, and Robert Brackenridge returned to Hagerstown with a bonus cheque in his wallet. The Italians were three in number, and their English was scanty. They had not become acquainted with the other workmen, who spoke English or Pennsylvania Dutch, and they looked down on the few Italians in Swedish Haven, who were pick-and-shovel laborers. George Lockwood's Italian woodworkers wore leathern aprons, but beneath the aprons were waistcoat and trousers, silk shirt, collars and neckties. As soon as the last of the other workmen had departed, the Italians went to work in the room that was to be George Lockwood's study, and even though they were alone in the house, they kept the study door locked, admitting no one but Lockwood himself.

The room as Brackenridge and his men had left it contained a large fireplace, to one side of which was a large closet door. Brackenridge had suggested another place for the closet, but Lockwood had overruled him. Now the Italians removed the door, cut away the ceiling and flooring of the closet, and installed a winding stairway that started in a closet in George Lockwood's bedroom, directly above the study, and continued down into the cellar. It was thus possible for George Lockwood to go from his bedroom to the cellar without using the main staircase or the kitchen stairs, and if he wished he could likewise go from his bedroom to his study unseen. The bedroom closet, which Brackenridge had described as enormous, was now reduced in size. The Italians installed a new closet wall, which was a large panel that fitted into grooves and could be rolled up to allow entrance to the hidden stairway. The original closet door in the study was replaced with paneling that matched the rest of the paneling, but it was still a door, hung on invisible hinges and opened by pressing a spring that was disguised as a gargoyle, one of a row of gargoyles that were carved out of the mantelpiece. The door could not be opened accidentally by a touch or a bump; the gargoyle had to be turned like a doorknob and then firmly pushed before the spring would be released. With a few drops of oil once a year, the mechanism would last as long as the house, and George Lockwood expected the house to last two centuries. Egress from the hidden stairway in the cellar was made through a sliding panel similar to the one in George Lockwood's bedroom. As in the bedroom, this panel was the back wall of a closet, which had been designated in the plans as storage place for old correspondence, receipted bills, cancelled cheques, and the like.

Full of compliments for the craftmanship, and with bonus cheques in their pockets, the Italians put index fingers to their lips and crossed their hearts, shook hands and grinned at George Lockwood, and went back to New York. The house was now almost ready to be shown to Geraldine Lockwood.

George Lockwood had a last look around the house, the four-car garage, and the grounds while it was still daylight on an afternoon in October 1926. Shortly after four-thirty o'clock he got into his little Packard roadster and moved toward the iron gates that now hung in place. Deegan, the temporary watchman from the detective agency, swung open the gates. "Goodnight, Mr. Lockwood," he said. "See you tomorrow."

"No, not tomorrow, Deegan," said George Lockwood. "Tomorrow I'm going to sleep all morning."

"Well, I take that for a good indication," said Deegan. "In other words, the job is finished satisfactory?"

"Now it's all up to Mrs. Lockwood."

"Well, all I got to say is it's a feast to the eye. I never seen such a beautiful house in all me life. A real residence, palatial, to my way of thinking. You've a right to be real proud, Mr. Lockwood. Real proud."

"Thank you, Deegan. Goodnight."

"A veritable dream come true," said Deegan. "Goodnight again, sir."

George Lockwood drove in the twilight to his old house in Swedish Haven, where he had been born; a square red brick house that seemed to rise suddenly in the center of a square lawn. He put the car in the horseless stable and walked around to the front door and let himself in. The sounds he had made brought May Freese from the kitchen.

"Any messages, May?"

"No sir, nobody called, and nothing in the afternoon mail."

"All negative."

"Only the papers. Where will I bring your tea to?"

"My study, and have we got anything like a piece of cake in the house?"

"We have what's left of that angel food, you had last night with the ice cream."

"All right. Bring me a piece of that instead of toast."

"You want a piece of angel food instead of your buttered toast?"

"Yes, May. A piece of angel food instead of my buttered toast. I'm not going to have buttered toast today. I'm going to have some of last night's angel food."

"Angel food," said May, leaving.

George Lockwood went upstairs, washed his face and hands, and changed to a velvet smoking jacket and cracked patent leather pumps. May brought in the tea tray and put it in front of him on his desk. "Notice there's four letters," she said. "Margaret took them out of the box while I was up doing the third story. The least she could do was tell me."

"I think the very least she could do," said George Lockwood.

"That angel food's a little stale. It gets stale if you leave it."

"I like it that way. I don't like it gummy."

"In another day it won't be any good."

"In another day it won't be here. I'm going to eat it all."

"How you can eat so much and don't get fat."

"I'm very active. I'm busy all the time."

"Yes. How's the new house?"

"It's finished. That's why I'm having the cake."

"It's all finished? Everything?"

"All finished. From here on it's Mrs. Lockwood's job."

"When are you going to take us out for a look? Margaret and I."

"When I'm good and ready."

"Do you know what I heard? Well, I didn't hear it, Margaret did, but she told me."

"What did Margaret hear and obligingly tell you?"

"I don't know if it's true or not."

"Well, you wouldn't want to repeat anything unless it was true."

"We heard that one side of the house settled."

"Settled? Oh, sank? Settled that way?"

"They're starting rumors already, before you get in. I heard another one myself. Let me think, what was it? Oh! Are you giving this house for a hospital? That's what I heard."

"Can you keep a secret?"

"Sure."

"I don't know. I haven't finally decided what I'm going to do with this house. The doctors want to start a hospital. That's probably what you heard."

"No, I heard you gave it."

"Well, I didn't."

"Is the new house settling?"

"I won't tell you."

"Then it is, huh?"

"I'm never going to deny or confirm anything about the new house, May. I've told you that before."

"They done nothing but talk about that house, ever since you started building that wall. It sure did give this town something to talk about."

"Was there ever a time when they didn't have something to talk about?"

"I guess people always find something to talk about."

"Yes indeed."

"That's what I was thinking. They always do find something. If it isn't one thing, then it's another."

"No doubt about it. Now what else is on your mind, May?"

"There *was* something."

"Yes."

"I did tell you about some things come by parcel post."

"No."

"All stuff from New York City, all addressed to *her*."

"Things for the new house, I imagine."

"Oh, now I remember what I wanted to ask you."

"Ah, good. What, May?"

"No, that wasn't it. I did ask you that. Oh! Yes! Margaret and I were talking, and the subject came up of Andrew and his wife. In the new place are they gonna have rooms over the grodge?"

"Why?"

"Well, I wouldn't mind, but Margaret said she wouldn't want to live our there in that lonely place if there wasn't a man there at night. Me, I'm used to it. I was born-raised on a farm, so I don't mind. But Margaret, she's used to town."

"You're a simple soul, May."

"Why do you say that? Maybe I am, and maybe I'm not. It depends on how you mean it."

"You are being used as a pawn. *Andrew* and his wife are the ones who really want to know about the garage. Andrew has been trying to find out for over a year. So he's got Margaret to get *you* to find out. Do you see that, May?"

"Oh. Well, yes, in a way I guess I do. Well, then, don't tell me. I'll just go back and tell Margaret I couldn't find anything out."

"I have no intention of telling you, or Margaret, or Andrew, until I'm good and ready. You and Margaret have been with me long enough to know that, but you never seem to learn."

"I learned. I told Margaret we wouldn't find anything out."

"But she thought it was worth a try."

"Yes, she thought it was worth a try. Almost her exact words."

"Yes, Margaret likes to be clever, forgetting that Andrew's even cleverer. All right, May. You may take these things away. I'm going to have my bath, and dinner at seven-thirty. What are we having for dinner?"

"Veal cutlets."

"Good, and while I think of it, I want to sleep tomorrow morning. Don't bring my coffee till ten o'clock."

"Ten o'clock?"

"Ten—o'clock. You'd better write it down on the slate, as soon as you get to the kitchen. 'His coffee at ten.' "

She smiled. "How do you know that's what I'll write?"

"Because I make it a point to know a lot of things, Mabel Christina Freese, born April 12, 1886."

"Don't tell Margaret the year."

"I won't."

"Thank you, sir." she said. At the beginning and at the

end of all their chats May Freese would remember to say sir, but the suspicion that he was enjoying himself with her made formality impossible during the in-between part. She was a strong, hard-working woman, who was beginning to realize that time was getting short for her, but in the not unpleasant routine of domestic service—the hours were long, but the tasks were simple—she postponed the positive action that she felt she ought to take. She was uncertain and vague as to what that action should be.

George Lockwood read the Gibbsville afternoon paper through, and refolded it and left it where May would find it. He rose, stretched, and was about to go upstairs when the telephone rang. He lifted the receiver and said: "Hello—all right, May, I'll take it. Hello." May, in the kitchen, hung up.

"Mr. Lockwood? It's Deegan, Matthew Deegan? Out at the place?"

"Yes, Deegan."

"Can you hear me all right? I'm calling from the shanty."

"Yes, I can hear you. What's the trouble?"

"I thought I better tell you, Mr. Lockwood. We'd an accident out here. It's a bad one."

"Yes, what kind of an accident? A fire?"

"No sir. It's a young lad, we don't know his name for sure, but he's dead. He was killed."

"Killed? On my property? How did he get in?"

"Him and another young lad, they climbed up a tree on the outside of the wall, the Richterville side."

"The west wall. Yes."

"This one lad, the dead one, he climbed up the tree and out on one of the limbs that extended over the top of the wall."

"There's no limb extending over the top of the wall that's strong enough to support a man."

"That's how he got killed. The limb broke and he fell on top of the wall. Two of them spikes went in him, Mr. Lockwood."

"Oh, Christ! Jesus! You mean he was impaled?"

"I didn't hear that, Mr. Lockwood."

"The spikes went through his body?"

"He let out a scream, and I ran in that direction, and there he was."

"Jesus Christ! Alive?"

"It was a terrible thing, Mr. Lockwood. Still alive, and I couldn't reach high enough to get him off the wall. I run to get a ladder, but by the time I found one in the cellar and got back to him, he was just lying there across the top of the wall. The poor little fellow, about twelve or fourteen years of age."

"Where was the other boy? Ran, I suppose."

"He ran before I could stop him. I yelled to him, but he kept going, and I didn't try to stop him."

"No, of course not. Then I suppose you telephoned for a doctor?"

"And the state police. One of the spikes went through near his heart, and the other broke his spine. He didn't have to suffer long, thanks be to God, poor lad. I guess they were after chestnuts."

"I doubt it. I haven't got any chestnut trees. Where is the boy now?"

"The staties had him taken to the undertaker's, in town."

"Town meaning here? Swedish Haven?"

"Yes sir. It shouldn't take them long to find out who he is."

"No, the other boy will certainly tell what happened. They must be farm boys."

"Yes sir. The lad that was killed, he was wearing a pair of overhauls, and them felt boots. Do you want me to keep you informed if I hear anything else? I guess the state police will come and see you."

"Oh," said George Lockwood. "Well, I won't be here, Deegan. I have to leave right away for Philadelphia. You tell your office that I'll be in touch with them in the morning, and if there's any legal matter to attend to, have the state police call Mr. Arthur McHenry, at McHenry & Chapin's. You know where their office is."

"Yes sir. If you want to give me your address in Philadelphia."

"Well, I'm not sure where I'll be. I'll telephone your office in the morning. I'm sorry this had to happen, Deegan. Very harrowing experience for you."

"Yes sir. I'm getting another man from the agency to stay here tonight. I couldn't last out the night thinking of that poor lad."

"Go home and try to think about something else."

"That's what I'm gunna try to do. Goodnight, Mr. Lockwood."

"Goodnight," said George Lockwood. He hurried upstairs and put on his shoes and jacket and packed a small bag. He went downstairs and through the kitchen. "No dinner. I've been called to Philadelphia on urgent business."

"You won't get a train now," said Margaret.

"I'm driving." He closed the door, started the little Packard, and was on his way. At Reading he drove to the Outer Station and after mentioning the names of two local directors of the line, gave the car keys to the stationmaster and boarded the next train for New York.

In a week's time the fuss would die down and he would not have been mixed up in it.

"I was just about to call the operator and tell her I didn't want to be disturbed," said Geraldine Lockwood.

"Who on earth would disturb you?" said George Lockwood.

She raised her eyebrows. "That's a thought. Who would? I always leave word that I don't want to be disturbed, but now that I think of it, there's no one that would call me at three o'clock in the morning, or five o'clock in the morning. You think of things like that."

"I can understand why you'd leave word that you didn't want to take any calls before, say, ten o'clock. But just leaving word that you didn't want to be disturbed—no."

"Every night since I've been staying here, I've called the operator, just before I turned out my light, and told her I didn't want to be disturbed. They're very nice, these operators."

"Yes, the whole staff are very nice. I told you you'd like this place. I've been staying at the Carstairs ever since it opened, twenty-five years ago. I like it because its big enough so they don't have to overcharge you, but at the same time small enough so that you know the people and they know you."

"My family always stayed at the Waldorf or the Knickerbocker."

"You and Howard always stayed at the Murray Hill."

"Nearly always. Sometimes the Waldorf. It seems so strange when I come to New York not to be staying at the Waldorf. I never became quite so attached to the Murray Hill. That was Howard and his family."

"It's a pretty good hotel, but lately they've been letting it run down. I hear it's going to pieces. Well, so is Howard Buckmaster, for that matter."

"Let's not talk about Howard. I'd much rather talk about what sudden impulse brought you to New York. If you're ready to tell me."

"I've already told you. The sudden impulse was to tell you that the house is all finished—and not over the telephone."

"Well, that's sweet, but I don't believe it. You do unexpected things, but you're not sentimental."

"I'm not?"

"I don't think so, George. You can be romantic, but not sentimental."

"What do you consider the difference?"

"Well—I can't just say offhand."

"Well, give me an example of the sentimental and an example of the romantic."

"I'm trying to think. A romantic man can be very romantic and still never lose his head. Thinking every minute. But a sentimental man is entirely swayed by his emotions. A man can be deliberately romantic, but I don't think he can be deliberately sentimental. You did a lot of romantic things. I guess we both did."

"Do you consider yourself sentimental?"

"No, perhaps not. But more so than you are. Howard was sentimental, but not a bit romantic. I think romantic people are probably more intelligent."

"Uh—I think intelligent people aren't likely to be sentimental," he said.

"That's better. I guess because you're so intelligent you couldn't possibly be sentimental, but you can be romantic."

"Well, then let's say that my coming to New York instead of telephoning was romantic, and not sentimental," he said.

"All right. I agree."

"Have you missed me?"

"The last few days, very much. All last week and the week before I went to bed exhausted. I told you that."

"Yes."

"It's true. I love shopping for myself. Clothes and things like that. But furnishing a house—I've done all the bedrooms and our dressingrooms, and the halls. And on the ground floor, the diningroom and the little sitting-room. And the hall. But the big room on the ground floor, you're going to have to help me."

"No, I want you to do everything but my study," he said.

"I don't feel right about it. That's where we'll entertain and that room should have more of you."

"You'll be the hostess."

"But you'll be the host, and for instance I saw a large Chinese vase. It's five feet high and comes on a teakwood base. Perfectly beautiful, and horribly expensive."

"How horribly expensive?"

"Five thousand."

"That's not too expensive for some Chinese pieces."

"But for a country house, and you're going to see it every day. It's blue, a deep blue but not sombre. Bright. And the design is carried out in a very yellowy gold and some black. It's an exquisite thing."

"Get it. You obviously love it. And the southeast corner of that room needs something like that."

"Oh, I wouldn't have it there. I'd have it on the right, just as you come in from the hall."

"Then you'd want something on the left."

"Oh, dear. That's just the trouble."

"What?"

"I have a confession to make."

"Confess."

"This vase is one of a pair."

"*Ten* thousand?"

"Eight thousand for the pair. I got them to come down."

"Then you have another confession to make?"

"Yes. I've bought them. Oh, this isn't the way I planned to break the news to you. George, you *make* me tell you things. You do somehow, you know. You look at me with those clear blue eyes and I hear myself saying things I had no intention of saying. But you will let me have them, won't you? I know just how I can save four thousand, on some guest-room rugs."

"The pair of vases will be a present."

"All right! Christmas! I'll have them for my Christmas present."

"No, that's not fair. I'll still give you a Christmas present. We'll consider it a reward for all those miles you walked shopping."

"Honestly, I'd love them for a Christmas present."

"As it happens, I've already ordered your Christmas present."

"You've ordered it? It's something you had to order two months ahead?"

"Yes, but don't start guessing." He rose. "I am now going to take my bath."

"Do you want me in your bed when you come back?"

"Yes," he said. He did not look at her again, and as he closed the bathroom door she snapped the bedside light. When he returned to the darkened room he picked up the receiver. "Operator, this is Mr. Lockwood in 1120. No calls before ten o'clock, please. Ten o'clock. Goodnight."

It was past eight o'clock when he awoke and looked at his

sleeping wife in the other bed. He got out of bed, shaved and had a shower, and as soon as he reentered the bedroom she opened her eyes. "Good morning, dear," she said.

"Good morning. Would you like to have some breakfast now? I'm going to have mine."

"What time is it?"

"Three minutes short of nine," he said.

"Oh, I slept so well."

"Yes," he said. "What about breakfast? Shall I order for you, or do you want to go back to sleep?"

"Oh, order for me, by all means. You do that while I wash my face."

"Good," he said. He waited until she closed the bathroom door behind her, then picked up the receiver. "Good morning. Mr. Lockwood, Room 1120. I want to order breakfast, but I still don't want to receive any calls. And instead of ten o'clock, make that eleven. No calls before eleven, please. And now will you give me Room Service?"

He gave the breakfast order; orange juice, toast, and coffee for his wife; orange juice, oatmeal, fried eggs and bacon, toast, jam, and coffee for himself. Geraldine was still in the bathroom when the meal arrived; the waiter left, and George Lockwood knocked on the bathroom door.

"Breakfast is here," he called.

She came out immediately. "I don't mind having a waiter serve my breakfast when I'm alone," she said. "But I hate it when you're in the room."

"Why?"

"Because I can't help but think what's going on in his mind. No matter how respectful they may seem, they're usually foreigners, and you know what they're thinking. Wondering whether we slept together."

"I'm sure that every foreigner assumes that something went on. If not the previous night, the one before that. Or will go on the next night. Or in our case, that I'm probably getting on in years, and that you have a lover."

"I have. You."

"Thank you, Geraldine. Shall I pour your coffee?"

"Yes, dear, please." She stood near him and drank her orange juice, took the coffee he handed her, and sat across the service table. "It's so long since we've had breakfast together."

"Well, you'd rather not."

"No woman of forty-eight is a fairy princess when she get up in the morning. Still, we miss something by not having breakfast together."

"Well, maybe in the new house. I'll have my bath and get rid of my beard, and you can do whatever you feel is necessary, and we can meet over the orange juice, so to speak."

"I like your tie," she said.

"Oh," he said. "I'll be here for about a week."

"You will? You didn't pack for a week, or are you having some things sent on?"

"I'd like you to do me a favor if you will. Will you go over to Brooks Brothers and ask for Mr. Huntington. I'll write this all down for you. Tell Mr. Huntington I'd like to have half a dozen shirts. He'll know what kind when you tell him who you are. And then will you bring them back to me?"

"Of course. Mr. Huntington will know the material and the sizes and everything? Would you like me to leave right away?"

"Well, finish your coffee, and it'd be nice if you put some clothes on," he said.

"Didn't you bring another suit?"

"Didn't have room, or time, or anything. I'll go to Brooks and get something later in the day, and if we go out in the evening, I always keep a dinner jacket and evening things at the club."

"So did Howard." She smiled. "I remember one time he didn't pack his Tuck, because he had one at *his* club. Then when he tried to put it on he couldn't button the trousers, he'd put on so much weight."

"Well, I haven't put on any weight."

"You're hurrying me, aren't you?"

"A little," he said.

"What's the matter with the shirt you have on?"

"Not a thing, but I want to get those other shirts in the laundry, don't you see? It's past nine o'clock, Geraldine, and I'm going to have to speak to Mr. DeBorio so that the shirts will get done today. Mr. DeBorio is the manager."

"I know. Funny little man, but perfectly charming."

George Lockwood looked at his wife.

"All right, dear, all right," she said.

He waited until she was gone ten minutes, then telephoned the Gibbsville lawyer, Arthur McHenry.

"It was a clear case of trespassing, George. The property is posted, so I'm told by Deegan, and you had a watchman, Deegan. I don't see any way that you can be held responsible. Liable. If you want to give the boy's family a few dollars, I can prepare some sort of quit-claim, a release, and I think that's the last we'll ever hear of it."

"How much, Arthur?"

"Oh, two or three hundred dollars. It's a large family, and I'll put it to them that you'd like to pay the funeral expenses. As you know, these people never have much cash, and a hundred dollars would cover the undertaker's bill."

"Give them five hundred."

Arthur McHenry chuckled. "If you give them five hundred the parents aren't going to be able to squeeze out many tears. That'll be a real windfall for those people."

"Well, I don't want any bad feeling, and by the way, I'm keeping this from Geraldine. Was there anything in the morning paper?"

"Yes. A little article on the front page. Nothing sensational."

"Would it be possible to have the deputy coroner finish up his investigation before we get back?"

"I shouldn't think that would be any problem. I'll speak to him, and I think we could rush it through, oh, within two or three days. They're performing the autopsy today. Cause of death is obvious. And no crime involved, except that the boy was trespassing. The deputy coroner is a young doctor named Miller. You may know him. Been in Swedish Haven about three years."

"I know him. He's one of those that approached me about turning over my old house for a hospital."

Arthur McHenry laughed. "Oh, my. What would you do if you were in Miller's position?"

"Yes, I see."

"This case is practically closed, right this minute, or as soon as I speak to Dr. Miller."

"Thank you, Arthur. Remember me to Joe Chapin."

"I'll do that, George. My best to Geraldine. Not now, though."

"I'll save it for some other time, Arthur. Thanks again."

George Lockwood looked hastily but carefully through the morning newspapers on the remote chance that the accident might be of news value to New York editors because of its particular gruesomeness, but neither the *Herald Tribune* nor the *Times* had seen fit to publish a word about it. Geraldine, followed by a bellboy, returned to the room in less than an hour.

"Thank you, Bob," said George Lockwood to the bellboy.

"Right you are, sir," said the bellboy, and placed the parcel on the luggage stand and departed.

"Mr. Huntington told me to tell you he could have saved

me the trip. All you had to do was phone him," said Geraldine.

"You were very prompt. Very efficient, my dear, and you don't know Huntington. Whether I spoke to him on the phone or whatever, he would have inquired about every Brooks customer in Lantenengo County, and my brother and my nephews and anybody else he could think of to talk about."

"That's why you made me go. I was wondering. But you always have a reason for things. I've learned that."

He rang for the valet. "Haven't *you?* I think everybody has."

"Not to the extent that you do, and you don't always explain what your reasons are. Consequently, you mystify people a lot of times."

"I've never mystified you, have I? At least I've never let you stay mystified after you ask for an explanation."

"No, that's true, dear. But sometimes I forget to ask."

"Then you can't really blame me, can you? When something I do mystifies you, just ask. As to other people, I simply don't give a damn. I owe no one any explanation for anything. Thought, word, or deed. And they love it. All those stories we heard about the wall. Why I had to have a wall. How much it was going to cost me. And why I discontinued the Dietrich farm. The people in the Valley and Swedish Haven—it's like giving them free band concerts."

"Why *did* you discontinue the Dietrich farm?"

"I told you."

"You gave me a funny reason. Humorous, that is. You said the prevailing wind was from the west, and we'd get tired of the odor of cow manure."

"That answer seemed to satisfy you at the time. What's more, it happens to be true."

"But there must be another reason."

"There is. Actually, two. One is that in a few years' time you'll find that the quail will be plentiful in that lower land, and we'll have some damn good shooting. A few seasons and the land will be all grown over and full of game. The other reason, of course, is that Dietrichs have farmed that land for so many years that they think of it as theirs, no matter who owns it legally. And the only thing to do was get rid of them, lock, stock and barrel. Good fences make good neighbors, they say. But I did more than build a good fence. I transplanted the neighbors to Lebanon County. I'm very fond of the Dietrichs, now that they're forty miles away. But Oscar wouldn't have made a good tenant, not on what was once his own land."

"I never would have thought it all out so carefully," she said.

"You didn't have to. I began thinking of these things when we were married. I knew you didn't like the old house in Swedish Haven."

"But I did. At least I didn't dislike it."

"No woman likes to live in a house that her husband's first wife lived in for twenty years."

"But it wasn't her house as much as it was yours. You were born there, and your brother. If it was any woman's house, it was your mother's."

"My grandmother's. Mother never liked that house. And in a few more years you would have liked it even less."

"Why didn't your mother like it?"

"I can only guess. My mother'd never tell any of *us* that she didn't like the house."

"You and your brother?"

"Children were children, and they stayed children till they were married. No matter what my father did or said, he was right, according to my mother, and there was to be no discussion or any criticism of anything the parents did. And I mean *no* criticism, even unspoken criticism. If we didn't like something they did, and were caught making a face, we'd get a good hard slap." He rubbed his newly shaved chin. "Those fat little hands could slap."

"I'm really glad we're past the age for having children. Or at least that I am."

"So am I. There'll be small ones around at Christmas for years to come. And any other time we want them, but *only* when we want them."

"Yes. That isn't exactly what I meant, but—"

"Oh, I know what you meant, Geraldine. You wouldn't want the task of bringing up a young baby."

"That's it. The responsibility."

"I knew that. Ah." The door was opened, simultaneously with a knock. "Peter."

"Good morning, sir. Ma'am. Heard you was stopping with us, sir. Pleasure to see you again, sir, Mr. Lockwood. How can I be of service to you, sir?"

"Good morning, Peter. See that blue box with the yellow edge? Half a dozen brand-new shirts in there," said George Lockwood.

"That have to go into the laundry before Mr. Lockwood wears them. Yes sir."

"I know it's past the time—"

"Oh, I think a special effort can be made, sir. Washed and ironed, no starch, and returned to this 'ere room by no later than eight o'clock this evening, sir? Unless Mr. Lockwood has some evening shirts amongst them? There I'd be inclined to be pessimistic, sir. Sorry."

"No evening shirts, Peter."

"In that case, I just take the box down meself and as one might say, exert a bit of pressure, sir. Very good sir, thank you sir. Ma'am."

"Thank you, Peter."

"Thank you, sir." The valet left.

"Thank you zah," said Geraldine. "Zah. He sounds as though he were saying czar."

"I think they learn that in the British army. Well, now, my dear, what shall we do this evening? Would you like to see a show?"

"You're not taking me out to lunch?"

"I thought you might have plans of your own, so I think I'd like to spend the day downtown."

"I'm having lunch at Henri's. Mary Chadburn, if you'd like to join us."

"God will bless you for being nice to Mary Chadburn, but I don't want to take anything away from your kind act. You lunch with Mary, and there'll be a gold star in the Good Book for you."

"I like Mary."

"Everybody *likes* Mary. What could anybody possibly have against her? I'll be at Lockwood & Company most of the day." He kissed her cheek. "I'm glad you ordered the vases. They sound just right," he said, and folded his topcoat over his arm and saluted her with his hat, and left.

George Lockwood's private office at Lockwood & Company was the smallest in the suite, but it was never used even temporarily by anyone else, and it was always kept ready for just such sudden, unexpected visits as that which George now paid. He went directly to his office, speaking to some of the staff on the way. As was customary, Miss Strademyer knocked on his door and asked if she could take any dictation. "Not this minute, Miss Strademyer. Maybe later. Is my brother in?"

"Yes sir."

"Well, I'll just go over my mail and then after I've seen my brother I may have some letters for you. After lunch, most likely. You're looking very well, for a girl that just had her appendix out."

"Oh, that was in August. I've almost forgotten about it."

"You should have had it done last spring, not during your vacation."

"I didn't want to have it done at all, and put it off to the last minute. Even then I thought it was swimming cramps."

"I told you last spring."

"Oh, you were right, no doubt about it."

"How is everything else with you?"

"Meaning?"

"Your life away from the office."

"I have somebody."

"Good. Who? Are you going to marry him?"

"I don't know. I haven't made up my mind. I couldn't stay here if I did."

"Why couldn't you?"

"Obvious reasons."

"Not so obvious, Marian. You don't have to tell him everything."

"No, but if he ever did find out *anything*. Men are men, and he'd never believe that it hasn't been going on all the time."

"He probably wouldn't, therefore why tell him at all? Ever. I can assure you *I've* never said a word to anyone. Not a word, to anyone. No one in this office ever had the slightest suspicion that I know of, and if they didn't know it here, where else would they know it? I think you're worried about me, Marian. That I might some day say something."

"No, I'm really more worried about myself."

"Then I suggest that you have a serious talk with yourself. Face the fact that you're exaggerating the importance of something that happened two years ago. It wasn't important then. You said so yourself at the time. Why make it important now? Be honest, Marian. The only thing that would have made it important was if you had fallen in love with me, and you didn't do that. The fourth time I wanted to see you, you very firmly refused, and did I ever bother you again?"

"No. You were very nice about that."

"Well, be that as it may. I think the trouble now is that you've fallen in love with this man, and hadn't been in love with anyone else in between."

"You're right."

"And there's something very self-destructive about the business of falling in love. I don't know exactly what it is, but men and women feel compelled to talk too much. I'm afraid the reason is that they want to test the other person's love, and they do it in a way that's cruel to the other person and self-destructive to themselves. Have you still got your apartment?"

"Yes."

"Would you like to meet me there at four o'clock this afternoon?"

"No, I wouldn't."

"Well, then you're free of me. It's as simple as that, Marian."

"What if I had said yes?"

"Would you like to try saying yes? You're just as attractive to me as ever."

"But there's nothing in it for either of us, is there?"

"Pleasure. That's all it was before."

"Yes, that's true. That's really all it was."

"And after me there were others that were no more than pleasure, weren't there? Before this man."

"Yes, there were two others. He knows about *them*."

"Then the reason you haven't told him about us was that you don't want to give up your job, for fear he'll think you're my mistress."

"I've never been anybody's *mistress*. I certainly wasn't yours, was I?"

"Hardly, considering the intervals between the three nights we spent together. As a friend of yours, and quite a bit older, I suggest that you marry this man and keep your job here, and put your trust in me as a gentleman. I mean that. I'll give you my word now that I'll never again ask to see you outside the office."

"I'm probably making too much of the whole thing."

"No, not if it bothers you. But I think you're so close to happiness that you ought to act decisively. Get yourself married, keep your job here, and let the future take care of the rest."

"I think that's good advice."

"You're a very attractive woman, Marian."

"You're a very attractive man."

"Come over here," he said.

"No, I don't think I'd better. And I think you'd better have one of the other girls take your letters, at least today."

"All right. Make it Miss Thorpe. She won't distract me."

She returned to the outer office, and Daisy Thorpe said to her: "What did he say this time?"

"Oh, he's always teasing or making jokes."

"Does he talk dirty?"

"George Lockwood? He's above that."

They saw him, a few minutes later, going from his office to the larger, more elegant room occupied by his brother.

"Hello, George," said Penrose Lockwood.

"Good morning, Pen. Are you free for lunch?"

"No, I'm not free, but you can come along. I'm having lunch with Ray Turner and Charley Bohm."

"What do *they* want?"

"Oh, don't take that tone. I don't know for sure what it is they have, but the way those two have been going, I want to be in on it. You don't have to come in if you don't want to."

"Are you going there for the Company or for yourself?"

"Both."

"I hope you go slow about involving the Company."

"Why?"

"Well, because before you involve the Company, I think you ought to hear what I have to say."

"I always do, but you've touted me *and* the Company off some pretty good things. You've been so God damn busy with this country estate of yours. How's it coming along, by the way?"

"It's finished. Ready to move the furniture in."

"October. Well, I'll give you credit. You said the first of November. But I started to say, why do you think your judgment is more reliable, sitting there in Swedish Haven, and I'm right here where things happen?"

"My judgment isn't more reliable, Pen, and I never claimed it was. And I never really touted you off anything."

"Oh, the hell you didn't."

"Now don't say that. I didn't. All I've done, and will continue to do, is make you count to ten, so to speak. And while you're counting, consider all the factors. In this market today, generally speaking, if you miss out on something good, something equally good will be along tomorrow."

"If you hear about it in time," said Penrose Lockwood. "It isn't quite as good, you know, if a lot of others have heard about it too."

"At the moment, almost everything is good, if you're not too greedy."

"Well, then, you can call me greedy if you like, but I've made money for you, haven't I?"

"Yes, and I've made some for you. But Pen, it isn't only a question of making money. I hear of all sorts of people making pots of it these days, so it isn't any great accomplishment."

"What is?"

"Holding on to it."

Penrose Lockwood laughed. "Holding on to it? What's this house of yours going to cost, if it's any of my business?"

"It isn't any of your business. I don't ask you what you do with yours, and you know damn well that isn't what I meant. Holding on to it means having it twenty-five, fifty years from now. For instance, things get a little bad in the automobile industry, and that man Ford orders an eight-hour day and a five-day week. He doesn't have anybody but himself to think of. But suppose all the big industries behaved that way?"

"It may not be so bad after all. He cut down over-production and made new jobs."

"That's what he wants you to think. But don't you see what this inevitably leads to? The immediate effect of course *is* to cut down over-production. But if every big industry followed suit, all production would slow down. All production, and this is a high-production country. You can't run this country on a five-day week. That is socialism in disguise. The labor union people know it, and they welcome it."

"I don't follow you."

"Look, Pen. Put this country on a five-day week, and you have to employ more men. But they won't be skilled men. They'll be incompetent, lazy bastards, getting the same money as the skilled men. That's the way I feel about spreading the work over a greater number of men. You have to hire the incompetents. That's something I've been learning with my new house. I don't mind paying a good carpenter good wages, but I've had to pay lazy men the same money I paid good men. I'm talking now about unskilled labor. I wanted some fences removed, so I hired some ordinary laborers. Were they uniformly good workers? No. About half of them did an honest day's work, and the other half did as little as they could, as slowly as they could."

"What's this got to do with the stock market?"

"Oh, Pen! What's any stock going to be worth if an industry has to overpay its labor? All materials will be overpriced because labor is overpaid, and the country will have inflation, just as they have it in Germany and Austria. You can buy a fine Mauser for fifteen cents today, in our money."

"Thank you. I've heard about their inflation."

"Well, then you know what I mean by holding on to it. I sometimes wonder if I want to make any more money in the market."

"What!"

"Oh, I will. I'm greedy, too. But I wish people like us would get out of the stock market and stay out for a while. We won't. It's foolish to think of it. But there are a great, great many stocks that are selling for much more than their earnings justify. That isn't healthy. What it means is that people like us, with money to buy stocks, are just as bad as labor. Labor inflates by being overpaid. We inflate by sending up the prices of common stocks, far beyond their real worth."

"I hear plenty of that down here. Bear talk."

"I don't see it as only bear talk. That's the trouble with being here, around the corner from the Stock Exchange. Any comment a man makes is either bearish or bullish. That's the only way you fellows think."

"I'm not a broker. Kindly don't confuse me with one."

"It's easy to. You talk like one. Frankly, I don't like the stock market. I don't like margin trading. I wish that I could find two or three investments. Buy the stock at the full price and hold on to it for twenty years, thirty years. But I don't want to pay these prices for stocks that aren't worth it: I say too many prices are already too high, and I just wish I were strong enough to resist the temptation to buy any more."

"You have no more objection to easy money than I have."

"I'm afraid not. I'm stingy at heart, and what I object to is being a sucker, paying fifty dollars for fifteen-dollar stocks. What's going on today, by the way?"

"In the market?" said Penrose Lockwood. "Have a look. Here's Allied Chemical, 124. Dodge Brothers, 22½. American Radiator, off two, at 108. Yellow Truck, 27½."

"I see," said George Lockwood. "Where are you meeting your cronies?"

"Ray's office. He's having lunch sent in. I ought to call him if you're going over there with me. Do you want to go?"

"They're not going to like what I have to say."

"Then shut up, or don't come."

"I'll shut up and listen, for a change," said George Lockwood.

Penrose Lockwood had his secretary call Ray Turner's secretary, to say that Mr. George Lockwood would be an added guest at lunch. "How is Geraldine? She came for dinner last week, you probably know."

"Yes."

"Wilma thought she looked a little tired."

"She was tired. She's been buying furniture for the new house. How is Wilma?"

"Fine. Do you want to come for dinner? How long are you planning to be in town?"

"About a week. I had to get the hell out of Swedish Haven."

"Why?"

"Some God damn farmer's kid got killed on my place."

"When?"

"Yesterday. Yesterday afternoon. The house was finally finished. The last Italian carpenters had left, and I went home and had tea. Just getting ready to have my bath and the watchman phoned. The kid fell from a tree onto my wall. Impaled on a couple of spikes."

"Impaled? On spikes?"

"I had spikes set in along the top of the wall. This kid fell on them."

"How horrible! How old was the kid?"

"Thirteen or fourteen. One of a large family. Farmers named Zehner. None of it was my fault. The kid was trespassing, probably wanted to see what he could steal. But I got the hell out of Swedish Haven because I didn't want to be questioned or have to appear at an inquest. I've spoken to Arthur McHenry and I'm legally okay. But I stay clear of any doings with the townspeople. Oh, our friends. But I've always avoided getting on familiar terms with the grocery clerks and people like that, and I didn't want to have to talk to reporters, or answer questions at the inquest. That's all been taken care of. By the way, Geraldine doesn't know a thing about this, so not a word to her."

"Of course not."

"The house would get off to a bad start. You know Geraldine."

"She's going to hear."

"But not right away. If I can put this thing in the past, she won't be shocked. If she'd known about it last night she might very easily have said she'd never live in the house. The Curse of Lockwood Hall."

"You're not *calling* it that?"

"Of course not, but that's the general idea. Romanticizing a nasty accident to a young thief," said George Lockwood. "What are you thinking about? Do you object to my calling him a thief?"

"No. He probably was," said Penrose Lockwood.

"Well, what's eating you? You're miles away."

"No I'm not. I'm right here," said Penrose Lockwood. "I have a problem of my own making. Nothing at all like this one of yours, but it's a problem."

"Can I do anything?"

"Well—yes. You've always been smarter than I am about women. Maybe you can think for me. I seem to have lost the power to think, at least about his. And I'm not so sure it doesn't affect my thinking about other things."

"Let's have it, Pen," said George Lockwood.

"Just don't call me the kid brother."

"It's all right if I think it, though, isn't it? I want to help, and there aren't very many people I can say that about. You have a lady friend."

"As long as I've been married to Wilma, that's well over twenty years, I've never had anything to do with any other woman. There were times when I think I could have had a fling or two. I very nearly did during the war, when I was stationed at League Island. A girl, a woman, in Philadelphia, wife of a friend of mine that you don't know. But we both saw how foolish it would be, and down deep she was in love with her husband and I was with Wilma. So we stopped seeing each other, and when I think of it, there was nothing that her husband or Wilma could object to. We just liked to talk, and I only kissed her once. That's when we realized that our affection for each other had this other side to it. And we stopped then and there."

"You never slept with her?"

"I told you. I kissed her exactly once. I'm not like you, George."

"You don't know *what* I'm like, but go on."

Penrose Lockwood stood up and went to the window, but it was at his past and not at Lower New York that he gazed. "Three years ago, a little over three years ago, I met a young woman. She was in her early twenties. Handsome. Quite intelligent. Some education, and I imagine came from a typical good middle-class family, not New York. I had occasion to see her quite frequently, and while I never thought of her that way, not consciously, I suppose that seeing her as often as I did, I was attracted to her physically. She was a young woman that was like a thousand other young women who have jobs in New York, and you notice them because they're pretty, but you never think of them again. But in this case, seeing her day after day, exchanging a few words now and then, she stopped being just one more anonymous pretty girl, and on days when I didn't see her, I *missed* seeing her."

"Propinquity."

"Of course," said Penrose Lockwood. "As you must have guessed, she, uh, had a job in the financial district, and one afternoon I gave her a lift uptown in a taxi, and since I was in no hurry, I stopped in for a drink at her apartment."

"This was three years ago?"

"Almost four, as a matter of fact. Until that day, there never had been anything personal in our relationship. She was *Miss* So-and-so, and I was *Mr*. Lockwood." He came away from the window and seated himself in the big leather revolving chair, folded his hands and looked at his shoes. "She was quite an extraordinary young woman. Although she was only twenty-three, she'd been married and divorced and had taken her maiden name again. Her husband had been a professional gambler in a city out West, but she didn't find that out until they went on their wedding trip. Saratoga. She saw the kind of men his friends were, and he admitted that he'd lied to her. He wasn't a bond salesman at all. He was an out-and-out professional gambler, and in less than a year she'd had all of that sort of life that she could put up with. *He* wouldn't change his ways, it was too late, he said. So she left him and he agreed to a divorce. He was in his late thirties and he'd been married three or four times, and in fact he'd lied to her about that and made false statements in applying for the marriage license. So naturally he didn't want any trouble, and he gave her the divorce readily enough. But she didn't want to go back to her home town and her parents, and so she took a course in shorthand and typewriting and with her looks and personality, and ability as a stenographer, had no trouble getting a job in New York. She's also had three years at one of the state universities, was far superior to the ordinary typist and was put in charge of several other stenographers."

"You're having a hard time getting to your part of the story, Pen," said George Lockwood.

"I've never told the story before, that's why. And I want *you* to understand that this wasn't a cheap, casual affair, either on her part or on mine."

"But it soon became an affair, I gather," said George Lockwood."

"We don't have to go into the details of that, do we? I'm not very proud of myself. I was forty-six years old, and with no reason to think that my life would be anything but what it was. Married to a fine woman. Good friends. Plenty of money. But whenever I was with this girl, at her apartment, I seemed to become another person." He swung his chair so that he again faced the window. "She had a piano in her apartment, and at home I never touched the piano. But she'd buy all the latest tunes, sheet music, and I'd play and she'd sing. She had a *nice* voice, contralto. And I began to spend every Saturday afternoon with her. I'm not trying to pretend that it was innocent fun, George. It was not. In that respect it was an entire new experience for me. I had never associated that experience with love, and I now realize that there was very little difference between my lack of sophistication and Wilma's. Wilma's—indifference, if you want to call it that—was largely my fault."

"The word love has just come into the conversation for the first time," said George Lockwood. "You were in love with this young woman?"

"I *am* in love with her, and that's the problem," said Penrose Lockwood. "She's going to marry someone else, and I'd do anything I could to prevent it."

"Short of marrying her yourself."

"*Not* short of marrying her myself."

"Have you asked her to marry you?"

"I have. Last summer, when she told me that she had someone else, who wanted to marry her. She went away on her vacation and while she was away she had appendicitis." He looked up quickly at his brother.

"It's all right Pen," said George Lockwood. "I guessed it a while ago."

"How? What did I say?"

"When you were talking about her ability, and her being in charge of other stenographers. I think I began to guess it even before that. You don't see many other stenographers day to day, and Miss Strademyer is certainly the most attractive one in this office."

"I've been alone with her once since last summer, and that was when she told me about her fiancé."

"Did you go to bed with her then?"

"No. I wanted to, but she wouldn't."

"And what did she say when you asked her to marry you?"

"She said she wouldn't. And she said she was going to resign her job here, and I'd soon forget her."

"What did you say to that?"

"I told her to take a leave of absence, stay away as long as she wanted to, but to come back."

"Why?"

"Because I know she was happy with me. If she wants to give marriage a try, then I have no right to oppose her. But I know she'll want what we had, and miss it. For over three years, close to four, we had a relationship that I didn't think was possible."

"Do you think she was faithful to you all that time?" said George Lockwood.

"In the beginning, no. But for three years she was."

"You have only her word for that, Pen," said George Lockwood.

Penrose Lockwood smiled. "I haven't even got that. I just know. That's where inexperience counts, George. You would be full of doubts because you've been what they call a man of the world. But being a man of the world has cost you something. You have to doubt people because you give them so much cause to doubt *you*."

"It's true that I have less faith in women than you have," said George Lockwood.

"Oh, you're completely cynical, not only about women."

"Cynical, but always hopeful. Well, you said you had a problem. What is the nature of the problem?"

"You know, I don't know that I have a problem now. I've poured it all out to you, and I'm grateful to you. But this has done me a world of good because I see everything more clearly. Marian will marry her young man, and I'll have to endure that for a while, but she'll be back."

"And then what? You'll marry her?"

"Yes. She'll have had the chance she's entitled to and that I can't stand in the way of."

"Well, then you have no problem. I hope you won't be sorry you confided in me," said George Lockwood.

"On the contrary. It's a great load off my mind."

"There's only one thing, Pen. What if she likes being married to this young man?"

"You're just as thorough as always, and I was wondering whether you weren't going to ask that," said Penrose Lockwood. "I've thought about it. Worried about it. But now I realize that those kind of doubts are inconsistent with what I really believe. Really know."

"Well, as long as you're that confident," said George Lockwood.

"Still the cynic, George. You miss a lot that way."

"Yes, I know I do. Come on, let's get over to Ray Turner's solid mahogany bucket-shop. Maybe I ought to say old oaken bucket-shop."

The brothers rose simultaneously. George Lockwood

helped Penrose on with his coat and they proceeded to George's office, where Penrose helped George. George then linked his arm in his brother's, and they went out to the elevator together.

Ray Turner's private office was neither mahogany nor oaken; it was in the newer fashion, knotty pine, and spacious enough for the caterer's table and service wagon. "George, I don't know when I saw you last. You don't get down here often enough, but I'm very glad you came today."

"Oh, I don't belong down here. I'm just a hick from the country," said George Lockwood.

"I hear you're becoming a country squire," said Ray Turner.

"Yes, I heard that, too," said Charley Bohm. "The hick from the country is making more money than any of us. How did you finally come out on that carburetor deal, if you don't mind my asking?"

"Not at all," said George Lockwood. "As the British say, we made a small packet. Pen will tell you."

"We won the patent suit. You knew that," said Penrose Lockwood.

"Yes. I saw that," said Charley Bohm.

"Well, then we sold our interest to Carlton-MacLeod," said Penrose Lockwood.

"Oh, *they* got it?" said Bohm.

"Yes, we got some common, some preferred—" said Penrose Lockwood.

"And some cash, I imagine," said Bohm.

"Oh, always some cash," said George Lockwood. "Always, always some cash."

"Well, that's the way I like to do business as a rule," said Bohm. I always like to see some cash in a transaction. You took the common instead of royalties, I imagine."

"We sure did," said Penrose Lockwood. "That's one less step in the bookkeeping. Funny things happen to royalties sometimes, but when you own common stock you have a better idea of where you stand."

"You do indeed," said Bohm.

"Does anyone care for a cocktail?" said Ray Turner.

"Nope," said Charley Bohm.

"No thanks," said Penrose Lockwood.

"Well, I'll have one, Ray. A Martini?" said George Lockwood.

"And I'll have one with you," said Ray Turner. "Stirred, or shaken?"

"Shaken vigorously is the way I like them," said George Lockwood.

"So do I," said Ray Turner. "Waiter, did you hear that?"

"Yes sir," said the waiter, going to work.

"Then you can come back in about an hour," said Turner. "We'll serve ourselves from the wagon. We're having lobster Newburg, gentlemen. Meet with your approval, George?"

"I'd be crazy if it didn't," said George Lockwood.

"Tell me about your new estate," said Ray Turner.

"Well, I've got about three hundred acres, all told. We're hoping to have some good shooting in a year or two."

"Horses?" said Charley Bohm.

"No horses. My wife doesn't ride and I don't any more. It isn't riding country."

"No fox-hunting riding-to-hounds?" said Bohm.

"Not within fifty miles. It's just a house on the hillside, woodland on three sides."

"What kind of a house did you build, George? We're thinking of either buying or building," said Turner.

"Lockwood Colonial, I guess you'd call it," said George Lockwood. "Red brick, two stories, an attic and a cellar. Doorway in the center. Very simple."

"How many rooms in a house like that?" said Bohm.

"In ours, which is deceptively deep, eighteen. It looks smaller than that sounds. Then we have two apartments over the garage. We have a tennis court and a small swimming-pool, and later on a house where people can change their clothes and, in a pinch, spend the night. We don't expect to do much entertaining."

"Well, you're all set," said Turner.

"Yes, we have plenty of water. Some game. A few deer. Fruit trees. We could subsist there if we had to. I always said that if I ever built a house I'd like to feel that I could be like the first Lockwoods that came to this country."

"When was that, George?" said Bohm.

"Well, our branch arrived here early in the Eighteenth Century. We believe he helped build the Conestoga wagon, and took a trip in one and settled in Central Pennsylvania. Am I correct, Brother Penrose?"

"Yes. He opened a store somewhere along the way."

"And was killed by Indians. Or at least Indians were

blamed. But now I've said enough. My brother cautioned me against talking too much."

"Go on. This is interesting," said Bohm. "Maybe not to Ray, but to me. My name was originally B, o, e, h, m. Pennsylvania name."

"Of course it is," said George Lockwood.

"I had an ancestor that was—I think he was governor of Pennsylvania. But then he got into some kind of trouble and went out West. He may not have been governor, but I know he was from Pennsylvania. We're all from Indiana and Illinois, my father and mother's people. But even so you could call this an all-Pennsylvania party. Shall we have another snort on that, George?"

"No thank you, Ray, but you go ahead."

"I never get the full taste of a Martini till I've had two. Help yourselves, gentlemen. Dig right in, and I'll be with you in two gulps." Turner drank two more cocktails, then finished his lobster Newburg ahead of his guests. No one wanted dessert, and they left the table and had coffee while seated around Turner's desk.

"Before you start, Ray. I'll be very polite and offer to leave if this is at all confidential," said George Lockwood.

"It's God damn confidential, George. But I don't want you to leave," said Turner. "This is something that Charley and I've been approached about. As you know, Charley and I aren't partners, but we occasionally go in on things together, so a lot of people have got to thinking we are partners."

"I don't have a nickel in Ray's firm, and he doesn't have a nickel in mine."

"Right. Neither firm is in on this thing, you understand, gentlemen?"

"Right," said Penrose Lockwood.

"Okay. Well now this is something that we heard about through a customer of Charley's firm out in Ohio. Charley's firm has a branch in Cleveland and one of his customers, not a big one but an old one, asked Charley if he ever put any money in a small business just starting out."

"Our customer is an elderly gentleman, living retired in a little town in Ohio. A country lawyer. Very highly thought of in his community, and through him we got several new customers. So I listened to what he had to say, that this friend of his wanted to start up a business, and then he handed me this. One of these." Charley Bohm took a cardboard box off Turner's desk, opened it, and extracted an object wrapped in heavy tinfoil. He handed it to Penrose Lockwood; took a similar object from the box and handed it to George Lockwood. "Go ahead. Open them up."

The Lockwoods removed the tinfoil. "It looks like a piece of candy," said Penrose Lockwood.

"It is. Take a bite out of it," said Bohm.

The Lockwoods ate the candy, nodding as they chewed. "Damn good," said George Lockwood. "I'm glad I didn't have any dessert."

"I never eat candy, but this *is* good," said Penrose Lockwood.

"Marshmallow, chocolate fudge, shredded coconut, and good thick chocolate coating," said George Lockwood. "But there's something else in there, mixed in with the fudge, I guess."

"Yes, you're right, there is," said Charley Bohm. "But I'll tell you frankly, I don't know what it is. I could have it analyzed, but what's to stop the chemist from making this himself? You agree it's good. I say it's as tasty a piece of candy as I ever ate, and I eat a lot of candy to keep from drinking booze. The recipe was invented by a woman in this town in Ohio, and I would like to put the God damn thing on the market. So would Ray. We're sold on it."

"To such a degree that we've looked into what it would cost to put on a national advertising campaign. First we think up a good name, and then we're off to the races. *Saturday Evening Post. Collier's*. Kid's magazines. Newspapers. Billboards. Car cards. We get somebody like Norman Bel Geddes to design the package and decide what shape the mould should be. The candy itself is going to cost nothing. The money is going into the advertising campaign. We'll create a demand before anybody ever sees the God damn candy, and that's why we need money. What do you think, Pen?"

"Well—I like the candy, but personally I wouldn't want to put up Lockwood & Company money for an advertising campaign. That can vanish into thin air, and if the candy is a failure, how much can you recover from an advertising campaign? Nothing. That's my opinion. George may differ with me."

"I don't differ with my brother, as far as Lockwood & Company are concerned. He has to think of various other individuals."

"Well, in other words, the answer is no," said Turner.

"I didn't say quite that," said George Lockwood. "How much money are you planning to spend, and how much are you going to need?"

"Well, George, the exact figures are confidential," said Turner. "But upwards of a million, and the lion's share goes into advertising the candy. That much I'll tell you, even if you don't think much of the investment."

"You can put me down for a hundred and fifty thousand," said George Lockwood.

"What? Are you kidding?" said Turner.

"I don't kid about a hundred and fifty thousand dollars," said George Lockwood.

"Well, say," said Charley Bohm.

"Pen, you ought to get in on this, your own money," said George Lockwood.

"I'm afraid not," said Penrose Lockwood.

"Fifty thousand?" said George Lockwood.

"Sorry, George. I believe in spending money on advertising when you have a product to sell, but this would be advertising without a product."

"You tasted the candy," said George Lockwood.

"But they're going to advertise first and manufacture later. If it was a new automobile, you'd at least have some scrap iron if the car was a failure. Sorry, George. No."

"Well, gentlemen, *I'm* in," said George Lockwood. "Pen you're excused. We're going to have a private meeting."

Penrose Lockwood rose. "I'll be a son of a bitch if I've ever known a more unpredictable man, and he's my own brother. Ray, thanks for the lunch. Charley. And good luck, all three of you. Maybe I'll be sorry, but maybe not. At least I won't lie awake nights when I see those ads in *The Saturday Evening Post*. So long." He departed.

"Now then, Ray, Charley let's see what you have on paper. Who else are in on this, and for how much, and have you signed up a man from one of the big candy companies? That's good candy. It leaves a good taste. It can be marketed for a nickel, of course?"

"In quantity, we can make money on a nickel," said Ray Turner.

"There'll be quantity," said George Lockwood. "Now there's only one hitch, and it isn't much of a one."

"What's that, George?" said Turner.

"As you can see, I'm going into this with great enthusiasm. I always do, and my enthusiasm will continue. But it's nobody's damn business what I go into and what I stay out of. So—publicly, my name stays out."

"That's easy," said Charley Bohm.

"The carburetor deal, that was Lockwood & Company, but my personal investments are another matter. I have no desire to broadcast my failures *or* my successes. Keep me out of print. With that understood, let's get down to business."

He remained with Turner and Bohm until past five o'clock, and the three men worked well together. George Lockwood asked the leading questions, Ray Turner would give the straightforward answers, Charley Bohm would embellish Turner's answers; but in Bohm's supplementary and lengthy remarks there was always some point of information that had not been included in Turner's terser replies. Turner had the bookkeeping mind and saw the enterprise as a structure of arithmetical figures. Bohm, it developed, had not at first seen the enterprise as a promising proposition, and had not tried to persuade Turner to invest in it. With him it was going to be a modest, sentimental speculation, in which he was thinking in terms of $25,000. But as he talked, Turner had caught some of his enthusiasm, and before long Turner was envisioning a business enterprise that could match the recent startling success of Eskimo Pie, the chocolate-coated ice cream that had become a legend.

"I thought of Eskimo Pie, too," said George Lockwood.

"Ah, you've had me wondering why you jumped right in with both feet," said Ray Turner.

"Oh, that occurred to me right away," said Lockwood. "This candy won't have the novelty that Eskimo Pie had, but it has something in its favor to make up for that."

"What are you thinking of?" said Turner.

"Ice cream melts," said George Lockwood. "This candy doesn't need refrigeration. You can put a stack of these candies on a cigar-store counter, and you can't do that with Eskimo Pie. The retailer won't have to buy a nickel's worth of extra equipment."

Turner smiled at Bohm.

"You're echoing what Ray said to me three months ago," said Bohm.

"Well, I'm a practical man, just as Ray is. I see the dollars-and-cents aspect. At the same time, though, my enthusiasm for this is partly based on a conversation Pen and I had this morning. After our conversation I was ripe for an investment of this kind. It's highly speculative, but it's an investment nevertheless. I'm damned tired of the stock market."

"I can't say I'm tired of it," said Charley Bohm. "But I'm inclined to be bearish."

George Lockwood looked at him before speaking. "Is that because you like being on the short side?"

"I go from short to long, whichever way I think is going to make me some money," said Bohm.

"Admit it, everybody knows you're generally bearish," said Turner. "Personally, I think we're in for a five-year boom."

"Beginning when?" said Lockwood.

"Beginning about now."

"You mean of course a stock-market boom," said Lockwood.

"Of course, although based on what I see going on all over the country. Expansion. New industry. Employment figures."

"But wouldn't you agree with me that stocks generally are too high?"

"Charley says that, but I don't think so, and even if they are a little high, the economy is going to catch up. We'll keep old Cal in Washington for another six years, and business will have a free hand."

"Well, Ray, I see that you and I are going to have to avoid one topic. The stock market."

"What are you complaining about, George? You've made plenty of money in it."

"Yes, and I'd like to hold on to it. That's why I'm investing in this candy, a business that I know absolutely nothing about, but that's at least a business. I think it made more sense to put money in Florida real estate. At least those people have a place to lie down."

"Am I to understand that you don't think it's wise to be in the market?"

"It's wise if you're willing to admit frankly that you're gambling. But it isn't wise if you think of it any other way. Because if you look at it any other way, you're deceiving yourself, and when you start deceiving yourself, you're not being wise. About anything." George Lockwood unconsciously looked at the door through which his brother had passed.

"I could point out that you may be deceiving yourself, George," said Turner. "A hundred and fifty thousand dollars' worth."

"No. I'm like that ancestor of ours that opened a store on the Conestoga Road. There was some risk, and he happened to lose. *But* he opened a store. *He went into business.* If he'd been luckier, he might have been as rich as the Astors. I'm going in the candy business, and I'm not risking my life, as our ancestor did. I'm not even risking bankruptcy. I could spend this money on a boat, speaking of Astor, but I don't care that much about owning a boat. I'm doing something because I'd like to prove a point to my brother, and to you too, for that matter, Ray."

"George, we're going to have our arguments. We won't be able to avoid it," said Turner.

"Oh, I'm pretty adroit at avoiding arguments, Ray. I never argue to convince anybody. Only to learn something or to entertain myself."

"Well, I hope you learned something today."

"Thank you, I did," said George Lockwood. "Life is a fascinating enterprise. Twenty-four hours ago I was congratulating some Italian cabinetmakers on some beautiful work they did for me. And not one thing that's happened to me since then would I have been able to predict. Why, this time yesterday I had no intention of coming to New York."

The three men agreed to meet again the next day, and George Lockwood walked up to Broadway and the office of Lockwood & Company. It was getting dark, and most of the office staff had gone home or were saying goodnight. Marian Strademyer was at her desk. "I have a message for you from your brother," she said, as George Lockwood was passing in front of her.

"And that is?" said George Lockwood.

"You and Mrs. Lockwood are dining at his house tomorrow evening, eight o'clock," she said.

"Thank you, Miss Strademyer."

"You and he were very chummy today," she said.

"Were we? Unusually so, did you think?"

"I thought so, arm-in-arm, going out to lunch," said Marian Strademyer.

"Oh, well, I suppose that was unusual, in the office at any rate. But we're very close," said George Lockwood. He turned his head in the direction of his brother's office, and continued, reflectively: "I don't know of anything I wouldn't do for him."

"That's nice," she said, then, lowering her voice slightly: "I changed my mind about this afternoon, if you're still interested."

"I said four o'clock. Now there isn't time," he said.

"Oh, all right," she said.

"You mustn't be disagreeable, Marian. I don't like disagreeable women. Have you any other messages?"

"No," she said. She took her purse out of her desk drawer

and angrily walked out. He went to his office and closed the door. "Miss Strademyer," he said aloud, "you are a nuisance." He seated himself at his desk and began speaking into the Dictograph, a summary of his conversation with Turner and Bohm. When he had finished he put the tube in his topcoat pocket. "I don't like you any more, Miss Strademyer," he said, and lightly tapped the Dictograph. "Not one damn bit."

The office was now deserted; the first of the cleaning women had not yet arrived. He went through Marian Strademyer's desk, carefully replacing everything he disturbed. None of the contents of the desk drawers interested him for long. He sat in her chair for a minute or two, and his next move was to the glass-partitioned bookkeeping room. He took down a large ledger stamped *Payroll* and placed it on a desk, and there before him was a complete record of Strademyer, Marian's, salary-and-bonus history at Lockwood & Company. He closed the book, and was about to return it to the shelf, but he reopened it, read the payroll accounts of several other employes, and discovered that Strademyer, Marian, had never had a deduction in her pay cheques for an advance salary payment. In this respect she was unique. No one else had managed to go through any single year without at least one salary advance; several employes on a slightly lower pay scale had seldom got through a fortnight without borrowing money from the petty cash account. Strademyer, Marian, had never borrowed a cent. She seemed to manage very well.

George Lockwood wandered about the office, walking from room to room, smoking his pipe. Then abruptly he stopped walking and took from his vest pocket a small, gold-cornered pigskin notebook. He opened it, and carried it, open, to the vault in the cashier's room. He read the combination from his notebook, and swung open the vault door. With the key at the end of his watch-chain he opened a file drawer marked Personnel Correspondence, and took out the Strademyer, Marian, folder. Soon he had a list of Strademyer, Marian's, charge accounts, which had required routine references from Lockwood & Company. For a young woman who was earning forty dollars a week she had found it desirable to establish credit at a considerable number of luxury stores. Lucetta Shay was a small, exclusive dress shop that made Geraldine Lockwood complain of its prices; Milestone & Leigh was a small, exclusive jewelry-silversmith that did not advertise; Kimiyoto & Company, Marchbanks Limited, Barney's Theatre Ticket Service, Edouard

Parfumier were Madison Avenue and cross-street institutions that were semi-secrets of the rich, the chic, the spenders. Marchbanks Limited did not even state its business on its letterhead.

It was six-thirty when George Lockwood closed the vault and took the subway uptown. Geraldine was lying in the tub.

"You'll have to get out of there," he said.

"I was getting ready to," she said. "Did you have a nice day with Pen? Tell me all about it, then you can ask me about what I did."

"Thank God we're going to have plenty of hot water in the new house," he said.

"Didn't we in the old? Wilma called and wants us for dinner tomorrow. I said yes."

"I know. Pen left a message."

"Where were you? I thought you'd be at the office, but they didn't seem to know where you were."

"Pen knew, but I guess he was being discreet. We had lunch with Ray Turner and Charley Bohm, then I stayed and spent the afternoon with them."

"Did you make a lot of money?"

"Potentially. Potentially. But I tied up a large amount of cash." He was undressing as she dried herself.

"I hope that's not intended as a warning. I went back and saw Mr. Kimiyoto. I told him we were taking the vases. Positively, this time. He wants to send them by van, and one of his sons is going along to supervise the unloading and uncrating."

"I should hope so. How was Mary?"

"Well, it shows what they think of them. Mary Chadburn? Weepy. Lawrence has T.B., and she was—"

"Lawrence? Who's Lawrence?"

"Her nephew. Doug's sister's oldest boy, but Mary is devoted to him."

"Mary gets devoted to anybody that will give her an excuse to weep."

"I know, but she does an awful lot of good, Mary."

"Well, maybe she can get the boy a new lung."

"I don't think that's nice, George. Shall I run your tub for you?"

"Yes, will you please?"

"Wait till I put something on," she said. "Mary wanted to know if everything was all right between Pen and Wilma. I said as far as I knew, yes. Then she gave me a sort of a patronizing look and I said well, I was just a hick from the country, but I couldn't pry any more out of her. Is there something I'm supposed to know? I didn't notice anything when I had dinner there, but I wasn't looking for anything."

"What kind of thing was she talking about?"

"Well, naturally I inferred that Wilma had a beau or Pen had a lady friend. One or the other."

"Mary threw the match in the gas tank and ran."

"But Mary doesn't usually gossip, unless there's something."

"Well, I was with Pen today, and he happened to say he didn't have any problem, so it isn't Pen. And if Wilma has a beau it must be somebody like old Rancid Martin."

"Ransome Martin."

"And at seventy-eight he's relatively harmless. No, you go back and tell Mary to give you more particulars or shut up. Not too warm, my tub. Just make it half and half."

"It is half and half. Your shirts are back from the laundry."

"Why do you tell me that? Was anyone talking about shirts?"

"I thought I'd say something to get you in a different mood. You've been very captious since you got here, and I don't enjoy that."

"I'm very sorry, Geraldine."

"I had too many years of every time something went wrong, I bore the brunt of it. I didn't marry you to go through that all over again. And I won't, George. Please make no mistake about that."

"You're really cross?"

"No, dear, I'm not cross. That's not saying I might not get cross. But let's have it understood that when I'm trying to be pleasant, which is most of the time, I don't like being snapped at. I loved every minute of last night and felt wonderfully all day. But you can make me unhappy, too. You can be very distant at times."

"I'm sorry, my dear. It's been one thing after another the past day or so."

"Have your bath, and then maybe you'll decide that it'd be nice to have dinner here and not go out. I'm perfectly willing to do whatever you'd like to do."

"We'll see after I've had my bath."

"You're the most attractive man I ever knew."

"Am I?"

"You know you are."

"After two years of marriage?"

"You'll always be attractive. I suppose I ought to thank those hundreds of women before you selected me."

"There was nothing like *hundreds* of women, Geraldine. A few, but not hundreds."

"Well—I'm just as much of a woman as any of them, although God knows I never knew that until three years ago. Maybe that's why you're so attractive, George. Any dull woman could be the wife of Howard Buckmaster, but I know they're all saying, 'What does *George Lockwood* see in her?' What shall I tell them?"

"You can tell them that I find you anything but a dull woman."

"Well, I would have gone on being one if you hadn't been so bold. 'Try me, sometime.' Who would think that a simple little remark like that could change my entire life?"

"The moment was right. I decided that you must be getting ready to try someone."

"That was really it. You read my mind before I was aware of what I was thinking. I was awful, wasn't I? I was so stupid. So embarrassed."

"No you weren't. You were yourself, not trying to be anyone else or anything else but what you were. That's the whole secret, you know. The stupid one was Howard."

"Oh, Lord. Poor Howard. Well, you go take your tub."

"And you're over being cross?" he said.

"I have to assert myself once in a while," she said.

They dined on antipasto and spaghetti at a speakeasy in Chelsea, where they were joined by a Princeton classmate of George Lockwood's. It was a family-owned restaurant, a single, long narrow room with both walls painted to depict a street scene in a small Italian town. Over the murals was placed latticework of white wood, in the hope of suggesting the illusion that the street scenes were being observed from inside a garden. The painting was so bad that no illusion was created, but the colors were bright, the latticework was spotless, and the artistic failure mattered less than the joyful intent of the proprietor and the artist. The Chianti had a slight metallic taste, indicating that it had reposed in an iron vat before being decanted into the straw-bound bottles; but the food was good and the service was kind. No one left before eleven o'clock, and only one young couple remained after twelve. Joe, the proprietor, stood behind the waiter whenever a dish was being served, supervising every last detail, then nodding and faintly smiling at the customers and leaving them to themselves. The clientele was largely middle-aged, built on the patronage of men who had once known Joe as a waiter at the Club de Vingt. They were men who were not unaccustomed to wine at their meals in the days before the Eighteenth Amendment, and they were orderly and solvent. Joe's political connections were excellent, and no police officer below the rank of lieutenant was ever seen in the place.

"George, the talk around town is that you're going to be asked to give a new dormitory," said Ned O'Byrne.

"What?"

"And call it Carlton-MacLeod," said O'Byrne.

"Oh," said George Lockwood.

"Or Carburetor Hall," said O'Byrne. "Why couldn't you have let a dear friend and classmate in on a thing like that?"

"No friend or classmate in his right mind would have gone into it when Pen and I first heard of it," said George Lockwood. "You're all so busy buying and selling stocks that you never even see. Pen and I nursed that thing along, you know, and the lawyers' fees would have paid for—well, a few tennis courts."

"Solid gold tennis courts, I heard," said O'Byrne. "Well, the next time you have something like that, let a fellow know."

"I wouldn't think of it, Ned. If it's going to be good, I want it all myself—with Pen, that is. And if it isn't any good, how could I ever face my dear old friends. What have *you* got for *me?*"

"Well, just to create good will, in the hope of *quid pro quo* in the future, I have got something in the way of a tip. It closed today at 11¼, and I'm going to hold on to it till it reaches an even 40. That should be around the middle of January, just about time to pay the Christmas bills."

"Is it on the big board?"

"No it most certainly is not, and as a matter of fact there isn't enough of the stock to attract a big investor like you, but I hope to make a modest fifty grand and then run."

"And then what will you do?"

"Well, I'm a speculator. I make no bones about it. I'm letting one or two friends in on it, and I fully expect them to reciprocate when they get something. This is pretty small stuff for you, George."

"Nothing in five figures is small, Ned. We've just finished building a house, and if I can get someone else to pay for it, I'll let them."

"Well, you're welcome to come in."

"No thanks, Ned. I might want to get out before you do, and if I started selling, you'd never forgive me."

"Well, of course I wouldn't want you to sell it all at once. You could start something that would upset my plans, so I guess you'd better stay out. But just between us, and since you're not going in, I'll tell you what it is so that you can watch it for the next three months."

"I'll keep my mouth shut," said George Lockwood.

"It's called Magico."

"Magic with an O on the end of it?"

"Yes. It's a radio set. Eight tubes, and it was designed by a couple of young fellows in Chicago. They have some kind of a gadget that eliminates most of the static in the cities, where the steel in the buildings and the electric power for elevators and so forth—you know. If what they claim is true, 40 is a low price to sell at. But I'll be satisfied with 40."

"Yes, and the question immediately arises, why haven't the Stromberg-Carlsons and the Atwater Kents perfected this thing? Why two young fellows in Chicago?"

"George, I didn't go to M.I.T., remember? And I'm not in this forever. I only know what I've heard, and I'm going to make a little money while the rumors are going around. Then I'm going to quietly get out, and as silently steal away. It may be a frost, but I'll be in sunny climes, literally and figuratively speaking. I have a goal set for myself, and when I reach that, in five years, I'm going to buy the village where my grandfather was born, in Ireland, and king it there. Catch salmon and drink whiskey the rest of my life. I haven't really got the acquisitive instinct. I'm not quite a bum, but I'm far from being an Andrew Mellon."

"I understand completely. I have no desire to live in Ireland. I'd be so outnumbered. But I'm doing what you're planning to do."

Geraldine Lockwood and Kathleen O'Byrne were carrying on a separate conversation, adventures in shopping the topic, and now Kathleen said: "George, I overheard the last part. What are you doing that Ned is planning to do? I'd like to know, because it would give me an inkling of Ned's plans."

"Aren't you in on Ned's plans, either?" said Geraldine.

"Either? You're always in on my plans, Geraldine," said George.

"No. I get announcements, but I'm not in on the planning," said Geraldine . . .

Later, in their room at the hotel, George Lockwood said: "That was a surprising remark you made, about not being in on my plans. Did you mean it, or was that just the Chianti? I think Joe fortifies his Chianti just a touch."

"Oh, I might have made that remark without Chianti. Without a cup of tea. Why?"

"Nothing. It was just one of those statements that women make in front of other people that they'd never make in private. When it's just the husband and wife alone, a statement like that would lead to an argument. In public, you try to avoid arguments. So, since you preferred to make it in public, you obviously wish to avoid an argument on the subject. Goodnight, Geraldine. I won't disturb you in the morning. I'm going downtown early and I'll be gone all day. I'll have my breakfast in the diningroom."

"Very well. Goodnight, George."

Dinner at Wilma Lockwood's the next night was followed by auction bridge, so that the formality between George and Geraldine Lockwood, that had carried over from the previous night, was not noticeable to the host and hostess. Back in the hotel room again Geraldine said: "If there's anything wrong between those two, I didn't notice it. What they're thinking about us is another matter."

"Quite. I'm going back to Swedish Haven tomorrow. Would you care to come with me?"

"No thanks. If you'll send the car, I'll drive down on Saturday."

"Saturday? Well, I suggest you have Andrew check and see what football games are being played Saturday. If there are games in Easton or Bethlehem, or Allentown, you'll run into traffic."

"I don't care how long I take."

"Very well."

"Maybe you'll have thawed out by then. But of course *I* may be quite cold, after that long drive and all."

"Both things are possible," he said. "If I don't see you in the morning, I'll see you Saturday. Goodnight."

In the morning he left a note for her:

G.—I shall send Andrew to New York today so that you can leave as early as you like tomorrow. Will tell DeBorio to reserve room for Andrew at Roosevelt Hotel. —G.L.

George Lockwood obtained the keys for the Packard from the Reading stationmaster and was home in midafternoon. "Wash the Packard, Andrew, and then I want you to drive to New York. There'll be a room for you at the Roosevelt Hotel, and when you get there, telephone Mrs. Lockwood. She's at the Carstairs, and she'll undoubtedly have a great many bundles to bring home. She'll let you know what time you'll be leaving tomorrow. Take the Pierce-Arrow. It has the most room."

"Mrs. Lockwood don't like the Pierce for long drives. She complains it's drafty."

"She'll need the Pierce-Arrow. If the weather's bad you can put up the side curtains, and take along enough robes."

"I was just thinking, the Lincoln contains as much room, if there's nobody else sitting in the back."

"Is that what you were thinking? *You* don't mind a little fresh air, do you, Andrew?"

"No, not me. Mrs. Lockwood, though. She does." He smiled.

"What's so amusing?"

"Well, just between you and I, and she wouldn't like it if I repeated this. But it isn't only the draftiness in the Pierce. She complains it makes her look older, riding in the Pierce. And when you think of some of the old ladies in Gibbsville with their Pierces—that car's an awful gas-eater, too, Mr. Lockwood."

"Who's been talking to you, Andrew? The Cadillac salesman? Fliegler? If that's the case, give up, I'll never buy a Cadillac, so you and Luther Fliegler stop conspiring. Now will you give my car a wash, and then get started for New York?"

"Nobody else will offer you seven hundred for the Pierce," said Andrew.

"It isn't worth seven hundred, therefore the Cadillac is overpriced."

"They only give Mrs. Hofman three hundred for her Pierce, the same year as ours. Old Mrs. Hofman."

"And that's all it was worth, today. Give up, Andrew. You may get your two percent, but not on a Cadillac. I won't have one in my garage."

"Well, if you say so, sir," said Andrew.

"While all this talking's been going on there was something I wanted to ask you," said George Lockwood. He stood before Andrew, who was taking off his shoes and getting into his gumboots. "Oh, yes. Was there any more about the boy that was killed?"

"They had the trial last night."

"You mean the coroner's inquest."

"Yes. In the paper this morning it just said accidental

death. They had the funeral yesterday. I heard you paid for it."

"Where did you hear that?"

"In town."

"Well, as a matter of fact I did, but people don't have to know those things," said George Lockwood.

"It was a good thing to do, in my opinion," said Andrew. "There's no law compelling you to do it, but people felt better about it."

"That isn't why I did it."

"Oh, I know that well enough. But that's why it was a good thing to do."

"Say it. What's on your mind?"

Andrew stood up. "Well, nobody could say it was your fault. I don't mean to hint that it was. But one or two said the wall was high enough to keep people out. You didn't need the spikes."

"I see. What else did they say?"

"That was all."

"I think there was more."

"Well, there was more, but along the same lines. They said the spikes weren't necessary. They said that last spring, and since Tuesday they said it all over again. Here you been living all your life in a house with only a little iron fence—I'm telling you what I *heard*. Not my opinion. All your life here, out in the open where people can see everything going on. Then all of a sudden you decide to build a house out in the Valley. You put up a high wall, and on top of the wall you put spikes. And to cap the climax, you knock all the houses down on Oscar Dietrich's old farm. One fellow said, what comes over a man that he wants all that secrecy?" Andrew paused.

"You know, Mr. Lockwood, as man to man," he continued, "I work for you, and you always treated me decent, so I stick up for you. But this is a different matter."

"Thank you for sticking up for me. What's the different matter?"

"Well, it isn't you I have to stick up for." Andrew looked questioningly at George Lockwood, silently asking him to help him out with the next statement.

"Well, who else, if not me?"

"Your wife. Mrs. Lockwood. Some are blaming her. You lived in this house all your life, your parents lived here, and I understand your father was born here. Some are saying that the new house, and the wall, and the spikes on top, and ruining Oscar Dietrich's farm—all that's only since you married again."

"The whole thing was my idea."

"Sure, but some you can't convince of that."

"I haven't tried to convince anyone of anything."

"I know. I'm just telling you what some people say. You never mixed much with the people in town, but they're used to you."

"My first wife didn't mix with them either, if they expected the present Mrs. Lockwood to get chummy."

"Yes, but with your first wife there was a reason. She was sickly, and they all knew it. The present Mrs. Lockwood is a strong, healthy lady. I'm just telling you what they say."

"Andrew, you came here from New York. Small-town life is still new to you."

"I like it, though."

"Yes, but you didn't know, for instance, that when my mother married my father and came here to live, the women in the town thought she was a snob because she'd only speak English."

"How do you mean, sir?"

"My mother came from Richterville, only ten miles away, and she spoke Pennsylvania Dutch and English, but my father didn't speak much Pennsylvania Dutch, so my mother spoke only English. The people in the town didn't like that. They'd speak to her in Dutch, and she'd answer in English. The point is, they'd have found some reason to criticize her, whatever she did or didn't do. Do you know why?"

"Well, I guess there could be a lot of reasons."

"One. She was the wife of Abraham Lockwood. My father. And he'd gone ten miles away to choose his wife. History is only repeating itself. But I'm very glad you stick up for me, and I assume you do for Mrs. Lockwood as well."

"That you can assume," said Andrew. "I had to hit one fellow a knock in the chin."

"For what he said about Mrs. Lockwood?"

"He took it back."

"I'm all for chivalry, Andrew, but don't get hurt. Goodnight."

"Goodnight, sir."

Geraldine Lockwood returned to the red brick box the next afternoon. "Good, a fire," she said, on entering George Lockwood's study.

"Is that all I get in the way of greeting?"

"If you mean, am I going to kiss you? No. I'm catching a

cold. I've been sneezing all the way from Easton. I could have revenge by passing the cold on to you, but I'm too nice for that. And besides—what right have you got to expect a kiss from me? You've been behaving like a bastard, George, and I don't like it at all."

"I guess I do, sometimes."

"Well, I don't like it. Really, I *don't*. I wish you'd at least say you're sorry."

"Would that cure your cold?"

"Don't try to blame my cold for the way I'm feeling. My cold has nothing to do with it. Although it has. Why didn't you send Andrew in the Lincoln?"

"Because I thought you'd be more likely to catch cold in the Pierce-Arrow."

"I wouldn't put it past you. I really wouldn't, the last two or three days. I'm going to have a bath and go to bed, and don't bother to come in to say goodnight."

"All right, Geraldine. Whatever you say."

"Where's my mail? Did any of my packages come?"

"Ask May."

■

ONE of the passengers on the evening train from Philadelphia on a day in late February 1921 was Bing Lockwood, George Bingham Lockwood Junior. He was a tall slender young man of twenty-two, wearing a light brown hat, a long raccoon coat that hung unbuttoned and revealed a very light grey Norfolk suit, plain-toed black shoes with a black saddle over the instep. He descended from the Pullman at Swedish Haven and looked about him to right and left, raising himself on tiptoe to see above the crowd. He stood on the platform, a splendid English pigskin kitbag at one side, a no less splendid pigskin tennis bag at the other. His clothes and accouterments were high fashion among undergraduates, but his present manner was far from carefree.

"Hello, Georgie. Home over Saturday?" The speaker was Ike Wehner, the baggagemaster.

"Hello, Mr. Wehner. You didn't see our Henry, did you?"

"No, I didn't. But I wasn't lookin' for him. I don't see your machine, neither. He may be along, you can't tell." Wehner moved on, and in a few minutes Bing Lockwood was alone on the platform. He waited five minutes, looked at his watch several times.

"Guess you're going to have to stretch those long legs of yours, Georgie, unless you want me to phone the house," said Wehner. "I'll phone up if you want me to and you can keep watch out here."

"No thanks, Mr. Wehner. I guess I'll walk."

"Anything wrong, Georgie? At the house? Your mother —no worse, I hope."

"No, nothing wrong, thanks. So long, Mr. Wehner."

Bing Lockwood walked the two blocks east and three blocks south to the family home. He let himself in, left his luggage and coat and hat in the hall, and went back to his father's den. "Hello, Father," he said.

George Lockwood put down the evening paper. "Hello, son."

"Well, here I am."

"Here you are, all right. Sit down. Don't stand there waiting for me to tell you what to do."

The son took a chair and lit a cigarette.

"When did you give up wearing garters? Is that the thing at Princeton now?"

"Are you going to start by criticizing my clothes?" said Bing Lockwood.

"Almost anywhere I'd start I could criticize, couldn't I?"

"Yes, I guess so. But Jesus Christ. Garters."

"All right. Forget the garters. We could start with your language."

"Well, I apologize for that," said the son.

George Lockwood got up and took a cigarette out of a silver box on his desk. He was about to light the cigarette when he hesitated, picked up the silver box and examined it. He then handed it to his son. "I was very pleased when you gave me this. But now I'm returning it to you."

"Why? I won it, and you admired it, so I was glad to give it to you."

"Yes, but *how* did you win it?"

"Oh, for Christ's sake, Father. This was tennis."

"You've been kicked out of college for cheating in exams. For all I know, you cheat in everything."

"It would be pretty God damn hard to win a tennis tournament on cheating alone. Did you ever notice those men on the big high chair? If you don't want the box, throw it in the wastebasket. I don't want it now, either."

"Why did you come home, I wonder? You didn't have to. You have some money. It's bad enough to bring disgrace on the family without being arrogant into the bargain."

"I see. You wouldn't let Henry meet me."

"Henry is off today."

"Then of course you wouldn't meet me yourself. In seven and a half years this was the first time I wasn't met by anybody."

George Lockwood snorted. "I declare, I think you expected us to meet you with a brass band."

"No such thing, and you know it, Father. I expect to be punished, and I hope I take it like a man. But picking on me for not wearing garters. And returning my cigarette box." The son's voice broke. "Honestly."

"Good God, not tears. You're certainly running the gamut, from swearing like a trooper to now, blubbering like a girl. If you're going to bawl, go on up to your room."

"I'm not going to bawl any more. I'll tell you once again, what I told you over the phone, I'd give anything if I could do over again. I'd rather flunk out than cheat."

"Or be caught cheating. I understand you got away with it once before."

The son hesitated. "I got away with it twice before. But I wish I'd let nature take its course and I'd flunked out."

"Yes, it would have been a lot easier to get you in some place else if you'd only flunked out. You could even have got back into Princeton. As it is, you've been turned down by Penn State and Bucknell."

"You mean you applied for State and Bucknell?"

"I spoke to friends of mine. I can get you in Bucknell *next year*. Your mother has a cousin, a Baptist minister in Wilkes-Barre."

"I don't want to go to Bucknell, or any place else."

"Oh, you've made your own plans. What are they, may I ask?"

"I'm going out to California and get a job."

"In a bank, I suppose."

"What are you trying to do? Kick me in the nuts? No, not in a bank. One of my roommates' father is more willing to give me a chance than my own father. I have a job on a ranch, and I'm leaving next week. I could leave tomorrow, as far as that goes."

"Well, why don't you? I won't stop you."

"You *couldn't* stop me. I hope I never see you again as long as I live. Good—bye, *Father*."

"Just a minute, before you make your dramatic exit. Your mother is waiting to see you. What are you going to tell her?"

"I'll tell her that I have a job in California, and that I have to leave tomorrow."

"Just so we get our stories straight, that's all I care about. Bear in mind when you go upstairs that this may be the last time you ever see her again. That is, if you plan to stay in California any length of time."

"How long?"

"If you stay a year. And if you do anything to excite her now, you may have to postpone your trip a few days. So don't be dramatic with her."

"Why couldn't it be the other way?"

"God damn you! Don't expect me to forget that."

"I won't," said Bing Lockwood.

His mother took off her boudoir cap as he entered her room. She was sitting in a high-backed chair, in nightgown and negligee, her satin-slippered feet on a carpeted circular footrest. She quickly ran her fingers through her hair and held out her hands. "Georgie, I'm going to turn you over my knee, that's all there is to it. Give me a kiss."

He kissed her, and sat in a matching high-backed chair on the opposite side of the fireplace.

"Smoke. Go ahead. And give me a puff," she said.

"When did you start smoking?"

"When did I start smoking? Exactly thirty years ago. Cubebs, when I was fourteen."

"Did they have cubebs then?"

"Oh, I don't know. I was only joking. I never have smoked, but I know *you* used to smoke cubebs. When you were fourteen, and even younger."

"Did you know it then?"

"How could I help knowing? You could smell them a mile away. Have you had your supper?"

"No."

"You must be hungry."

"Not very. I had an oyster stew in the Reading Terminal."

"You've been talking with your father, I know. I could hear your voices, but I couldn't make out what you were saying. He's very upset, of course. But he'll come around. Do you remember Cousin Charley Larribee? I don't know whether you'd remember him or not. He was my second cousin, and he came here one time to preach at the Baptist church. He spent the night with us, but you couldn't have been more than three or four. Well, he's done very well in the ministry, the Baptist ministry, and I happened to remember reading somewhere that he was a trustee at Bucknell. So I suggested to your father that we might write and tell Cousin Charley all the circumstances. Not holding back anything, but putting it to him as a Christian minister—"

"I know, Mother. Father told me."

"He did? Well, I knew he was going to. And you've been accepted for next year. At least, you will be. They'll take you. And you'll have a degree. It's only for a year, dear."

"A degree doesn't mean that much to me," said the son. "I'm through with college."

"I was afraid you'd say that. But you mustn't make up your mind now. I know what you're thinking. That they're showing favoritism in taking you at Bucknell. But wherever you go, it's going to be much more difficult for you than for anyone else in the school. They'll watch you like a hawk, and at the first sign—well, you know. But for that reason you ought to go. That's the best possible way to make up for what happened at Princeton. Erase the bad mark on your record. Bucknell is willing to give you that chance, and I hope you'll go there and get your degree and show them at Princeton that you profited by your mistakes."

"Well, I'm going to, Mother. But not by going to Bucknell. I'm sure they're very decent to give me the chance, but I'm fed up with college. Look at my marks all the way through. Barely passing, and I cheated last year too. I never should have gone in the first place. It was a waste of time and money. Maybe it's a good thing I got caught, although a hell of a thing to happen when I was almost through. Four more months."

"Then maybe it is a good thing. If you'd got through by cheating, I wonder how that would affect the rest of your life. Well, what are your plans?"

"Steve King my roommate's father says he has a job for me."

"In California? All the way out there? It takes a week by train, dear."

"Well, I thought of going to China, and I don't know how long it takes to get *there*."

"What would you do in California?"

"Work on Mr. King's ranch."

"A cowboy?"

"No, it isn't a cattle ranch. He raises fruit. Oranges and things like that."

"Would you like that?"

"I won't know till I try it."

"What would you do? Pick oranges?"

"I guess I will at first. He says I'll start at the bottom. Manual labor. Hard work. But if I want to make something of myself, he says this is my chance."

"You've talked to Mr. King, the father?"

"I had a letter from him. He doesn't say much about the kind of work I'd do, other than to say it'd be hard work, and I know from Steve that when he says hard work he means it. Rowing is nothing for Steve after a summer on the ranch."

The mother's hand hung limply over the arm of the chair. "When do you leave?"

"Tomorrow."

"Yes, I knew it. I knew it. I knew you were coming to say goodbye. Stand up, Georgie. Let me look at you. Turn around. Oh, my dear. My *dear!*" She put out her arms and he knelt to come within her embrace.

"Don't cry, Mother. It isn't as far as China."

"Yes it is. For me it is. But at least it isn't a war. Four years ago I'd have been terrified for you. But this isn't a war. This is a wonderful new start for you. You think of it that way, don't you?"

"Yes."

"Maybe you'll meet a nice girl out there."

"Well, that's a long way off, Mother."

"No. You're older than you think. You had a good time, you had a lot of fun, with your tennis and your friends. But I think that's over for you."

"I do, too."

"Sit down now, and I'll tell you something about your father. I *know* you know about *me*. You treat me as though I were fragile, and that's how I know. Your father has told you, hasn't he? Oh, that's not fair. Let *me* say it. My heart is bad. I may never go downstairs again. But you can't stay here waiting for me to have a final attack. I may go on for years this way. Now, about your father."

"Are you going to tell me that he's not my father?"

She laughed. "Oh, he's your father, there isn't the slightest doubt about that. But think how times are changing when you can *ask* me such a question. If your Uncle Pen had ever asked your grandmother a question like that!"

"Times haven't changed. You and I have."

"Well, maybe. I guess there are things like that in Shakespeare. Anyway, to understand your father, Georgie, I must tell you something about him. It's nothing terrible, or scandalous, it's just something in his character. He thinks too much."

"He thinks too much?"

"Yes. You're more like me. I've noticed that since you were a little boy. But your father is all wrapped up in himself, always thinking, thinking, thinking. Never does anything without thinking about it. And gets more pleasure out of planning a thing than doing it. By the time he's ready to do a thing, he's lost interest in it. He'll even make a study of a thing, big or little. Notice him ordering a meal in a restaurant. He takes hours to order, but he doesn't seem to enjoy eating. Ordering a new suit. He'll have six fittings, and then the suit will hang in his closet for months before he wears it."

"I know."

"This is something that perhaps you know and perhaps you don't. But you're going out in the great wide world now, so I'll tell you. It isn't terrible, or it isn't scandalous. But your father hasn't always been faithful to me."

"You mean he's had affairs with other women?"

"Yes. Not many, but more than one. But they don't last. The pursuit, the planning—he'll spend a year on that part of it. But then he loses interest."

"What kind of women?"

"Different kinds. I haven't always known them, or who they are, but I can tell."

"And you never let on?"

"The first one, yes. That *was* someone I knew. A friend. I thought my life was over, everything ended, especially because I was having Ernestine at the time."

"What a terrible thing to do to you."

She shook her head. "No. Not really, not when he explained it to me."

"How could he explain a thing like that?"

"Well, he did, and *after* he did I realized that I'd married a man with so little feeling that it didn't much matter."

"I'll say."

"It didn't matter, because—well, there were certain things you didn't discuss. A man and woman could be married for years and years, and have children, but never discuss that side of their marriage. We didn't, your father and I, until he had an affair with another woman. Then we did. He admitted the affair, and he explained it in a way that showed me how little feeling he had. I guess by feeling I mean love. Yes. You see, his explanation was that a man had to have relations with a woman, once he'd started. And he picked someone in our own circle of friends because she'd have as much to lose as he if she made a fuss."

"Did he always have his affairs in your circle of friends?"

She smiled. "Oh, no. There weren't *that* many unfaithful wives."

"So he had some other explanation for the others?"

She shook her head. "No. I never asked him for one. He was so cold-blooded about the first one that I realized that he was telling the truth. The truth about himself, more than he realized. More than he realizes to this day. It was just as though he'd told me he had some sickness. I, for instance, have a bad heart."

"And he has no heart at all."

"In that sense, no, he hasn't. But I want you to understand that in other ways he's been a good husband. I wouldn't change places with any woman I know. He's been generous, considerate, gentle, and not only since I had my heart attack. Always. And I know what the other women have to find out for themselves—that he's never loved anybody, because he can't. When *they* find that out it must make them unhappy. I'm sure it must. But I found it out ever so many years ago."

"But Mother, what's the purpose in telling me?"

"I have a purpose. It isn't just to gossip about your father. It's to try to make you understand some people. You're going away, a long distance. Strange people. Don't be surprised if you can't understand the actions of some people. And never be surprised at anything your father does. He lives entirely in his mind. A very sad man, to have missed so much in life."

"I guess I'll understand this later."

"Don't try now. Wait till you come across somebody you don't understand, then remember what I've told you. There are some women who are that way, too. It isn't confined to men."

"Were you ever in love with anybody?"

"Your father. Six years. Then I found out what kind of man he was and I stopped loving him. By that time I had you and Ernestine to love, so I didn't really miss loving your father. I want you to go to California full of hope, but prepared. People can disappoint you. Someone you love can disappoint you. If that happens, remember that I lived for fifteen years with a man that I'd stopped loving, and nobody ever knew I was unhappy. Most of the time I *wasn't* unhappy. Only when I thought back on the six years that I was in love. You never thought of me as an unhappy person, did you?"

"No. But I did use to wonder how you could be happy with Father. I guess that's as close as I ever came to thinking you were unhappy."

"I'm glad you didn't come any closer. Children should believe in their parents' happiness. But now you're older, about to go it alone, so I don't mind disillusioning you a little bit."

"I haven't as many illusions as you might think. Especially now. I have none about myself. I thought I was honest, till last year. Then I discovered that I wasn't."

"You were, and you still are. But you may be weak, in some things. Most of us are. Haven't you ever read about men who led quiet, respectable lives, and then one day they can't resist temptation? They take all the money out of the cash drawer and run away? Well, you're twenty-two instead of forty-five. And of course what you did has harmed no one but yourself. No real harm will come to anybody else because you were asked to leave Princeton. Your father talks about the disgrace, but he's made such a practice of staying aloof from people that they don't know much about us. He's not going to say anything now, to the people in Swedish Haven, but he never has, so there's nothing very different about that. If he'd been a more friendly, convivial man, his silence now would be noticeable. As it is, there won't be anybody outside this family that knows why you left Princeton."

"Yes there will."

"I'm talking about Swedish Haven."

"I'll never be able to go back to Princeton, or face my Princeton friends."

"Who came to say goodbye to you when you left?"

"Oh, four or five fellows."

"Then remember them and forget about the others. Those four or five will defend you, and the others don't matter." She sighed. "Nobody matters."

"Are you getting tired?"

"Yes I am, a little. I think there must be something else wrong with me besides just my heart. Not that my heart isn't enough. What a nuisance it is, being an invalid."

"I'll let you sleep."

"All right. Come in before you go to bed, I'm usually reading. I'm reading a book about a woman that got a new start in life, but her story isn't at all like yours. She goes away with a man, and comes back home without marrying him. Before she goes away she was like Cinderella, the ugly duckling, but my! what an illicit romance does for her self-confidence. It was written by a woman, but I don't believe a word of it. And that Princeton book they're all talking about. Don't they ever study there?"

"As little as possible. That's why some of us have to cheat in exams."

"Oh, Georgie—well, it's on your mind."

He saw from the second-story landing that his luggage had been taken to his room. He went downstairs and noticed that only one place was set at the diningroom table.

"Hello, May. Hello, Margaret," he said, in the kitchen. "Is the table set for me or for my father?"

"Welcome home," said May. "It's set for you. Your father's having his dinner at the Gibbsville Club. He has some meeting he has to go to, and he couldn't wait."

"All right. I'm ready any time you are," he said. "Oh—is Henry around?"

"He has the day off."

"I thought I saw his light on."

"He's in his room, but it's his day off," said May.

"Is that so?" said Bing Lockwood. He went to the wall telephone and pushed the Garage button. "Henry, this is George."

"George Who?"

"George Bingham Lockwood Junior."

"It's my day off."

"I won't be bothering you very often after tomorrow. My trunk is coming from Princeton, New Jersey. I want it readdressed to me, care of—write this down now, please—care of Jack King, Rancho San Marcos, San Luis Obispo County, California."

"You're going too fast for me. All that Spanish."

George gave him the address more slowly. "Have you got it now?"

"Care of Jack King, Rancho San Marcos. San Luis Obispo County. California. You don't want me to bring the trunk home. Just readdress it and have it put on the next train. Who's going to pay for this?"

"I'm sure my father will be glad to pay for it."

"Don't you know some way you could put it on your ticket?"

"I haven't bought my ticket."

"Well, buy it, and tell Ike Wehner to readdress the trunk. That would simplify matters. And save a lot of money. If you knew you were going all the way to California, why didn't you have the trunk sent from Princeton, instead of this roundabout way?"

"I wasn't sure I was going to California. Now I am." He hung up.

"You going all the way to California?" said May.

"All the way."

"What happened? Did you get in some kind of trouble at the college?" said Margaret.

"I sure did. I cheated in my exams."

"Aw, now, tell us the truth. What did you do?"

"I told you. I cheated in my exams."

"All right, if you don't want to tell us. Did you get in trouble over a girl?"

"Liquor, more likely," said May.

"Why more likely liquor?" said George.

"Because they don't take girls at your college," said May.

"There's the other kind, that always hang around where the young fellows congregate," said Margaret. "Anyway, we're not gonna get it out of him what it was, women or booze."

"Or maybe both. My nephew is attending the Penn State, and those frats. The things that go on there you'd never believe. The Princeton frats would be worse."

"Why?" said George.

"A wealthier class of boys go there and they have more money. They're much worse."

"No, only during one week," said George.

"One week?" said Margaret.

"Yes. Once a year they have a custom at Princeton called Orgy Week, and you're allowed to have as many women as you like in your room."

"Staying there?" said Margaret.

"Of course. Anything is allowed during Orgy Week, except to have a professor's wife in your room. If you're caught with a professor's wife you have to translate fifty lines of Horace."

"I don't believe it," said Margaret.

"I don't know whether I believe it or not," said May.

"Ask my father. Ask him sometime if he ever had to translate fifty lines of Horace."

"Fifty lines of horrors? What does that mean?"

"It probably means you have to write down fifty lines of horrible things," said May.

"Well, *I* knew *that,*" said Margaret. "Fifty lines of horrors, what else could it mean? But is there some book that has all these horrors in it?"

"I'll send you a copy."

"Not to me. I don't want the postman knowing I got such a book," said Margaret.

"I have an old one upstairs," said George.

"I never saw it," said May. "Did your father get caught with a professor's wife?"

"Just watch his face when you ask him."

"I might get fired," said May.

"You might at that. Princeton men aren't supposed to talk about Orgy Week, not to outsiders."

"When is this week?"

"When is it? It varies from year to year. Sometimes in the fall, sometimes in the spring. The student council decides. You get an announcement that Orgy Week is going to start on such-and-such a day. Most of the professors' wives leave town, just to be on the safe side. But there are always a few of them that stay."

"The young ones, I guess. The pretty ones," said May.

"Mostly the young and pretty ones," said George. "But I wouldn't have anything to do with a professor's wife. Fifty lines of Horace—not worth it."

"You'd be better off if you stayed away from women entirely," said Margaret.

"He's old enough. Twenty-two," said May.

"I don't care how old he is or how young he is. Look at the trouble he's in already, going to California."

"What's the name of this week you're talking about?" said May.

"Orgy Week. It was named after John W. Orgy, he was the professor of pederasty at Princeton in 1865 and he started the whole thing. Professor John W. Orgy. Easy name to remember. There's a statue of him in Nassau Hall."

"Huh. I don't swally it," said Margaret.

"I suppose John W. Orgy wasn't professor of pederasty?" said George. "I suppose there's no statue of him in Nassau Hall?"

"Well, maybe he was a famous professor of that thing, but don't try to make me believe a professor would start a thing like that," said Margaret.

"Not an ordinary professor, maybe, but a professor of pederasty would. I don't think you know what pederasty is, Margaret."

"I heard of it. It's some kind of a medical subject. The bones in the human body," said Margaret.

"See, you don't know. You've got it confused with orthopederasty. The two aren't the same at all."

"Well they sound almost the same," said Margaret.

"That's just the trouble. What are homiletics, for instance?"

"Why, I know what they are but I'd rather not say. Like Artie Minzer?"

"Well, there you are. You did know about homiletics. But not about John W. Orgy, the professor of pederasty. His subject. He believed in absolute freedom of the individual, and he conducted this experiment of allowing complete freedom for one week. It's been going on for half a century."

"Well, it didn't do *you* any good," said Margaret.

"It's too soon to tell," he said.

On his last night in the house where he was born, George Bingham Lockwood Junior dined alone on a meal that he had not ordered and would not have chosen. His mother was asleep when he went to her room, and he telephoned three girls in Gibbsville, but they all seemed to be at a bridge party and were not expected home much before eleven-thirty or twelve. He unpacked and repacked his kit-bag, took a bath, and fell asleep while reading in bed. He did not hear his father come in; he did not hear his mother when she came to his room, opened the windows, and turned out his light.

He was awake at six o'clock. He shaved and dressed and had a last breakfast in the kitchen, with Margaret urging more food on him. After breakfast he went to his mother's room, knocked, and entered. "You're making the eight-forty-six?" she said.

"Yes. Thanks for opening my windows. You did it, didn't you?"

"You were sleeping so soundly. You needed that sleep. Write to me on the train. You go by way of Chicago, I suppose, but I guess you wouldn't want to look up any friends of ours."

"No, I don't think so."

"You can make a list of things you'll want us to do. I'll have your fur coat put in storage. You won't need *that* for a while. And when your trunk comes I'll have Henry—"

"I've done that."

"Send me a telegram when you get to California, and write me when you're settled. I want to know everything. Do you need any money?"

"No thanks."

"Well, if you ever do."

"I know. I'm traveling very light, because when I get there all I'll have to have will be work clothes. Blue jeans."

"Blue jeans?"

"They're like overalls, without the bib. They call them Levis out there. A store in San Francisco owned by a man named Levi. I got all this from Steve."

"Is Steve's mother living where you're going? On the ranch?"

"I believe so, yes. But don't write to her, Mother. Not until I've been there a while and there's some occasion for it. I'll give you the address now, but you understand why I don't want you to write Mrs. King."

"Of course. I'll say goodbye to Ernestine for you."

"Do that, yes. Well, I think I hear Henry."

"Yes. Well, I guess there's nothing more."

"No, and I'm not the one they hold the train for. Take good care of yourself and I'll write to you and you write to me."

She looked at him appraisingly. "This is all for the best. I know it is. You're not leaving anything that you'll really need. My love goes with you and stays with you. You know that, my boy."

"Yes, Mother. I know that." He leaned down and kissed her and just once she stroked the top of his head.

"Hurry, and God bless you."

He barely caught the train, and he was on his way.

In his mother's room his father was standing at the window. He was fully dressed. Presently she came out of her bathroom and got back into bed.

"Good morning, Agnes," he said.

"Good morning," she said.

"He's gone."

"Yes, he's gone, and I'll never see him again."

"That isn't necessarily true."

"It's as true as anything you ever knew," she said. "As true as the fact that I'll never forgive you for last night."

"Agnes, listen to me, please. There are two sides to this, and be fair."

"No, there aren't two sides to it, and there's no question of fairness, George. This was the one time in your life when you didn't have to think-think-think. And what good has your thinking done? You made it impossible for my son to stay another night in this house. I might have been able to do something for him if *you'd* gone away for a week or a month. But whatever you said to him, you made it impossible. If you didn't want to be nice to him, at least you could have gone away while I tried to make him feel less like a leper."

"He said in so many words that he wished I would die."

"What did you say to provoke him? Don't tell me. I don't want to know."

"I'm very strongly tempted to tell you."

"Well, don't."

"You're taking advantage of your illness."

"What advantage? What advantage have I got to take? I know what's going to happen to me. I know how long I've got, a year at the most. What if you shorten that by a few months? What can you possibly say that would be as bad as what you did last night? You mean that you could say something that would give me another attack? And you're not saying it because you don't want to take advantage of my illness? What a hypocrite you are, George Lockwood. Really and truly."

"Thank you."

"I've learned something about you. Too late, but at least I'll die knowing it. You pretend not to care what people think about you, but in fact you care more than anyone else in the world. You're not a snob, you're not an aristocrat. You're nothing more than a cowardly person that doesn't want anything known about him, good or bad. So afraid that if the good became known, the bad would too. That's all it is."

"Oh, there is some good about me?"

"Why yes. I even told your son that you were generous, considerate, gentle."

"I'm sure that fell on hard ground."

"I didn't do it for you. I did it for him. He has your blood, and the boy is going to wonder about himself, these next few months and years."

"Well, he wants me dead."

"And *you* know what *that* can be, wishing someone would die, but unable to hasten the event."

"I consider that insulting and ungrateful. I'd hoped you and I could discuss some plan for George."

"Nobody's listening to you, George. The effect is lost."

"Perhaps so, Agnes. But you always talk as though you were absolutely sure that God is taking down every word. In the long run maybe we're both cowards. Both of us."

"Please go," she said.

Agnes Lockwood survived the winter, was sustained through the spring by the letters from her son and daughter, but could not endure the heat of August. She was not helped by the last few letters from her son, which came at irregular intervals and contained over-casual references to a girl called Rita and descriptions of the San Luis Obispo County weather. Rita had no last name; George seemed to have proceeded on the notion that he had fully identified her in an earlier letter. As to the California weather, the heat was continually of such intensity that only the nearness of the Pacific Ocean made it bearable. "Occasionally Rita and I seize the opportunity to go for a swim." Agnes Lockwood would hint for more information about Rita, but it was not forthcoming. "She sounds Spanish," said Ernestine Lockwood. "There are a lot of people of Spanish descent in California."

"I wouldn't want him to marry a Catholic," said Agnes.

"Well, I'm only guessing. And he hasn't said anything that makes me think he wants to marry her."

"*She* may want to marry *him.*"

"She'd be crazy if she didn't, but he'd let you know, Mother."

The girl watched her mother's struggles with the lowland heat of the dog-days. Agnes could not sleep with the electric fans humming, but she could not breathe unless the air was circulated, and one Friday evening late in August she simply dropped her chin on her chest and her life was at its end.

Ernestine Lockwood sent her brother a telegram:

MOTHER DIED FUNERAL MONDAY LOVE

ERNESTINE

A week later a telegram came from her brother:

HAVE BEEN AWAY TELEGRAM RECEIVED TODAY PLEASE WRITE LOVE

GEORGE

She wrote him at length, and in two weeks she had his reply.

Sept. 20, 1921

Dear Tina:

You have been very sweet to write and I also appreciate your sending the newspaper clippings concerning Mother's death and funeral. It was expected but when it finally came I discovered that I was not prepared for it. It must have been a dreadful experience for you but we can console ourselves with the thought that she could not have suffered very much. Most of her suffering was in being an invalid, confined to her room and I sincerely believe that she preferred dying to another year of that.

I have some other news for you of a more pleasant nature. The reason I did not get your telegram sooner was that I was taking a few days off to go on a honeymoon. Yes, I was married on the 18th of August to Rita Collier. I mentioned her several times in letters to Mother so it would not have been a complete surprise to her (or to you either, I guess). She is a fine girl, one

year younger than I am, graduated from Mills College cum laude (unlike her husband). Taught school near here. Her father and mother are Mr. and Mrs. David B. Collier, who live in Los Angeles. Mr. Collier is a chemist with the San Ysidro Petroleum Corporation. Originally came from Cleveland, Ohio, and is a graduate of Western Reserve University (Phi Beta Kappa). Mrs. Collier is also from Cleveland. Her maiden name was Ethel Van Meter. She was also a Phi Bete at Western Reserve. So you see I married into an intellectual family. I told them why I was kicked out of Princeton but they had already written to a friend of theirs on the Princeton faculty when they saw that Rita and I were getting serious. So they knew, but were willing to let us be engaged until I could support a wife.
That has now happened. I did not want Mother to worry but the work I am doing is not ranching. Mr. King is in the oil business. His ranch, which I gave as my address, is a hobby. The first two months I was here I drove a truck, carrying pipe, etc., then was promoted to stock clerk. I am on the payroll of the San Marcos Petroleum Company, Mr. King's company. I have been living in a boarding-house in San Luis Obispo but we have rented a small house. Address above. I received a cash bonus for introducing a new system of checking on supplies so that anyone can find out immediately how many drills, etc., are on hand and where "out" tools are located. Mr. King was the only person here who knew I had any other income until I told Rita and her parents. My next promotion will probably take me out in the field to really learn something about the oil business. Mr. Collier has recommended several books on the subject, which I bought, but they are hard going. Rita helps me with my "home work" but I confess that I often fall asleep in the middle of a sentence. Don't know when I will see you again unless you get out this way on a trip, but I hope you will meet Rita before long. I inclose several snapshots. Please write and let us know what you are doing.

Love,
George

Also inclose check. Please have the florist put flowers on Mother's grave on her birthday, Oct. 22. No name. Perhaps she will know.

"Of course she'll know," said the girl.

■

AN American family history customarily has two beginnings: the one, not always so easily determinable as the other, has to do with the earliest progenitor and his arrival on this soil; the other, about which there are no doubts, has to do with the first member of the clan to distinguish himself. So many family records were destroyed by fire or the plow that guesswork has been a considerable factor in most family histories that go back beyond the War of the Revolution. Few family Bibles, tax rolls, church records of pre-Revolutionary times survived the numerous fires. An overturned candle, a glowing ember from the hearth would start a fire, and there was nothing to stop it; nearly everything in a household or a church was highly flammable, and only the lucky citizens got out alive, with their lives and nothing else. They, and their neighbors if they had any, could stand outside and watch the burning of their possessions. The farmer with his plow and the surveyor with his transit were unsentimental about disturbing buried bones and their identifying headstones; furrows had to be straight, roads had to be built *where* they had to be built and the road-builder would make a curve around a solid rock but not around a long-dead citizen's remains. The materials used in building and furnishing jails were more effectively fire-resistant than those thought suitable for the private residence, but prison records were often inaccurate and in any event not sought after by the descendants of the men and women recorded. Thus it was that flame and cast iron obliterated the provable line between many an early ancestor and his living, proudly curious namesake.

George Bingham Lockwood and his brother Penrose were agreed that while the Robert Lockwood who emigrated to Watertown, Massachusetts, in 1630 and later settled in Fairfield, Connecticut, was in all probability their first American ancestor, their claim could be disputed by numerous other bearers of the name whose connection was, in a manner of speaking, fireproof. They had better reason to believe that their Eighteenth Century ancestor worked on the Conestoga wagon and was slain by Indians or other hostile persons. They had evidence to show that a Lockwood worked on the Conestoga wagon, lost his life in violent fashion in Central Pennsylvania, and was survived by several sons. Presumably, and almost logically, at least one of those sons settled in Nesquehela County, and when George Bingham Lockwood and his brother Penrose claimed descent from the Nesquehela County Lockwoods, they were on safe ground. Their father, Abraham Lockwood, was the son of Moses Lockwood, who was born in Nesquehela County, and there were many family Bibles, church records, and gravestones to support that claim.

Actually there were, in the brothers' childhood, many living residents of Swedish Haven who had known Moses Lockwood when he arrived from Nesquehela County, and Moses Lockwood was almost surely the grandson of John Lockwood, who was born in 1761 and miraculously escaped death at the hands of the Indians who killed his father. George and Penrose Lockwood readily conceded that the 1630-Watertown Lockwood might not be their kin; and they privately admitted that the 1761-Indian-murder John Lockwood was not incontrovertibly proven to have been their grandfather's grandfather. But Moses Lockwood was certainly their grandfather—unfortunately born in 1811 rather than in the previous century—and the first to gain distinction, which he did by making a great deal of money. When he died he left a fortune of more than $200,000 in Swedish Haven real estate, coal-dredging operations, farm mortgages, a distillery, and bank stock. He left every penny to his son Abraham, who was already well on the way to a considerable fortune of his own. Thus in two successive generations the richest man in Swedish Haven was a Lockwood, and the validity of the next generation's claim on New England origins was a topic of family conversation only. In Swedish Haven thrift was a word that was pronounced as reverently as the name Jesus, and the ability to accumulate so much money conferred its own distinction. And not without reason, especially when the second moneyed generation had inherited the ability. The citizens of Swedish Haven, who had made Moses Lockwood rich, took pride in the fact that he lived in their town; and their pride was in no small measure due to the fact that Moses had intended to settle in Gibbsville, the county seat and metropolis, which they hated. Moses, according to the legend, was on his way from Fort Penn to Gibbsville on horseback, and was only four miles away from his destination when a cloudburst fell and he was compelled to take refuge in the Five Points Tavern, the only inn in Swedish Haven. During the night he awoke to hear someone moving about in his room, and when he challenged the intruder, a man rushed at him with a dagger. But Moses Lockwood had drawn his pistol from beneath his pillow, and he shot the man dead. The man was a known ne'er-do-well, a brawler, frequenter of taverns, card-player and native of Gibbsville. The would-be thief was in his stocking feet, the dagger was recognized as belonging to him, and he had no right to be in Moses Lockwood's room at three o'clock in the morning. There was no need for a trial; the chief burgess made a notation in his journal—"blotter"—and so many citizens congratulated Moses Lockwood on his narrow escape and his brave dispatching of the criminal that he decided to remain in Swedish Haven an extra day.

He never left. The dead man was said to have several vindictive brothers in Gibbsville, who had publicly sworn to avenge his death, and Moses Lockwood was urged to stay away from the county seat. He continued to postpone his departure, but his money was running low and he told his new friends that he had to find employment, which he was more likely to do in the larger town. He had made so favorable an impression in Swedish Haven that he was offered, and accepted, the post of roundsman. The pay was not much, but the borough provided lodging in the borough hall, and the Five Points Tavern fed him at the common table with its other guests. Moses Lockwood had no experience in police work, but he had proven himself courageous and cool in a crisis, and a dead shot with the pistol. He had accepted the job gratefully, but conditionally, it being understood that when a more attractive proposition came along, he would take it. In the next election he opposed the chief burgess, who, more than anyone else, had been influential in getting him the job. Moses Lockwood won the election on the single issue of economy; he could do the chief burgess's job and be the roundsman for the chief burgess's pay, plus fees. It had not escaped his notice that the office of chief burgess paid a miserably small salary, but that the fees were an attractive proposition, partly because his predecessor had made them so. As chief burgess, Moses Lockwood, following precedent, charged fees for all the customary services of notary public and justice of the peace, and now charged extra fees as rent collector, process server, and collector of delinquent taxes. He also raised court costs for hearings conducted in his office, which he pocketed, and for writing legal letters for citizens who felt they could not afford attorneys. He then married the younger daughter of the chief burgess, and Moses Lockwood and his father-in-law soon had a monopoly on real estate transactions, fire insurance, and borough government, alternating as chief burgess every second year. They established the first stage line between Swedish Haven and Richterville, eleven miles to the west, and they built a whiskey distillery on the river bank. They contracted to feed and house the workers on the new Philadelphia-Gibbsville canal, and when the work was finished, converted the barracks into two tenement blocks.

Moses Lockwood did not proceed unopposed, and in 1848, through a business quarrel, he shot and killed a second man. It was then brought out that he had not left Fort Penn of his own accord, and although his lawyer objected and the objection was sustained, Moses Lockwood was forced to listen as the district attorney attempted to show that the earlier fatal shooting of the sneak thief in the Five Points Tavern was in fact a deliberate murder. According to the district attorney, Moses Lockwood had known the thief was planning a robbery in Gibbsville. The witness was one of the dead thief's brothers, and Moses Lockwood's attorney succeeded in having most of his testimony stricken from the record and discrediting most of what was allowed. Nevertheless the spectators in the courtroom were treated to the makings of a scandal.

The second fatal shooting, for which Moses Lockwood had to stand trial, took place in daylight on Dock Street, Swedish Haven. Calvin Lichtmann, a Richter Valley farmer, on whose farm Moses Lockwood and his father-in-law had threatened to foreclose a mortgage, was walking a few steps behind Lockwood on Dock Street, and carrying an old rifle. He called out a few words to Lockwood, who knew very little Pennsylvania Dutch. Lockwood turned, saw the rifle, drew his pistol and shot Lichtmann in the chest. Some Dutch-speaking pedestrians who heard the dying man's words swore that he wondered aloud why Lockwood had shot him, that he had meant no harm. It developed that Lichtmann had brought the rifle to Swedish Haven for repairs to the firing-pin and had no intention of harming Lockwood. It was claimed for Lockwood that in the circumstances—the rifle, the threat of foreclosure, the suddenness of Lichtmann's calling to him—he had reason to believe he was being attacked. Moses Lockwood was acquitted of manslaughter, but the judge, while finding no fault with the verdict, delivered himself of a few hundred sardonic words on the subject of men who go armed with a concealed weapon in the ordinary course of business. He then permitted Lockwood's attorney to say, for the record, that Moses Lockwood was a peace officer as well as a business man, since he was also chief burgess of the thriving Nesquehela County community of Swedish Haven. "The court trusts," said the judge, "that the peace-loving community of Swedish Haven will continue to thrive, and if the learned counsel has concluded, I declare this court now closed." He rose and ignored Moses Lockwood's outstretched hand.

Moses Lockwood was now thirty-seven years old, father of two daughters and a son, Abraham Lockwood. He did not again run for public office, and instead of soliciting business as had been his practice, he handled his affairs in a one-story, two-room building. He stayed in the back room, which opened on an alleyway. He kept the door key on his person at all times and as an extra precaution the door was bolted. From his desk he had a view of the front room and beyond it, through a large multi-paned window, of the passers-by. In spite of the judge's remarks, he continued to go armed. He built another house; this one a square red brick dwelling in the center of an acre of ground, and all around the property he put up a brick wall, eight feet high, with spikes embedded along the top. It was said that the wall had cost more money than the house, and older citizens recalled that the original Swedish Haven settlement had been wiped out in an Eighteenth Century massacre by the Lenni Lenape tribe. Plainly, Moses Lockwood would be ready if the Indians ever came again. The most obtuse citizens could guess the reasons behind Moses Lockwood's zeal for self-protection: the Bundy brothers, three in number, were only four miles away and they unanimously glowered at mention of the name Lockwood. The threat of a perjury charge against Josiah Bundy for his testimony in the Lockwood manslaughter trial had reactivated the brother's animosity, and citizens remarked that regardless of how much truth there was or was not in Josiah Bundy's accusation, the brothers now firmly believed—or convincingly pretended to believe—that Moses Lockwood had lured their brother to his room and murdered him. They were violent men, ever in and out of trouble with the Gibbsville constables; and to give substance to Moses Lockwood's story of the shooting of their brother was the family reputation for preying on drunken men. In so far as the Swedish Haven citizens were concerned, Moses Lockwood was given the benefit of the doubt; but a doubt had been created, and not everyone in the town believed that Moses Lockwood's anxiety for safety emanated from a clear conscience.

There was the matter of his departure from Fort Penn, the capital of the Commonwealth and one of its larger cities. Swedish Haven, in 1833, when Moses Lockwood first arrived in the town, was still very much a town in the wilderness. True, there was farming to the west and the south, and only four miles to the northwest lay Gibbsville, with a population of more than 8,000. Gibbsville was reachable by highway, railway, and the canal, but these transportation lanes had been cut through a dense forest; snake, panther, and wildcat country, and on occasion, bear. Strange men, of whom no questions were asked, went from town to town, and these floaters were quite sensibly blamed for the fairly frequent highway robberies and senseless killings that occurred in the area. Moses Lockwood had said he was on his way to Gibbsville when the cloudburst detained him at the Five Points Tavern; but he never told anyone why he was going to Gibbsville. Citizens had to supply their own answers to the questions, and they could invent the answers out of what they knew of Moses Lockwood after the manslaughter trial.

The district attorney had called a witness, who was sworn and gave his name, Adam Yoder, Fort Penn. Immediately Moses Lockwood snatched his attorney's arm and whispered to him, but before the attorney could get his objections sustained, Adam Yoder was able to say, in response to the district attorney's opening question, "Yes sir, I arrested Lockwood back in 1833." The defense attorney shouted his objections so that the next words of Adam Yoder were not audible, but it was thereafter common knowledge that Moses Lockwood at least once had been charged with a misdemeanor or a felony. Several business men of Swedish Haven and Gibbsville then went to the trouble of ascertaining by correspondence the nature of the young Lockwood's offense. It was burglary. Specifically, it was the theft of a cash box from a tavern of dubious reputation in Fort Penn. Moses Lockwood was arrested and put in the lockup, but the tavernkeeper changed his mind about pressing charges and Lockwood was released. Informally, however, he was ordered to leave town, never to return.

This information came too late in Moses Lockwood's career to be of value to his business competitors. His rise had been rapid, and men who had been on an equal footing with him during his earliest years in Swedish Haven now owed him money or would in all likelihood some day want to borrow from him. Moreover, in doing business with Moses Lockwood they had had to reveal some sharp practices of their own; and what Moses Lockwood did not know of his own knowledge, he could easily find out from his father-in-law, the alternating chief burgess, who possessed a complete record of the citizens' sins. It was time to concede that Moses Lockwood had reached a new level of importance, that put him out of range of cobblers and blacksmiths, bricklayers and harness makers. Now his dealings were in money, real money, or in its mysterious, capricious ghost, Credit; and the citizens were finding it difficult to remember him as a young roundsman, going about the town in the night, trying doors and keeping the peace.

He had his defenders, if he had no real friends. Whatever he had been or whatever he had done in Fort Penn, he had given good value as a roundsman and in his other enterprises; when he agreed to do something, he did it, promptly, efficiently, and to the extent he contracted for. He was firm in money matters and there was no doubt that he took advantage of his official positions to create business opportunities for himself; but none of this was against the rules that applied in business or politics, and it all gained him respect, the respect for the strong-growing-stronger that silences ethical considerations. He joined a church, attended Sunday services with his wife, and contributed increasing amounts as he prospered. Every man in the borough had his own personal set of ethics, and those who were possibly in a position to be critical of Moses Lockwood's made a compromise: Moses Lockwood was prospering, perhaps at the cost of strict adherence to a code of honorable conduct, but he was behaving himself, living respectably, and doing so despite and practically in defiance of the man he had been on first arriving in Swedish Haven. He had come to town with a pistol in his pocket, alone and unknown, and he had been set upon by a thief with a dagger; he had killed the thief, he stayed in the town, he took work, he married, he prospered. The second killing was a tragedy of errors, but could not be held against Moses Lockwood. Nor was it, except secretly by every man in the town. In their very midst, in daily association, he was an outcast. No one wanted Moses Lockwood's friendship after he had killed twice, and the citizens' efforts to hide that fact—sometimes from themselves—were soon apparent to him, with the curious result that he became more and more devoted to his family, his wife and three children. Every day he tried to make money for them, and most days he was successful.

In 1861 he organized a company of militia, uniformed and equipped out of his own pocket, and as Lockwood's Rifles they were absorbed into the 70th Pennsylvania Infantry. Lieutenant Moses Lockwood was home three months after leaving Swedish Haven, badly wounded in the chest and disfigured by the loss of the lower half of his left ear. He had participated in the battle and the rout at Bull Run. He was past fifty years of age, had learned that war is for young men, but was determined that one young man, his son Abraham, would see none of it. Abraham, now twenty, was at the University of Pennsylvania, where the members of his fraternity were agitating for the mass enlistment of the entire chapter. Moses Lockwood wrote his son:

> You have seen what can happen in one battle. I am a comical figure with my cropped ear but not so comical when I try to breathe. I beg of you to heed my advice. Do not enlist now. Finish your schooling for it is to be a long war. Our troops do not posess the fighting spirit of the rebels because the latter are defending there home land & they will fight us to the last man. This war is certin to last another year. Time enough a year from now to enlist. Maybe 2 yrs if England & France join in on the side of the rebels. Also your Mother & Sisters will need you if anything happens to me. You would be head of the Family then. Yr loving Father, Moses Lockwood.

When it became apparent that his prediction of a two-year war was optimistic, Moses Lockwood persuaded his son to apply for a commission. He then, unbeknownst to Abraham, got in touch with Jacob Baltz, member of the House of Representatives for the Lantenengo County district, and talked straight: Baltz would see that Abraham got a commission promptly and was assigned to duty with the War Department in Washington. If this was not done, and done promptly, Moses Lockwood would use all his money and his new prestige as a wounded soldier to run against Baltz. Baltz was amenable, and Abraham Lockwood, second lieutenant, served his country as an aide to a general in the Quartermaster Corps. He was particularly useful as a handsome young guest at the social functions in the foreign embassies. His French was more than adequate to these occasions, and he was a welcome relief from the aging colonels and generals who represented the North at the diplomatic balls. He knew that he had not been chosen accidentally, but he bore his father no resentment. In 1865 he was still alive, and that could not be said of more than half the men in his fraternity.

Abraham Lockwood, not slender but thin, not humorous but witty, not affectionate but concupiscent, had grown from boyhood to manhood in the atmosphere of withdrawal and vigilance that followed his father's acquittal on the manslaughter charge. Abraham himself was by nature outgoing and gregarious, and he was free to play with boys his own age; but every day he saw his father's derringer lying beside his watch-and-chain, notecase, pocket handkerchief, small change, and he knew that in the desk drawer at the office and bureau at home his father kept full-size "horse pistols," always loaded. The business of locking up at night was not a casual routine; and at the new house, after the spike-topped wall was built, Abraham Lockwood's playmates repeated the fortress jokes their fathers made. He was sometimes proud, sometimes ashamed of the fact that his father had shot two men to death; no other father had participated in a shooting, and Abraham Lockwood was conscious of his playmates' admiration of his father; but it was *his* father, not theirs, and he did not like his father to be so very different from other fathers. It would have embarrassed him, too, if his playmates had known that in the privacy of the home his father was gentle, considerate, and generous; while conventional sternness and aloofness and overt cruelty kept most of his playmates in continual fear of their own fathers.

At the University, away from his family, Abraham Lockwood identified himself with the campus social life rather than with the bookish. He had a large allowance, spent it freely on his wardrobe and the entertainment of his new friends, and the money enabled him to participate in games of chance for comparatively high stakes. He learned to play whist, and was invited to join a club at which the new duplicate whist was played. Membership in this club was a major social triumph for Abraham Lockwood of Swedish Haven; the other members were undergraduates whose families were the *bon ton* of Philadelphia and nearby Delaware, Maryland, and New Jersey. As merely a good whist player Abraham Lockwood could have been ignored; the invitation signified the members' unanimous approval of Abraham Lockwood as a good fellow. He wore the club badge, a golden scarf pin in the shape of a question mark, like a decoration, which indeed it was; to be made a member of The Ruffes was a more promising augury for the post-college future than his membership in Zeta Psi.

It had been taken for granted at Zeta Psi and among The Ruffes that Abraham Lockwood—handsome, clever, well supplied with funds—was related to certain other Lockwoods of substance. *He* seemed to take for granted that everyone would assume he was one of *those* Lockwoods; consequently he was not asked the direct question and was not compelled to give the kind of evasive answer that would immediately have made him suspect. His only lie, in that respect, was to say offhand that most of his people had gone to Yale, although his father had not. In a sense he was telling a half-truth; the closer descendants of 1630-Watertown Robert Lockwood had gone to Yale in abundance, and it was not then or ever established that Abraham Lockwood was not somehow connected with 1630-Watertown Robert. In any event it seemed altogether likely to the members of Zeta Psi and more particularly to the members of The Ruffes that Abraham Lockwood, son of the upstate magnate, was all they made him out to be—a gentleman.

The Ruffes, who were twelve in number, had an arrangement with a Miss Adamson that made her, in effect, the club's mistress. She had a house in Juniper Street where she lived alone with a maid. Unlike the Greek-letter fraternities and the upperclassmen's societies, The Ruffes had no secrets of ritualistic nature; even the name was quite obvious to anyone who had ever heard of the game of whist; but it was understood by the members that anything and everything said or done during gatherings of the club was not to be talked about with outsiders, and the arrangement with Phoebe Adamson was in the same esoteric category as the stakes the members played for. Under the arrangement, any member of the club could go to Phoebe whenever he felt the need, and she would accommodate him. If too many—more than two—members desired to be accommodated, Phoebe would dispatch her maid to bring in other girls who were on her carefully selected list, and who were regularly employed as hotel chambermaids, housemaids, and salesladies in the stores and who wished to augment their salaries. Phoebe, through her own maid, could round up a dozen young women in a couple of hours.

On such occasions Abraham Lockwood was splendid company. He was extraordinarily well equipped by nature and immediately and inevitably was nicknamed The Stud-Horse. His fellow members of the club would time him with their watches to test how long he could postpone orgasm; and when Phoebe was introducing a new girl, the members would gather around to watch her amazement when she saw him stripped. Away from Phoebe's he was discretion itself; his dignified conduct was given credulity by his appearance, his blameless complexion, his innocent wavy locks, his unworldly look of slightly bewildered friendliness. "It's hard to believe it," his fellow members would say—and Abraham Lockwood himself became one of the few club secrets.

His army assignment in Washington was a post-graduate course in the amenities he had so quickly mastered at Penn. His Pennsylvania Dutch was offensive to the German-speaking diplomats, but he at least could understand a great deal of their conversations; and at the University he had liked and done well in French. Having been partly bilingual since boyhood, he was less self-conscious about using a foreign language than his fellow students; consequently he seemed a more alert, interested student and, in turn, his professors reciprocated with an interest in him. His accent and intonations needed practice, but he could understand and make himself understood for hours at a stretch. This was not an unimportant attribute; any effort, large or small, that succeeded in making the French nation hesitate to help the Confederacy was worthwhile. Abraham Lockwood was fed harmless military information to be passed along at the parties he attended, in the hope that it would be carried back to the French embassy. There was no way to estimate the efficaciousness of this minor propaganda scheme, but the French stayed out of the conflict. Abraham Lockwood was the more effective because the highly sophisticated French diplomats regarded him as a completely ingenuous Yankee, who possessed some small skill at cards but was otherwise little more than a dancingman in a blue uniform.

One result of his Washington experience was Abraham Lockwood's discovery that Philadelphia was not the capital of the world and the Philadelphians, even the families that were represented in The Ruffes, were not taken at their own valuation when they journeyed away from home. It was true that in diplomatic-society small talk Abraham Lockwood was often asked about individual Philadelphians who were acquaintances of the foreigners, but it was as individuals and not as Philadelphians that they had made an impression. Abraham Lockwood never forgot this lesson, and its immediate effect was to keep him from making a fool of himself.

No young woman in Swedish Haven had attracted the young buck as a suitable nubile prospect. He had gone to Washington with the thought that when the war was over he would live in Philadelphia and in due course marry some sister of some University friend. He discarded the plan after he had begun to see Philadelphia from another perspective. Philadelphia was only Philadelphia, and a marriage of convenience could turn into a lifetime of boredom, convenient only as a means to achieve high standing in a city that had begun to disappoint him. With this thought came two others: in Washington he realized that he had not often been invited to visit the homes of his fellow members of The Ruffes, and that on the rare occasions when he dined with his clubmates' families, the daughters of the house had not been present. He slowly found an explanation for this careful oversight: his antics at Phoebe Adamson's.

The other thought, which came as he projected his plans into the post-war future, evolved into the scenes that would take place if he got himself engaged to a Germantown girl and there was an exchange of visits by the two sets of parents. Moses Lockwood in his middle fifties had acquired dignity through success and suffering and reticence through his fears, but he had no polish and he did have, literally, half an ear. He was bothered by phlegm, and his efforts to clear his throat stopped conversation until he had caught the bothersome wad and spat it, when luck would have it, into one of the brass spittoons that were in nearly every room in the house. When there was no spittoon he would leave the room, saying, "I gah geh rih oh this," and get rid of it. Abraham Lockwood's mother could read and write and play a few favorite hymns on the organ, but she had never been to Philadelphia, never read any book but the Bible, never seen a play, never danced, and never had guests for a meal. In the red brick house she had employed her first help, a woman to do the laundry; but despite her husband's prosperity she did all the cooking, cleaning, mending and fancywork. Abraham Lockwood's sisters took Louis Antoine Godey's *Lady's Book,* and they had been to Reading and Gibbsville, but they would add neither beauty nor social charm to the hypothetical visit of the imaginary Germantown girl's parents. Daphne Lockwood looked exactly like her brother, was the same height, had no bust and had a scramble of incisors that made her speech inaudible, made extra-inaudible by her habit of covering her mouth with her fingers. Rhoda Lockwood, the other sister, was dumpy like her mother, and washed her hands and face only when specifically ordered to do so. Long past the age when it was excusably childish, the sisters would giggle together whenever any visitor came to the house. There were other problems the sisters might create: Rhoda, at fifteen, had once slapped her mother when Abraham kissed their mother goodnight. Daphne, when late for a meal, could usually be found locked in the privy.

Thus from his reappraisal of Philadelphia had Abraham Lockwood gone to a realistic appreciation of his own situation. And realistic it was, for he saw that only as an upstater coming to Philadelphia could he count on the continuing friendship of his University chums, friendship that could be extremely useful in a business way; and he now was determined to make money and look toward Gibbsville for a suitable partner in marriage. He came home from the army, and delighted his father with the announcement that he had decided to cast his lot with the Lockwood enterprises.

Abraham Lockwood was so much smarter than the men with whom he was soon doing business that he found that he could afford to be somewhat less ruthless than his father had become. The result of his calculated kindness was that people preferred to do business with him. He made no large-scale moves without his father's approval; now it was a case of building a more amicable relationship—good will, it was called—while the methods and aims remained essentially the same. Abraham Lockwood did not foreclose as quickly as his father and grandfather had done, but a farmer who needed more time would find that in exchange for time he had given time and money. The interest rate would be the same; the farmer would simply go on paying it an extra year or two, and *en passant* be advised to make all purchases—harness, gunpowder, tobacco, salt, nails, molasses—through the Swedish Haven Mercantile Company, a Lockwood concern.

The establishment of a bank was long overdue in Swedish Haven; it could not, however, be established without the knowledge of the Lockwoods, father and son, who were themselves very much in the business of lending money.

They were therefore prepared for the invitation to discuss the formation of a bank, and when the invitation came they surprised the somewhat timid merchants by agreeing to participate. The new institution was an accomplished fact before the merchants fully realized that the Lockwoods controlled it, while continuing their own business of lending money at higher rates. The bank got exactly as much business as the Lockwoods chose to allow it, and no one would be so foolish as to dream that Swedish Haven could support a second bank.

If only indirectly, every citizen of the borough and its environs contributed to the financial well-being of the Lockwoods. Three years after Appomattox, Abraham Lockwood decided that things were going well enough for him to reinvest some of the family cash. His father demurred; he knew the value of a front foot on Dock Street and an acre of high timberland in the Richter Valley, but he was suspicious of the world of stocks and bonds. He had seen where waste and graft and plain theft reduced the profits of the railways and the canal, and as for buying shares in far-off enterprises, he protested that it was giving strangers the combination of your safe. "You forget that I have friends," said Abraham Lockwood. "I wouldn't be going to strangers. They would be men who would want to make a profit out of us, but they're entitled to it if our profit is bigger."

"I would like to see the money stay here. Maybe we could build a factory around here."

"Later on, Father. Let's stay in the money business for the time being."

Abraham Lockwood, not to show his hand, waited for the annual dinner of alumni members of The Ruffes. Half the members had married since leaving the University and for most of them the intimate frolics were a thing of the past (and possibly of the future). This circumstance was a fortuitous one for Abraham Lockwood, in that his reunion with his friends was conducted on more dignified terms, and the conversation quickly got around to the kind of life the clubmates were living and thus to talk of business. "I have my fingers in a lot of pies," said Abraham Lockwood, when it came his turn. "My father and I of course have the bank, and I've got him to put his money in this and that. Nothing that would seem big to you fellows, but in our part of the world a man with a thousand dollars is very well off."

Among his listeners were young men who knew a great deal about his part of the world through their holdings in coal and railways. One friend in particular, Harry Penn

Downs, admitted to having passed through Swedish Haven twice in the past year while on business in Gibbsville. He was mildly apologetic for not having stopped over in Swedish Haven. "Oh, I understand, Harry. And even if you'd stopped over I might not have been there. I'm away a lot, looking at this and that for possible investment." He did not mind lying to Harry Penn Downs if a lie asserted his independence of Philadelphia and Gibbsville. "To tell you the truth, I've been here a few times on my way to New York. Just between trains."

"New York?" said Downs.

"Philadelphia isn't the only place. And I doubt if the Drexels are aware that my father and I exist."

"Well, the Drexels aren't the only bankers in Philadelphia. You ought to know that."

"Are there others? One thing they all have in common with the Drexels—they've never heard of us either. On the other hand, we've had very pleasant dealings with a New York concern."

"What concern, may I ask?" said Downs.

"You may not. And in any event, why are we mixing business with pleasure? At home all I ever get to talk about is business. Harry, you? What do you do for relaxation?"

"Oh, I imagine I'm like the others here. Morris has his City Troop, and we all see each other at the dancing parties. But most of us are like you. Working hard. This is the time, you know. The next ten years tell the story, wouldn't you say, fellows?"

The others agreed.

"What story?" said Abraham Lockwood.

"Well, this is the time of our lives when our families overload us with work. Make us learn the game. And what we do now, the next ten years, determines a man's ultimate future. Not that it's all business."

"No, indeed," said someone.

"But it's work. Charity work. Committee work. And going out in society. Not one of us can say his time is his own."

"Hear, hear," said someone.

"And of course we're increasing the population, most of us," said Harry Downs. "You're not, though, are you, Locky?"

"I hope not," said Abraham Lockwood. "And I don't do much in the charitable line. My father contributes to this and that, but I prefer to put my money to work. Later, when I've made a little pile, I'll pick my own charities."

Everything he said was calculated to make them think, to make them think and remember him and want to do business with him, and to recall that he was so far from using his old friendships that he was bypassing Philadelphia for New York. Any earlier suspicion they might have had that he was a climber was now being allayed. Before the evening was over Harry Downs and Morris Homestead separately invited him to lunch before returning to Swedish Haven. He declined both invitations because, he said, he was taking an early train to *New York*.

As he had anticipated, he received letters from Homestead and Downs. He arranged to meet Downs at the Gibbsville Club on Harry's next visit to the region. He dismissed Homestead with a friendly but vague reply; Homestead was not his man. Morris Homestead would never need money himself and would not be eager to make it for anyone else. He was interested in fox-hunting, food and wine, club life and his family. He had not even been a particularly good whist player, and his membership in The Ruffes was due to the fact that he could not be left out of any good club in Philadelphia. He was a quiet, clean-cut, well-bred, courtly bore, already worth eight million dollars and with as much again to come his way when his mother died. There was not even much use to cultivate him for the future, when Abraham Lockwood might seriously cock an eye at the Philadelphia Club. Morris Homestead would never support the candidacy of anyone who was not automatically qualified, as Abraham Lockwood had reason to know from experience in The Ruffes' deliberations.

Harry Downs was another story. He was extravagantly proud of the Penn in his name, but his family during the post-Revolutionary years had never had a considerable fortune. He played cards to win, so much so that in college days he was the most intense and abstemious player, drinking almost nothing, and impersonally critical of his partners' play. For three years he had been the most consistent winner, if not the most congenial member of The Ruffes. His money-making was postponed by the War, during which he was brevetted major and wounded by mortar fire at Gettysburg. After the War he became frenetically dedicated to the making of money, and he was Abraham Lockwood's man.

They dined together at the Gibbsville Club. "Locky, you hurt Morris Homestead's feelings," said Harry Downs.

"Why?" said Abraham Lockwood. He was a little surprised that Harry Downs would know of Homestead's overtures. "Or should I say, how?"

"It's a great privilege to be asked to become a client of Homestead & Company."

"I wasn't. I was asked for lunch, and I couldn't go."

"Well, it's a great privilege to be asked to lunch by Morris Homestead. Some people would cancel a trip to New York."

"Morris is a nice fellow, but as you said that night, these are the years that count. Why did Morris ask me to lunch?"

"Possibly because he thought I was going to. He doesn't go after new business, but he feels that Homestead & Company have every bit as much right to you as we have."

"As you have? Are you after new business, Harry?"

"Yes, Locky. Yours."

"Where did you get the idea that our business would be worth going after?"

"From you, first, and then I've been hearing reports right here in this club. Our friends here tell us that you and your father have a miniature empire in Swedish Haven."

"It's miniature, I assure you."

"I wonder. I'm told that both you and your father have turned down directorships in the Gibbsville Trust Company. Very wise."

"That was my father's decision. We'd have nothing to gain. We don't want Gibbsville men encroaching on our territory, so to speak. But we couldn't keep them out if we were fellow directors. You know how those things are. For the same reason we haven't had anything to do with Philadelphia. Philadelphia money is all over this county—except Swedish Haven. We would like to keep that for ourselves, and we're going to, if we can."

"You won't be able to forever. I say that in a friendly spirit."

"You say it as a friend, but I detect a warning note."

"Yes, Locky, there's a faint warning note."

"From Philadelphia? All the way from Philadelphia?"

"No. From Gibbsville, only four or five miles. There are some Gibbsville men who don't see why you should have it all."

"How much are you going to confide in me, Harry?"

"I've already told you as much as I should as a friend."

"Yes, and I thank you. But from now on, it's business?"

"Yes," said Harry Downs. "Your New York people won't help you, at least as much as we could."

"Oh, you're implying that we need help?"

"Not yet, but if you did need help, would New York come to your rescue?"

"No. We haven't given them that much business, and I

have to tell you now, Harry. My father isn't in the New York transactions at all. It's all me, my own money."

"I could almost guess that, from what I heard of your father."

"So we can leave him out of this discussion."

"That's fine. I'd rather. Now I'm dealing with the principal himself. All right. Why don't you just forget about New York and let me try to make some money for you?"

"You surely don't expect me to say yes or no right away? As you said, Harry, a while back this became business, not two friends."

"Said it and meant it, and we'll be friends whatever the outcome of this conversation."

"Always, I hope. Now you've asked me to do business with you, a compliment, because you don't know what kind of business I'd bring you. It won't be large, at least at first, and never large by Philadelphia standards. But the character of the business. You don't know anything about that, so I'll tell you. I am interested in one thing—making money. Two things—making money and making it quickly. Therefore, the character of my business would be, simply, speculation. Does that interest you?"

"Very much. We can always find customers for conservative investments. That's the bread-and-butter business. Trust funds. Large estates. Elderly people. People that are satisfied with small returns on their money. But as you know, the big, quick money is made in speculation. *And lost*. Your father has made his money one way, you want to make yours the other. I lead a double life, Locky. I'm a conservative, three-percent man when I come to Gibbsville. But part of the time I'm a gambler."

"How have you done, as a gambler?"

"So far, I'm ahead of the game."

"Why?"

"Why? Oh, I see. You want to know if it's on my own hook or through private information. Frankly, it's mostly on my own. I watch a stock until I know its fluctuations. At a certain low, I buy it. At a certain high, I sell. And I do it on margin. I couldn't afford to do it otherwise. Everybody does what I do. Nothing unusual about it except that I may be a little more attentive than most fellows."

"I'm sure you are. Well, is it your idea that I turn over a certain amount of money for you to speculate with?"

"Yes."

"To you, and not to the firm of Haynes & Webster?"

"If you want to do your own trading, you could do it through

Haynes & Webster. But if you decide you want to gamble, that would be through me. My personal account. I would take your money and gamble with it, and at the end of a stated period, six months, a year, we cut up the profits."

Abraham Lockwood smiled. "Not very businesslike, is it?"

"No. For all you know, I could use your money to gamble with, never risk a cent of my own, and still take half your profits."

"That's what I was thinking."

"That's what I knew you were thinking. But not if I told you what stocks I was speculating in. Then you'd know to the penny."

"But if you told me the names of the stocks, I wouldn't need you at all, would I?"

"Of course not. In this kind of transaction we have to trust each other. For example, if you turned over $5,000 I would then tell you the names of the stocks I was buying. But I would be trusting you not to speculate in them on your own. In other words, Locky, you could buy my information for $5,000, but trade on your own with a much larger sum of money."

"I thought of that."

"Naturally. And you might make a very large profit, much larger than I would make. But—that would end our association, and I hate to think what it would do to our friendship."

"Of course. Then I take it that we can forget all about Haynes & Webster."

"For the moment."

"You and I would be partners? Equal partners?"

"No, not if we each put in the same amount of money. Sixty-forty. On a basis of $10,000, you would put up six thousand, and I would put up four. We would split the profits evenly."

"You take 16⅔ percent of my investment for your information. Isn't that high?"

"I think it's fair. It's the only way I'd do it. My 16⅔ percent is at the start. It becomes 50 percent at the division of profits. But only fifty percent."

"Only?"

"Only. You wouldn't be doing the trading. I would."

"And the losses?"

"You have lost $6,000 as soon as you go into partnership with me. That's the way you have to look at it in these speculations. I never want you to speculate with money you can't afford to lose."

"Ah! Now I like the whole thing better. I kept wondering whether you'd ever get around to that, Harry. I wanted to hear you *say* it."

"It's the first time I had a chance to. Well?"

"Six thousand dollars?"

"Six thousand dollars, and I'll put up four."

"I'll send you a cheque tomorrow."

"All right. And now I'll tell you the name of the stock I'm watching at present. St. Paul Paper Company."

"What's that?"

"They make paper for magazines and newspapers. The stock was selling at 6½. Too high to buy. The minute it goes under 5, I will buy. The minute it touches 9, I sell. It has gone to 10½ in the past year, but that's a little too much."

"Do you own any of it now?"

"Oh, no. I've just been studying it for two years. I got interested in it because I happened to notice that three of the Philadelphia newspapers buy their newsprint there. Haynes & Webster have a financial interest in one of the papers and may take over another. Until then I'd never paid any attention to the St. Paul company, but they're almost a monopoly. Oh, the stock will go much higher some day, but you and I will be trading in something else."

"Yes. Now, what Gibbsville men were going to encroach on our territory?"

"That man sitting over in the corner."

"Peter W. Hofman?"

"Yes. He had some very unpleasant things to say about your father, Locky. Not so much about you as about your father, although you didn't get off scot-free. He's going to help some of your townsmen start a bank."

"We'll see," said Abraham Lockwood. "He's king here, but not in our little empire. But thanks for telling me, partner."

■

IT was only fifteen miles from Richterville to Gibbsville, the county seat; it was thirty-five miles from Richterville to Fort Penn, the capital of the Commonwealth; but it was easier to get from Richterville to Fort Penn than from Richterville to Gibbsville. Richterville thereby came within the Fort Penn sphere of influence rather than the Gibbsville.

To go from Richterville to Gibbsville the traveler was well advised to proceed on horseback. There were four steep hills and one mountain intervening and the road that had been scratched out of the mountainside was two frozen ruts in the winter and liable to be a morass at other seasons of the year. No light rig or cutter, only wagons and wide-runner sleds, could be expected to get through without having a wheel or cutter-runner snapped off in the ruts. The mountain road was so narrow that for most of its length one vehicle could not pass another. As a precaution the driver of a wagon, about to enter the road, would blow his horn—literally a horn, cut from a cow and hollowed out—and wait for an answer. If there was no answer he could fairly assume that no other wagon was coming from the opposite direction. If there was an answer he would wait until the oncoming wagon had come along and made the road clear. If the wind was wrong—howling, blowing in the wrong direction—and the warning horns unheard, the two wagons might meet, creating their own impasse. There would be a consultation of the two wagoners; a coin would be tossed. The winner of the toss would then help the loser to unhitch his team, unload the wagon, remove the wheels, and lift the empty wagon-box to a place behind the winner's wagon. The loser's wheels would be replaced, his team hitched up, the wagon reloaded, and the two parties, delayed an hour or two, would be on their separate opposite ways.

After Moses Lockwood established the Swedish Haven—Richterville stage there was an alternative method of getting from Richterville to the county seat: by stage to Swedish Haven, by rail from Swedish Haven to Gibbsville.

As against these inconvenient and hazardous routes, the steam railway line directly connected Richterville and Fort Penn. Richterville, solidly Pennsylvania Dutch, was the trading center for farmers and trappers to the east and south, coal miners to the north, farmers and iron miners to the southwest, horse and pony breeders to the west. In the town were a tannery, a foundry, a brick kiln, a wagon works, two grain mills, and the end-of-rail for the all-important Fort Penn, Richterville & Lantenengo Railway. There was not a Catholic, Episcopalian, or Presbyterian in the town, although there was a Baptist church for the sizable Negro community, many of whom were Pennsylvania Dutch-speaking. There was no high school prior to 1855.

The numerous Hoffners in Richterville were headed by Levi Hoffner, who had six daughters and was unhappy that he could not make a boy. Adelaide Hoffner, the second daughter, was the prettiest, but she was as determined as her father that she would not be married for her money. In due course three of her sisters were matched to suitable young men and in 1870 she had become the oldest unmarried Hoffner girl, still the prettiest, still determined to remain single until she could marry a man who would appreciate her good looks, of which she was fully conscious. It was beginning to look as if she might become the richest spinster in Richterville when Abraham Lockwood came into her life.

As a small boy he had been taken for rides in the family-owned stage. It was a two-hour journey, if all went well. At Richterville the stage would change horses for the return trip, and while this was being done Abraham's father would take him to Mohn's Hotel for dinner, transact whatever business was to be done in Richterville, and go back to Swedish Haven on the afternoon stage. Abraham Lockwood as a consequence had no acquaintances in Richterville except Ted, the Negro hostler at the stage stable, and Chris Mohn, owner of the hotel. At age fifteen the novelty of the trip had worn off for Abraham Lockwood, and he did not again go to Richterville until he was in his thirty-first year, in 1871.

The occasion then was a wedding, the marriage of Sarah, the fourth Hoffner daughter, to a Gibbsville young man who had been a Zeta Psi at the University. Samuel Stokes was younger than Abraham Lockwood and no close friend, but it was an important wedding. A two-coach special train took Gibbsville guests by way of Reading and Fort Penn, a distance of 105 miles by rail. Abraham Lockwood and six other Swedish Haven guests made the eleven-mile trip in the newer of the Lockwood stages.

The ceremony took place at noon, followed by what was called a banquet on the Hoffner lawn. There was champagne in barely sufficient quantity for the wedding toasts, but there was no dancing. It was a hot day, and the out-of-town guests, their duty performed, were beginning to look homeward. Abraham Lockwood, looking at his watch, was about to round up his fellow passengers for the trip back to Swedish Haven when Adelaide Hoffner, in her bridesmaid's dress, came up to him. "I saw you look at your watch. Are you going home already?" she said.

"I'm afraid we must, Miss Hoffner. I think we're in for a thunder shower."

"That's too bad, then. I was tolt to inwite you to a party. Coultn't I persuate you to stay a while?"

"Well, if anyone could, you could."

"Ach, now."

"Who's having the party and what it is and where is it?"

"Some of the young ones, we're going ower to Barbara Shellenberger's place. Stay a while. There'll be a lot of pretty girls and Mr. Shellenberger bought more champagne. More than my father bought."

"Who told you to invite *me?* I'm not one of the young ones."

"I was tolt to inwite anyone I felt like, you forced me to atmit."

"Well, in that case I couldn't possibly say no, could I?"

"You better not."

"Do we walk? Is it far?"

"There it is, so. The white brick on the corner. Can you walk it?"

"I can walk it."

"I was afrait you't say it was too far for such an olt person like yourself."

Abraham Lockwood arranged to have the others return to Swedish Haven without him, and he accompanied Adelaide Hoffner to the Shellenberger party. The house was cool, even with the two dozen young men and women who were enjoying the unexpected release from the sobering presence of their elders. The young men were from the colleges—Lafayette, Muhlenberg, Franklin & Marshall, Lebanon Valley—and wore their fraternity pins on their lapels. Soon they would return to their shyness, but at the moment they and the girls were chattering, being reintroduced, getting names straight, laughing over nothing, rather desperately wanting to be gay together.

"As you can readily see, I shouldn't have come," said Abraham Lockwood. "To them I'm an old fossil."

"But not to me. I'm older than those girls."

"Yes. You must be two years older than some of them."

"You and I will go sit in the hall, say?"

"That's fine," said Abraham Lockwood.

"I wonter where is the champagne? Ah, here it comes. Take two glasses and then you can have mine."

"Don't you like champagne?"

"I had enough. I took an extra to give myself the courage to inwite you to the party. My Daddy was watching me to see if I drank too much of the toasts."

Abraham Lockwood lifted two glasses from the tray offered by the Negro maid. He handed a glass to Adelaide Hoffner. "Well, here's to us," he said.

She touched his glass with hers but did not drink.

"Not drinking?"

"You don't want me to get intoxicatet, do you?"

"No, not if you don't."

"I don't. Do you like Sam?"

"Sam? Oh, Sam Stokes. Yes, I like him. I don't know any reason why I shouldn't like him. Do you have reservations about him?"

"No, not for Sarah. My sister. But I wouldn't marry him."

"Well, you never will now, that's sure."

"I newer would ewer. Gootness, I'm having trouble with my wees and my wubbleyews. I'm so Dutchy already yet. My Daddy wasted his money at Miss Holbrook's."

"Miss Holbrook's in Fort Penn?"

"I went there two years as a boarting stutent already yet."

"Now you're putting it on. What's the matter, Adelaide? You are Adelaide, aren't you?"

"How dit you know?"

"I deduced it. All the girls and most of the young men

called you Adelaide, so I deduced that that was your name. What's the matter?"

"Nothing serious. Just thinking about Sarah. Now she's locked together with a man. What if she doesn't like it? She's still locked with him. For that matter, what if *he* doesn't like it?"

"Well, that *is* serious."

"Yes, it is. I didn't mean it wasn't serious. I meant it wasn't anything for me to fret about. Is that why you're still single?"

"Maybe. I haven't had time to think of matrimony."

"Then you must have thought about it a great deal."

"Why?"

"Well, you're handsome and wealthy, and the only way you could have stayed single was by making up your mind to. Therefore, you gave it a lot of thought, so?"

"You're right."

"She turned and faced him. "You're experienced, aren't you?"

"Yes."

"I knew that, all right."

"How?"

She smiled. "How? I could tell by the way you looked at the girls. A man without experience doesn't look at the girls that way."

"How *should* I look at them?"

"You can't change the way you look at them, not now any more. That's what experience does to a person. And girls know when a man is experienced."

"Woman's instinct?"

"Yes. It warns them. But the warning doesn't always do any good."

"Where did you learn all this? At Miss Holbrook's?"

"There I never learned anything. Yes, how to serve tea. How to curtsey if I ever meet the Queen of England. I didn't *learn* at Miss Holbrook's. I *taught*." She laughed.

"You taught?" he said. "What?"

"I'd rather not say. Certain things you learn on the farm. My Daddy has a farm two miles out."

"Oh, I understand. And you taught the girls at Miss Holbrook's about a calf being born."

"Calf? *Babies*, yet!"

"Well, that's something I've never seen. Would you like to teach me?"

She blushed and looked at him with alarm. "No." The

word was more a protest than an answer. "I talk too much for my own good."

"Are you afraid of me? You look it."

"I don't know. Yes, I guess so."

"Would you like me to leave?"

"Stay, but don't talk such a way. It was my fault."

"Would you like to kiss me, Adelaide?"

"Sure, but I'm not going to."

"Would you like me to kiss you?"

"Stop doing that."

"I'm not doing anything. I'm asking you a question."

"You're experienced. You know what you're doing."

"Yes, I do. And you do want to kiss me, don't you?"

"Yes, but I'm not going to."

"And you want me to kiss you, don't you? To put my arms around you."

"Yes."

"Tight. You against me."

She nodded, and she was breathing like a tired swimmer.

"Have you ever kissed anyone?"

"No," she said.

"But when you do, it will be me, won't it?"

"Yes. I guess so."

"When?"

"I don't know."

"It would be nice if we were alone, wouldn't it?"

"Yes."

"Are you still afraid of me?"

"I don't know. Yes."

"Do you think I'm bad, Adelaide?"

"Yes."

"Wicked?"

"Yes."

"Evil?"

"I don't know. Let me go."

"I'm not touching you. I haven't touched you."

She looked at her arms, one, then the other, and then she straightened up. "Let's go and get some fresh air," she said.

"All right, but you made a promise."

"I know."

"I'm going to see that you keep it."

"When I kiss somebody it will be you, but maybe I don't want to kiss anybody."

"We know better. Both of us," he said.

He left the party while she was still disturbed by their

conversation, reintroduced himself to Chris Mohn, and engaged a room at the hotel. Then, not to waste the visit, he called on the blacksmith, hay and feed dealers, and the owner of the wagon works—all men with whom the stage line did business. The stage was an enterprise that Moses Lockwood administered personally, but Abraham Lockwood was Moses Lockwood's son, and the men were accordingly pleasant. In the course of his conversations with them he learned more about the Hoffner family, the *Levi* Hoffner family, and came away convinced that—modesty to one side—they were the Lockwoods of Richterville, with a larger share of good will than the Lockwoods could claim.

In a week Adelaide Hoffner, the emotional girl, was less in his thoughts than Adelaide Hoffner, daughter of Levi. Marriage was one of the items in Abraham Lockwood's consideration of his future, along with the death of his father, which could reasonably be expected in a few years. Moses Lockwood was now in his sixty-first year, shrewd enough in business matters but easily exhausted by physical effort. From now on any time was his time for dying, and he knew it. When one of the Bundy brothers was found drowned in the canal Moses Lockwood said to his son, "One more to go. I want to outlive those bastards, and I want to see my first grandchild. That's going to be up to you, son. The girls will never get a husband, neither one of them. I wrote you during the War. If anything happened to me, you were going to have to take care of Mom and the girls. Mom is all right, but one of these days we're going to have to put Daphne away, and maybe Rhoda too. If they was farm girls they could be farmer women. A farmer woman works like a mule all day and night-time comes and she does something else like a donkey, and that's all their life is. All they got to look forward to. But our girls have a well-to-do father, never had to work, don't show any tendency to work, can't hardly read or write as good as their mother. I doubt if any farmer would have them, and the Lord knows none of the town fellows want them. So that's up to you, too, son. Be nice to them till they have to be put away, the poor miserable creatures. Poor, miserable creatures. And their mother was pretty. Your mother was a pretty young woman. Bright, too. Bright as a new pin. Spunky. All them things. But the girls didn't get any of it. Daphne hiding herself down-cellar or locking herself in the privy. Rhoda doing things if I didn't know them I'd never believe them. Their father. There'll be the money to take care of them. I saw to that. But when all is said and done, I wonder if they wouldn't of been better off poor. The poor can't be so particular when they're picking a wife."

His father's observations alarmed Abraham Lockwood: the rich could be particular in picking a husband. Sam Stokes was somewhat of a catch, in all honesty as much of a catch as Abraham Lockwood would be. No single branch of the Stokes family had more money than the Lockwoods, father and son; but the Stokes clan and the mighty Hofman clan, who were closely related, and the Chapins and the Walkers were now suddenly united with the Hoffners of Richterville. Abraham Lockwood, counting his trump, was now not so sure he had enough to win.

"Father, he said, a few days after the preceding conversation, "I have a young lady picked out to marry. Levi Hoffner's daughter."

"Well, he has enough of them. One fewer than a month ago, but he must have a few left. You like one of them?"

"Yes. I met her at the wedding."

"Pretty and all that, I guess, or you wouldn't show no interest. Well, why are you telling me?"

"Let me have the stage line. That will give me an excuse to go to Richterville."

"The hell with the stage line. Levi Hoffner could build a railroad to Swedish Haven if he wanted to. Well—halfway. But why do you want to let those people think of you as a smelly stage driver, or black Ted, our hostler there? That's what they'll think of you as. That's no way to do it, son. Go to Levi with something big and important. Did you talk to him at the wedding?"

"No."

"Glad to hear that, because if you'd of talked to him you'd of sized him up for a different kind of a man. Not a man that gives a damn for a stage driver for a son-in-law. He knows me, Levi. But he would of thought right away you weren't as smart as your old man. And you are. In some ways smarter, but not always. Levi Hoffner could have stopped your Grandpa and I from putting the stage into Richterville."

"How?"

"How? A dozen different ways. Refusing us stable room. Ordering the blacksmith and the wagon works to refuse us. Give us trouble with the law. Or just poison our animals."

"He'd have done that?"

"Levi Hoffner and his father, Jake Hoffner, wouldn't of sat and waited for the Bundy brothers. They would of rode up to Gibbsville and had it out with them right out in the street. I couldn't do that. Nobody knew me. I didn't have nobody I could ask to go with me. But Jake and Levi had all them Hoffners, livin' here since back in George Washington's time. I was the one and only Lockwood in the whole damn county till your mother took the name. The only way we put the stage in Richterville was because the Hoffners let us. And they was sure we'd go broke. We would of, too, if we didn't have other money. We lost money on the stage line the first four years. No mail contract. Philadelphia bastards didn't want us to get the mail contract. They wanted the mail to go all the way around by way of Fort Penn and Reading. No, don't go to Richterville as the owner of the stage line. Who invited you to that wedding? Not the Hoffners."

"No. Sam Stokes was a fraternity brother of mine."

"You bet. The Hoffners wouldn't invite the Lockwoods. You see what I mean? When you go to call on Levi Hoffner, you want to be able to look him in the eye as an equal."

"We have more than they have."

"Now we have, but that ain't the way he remembers it. You sure we have more?"

"I did some scouting."

"Good boy. Better scouting and maybe I'd have my whole ear. But even if we do have more, son. We don't have something they do have. A big family and over a hundred years in the one neighborhood. We don't even count in Swedish Haven yet. Only our money, our property. But marry this Hoffner girl and by Jesus we'll count. I'll put my brains to work. I know Levi Hoffner, and you don't."

Moses Lockwood sat silent for so long that his son thought he had gone to sleep with his eyes open, but presently he spoke. "Son?"

"Yes sir."

"Go tell Levi Hoffner you want to start a railroad."

"Between Swedish Haven and Richterville?"

"Levi Hoffner is a stockholder in the Fort Penn, Richterville & Lantenengo. Now listen to me, son. There's only one reason in God's world why the F. P. R. & L. don't come all the way through to Swedish Haven. You know why?"

"Money."

"It's always money, son. But why didn't they? Because there's nothing but farms and a few farmers from here to Richterville. That's why there's no money in it. A few head of cabbage, once in a while a farmer. Christ Jesus, I thought this out ten years ago, and I ain't a railroad man. No coal, no heavy freight to speak of. Such a line would never make money."

"No. Therefore Levi Hoffner wouldn't think much of me as a business man."

"Not right off, he wouldn't. But you'd have to make him wonder why you want to start a railroad. He'd start wondering, and you'd have to start play-acting."

"How?"

"Let on to him that you have some secret information. You don't have to tell him an out-and-out lie, but you can hint. Hint around that you got secret information that the Philadelphia, Reading & Gibbsville is thinking of building a line from Swedish Haven to Richterville."

"He'd see through that right away, Father. He's a stockholder in the F. P. R. & L., and they're owned by the P. R. & G."

"Hell, I know that, son. I just told you. But I know Levi Hoffner. He's going to say to himself what do you know? Young Lockwood knows more than he does, and he's a stockholder."

"All right. Go on."

"But you don't tell him anything, only enough to let him smell the money. That's when he'll start thinking of you as a big man. He'll try to get your information out of you. He'll invite you to his house. And you go after his daughter. That part is up to you."

"It sounds fantastic."

"Well, I don't know what that word means, but I know Levi Hoffner. And I guess I know you, son. If you want a woman, you know how to go after her. Anybody that can stay single as long as you have, they know how to handle women."

"This imaginary line that the P. R. & G. is supposed to be building."

"Make Levi believe that you build yours first and then sell it to the P. R. & G."

"That's what I thought. Now I see the whole scheme. Maybe it wouldn't be such a bad idea."

"Well, a good lie has to have some truth in it."

"Yes. If I marry this girl—"

"Then you can tell Levi that you got secret information that the P. R. & G. changed their minds."

"Won't he try to get information through the Fort Penn people?"

"An honest man would. But Levi's as crooked as anybody.

Thinks everybody else is crooked. And he's going to think that the Fort Penn people are giving him a dirty deal. The last thing he'll ever think of is that we cooked this whole thing up so you could marry his daughter."

The scheme worked. Adelaide Hoffner and Abraham Lockwood were married in November, and although it was a blustery day, the wedding was the largest ever in Richterville, attended by large delegations from the recent family connections in Gibbsville, selected substantial citizens of Swedish Haven, and all the solvent and some insolvents of Richterville. The small number of family connections of the groom was overlooked in the delighted surprise of the knowing at the prestigious names of his ushers, all of whom wore golden question marks in their cravats. Daphne Lockwood was not there; she had been put away. Rhoda Lockwood was not there; she was dangerously ill at the family home in Swedish Haven.

Someone sent Adelaide Hoffner Lockwood a book to take with her to Niagara Falls, a book called *Their Wedding Journey*, by a man named William Dean Howells. She unwrapped the book on the train from Fort Penn to Buffalo, glanced at the title, and threw it out the coach window. "Why did you do that?" said Abraham Lockwood.

"I know what kind of a book that would be," said Adelaide Lockwood.

"How do you know if you don't read it?" said her bridegroom.

"I chust know, that's how. *Their Wedding Journey*. I forgot to look who sent it to me."

"You think it's spicy?"

"Wouldn't you think so?"

"Well, it might be. But now that you're married you can read what you please."

"You wouldn't mind if I read a book like that?"

"What's a book? Something to pass the time. No, I wouldn't mind. Did it have any pictures in it?"

"I didn't take the time to find out."

"I don't see how you could throw away a book without looking inside it. I hope I haven't married a prude, have I, Adelaide?"

"A prude? No, I'm not a prude, but I won't say I want to read a book with that title. *Their Wedding Journey*. Huh."

"Maybe you'll want to write your own book, eh?"

"Please don't make such talk, Abraham."

"Are you afraid of me, Adelaide?"

She shook her head. "No. You're experienced."
"Shouldn't you be jealous because I am?"
"You didn't marry them. You married me."
"Yes, and I love you."
"And I love you. I love you more than you love me, but you loved me enough to marry me. And I loved you enough to marry *you.* We'll make a home and have family, and we'll love one another the same. You as much as me."
"You're *not* afraid of me, are you?"
"No."
"You're not altogether sure. What are you thinking?"
"It hurts the first time, doesn't it?"
"I hope it won't."
"That's why it's better that you're experienced."
"And if you're in love. If the girl is in love she doesn't notice the hurt so much."
"I wish we were there and it was tomorrow."
In their hotel room during their first love-making she lay with her eyes open, staring at him, wincing with the first pain but determined to go through with the necessary ordeal. But when his excitement took control of him she forgot the pain in her wonder at his passion. She was converted to passion immediately, and wanted to repeat it before he was able. "This time I'll do it right," she said.
"In a little while," he said.
For her the real novelty of the experience was in his passion. She knew the mechanics of erection and orgasm, but she had not been prepared for his eager grabbing of her and his outcries, demonstrations that her past knowledge of this cold thin man had not led her to anticipate. Then, just before they were leaving Niagara Falls, she herself experienced orgasm, and life and the world changed for her and Abraham Lockwood became a hero. There could be no other man, this man was Man.
At first they lived in a house of their own, across the side street from the walled square containing the red brick box. There had been no way to avoid telling the Hoffner family that Daphne Lockwood was in the crazy-house, the *In*sane, as it was also called; but Rhoda's advanced condition had been a secret. Every family had someone who behaved strangely; one of the Hoffner girls had taken a long while to recover from the birth of her first child. But Levi Hoffner had been kept in ignorance of the true illness of Rhoda Lockwood, and it remained for Abraham Lockwood to tell his new wife that Rhoda did not "go out." A person who suffered from a chronic ailment such as consumption was

"poorly"; one who had something wrong with the brain "didn't go out."

"Is she like your sister Daphne?" said Adelaide.

"She's worse. She'd go after you with a pair of scissors."

"Then why isn't she put away?"

"She's going to be."

"What's holding it up, if she's dangerous?"

"My mother. She doesn't want to see her go."

"How old is your mother?"

"Fifty-five or-six."

"She'd be lonely, is that why?"

"Yes, I guess so. But Rhoda hates her. She hates all females."

"But not all males?"

"That's what her trouble's been."

"Oh, there was one like that in Richterville. When did it start?"

"Oh, maybe ten years ago."

"The one at home, too. It started about the same age for her. Fourteen or fifteen?"

"Yes."

"There's nothing you can do for them except put them away. They don't like men, either, you know. The one at home did a terrible thing to a man."

"What?"

"I won't say."

"You know so much, and you know so little."

"That's the trouble, Abraham. You're told to act like a lady, but you see things and hear things. But ask anybody a question and they tell you to shut up. One day Sarah and I were in the backyard, sitting in the swing, and we heard some voices in the alleyway back of our barn. We went to see what it was, and there was a man sitting on a log. There were two other men with him. And the girl I told you about, she was doing something to the man. Out in broad daylight. I told Sarah not to look, but she saw. Broad daylight. I thought I was going to faint."

"Weren't they afraid of the constable?"

"That's *it*. One of them *was* the constable. They weren't boys. They were all men. It isn't funny, Abraham."

"I guess it isn't, but I have to laugh. Your father, with six daughters, protecting them from the world, and there in his own back alley, in broad daylight. The constable."

"Your father killed two men, didn't he?"

"Yes. Why did you bring that up all of a sudden?"

"I don't know. Thinking of us girls, and what we saw in the

alleyway. And you, so elegant and stylish, but your father killed two men. I often think of things like that. Sin isn't only in New York, or Europe. They try to make us believe that, but it's everywhere. I guess there's just as much in Swedish Haven, and *Gibbsville!* I heard such things about the Railroad Street in Gibbsville that would turn your stomach. When we have our children we mustn't pretend as if sin was every place else. I want our children to face the truth. We're not much better than other people, just because our fathers are rich. The girl, the one I was speaking about, she's related to me. Her mother was a Hoffner. They weren't the Close Hoffners. That's what my father and mother called the ones that are related to us closely. But they were Hoffners, all right."

"It makes me feel better, to hear that you have some family skeletons too."

"Don't tease me, Abraham. My grandfather got rich because he could read and write. He rooked people. I know, because my father bragged about it. He wouldn't to you, but at home he did. Do you know why we were married in the Reformed? Because my grandfather was expelled from the Lutheran. Somebody that couldn't read took a paper to the Lutheran preacher, some kind of an agreement with my grandfather. And when the preacher read it, it was a scandalous thing. Dishonest. And Grandfather Jacob Hoffner was expelled from the Lutheran Church. Didn't they ever hear that over in Swedish Haven?"

"They were too busy talking about my father, I guess."

He believed himself when he told her that he loved her. He was becoming accustomed to her Pennsylvania Dutch sing-song and her trouble with v's and w's; d's that came out t; j's that came out ch; s's for z; z for s; the diphthong in *how* made to sound like *hah;* and the words and constructions that Miss Holbrook's School had not corrected. He had grown up with the Pennsylvania Dutch patois as part of his own speech, and he was accustomed to the accent that it left on the English speech of his fellow citizens; but his father did not have it, his mother had only a trace of it, and he himself had largely got rid of it during his years at the University and as an officer in the army.

The manner of her speech was a strong, if subtle, factor in the growth of love. Her voice was low, without being especially deep by nature; and the sing-song character of the Pennsylvania Dutch accent retards the speed of speaking. Thus she communicated her words to him in quiet tones and at a rate of utterance that made her delivery always gentle and required a slowing down of his listening faculties. It made what she had to say seem thought out; well considered and deeply felt, even when the most trivial things were being discussed. As against that easy, not unpleasantly musical enunciation was the trusting violence of her love-making, so that he often found as he listened to her that he was thinking as much of the contrasts as of the things she had to say. It was indeed as though the way she spoke of everyday things was an agreed-upon deception, a secret of their own that hinted at a more esoteric secret that they revealed to each other—and she especially to him—when they would make love.

The love was genuine enough on her part; on his it was a gradual development. She had been disturbed by him from the first, and it came as a happy discovery that she could have such deep feelings for a man who already met her first requirement for marriage, namely, that he would not be marrying her for her money. The said requirement receded into forgotten unimportance as she saw him more frequently and as he courted her. There was, of course, an element of gratitude in her love; she was thankful that his look and presence made him desirable enough so that his economic status in relation to hers could be so easily dismissed, and she could enter into romance unhindered. Then after their first week of marriage Adelaide Lockwood acquired a female pride in the new knowledge that while he was in control of their store of ecstasy, she could make him eager to share it.

Abraham Lockwood's experience with women, wholly a matter of satisfying sexual needs, had paradoxically been preparing him all his mature life for just such a love as began to grow in him. From the whores at Phoebe Adamson's place in Juniper Street he had gone to the whores in Washington; and in later years, after his return to Swedish Haven, he had used a dressmaker in Gibbsville. Arrangements with her had to be made in advance and by letter. Annabella Crowe's house was in Second Street, only a square away from the main business thoroughfare. On the first floor of the house she had a room in which her lady customers could examine materials and make their decisions; a second room where they could be measured and have their try-ons; a third room, in which her sewing women worked; a fourth room, a kitchen, which also served as her dining room. Annabella Crowe's living quarters were on the second story, more than adequate since she lived alone. She was a woman in her early thirties who had been deserted by her husband and had been briefly and secretly the mistress of a county judge, who set her up in the dressmaking establishment before parting company with her. In the vicinity of the railway and canal station there had been whorehouses for several decades when Abraham Lockwood returned from the War, but none of them had been operated with any sense of discretion, and he avoided them. A Gibbsville lawyer introduced him to Annabella Crowe. "What do you do for a piece of tail," Abraham Lockwood had asked. The lawyer answered evasively, but optimistically, and shortly thereafter, he gave Lockwood the name and address of Annabella Crowe. "Go there at ten o'clock Tuesday night," said the lawyer.

At the appointed hour he knocked on the door, which was swung open immediately and quickly closed. A woman he could not see said, "Go upstairs where you see the light." He mounted the stairs, and the woman, who followed him, said: "To your left." It was the middle of three rooms on the second story and the only one in which there was any illumination. It had a single, heavily curtained window, a large, ornately carved double bed, with a wardrobe, dresser, and chairs belonging to the same suite. "I'm Mrs. Crowe, and I know who you are but I don't know much about you. You're single?"

"Yes."

"Are you courting anyone?"

"No."

"Are you a drinker?"

"Some. Not much."

"I don't like to have friends of mine that get drunk and tell everything they know."

"I can understand that."

"And I never let a friend of mine come here without he makes an appointment ahead of time. I don't open my door if I'm not expecting a person. I don't care whether he's been a friend of mine before. He don't get in. You understand that all right?"

"Yes."

"Another thing you have to promise, if you get to be a friend of mine, don't ever tell anybody you're a friend of mine before you ask my permission."

"I see."

"One other thing. Don't ever come here inebriated, regardless of whether you have an appointment. Don't come here inebriated. Did our friend say how much a visit?"

"No, he didn't."

"Twenty dollars a visit."

"Twenty dollars?"

"And always have the money with you. I don't extend any credit. This isn't a *place,* you know. I only have a very few friends. You agree to everything?"

"Yes."

"Then hang up your clothes in the wardrobe and I'll be back in a couple minutes. Oh, I almost forgot. No cigars. Never light a cigar while you're visiting me."

She went out and he undressed and hung his clothes in the wardrobe and sat on the edge of the bed. She returned, wearing a bathrobe, which she quickly took off and hung on the back of a chair.

"Say," he said, admiring her body.

For the first time she smiled. "Worth it, huh?" She made a complete turn.

"Just about perfect, " he said.

"I had one friend of mine wanted to carve me in marble. He said I ought to be carved in marble."

"He's right."

"Well, a woman likes to hear compliments. You waiting for me to get in?"

"I guess I was."

"Let me have a look at you first. Oh. Our friend didn't tell me about this. You're young, aren't you? Twenty-six? Twenty-seven?"

"Almost twenty-seven."

"I have mostly older friends. I guess you're the youngest. Well, lie down, honey, and we'll get used to each other. Would you like that, honey? We get used to each other? The first couple times we got to get used to each other's ways."

In 1871 she said to him, "Well, I guess I'll be losing you as a friend, Abe. I heard my customers talking about you courting a young lady in Richterville. Is that true?"

"Yes."

"Well, tell me when it's our last night and I'll give it to you for a wedding present."

"I want to give you a present."

"All right, if it's cash. You know me, the only kind of presents I take are cash."

"Oh, it'll be cash."

"A young fellow getting married—if you wanted to make me a present of five hundred dollars, I'll agree to have you be a friend of mine for a year, in case the young lady's hard to get along with. Some are, and I had a friend of mine wish to visit me again, but I only take so many."

"All right, I'll give you five hundred dollars."

"My downstairs business is getting bigger, and I just as soon weed out some of my friends, but I can't afford it yet. When I have enough saved up I'm going to move away. Sell the downstairs business and go live in New York City. I want to get some millionaire for my keeper before I start getting old. But first and foremost I want to leave here respectable, no talk about me. If I don't find a millionaire I may open up a high-class place, and that'll take money. Be the best in the long run, pay better, because I'd run the place as long as I live. But it takes money and you have to know the right people. You can't just open up somewhere. My dream come true would be if I found a millionaire and he knew the right people, and maybe put up enough to get me started. A place where a lady could go. I know ladies right here in town, if they had a place to go, they'd go there. I had a lady, one of my downstairs customers, she keeps hinting around that she'd like to see my upstairs rooms. I know what she wants. She wants to see if she can trust me, and then make me an offer to use these rooms. But women are big-mouthed. So are men, but I never had a friend of mine talk, so far. I don't want *any* women up here, only me. I spend an hour every day keeping these rooms neat and clean so I don't have to hire a servant-girl . . . So you're going to leave me, Abe? Well, if it's who they say it is, five hundred dollars won't break you, and maybe you'll want to come back. But that doesn't say I don't wish you luck. And maybe some time she's in the family way, you can come and see me. You'd be much better off with me instead of somebody you didn't know."

"Thanks, Annabella."

"And, like I just said, five hundred won't break you."

"I'll have it with me the next time I come to visit you."

"Where's she getting her wedding dress, your bride-to-be? Do you know?"

"No. Fort Penn, I guess. Why?"

"Well, it'd be funny if she got it here. I could get a good look at her before you do. I could tell her a few things, too, couldn't I, Abe? Maybe if she knew what I know she'd run like a cat shot in the behind."

"Now, Annabella."

"Oh, don't worry. I'm only teasing you."

With no question of fidelity involved he had yet been faithful to Annabella Crowe for nearly five years. All during that period he had known that Mrs. Crowe was going to bed with—as well as he could figure out—three other men and possibly four. But he had known this from the beginning, and he neither felt jealousy nor expressed any desire for exclusive rights to her services. The machinery of a well regulated need and its satisfaction created neither lasting gratitude nor masculine vanity nor any other item in the stuff of love. Spontaneity was, of course, entirely absent because of the precautionary appointment arrangements, and Annabella Crowe was so candidly in the business of hiring out her lovely body that she could not more effectively have thwarted romantic notions. After an hour in bed with a man she would sit in her wrapper, holding his folded banknotes in her hand as he dressed, sometimes fanning herself with the money, sometimes using it in gestures, chatting amiably until it was time to lead him to the front door and close it behind him for the night.

But the sexual act with Adelaide was so unlike the brief, calculated meetings with Annabella Crowe that it was a relationship and not a transaction, similar only in the union of their bodies. There was never, when a variation was tried, the suspicion that the variation had originated with Adelaide and another man. It was all, all new and unique with Adelaide, and here was the beginning of love. Abraham Lockwood chose to think of himself as a man of experience, but for the first time in the more than thirty years of his life he was living with a woman and not visiting her. If it was seduction by marriage it was still the larger experience of living with her, and the marriage as a personal institution gained and was strengthened and finally became love. When it happened Adelaide knew the difference, but she made no comment. She only loved the more.

Abraham Lockwood's mother died of weariness a few weeks after Rhoda was put away. Weariness, some shame, uselessness, hard work, an uninspiring future, a too demanding past, and, on the death certificate, quinsy. It was not an easy death, to strangle slowly and look into the eyes of husband and son and read so plainly their wish to have the laborious breathing come to an end. Within a week Moses Lockwood had pleaded successfully with Adelaide and Abraham to move into the red brick box, and there, in 1873, their son was born. He was called George Bingham Lockwood, in honor of the Governor of the Commonwealth, who was a close friend of Levi Hoffner's.

■

When George Lockwood was about five years old and his brother Penrose an infant, their grandfather's health was bad. He had become so enfeebled that he seldom made the effort to walk the few squares to his office in Dock Street, and business matters that required his attention were taken care of at his desk in the den in the red brick box. All of his day was spent in the house or in the yard. He was up early in the morning, and the servants who were hired soon after his wife's death took turns rising at five o'clock to get him his tea. On fair days he would be out in the yard, carefully dressed in the clothes he might wear for a business day, and walking a few steps at a time, from rose bush to elm tree, sometimes touching the petals of a rose, sometimes studying the tree from ground to topmost branch, pausing to rest in the rough-hewn oaken chairs and benches that were strategically distributed about the yard. On days when rain or snow or bitter cold kept him in the house he would walk about from room to room, stopping to study a statuette, a bit of porcelain, and often colliding with a servant on her cleaning rounds. The household was now a busy place, with Abraham and Adelaide and their two young children, and the two servants and nurse, and a coachman in and out of the kitchen; and yet wherever Moses Lockwood went in the house he would bring quiet with him; his entrance into a room would suspend conversations and the people would wait respectfully for him to tell them what he wanted;

but most often there was nothing he wanted and he would take their continuing silence for the dismissal that indeed it was.

Moses Lockwood did not like the coachman, Rafferty, who made him feel on visits to the stable that he was spying. Moses Lockwood was thus deprived of the company of the horses, of which he was not over-fond but which were at least living beings and would hear him if he said a few words. Abraham Lockwood, the only survivor of the four human beings with whom Moses had passed most of his life, was off in a hurry every morning, frequently gone for the day, fairly frequently gone for two or three days with his new interests in Philadelphia. Adelaide Lockwood, a pleasant little piece, had the children and the household on her mind, and she would almost never spare a few minutes just to sit down and converse. The servants were a pair of colored women, sisters, from Richterville, and they had a way of looking at a white man who conversed overlong that told plainly and embarrassingly their suspicions of him, although he was sixty-five years of age and weak in the knees. There was only one person in the household who had any time for Moses Lockwood, and that was his grandson, George. And what with the new baby and his mother's preoccupation with it, and his father's being engrossed in his business, the boy and his grandfather were mutually interdependent for stimulating company. The old man told stories, semi-inventions out of his early past, of which the boy soon had several favorites and in which, in the retelling, he would correct the old man's departures from the original versions. ("Grandpa, you told me the Indian had a rifle, but before you told me he had a tommy-hawk. *Then* you shot him.") The differing versions and the boy's corrections made the storytelling sessions into a game, and the old man began deliberately to introduce new details into the basic stories to challenge the boy's alertness. Momma was Momma, Poppa was Poppa, but Grampa was Grampa, the storyteller with the funny ear and fascinating spitting and interesting sore on his left temple. ("Did the bullet go through your ear and then they cut off the bottom part? Or did the bullet shoot it all off?") Sometimes they would go to the privy together, the old man sitting on the elevated hole, the boy on the lower, smaller one. The boy would finish his business quickly and watch while his grandfather strained and grunted. ("Wait outside, boy, this is going to take a little time.") The boy would pick a capful of cherries, which the old man could eat with him. The old man could not bite into an apple, but he would peel one with his pocket knife, in a long continuous curl, and cut the apple up into small bits that they would share. Always there was something to talk about when they were together. ("Why don't you want me to touch your sore? Does it hurt? Is that from a bullet, too, Grampa? Grampa, let me see your teeth. Did you have to buy your teeth when you were little?") The old man taught the boy about money ("This is a penny. Here's one, two, three, four, five, six, seven, eight, nine, ten pennies. All these pennies are worth one of these. One of these will buy as many sourballs as all these pennies.") and a little bit about flowers ("Never twist them off, cut them off with a scissors or they won't grow again.") and some American history ("Mr. Lincoln was shot because he made John Wilkes Booth give up his slaves.").

Because of their companionship the boy was on his grandfather's side during the worst fight he had ever witnessed in the household. His mother started the fight. "Mr. Lockwood, when are you going to be as good as your word and tear down the wall?" said his mother.

"As long as there's a Bundy alive—"

"The last Bundy died two years ago, and the wall is still up yet," said Adelaide Lockwood.

"Well, don't hurry me, young lady."

"Two years is time aplenty. You promised you'd tear it down."

"I don't remember no promise. I said we'd talk about it."

"Mr. Lockwood, that's a falsehood. You're prevaricating."

"Call me a liar and be done with it, why don't you?"

"If the boy wasn't present—George, run out and play." The boy, trained to obedience, left the room but stayed in the hall outside the den. "Now, Mr. Lockwood, either that wall comes down inside of the next six months or we move out of this house." Adelaide was getting Dutchier by the second: "We moo otta this hahs," was the way she pronounced the threat.

"My son won't move."

"There is where you're wrong, Mr. Lockwood. Abraham wants the wall down as much as I do. I won't have my children raised in such a penitentiary with a prison wall around it. Now mind, you listen. Six months, Mr. Lockwood."

"Who's going to pay to have the wall torn down and them bricks carted away?"

"With my own money it won't cost you."

"There's better things you could do with your money."

"I don't take orders how I spend my own money, Mr. Lockwood. Such as I could build a new house and take my boys and my husband and let you sit behind your wall."

"Tear it down and be damned to you."

"Will you order the contractor?"

"I'll order the contractor. And I'll pay the money."

"Mr. Lockwood, I'm not a mean person, but I don't like my boys growing up in such a penitentiary. They make jokes about my boy George, and they'll make jokes about the baby too."

"I never heard any jokes about my grandson."

"You never see anybody any more. But they say is my boy like you-know in the *In*sane."

"Not a mean person, you call yourself, but you say a thing like that."

"Well, it's what they say and I won't have it said about mine."

Little of the conversation had much meaning for George, but a few days later workmen appeared on the property and began the long, noisy, fascinating task of taking the wall apart, stacking the freed bricks that would be carried away by the wagonload. The boy could not persuade his grandfather to come out into the yard to watch the workmen; the old man would not leave the house nor look out the window to see how strange the yard seemed without the wall, not even to observe the men when they began putting up an iron fence that was not much higher than the boy himself. The old man now spent most of his time in his room, taking his meals alone there, and he no longer had time, he said, to tell the boy any stories. So matters stood for about a month, and then the grandfather changed his habits. Every day he would leave the house in the morning, go to the barber shop and from there to the Exchange Hotel bar and remain until late afternoon, when Rafferty would bring him home in the cut-under and assist him to his room. In a year he died, without ever telling his grandson another story, but by that time George was in the first grade, in the company of boys and girls his own age. A lot of soldiers were at his grandfather's funeral and his grandfather was in a box that was covered by an American flag and instead of a hearse the box was on a sort of cart drawn by four horses, two ridden by soldiers, and at the cemetery the soldiers shot their guns in the air and another soldier played a bugle. George's father was in a soldier suit and so were a lot of other men who were not soldiers. After the funeral was over George saw a lot of the real soldiers from out of town and many of them were drunk.

An old man named Mr. Baltz had supper with his mother and father and all he seemed to do was shake hands with everybody that came along. George Lockwood had never seen anyone shake hands so much.

His other grandfather, in Richterville, was not a teller of stories, but it was pleasant to visit him even so. Near Richterville there were two pony farms, and Grossvater Hoffner, as he preferred to be called, usually took George to look at the ponies and ride around in the shiny wagon that was drawn by a four-pony hitch, always promising George that when he got a little older he could have a pony of his own. At Grossvater Hoffner's house George would sometimes be visiting at the same time his cousin Davey Stokes, a year older, was visiting. "Are you going to get a pony from Grossvater?" George once asked his cousin.

"He says I am, but I don't believe him," said Davey, who then reported to George that several other cousins, one of them eleven years old, had been promised ponies, but that Grossvater always kept putting off the actual purchase. Their cousin Leroy Hoffner, the eleven-year-old, was still being taken out to look at the ponies and ride around in the wagon, but had been given no pony of his own, and soon would be getting too big to have a pony. George hated David Stokes for telling him these things and went on believing Grossvater. He discussed the matter with his mother, and on his next birthday he got a pony, a set of harness, a trap and a cutter. Within a few weeks David Stokes likewise had a pony, and so did Leroy. "Did Grossvater give me the pony?" George asked his mother.

"You might say he did."

"But did he?"

"You might say so. Why do you care, as long as you got it?"

"Because I want to tell Davey."

"Well—no. Poppa and I gave you the pony, but Grossvater gave me the money for my share, so you might say he gave you the pony too."

"But do I have to thank Grossvater too?"

"No, you don't have to thank him."

"Then he didn't give it to me, or you'd make me thank him."

"You're like your Poppa. You can twist around with your questions. Just don't say any more about it."

Davey Stokes, when he got his pony, told George that their Grossvater had not bought it, that it had been bought by his parents, and that Leroy Hoffner was getting one from *his* parents. "Grossvater is a big liar," said Davey Stokes. "He's a dumb-Dutch big liar, that's what my father says. My father says all the Dutch are stingy."

"Your mother's Dutch."

"Not any more."

"She talks Dutch."

"She does not," said Davey Stokes. "My father won't let her."

"She does so. She talks it to my mother. My mother is your mother's sister."

"Anybody knows that."

"Anyway, your mother talks Dutch to my mother, so you don't know everything."

"Anyway, my grandfather didn't kill two men and your grandfather did."

"My grandfather was a soldier in the War."

"That's all you know. Ha ha ha ha. Your grandfather killed two men."

"He was a soldier, that's why. My father was a soldier, too."

"Ha ha ha. Your grandfather killed two men before he was a soldier. He was arrested."

"He was not. He killed an Indian."

"He did not. He killed a man that owed him money. Ha ha ha ha."

Davey Stokes was so sneering and positive that George Lockwood asked his father about Grampa. "Poppa, did Grampa kill a man? Two men?"

"Where did you hear that?"

"Davey. He said Grampa was arrested."

"Oh, your uncle's been talking. Well, it had to come out sooner or later," said Abraham Lockwood. "Yes, Grampa killed two men."

"Not Indians?"

"No, not Indians. White men. Long before I was born, one man tried to rob your Grampa, sneaked into his room in a hotel, with a dagger, and Grampa shot him to save his own life. That was long ago, before I was born, when it wasn't safe to go out at night. In fact, your Grampa was what you might call a constable, a policeman."

"Then they couldn't arrest him if he was a policeman, could they?"

"Yes, a policeman can be arrested. Anybody can be arrested. Even somebody named Stokes can be arrested."

"Was Uncle Sam arrested?"

"No. But that's not saying he couldn't be. Or that no Stokes ever was arrested. Anybody at all can be arrested."

"Was Grampa?"

"Yes. He shot another man. He thought the man was going to shoot him, and Grampa shot first."

"Is that why they arrested him?"

"Yes. You don't know about courts, yet, do you?"

"About what?"

"In a court a judge decides whether a man is guilty. A judge and a jury. Twelve men and a judge. They decide if a man is guilty, and they decided Grampa was *not* guilty."

"Didn't the man die when Grampa shot him?"

"Yes, he died. But Grampa wasn't guilty. I'll have to explain these things when you get older. You're too young to understand it now."

"Davey understands it."

"No he doesn't."

"But he told me Grampa shot two men, and you said he did too."

"He still doesn't understand about the law, and court. His father neglected to explain that. It's too bad his father had to say anything at all."

"Are you mad at Uncle Sam?"

"Oh, no. No, of course not, son. But Davey shouldn't listen to grownups' conversations. Little boys never should. They hear things they shouldn't hear."

"Are you going to have a fight with Uncle Sam?"

"Of course not."

"Poppa, didn't Grampa ever kill an Indian?"

"No. He killed some Rebels, but not Indians."

"He told me he did."

"Oh. Well, I don't know what stories Grampa told you, but he made up most of them."

The boy remembered that his grandfather's stories varied from telling to telling, but basically the stories had been the same. He wanted to ask his father how he knew that Grampa had made up the stories if he did not know what stories Grampa had told; but the question was too complicated to present.

The disclosure of the conversations in the Samuel Stokes household was a disconcerting one to Abraham Lockwood. Sam's marriage to Sarah Hoffner, followed by Abraham's marriage to Adelaide, had seemed to Abraham Lockwood to have the immediate effect of connecting Richterville, Swedish Haven, and Gibbsville in an alliance that was momentarily a merely social one. But since the alliance plainly did connect the first families of Gibbsville, *en bloc,* with the first family of Richterville and the first family of Swedish Haven, Abraham Lockwood's early decision to marry an upstate girl would seem to have been extremely sapient in his long-range plan to be an important, if not dominant, figure in the life of the county. He had accomplished a desirable union with the Gibbsville oligarchy without incurring their suspicions by courting a Gibbsville girl. He had, in fact, by marrying a Richterville girl, made a move that should have disarmed the cynical. He thought of himself as having made his way into the Gibbsville oligarchy modestly, through the back door. Now it appeared from the revelations of the conversations in the Stokes household that he had not made his way into it at all. For he attached greater significance to the remarks of Davey Stokes than those of an eavesdropping child. Sam Stokes was a full-fledged member of the oligarchy, and as he grew older a place would be made for him in the business and social life of Gibbsville; but meanwhile he was very much a lesser member of the Stokes-Hofman-Chapin clan, not likely to express opinions that were contrary to the prevailing mood of the important senior clansmen. He would never be a major figure in the town of Gibbsville or the county of Lantenengo, and Abraham Lockwood had long ago dismissed Sam Stokes as a possible threat to his own ascension to the place occupied by Peter W. Hofman.

Once, and only once, Abraham Lockwood had done something to displease Peter Hofman: after the warning by Harry Penn Downs in the Gibbsville Club the Lockwoods, father and son, paid special attention to the affairs of the Swedish Haven bank, particularly in regard to the decreases in deposits that would give a quick clue to the identity of Swedish Haven business men who might be hoarding money to establish a second bank. Four merchants' names stood out, and Moses Lockwood was in favor of drastic action; but Abraham Lockwood, the second-generation advocate of good will, had a talk with each of the men. He said he had "received information" that the man was negotiating with Peter Hofman to open a new bank—a complete invention, since he had received no information whatever. He then would pretend to be sympathetic; if the man wanted to start a second bank with *out-of-town* assistance, there must be some reason. If, on the other hand, the reason was no better than merely that the man wanted to help a *Gibbsville banker* to go into competition with the *Swedish Haven bank,* Abraham Lockwood and his father were grievously disappointed. Abraham Lockwood avoided the appearance of a threat to the man. What he wanted was some admission on the man's part that he was in cahoots with Peter Hofman. In three of the four cases his guess was correct, and he had three names to mention when he paid a call on Peter Hofman.

"Good morning, sir," said Peter Hofman. "What can I do for you?"

"A great deal, sir," said Abraham Lockwood. "But the question is, will you? A few years ago my father and I opened a bank in Swedish Haven—"

"Just a moment, sir. I believe the bank was started by some other men, and you and your father came along later and took control."

"That is the impression, I know, sir. The facts prove otherwise. My father and grandfather, and later my father and I had conducted a business that was for many years the only banking service in Swedish Haven."

"Yes indeed, and a highly profitable business it was."

"Oh, yes. My grandfather and my father and I are not in business for our health. Neither were the men that borrowed from us, over those years. Neither are you, Mr. Hofman."

"Indeed not."

"Agreed. Now of course any profitable business creates its own imitators. You yourself have seen that in the leasing of coal lands. You and your father used to have that pretty much to yourselves, but others, especially Philadelphia and New York men, have known a good thing when they saw it, and you have a lot of competition."

"Competition is the life of trade, so they say."

"And the death of some tradesmen, when the competition gets too fierce. But may I continue, sir? In Swedish Haven there was a movement started to open a bank. Now, Mr. Hofman, who started that movement? That movement was started by some men who had been borrowing money from us, prospered, and decided that now that they were enjoying some prosperity, why not take that business away from the Lockwoods and share it among themselves?"

"Logical. Understandable."

"But very little goes on in Swedish Haven that my father and I don't hear about. And we knew inside of a week that a few men wanted to give us competition, but they were going to call themselves a bank. We had never thought to call ourselves a bank. That would have been presumptuous on our part. We weren't a bank. It was always either my father and grandfather, or my father and I, lending our own money and not the money of anyone else. This little group of men proposed to lend the money of their depositors, and that worried my father."

"Indeed?"

"Yes. It wasn't only that some of these self-styled bankers were pretty small potatoes, and not entitled to much credit with our firm. The thing that worried my father was, what if this new bank should fail? Who would suffer? The depositors would suffer."

"Moses Lockwood was worried about the depositors of this new bank? A touching concern, my dear sir. Very touching."

"I'll ignore that, sir. Just hear me out, please. Common courtesy. I don't argue that my father was worried for sentimental reasons. He was worried for business reasons. If that bank failed, *we* failed, because it could very well be the end of Swedish Haven. If the people that worked for us put their money in this new, risky bank, and the bank failed, who would be able to pay us our rentals? That's just one source of our income, but a big one. You know what our holdings are."

"I can make a pretty good guess."

"Therefore, my father and I stepped in, got rid of those we knew were not good business men, and, as you put it, took control. But without us there'd have been no bank."

"Meanwhile, of course, holding on to your money-lending business."

"Naturally. We could afford to take risks with *our* money that a bank could not."

"Oh, that's the way you put it? How interesting."

"I challenge you to put it any other way. Because those are the facts, my dear sir. The facts. The hard-cash facts."

"As seen by you, my dear Mr. Lockwood."

"As seen by my father and me, who are in a much better position to know the facts than anyone else, whether they're merchants in Swedish Haven or magnates in Gibbsville. I invite you to dispute anything I have told you."

"I could dispute it all, if I chose."

"Oh, you could dispute anything, just for the sake of argument. But would you care to deny that you are now contemplating giving assistance to another group of men, to help them start a second bank in Swedish Haven?"

"My dear young sir, who are you to come to my office and challenge me to dispute this or deny that?"

"Who am I? Well, I'm the legitimate son of a man who

made his own way in the world, served his country and was badly wounded in the service of his country. One of the very first. A man who has shown great courage, and without it wouldn't be alive today. And, in this discussion, most of all, a man with an unblemished business record. Unblemished, Mr. Hofman. Unblemished, I repeat that. Would you say the same for Paul Ulrich?"

"Paul Ulrich?"

"Oh, come now, Mr. Hofman. Paul Ulrich is one of the men you are in cahoots with."

"I don't like that word at all, cahoots."

"What word do you like? You wouldn't like any word I use, not when I accompany the word with the name of one of your cronies."

"I don't like that word, either, and I don't like your manners."

"I'm told my manners are very good. I had them polished at the University and brought to a high gloss in Washington society. Please don't complain about my manners, Mr. Hofman. Paul Ulrich's manners aren't outstanding. Neither are Cyrus Reichelderfer's. Did you find Cyrus Reichelderfer another Lord Chesterfield? When he's come to me for money I always have to open the window. Cyrus has something that the medical students used to call animated dandruff. But I've done business with him, helped him out from time to time. I don't object to his manners or the things that grow on him, Mr. Hofman. I do object to his underhanded dealings with you."

"How dare you, sir?"

"Well, I'm doing you a favor. If he'll go behind my back, he'll go behind yours. Shall I give you some more names, Mr. Hofman? I know you thought you were working in great secrecy, but here I've already given you the names of two of your conspirators. I have more."

"You are insulting, sir. I must ask you to—"

"To leave your office. Very well. And do you know where I think I'll pay a call when I leave? When I get back to Swedish Haven I may pay a business call on Wilhelm Strotz. Wilhelm Strotz. I'll explain to Willy that you wouldn't admit to having any dealings with him. Mr. Hofman, I've never tried to take any business away from you, but I'll take it away from you if you try to take it away from us. I know my people. Good day, sir."

The second bank was not again heard of in Swedish Haven, and Peter Hofman, while not cordial, usually nodded and spoke to Abraham Lockwood by name when they visited the Gibbsville Club. Abraham Lockwood accordingly assumed that no rancor remained from the bank dispute, but he was a young man, not so liable to remember the unpleasantness of the discussion. Moreover, the dispute had ended in a triumph for him in his first encounter with the Gibbsville oligarchy, and while the triumph was extremely satisfactory and encouraging, Abraham Lockwood was too ambitious to rest there. With his eye on the future he overlooked the damage his triumph had inflicted on Peter Hofman's hitherto unchallenged self-esteem. Abraham Lockwood, it was true, knew his people, but he really knew next to nothing of Peter Hofman. But he was learning. The low-ranking Samuel Stokes had inadvertently told Abraham Lockwood that the Lockwood link with the ruling clan of the county consisted of a single, tenuous connection by marriage, a marriage to an in-law of the same low-ranking Samuel Stokes. Abraham Lockwood had made the kind of mistake he seldom made in business: he had overrated the worth of something.

But he rarely made the same mistake twice. The discovery that his marriage had accomplished so little did not alter his determination to take advantage of everything in his favor. Abraham Lockwood at this time was on the outtermost edge of the Peter Hofman oligarchy; the time would come when it would be a Lockwood oligarchy, and the importance of any individual would depend on his closeness to the Lockwood line. Abraham Lockwood was not convinced that this reversal would occur in his own generation; he himself might not live to become a Peter Hofman. The Hofmans happened at the moment to be in the ascendancy in Lantenengo County, and besides their Lantenengo relatives they had kinship with Muhlenbergs and Womelsdorfs in the counties to the south, pre-Revolutionary families of distinction. Abraham Lockwood, not positively certain of the identity of his own grandmother, fully appreciated the size of the task he had set himself; but now that he had two sons, George and Penrose, he might at any rate live to see one of them—or both—the acknowledged symbol of power in the county. His ambition, of course, did not stop there. In some distant day men of his blood would have national and international renown; too late, perhaps, for him to share in it; but he was building toward it.

Abraham Lockwood had learned that as the leading family of a region his children and their children would carry more prestige than as members of one more family in New York or Philadelphia. Peter Hofman was an unimaginative man, who apparently had no ambitions beyond Lantenengo County. Abraham Lockwood wanted to overtake and pass Peter Hofman in the county, and go on from there while still remaining a Lantenengo County citizen. Future Lockwoods would always have Lantenengo and Swedish Haven to come back to; they must never abandon their Pennsylvania, Lantenengo County, Swedish Haven, identity, for to do so would be to lose their uniqueness. Abraham Lockwood was, in effect, granting himself a title and his children a dukedom. And an attractive feature of his long-range plan was that while money in large quantity was an essential, it did not have to match one of the great fortunes that were being amassed in Philadelphia and New York. He would bring up his sons so that they had respect for money and at least an inculcated sense of how to make it; but the model he secretly chose for imitation by his sons was Morris Homestead. Morris Homestead was not Abraham Lockwood's choice of the man with whom he would do business, since Morris Homestead was not inclined to make more money, or to make it quickly, or to make it for anyone else. Nevertheless Morris Homestead was the *kind* of millionaire Abraham Lockwood wanted his sons to be. Abraham Lockwood had justifiable confidence in his own ability to make money, to establish a fortune; then once having taught George and Penrose how to take care of their inheritance, they could remain in comfortable, affluent obscurity while deciding which boards to sit on, which ambassadorships to take, what games to play, whose women to sleep with.

Now, with only twenty years of the Century remaining, Abraham Lockwood had nothing to fear from the Gibbsville oligarchy, despite the knowledge that his concept of a Gibbsville-Swedish Haven-Richterville axis (which he would rapidly control) was an error. He had misjudged Peter Hofman, and he had taken too much for granted as regarding the three-town axis; but his inheritance from his father and the money he was making through his own efforts gave him protection from the Gibbsville money-men. Knowing what they thought of him, he could afford to be nice. His father, and his father-in-law, Levi Hoffner, would have declared war on the covertly hostile Gibbsville men; but Abraham Lockwood was an original strategist. And while he conceded that he had misjudged Peter Hofman, he was convinced that he had not misjudged the others in Gibbsville, whom he held in lower esteem, a judgment based on the knowledge that among the others there had not been in thirty years a single man who seriously challenged the placid despotism of Peter Hofman. The only threat to Peter Hofman's dominance had come not from Gibbsville but from outsiders, from Philadelphia and New York. Abraham Lockwood therefore asked to call on Hofman, knowing that the old man's curiosity would overcome his impulse to refuse to see him.

Hofman did not rise when Abraham Lockwood entered his private office. The old man turned in his swivel chair and folded his hands across his belly. "Good afternoon, sir," said Peter Hofman.

"Good afternoon, Mr. Hofman."

"Well, what have you got up your sleeve this time?"

Abraham Lockwood made an elaborate business of looking up his sleeve. "A pair of slightly soiled cuffs, and a pair of cuff buttons that my dear mother gave me when I graduated from the University. However, if you ask me what I have in my billycock, I'd have another answer."

"A rabbit, no doubt," said the old man.

"No, sir, I'm not a magician." Abraham Lockwood took some papers from his hat and extended them toward Hofman, who did not hold out his hand.

"Tell me what they are. My eyes are tired."

"These are the plans of a toll bridge. Rough drawings, but the figures are accurate."

"A toll bridge?"

"Where the river bends, between here and Swedish Haven, you know where the river bends and the road follows the curve of the river, then goes up a steep hill below Klauser's farm?"

"I know the spot."

"This bridge would shorten the distance between the two towns by almost a full mile, and eliminate the two steep grades that a team with a heavy wagonload has to rest on. This toll bridge could be built for about $35,000."

"And be washed away in the first flood."

"Not this bridge."

"Well, go ahead and build it," said the old man.

"It's going to make money, Mr. Hofman. It's going to make money now, and it will make more and more as the two towns grow. In due course the county or the Commonwealth will have to buy this bridge."

"Well, you have $35,000. You inherited a great deal more than that from your father. It's not all gone, is it?"

"Far from it. I have more than doubled the money I inherited from my father."

"You have? That's a most unusual statement to make."

"I wouldn't make it if I weren't convinced that you're well aware that it's the truth."

"I believe I did hear that you've been having some luck with some speculation of yours."

"Now only mine. Your friends in Drexel & Company have been in on some of these speculations."

"Have they indeed?"

"Mr. Hofman, it's now obvious that you don't want to hear any more that I have to say."

"I'm only curious as to why you came to me, Mr. Lockwood. You can build this bridge without my help or anyone else's, and I must say I think it appears to be a promising investment. Why *did* you come to me?"

"As a courtesy. You're the leading citizen of Gibbsville, and this toll bridge should make our two towns come closer together. The money it will make won't have any great effect on your fortune, nor for that matter on mine."

"I take it then that you consider yourself the leading citizen of Swedish Haven."

"Well, I have more money than anyone else. Than any *two* citizens of Swedish Haven. Possibly any *three*. And I've begun to follow the example set by you."

"Explain that, please."

I *give* more money to the people of the town than anyone else. You do that in Gibbsville. I do it in Swedish Haven, now that I can afford to."

"I was *brought up* to believe in sharing."

"So was I, Mr. Hofman. Perhaps you don't know it, but my father built the Lutheran church, and we put up the money for the South Ward public school. I say perhaps you don't know it. I know you don't know it, and very few people do. I am interested in the future of Swedish Haven, and I believe that the future of Swedish Haven and the future of Gibbsville are bound together, one with the other."

"I should like to ask you a question. Why do you stay in Swedish Haven, when you could make your fortune in one of the large cities?"

"I suppose for the same reason that you stayed in Gibbsville. A man can love his home town, and if he doesn't there must be some reason. I have every reason to be fond of Swedish Haven, and I'll never leave it."

"You surprise me, Mr. Lockwood."

"I don't see why I should surprise you, Mr. Hofman. You don't know me very well. You scarcely know me at all . . . Well, I've taken up enough of your time, and we both have other things to do. Good day, sir." He stood up, tossed the papers back in his hat, and turned to go.

"Mr. Lockwood, let me have a look at those drawings," said the old man.

Now at last they were in a joint venture. The news caused new hostility toward Abraham Lockwood, but of a different kind; and the hostility among jealous relatives of the old man was offset by a gain in local prestige. The old man let it be known that the idea for the toll bridge had originated with his younger partner-of-the-moment, and when Peter Hofman addressed the younger man as Abraham, the minor members of the clan went him one better and called him Abe. At the ceremonies of the bridge opening, where George Lockwood cut a red ribbon, Abe Lockwood smiled in his friendliest fashion at Samuel Stokes, who would not have dared to be absent.

■

THE father without a plan ruled because he was the father; the father with a plan, an Abraham Lockwood, was more likely to extend the scope of his supervision to take in the small and large things as they advanced or hindered his plan. The father who confided his plan to his wife was acting voluntarily; even the most unreasonable actions often went unexplained and unjustified, for in that time and especially in that geographical-sociological area the husband and father was impervious to criticism—or the wife's criticism was made at her own risk. Divorce was almost nonexistent, and the wife who endured the intolerable could not count on the support or encouragement of her parents, let alone of her friends, if in her desperation she went to law. Having taken that step she still had to put her case before a judge who in all probability was opposed to any and all divorce. A woman who wanted to be free of her husband at any cost could achieve her freedom at the price of her reputation: she could be so flagrantly adulterous that the husband would sue, and he would win.

Under such conditions marriage was permanent and the rule of the husband and father was absolute, and these things were understood by all nubile girls. If Adelaide Hoffner questioned her sister's chances of compatibility with Samuel Stokes on Sarah's wedding day, the questioning was academic. Academic and forlorn, so far as correction of a condition might be concerned. Marriage was entered into joyfully, as the realization of an ambition; but the finality of the new status was as much a source of apprehension as the hazards of the physical union. A lucky, attractive girl might have her choice of suitors, but they seldom numbered more than two or three, and the maiden's true preference of one to the others was often discouraged. Love was not regarded seriously as a determining factor, since the girl's mother in all probability had not been allowed to marry for love. The delightful novelty of the use of the expression, "a real love match," was unintended evidence of the rarity of the phenomenon; it did not often apply. Sometimes love—as always promised—came into being after the marriage was an accomplished fact, and the marriage then could be considered a happy one; but love itself could be threatened by the propinquity that had originally brought it into being.

Thus Adelaide Lockwood, in love with her husband after the first months of their marriage, was confused by his unexplained, intense concern for their children. The greatest pleasure in many women's lives was their right to mother their young, and they mildly resented paternal interference. The father could stay out of the nursery; time enough to exercise his authority when the children were grown. Abraham Lockwood, however, had shown an interest and made decisions governing the upbringing of his sons from their birth. Their diet, their sleeping habits, the temperature of their bath water, the selection of nurses, the children's exposure to sunlight, the degree and method of punishment and reward—nothing escaped Abraham Lockwood's attention, and the only explanation he offered was that he was one of the "new" fathers, who took a more active part in the raising of the children. Adelaide, unable to protest on any reasonable grounds, did not accept her husband's explanation. She deduced that her husband had ambitions for their sons, but this was as close as she ever came to comprehending his plan.

The evolution of the plan had commenced earlier than Abraham Lockwood's decision to stay out of Philadelphia society. In spite of his election to membership in The Ruffes he had not long deceived himself as to his actual standing in the off-campus life of his clubmates. He did not agree with Thomas Fuller (1608-1661) that manners and money make a gentleman, nor with the contemporary John Cardinal Newman that a gentleman was one who never inflicted pain. Abraham Lockwood's association with the University bucks had taught him that Fuller was overly cynical and Newman not cynical enough, and that both had failed to define a gentleman. At the University, then in Washington, then in the post-bellum years, Abraham Lockwood had been evolving his plan with more thoroughness than the time he spent thinking about it might indicate. He had been fortunate in the kind of woman he made his wife—sound breeding, financially well off, adequately educated—but he realized at some undeterminable stage that his plan was not merely to raise his sons to be gentlemen. They would be gentlemen according to Fuller, but for them to be gentlemen was not the ultimate desideratum; it was only a phase, a step toward the family status in the generation that would succeed his sons'. Abraham Lockwood knew that his grandsons and great-grandsons would have no titles, but if his plan was successful, "Mr. Lockwood of Swedish Haven" would be sufficient, and he was becoming convinced that what he sought to achieve could be accomplished in the third generation, the second after his own.

Abraham Lockwood's plan was more than a plan—which was only a method—and more than an ambition—which was only a desire. It was a Concern, in the Quaker sense of the term. Although he was not a Quaker, he had heard of the Concern, which was the name given to obsessive act or thought, or both, of a religious nature. A Quaker who accosted strangers on the street, a Quaker who used his money for special missionary purposes—each was said to be influenced by a Concern. Abraham Lockwood's Concern was the establishment of a dynasty of his own line, beginning with Moses Lockwood, and apart from and independent of the 1630-Watertown line. He would proceed, and was already proceeding, with his Concern as the theme and motivation of his life and of the lives of his family. The gentlemanliness of his sons was not an end in itself but only a desirable, minor characteristic. Its place, its value in Abraham Lockwood's Concern was quite possibly inferior to the place and value of the two fatal shootings in which Moses Lockwood had been involved. Assuming that his father had killed two men in cold blood, Abraham Lockwood felt no shame or even lasting embarrassment. Murder had never disqualified a family from a position in history; it was the method by which kings became kings, barons became dukes, and in the year 2000 the only Bundy and the only Lichtmann worth remembering might easily be the early Nineteenth Century victims of Moses Lockwood's quickness on the trigger. Then, too, assuming that there would be a friendlier appraisal of Moses Lockwood, the historian could make much of the man's bravery in the first Battle of Bull Run. For the present, Abraham Lockwood would have his father remembered as a hero and a man of action, for of such stuff is family pride fashioned; for the present and the near future Abraham Lockwood would have himself regarded as a man of business and leading citizen; for the more distant future he would have his sons regarded as gentlemen, men of affairs, patrons of the arts, third-generation leaders of their community and the first generation upon which the national public would bestow the title, Lockwood of Swedish Haven. He sometimes hoped for more sons, so that he could direct them into the professions—the law, medicine, the clergy, the army—but a larger family naturally increased the chances of breeding a scoundrel, and he could not give to five or six boys the same supervision that he could concentrate on George and Penrose.

Abraham Lockwood, as stated, had heard of the Quaker Concern, and he was aware that his great plans could be called a Concern, but he did not so refer to them, or it. He gave no name to it. A concern. A cause. A campaign. A plan. A strategy. An obsession. A purpose. A mania—it did not matter that he gave it no name. It could have mattered if he had given it a name, since a designation, a definition would have inhibited his actions within the meaning of the name. It was so constantly in his thoughts and took so many forms of action that an action that could be called loving was sometimes followed by an action that could be called cruel, and neither modifier would be applicable to a third action. Since the Concern was Abraham Lockwood's secret it did not need a name. Adelaide would have understood a father's ambition to have George become a lawyer and Penrose a banker, but Abraham Lockwood could not make the daughter of Levi Hoffner understand the Concern, and he did not try. There was, after all, the danger that Adelaide might not agree with her husband's plans for her sons' future, and Abraham Lockwood had a respect for her potential influence. The boys loved her, and properly so. She was prettier than most mothers, she was strict but kindly, she bound their wounds and calmed their fears, and her education had not taken her so far from their mental level that she was unable to comprehend their small, daily discoveries. She was extremely useful to their well-being and as a symbol of gentle discipline, which prepared the boys for unquestioning obedience of their father's orders. He could, moreover, count on her support even in situations where she was not sincerely on his side.

George wanted a dog, but Abraham Lockwood had seen

dogs go mad with hydrophobia, racing up and down the street until someone brought out the shotgun. Therefore George was denied a dog, although Adelaide had all but given her consent to the purchase of the red setter that he asked for.

George did not want to go to school in Gibbsville, although the trip back and forth every day meant a ride on the railroad train. "Naturally, he doesn't want to go to private school. The school he's going to now doesn't start till October and ends in April," said Abraham Lockwood. "And if he stays in public school here, pretty soon you and I won't be able to understand him, he's so Dutchy."

To Adelaide it did not seem fair that once a week George had to remain late in Gibbsville for his piano lesson with Professor Fischer. "He doesn't get home any day before the four-twenty-five. That doesn't give him much time to play with his chums," she said.

"He has all the other afternoons and all day Saturday. You wish you could play the piano, and I wish I could," said Abraham Lockwood. So matters stood until several months later.

"Poppa, George wants to tell you something," said Adelaide one evening before supper.

The boy was flustered.

"Go ahead and tell Poppa," said Adelaide. "I'll leave you two alone." She went out.

"What is it, son?"

"Poppa, I don't like Professor kissing me all the time. He makes me sit on his lap and kisses me."

"Professor Fischer?"

"Yes sir."

"What else does he do?"

"He squeezes my behind."

"In front, too? Your pecker?"

"Yes. He wants me to squeeze his pecker, too. I don't like him. I don't want to squeeze his pecker, but he makes me. Do I have to take piano lessons, Poppa?"

"You can stop taking them from Professor."

George's study of the bass clef was resumed under Miss Bessie Auchmuty, organist at the Swedish Haven Lutheran Church. Abraham Lockwood concluded that it was not his duty to inform the Gibbsville parents of Fischer's overtures. The joint venture between Abraham Lockwood and Peter Hofman entailed no such responsibility. The Gibbsville parents could safeguard their own young, and Abraham Lockwood would do the same for his. It was altogether possible that the Gibbsville parents had deliberately refrained from warning him that Fischer was a degenerate, and in any event Abraham Lockwood, in undertaking to build a toll bridge that would mutually benefit the two towns, had not committed himself to a program of furthering the interests of a town where so many leading citizens still looked down their noses at him. If any Gibbsville parents should ask why he had changed piano teachers, he would tell the truth; otherwise he would remain silent. (As it happened, the Gibbsville parents, without having had any information from Abraham Lockwood, subsequently banished Fischer, and for several years musical education of the very young was at a standstill.)

The boys' religious training was left to Adelaide; Abraham Lockwood was not on sure ground in such matters. He could not convincingly give the fundamentalist answers to their inevitable questions, and attendance at church on Sunday was as far as he cared to carry his recognition of the place of formal religion. For a time he considered the desirability of subsidizing an Episcopal mission in Swedish Haven. The Episcopal was the church of fashion, increasingly so in the East and especially so in Philadelphia and Gibbsville. There were not enough potential Episcopalians in Swedish Haven to warrant the forming of a parish, but Trinity Church in Gibbsville served a mission in Collieryville, which was the same distance from Gibbsville as Swedish Haven. A Trinity Church curate conducted weekly services in the Collieryville Odd Fellows Hall, and Abraham Lockwood had no doubt that he could persuade the rector of Trinity to provide the same facility for Swedish Haven. But Abraham Lockwood, after viewing the project from the point of view of his Concern, decided that the boys were better off as Lutherans, at least until they were ready to go away to boarding school. He and his father were forever on the records as donors of the Swedish Haven Lutheran Church, and it would be foolish to toss away such a respectable bit of family history. ("My grandfather gave the Lutheran Church.") The boys already were third-generation Lutherans. Then too, the Lutheran faith was, in a manner of speaking, the indigenous denomination of Swedish Haven, comparable to the Society of Friends in Philadelphia, or even the Catholics in New Orleans. In Abraham Lockwood's view it was all the same God when you came right down to it, and when the boys sang about the Faith of Our Fathers they were stating a historic fact. The Lockwoods of Swedish Haven would naturally be Lutherans, and it was no more inconsistent for

Lockwoods to be Lutherans than for the important German-name brewers and meat packers to belong to Trinity Church in Gibbsville.

At this stage of their growth the boys chose their playmates among their contemporaries, without regard to the economic or social status of the playmates' parents. During the school day George and, later, Penrose were in the company of boys whose families could afford private schooling; at home in Swedish Haven, George had for chums the sons of a minister, a physician, a grocer, a railway brakeman, and the Negro porter at the Exchange Hotel. Penrose's playmates were from the families of the physician and the grocer, and the others were sons of a jeweler-watchmaker, a widowed schoolteacher, and a second cousin of the notorious Bundy brothers. There were certain areas where the boys were forbidden to go: the railroad yards, the quarry pond, and the jungle north of town which was snake-infested and full of treacherous water-holes. The boys learned to swim and to skate at the canal, and to skin-the-cat in various barns, steal plums and cherries from various orchards, hop ice wagons, experiment with stogies and chewing tobacco, attempt sexual intercourse with the grocer's daughter, commit vandalism in the week preceding Hallowe'en, and try Roman riding with George's and the physician's sons' ponies. George skinned his forehead and nose in a dive at the quarry, and Penrose fractured his left arm in a fall from a chestnut tree. Punishment was by spanking; bare-handed by Adelaide when they were young; with an old trunk strap by their father when they were older.

Ostensibly the boys throughout the grammar school years led lives that were no different from their contemporaries'. Abraham Lockwood was not making a conscious special effort to teach the boys equality. On the contrary, his eventual purpose was to send his sons to boarding school at the earliest possible age, and so to arrange their vacation schedules that they would have very little time to spend with the sons of the brakeman, the porter, the schoolteacher, and the cousin of the Bundy brothers. But he did not want his sons to grow up as bookish freaks, as sissies, as latchers-on-to-Momma's-apron-strings. It was likewise his wish to let his sons have an early acquaintance with all classes in the town, so that when the time came for them to assume the position they would occupy according to the Concern, they would not do so as strangers or virtual newcomers. His own father, and even more so his own grandfather, had mental records and working acquaintance with every citizen in the town, and so had he himself. His sons would not be absentee landlords; they would follow the proprietary tradition of the resident gentry, who knew their people, and George and Penrose were off to a good start.

Abraham Lockwood's Concern was not a bothersome thing, a chore, and it interfered amazingly little with his business career. With the Concern to guide him it was easy to make small and great decisions governing the raising of the two boys, despite the mystification of and occasional opposition from their mother. Nearly everything relating to the boys' present could be related to the future of the Concern: the boys' education, manners, attire, appearance, and the subtler items of pride, hauteur, independence, honesty, self-control, moderation and ambition. Oddly, as they grew older into adolescence, the boys developed a filial love that was to Abraham Lockwood quite unexpected, and to their mother seemed somewhat perverse. They went to her for warmth, but they esteemed his approval. This thin, sharp man, who said no to so many of their requests, was nevertheless a positive factor in their daily lives, omnipresent even when they were secretly disobeying him, and always the adult they were most eager to please. Their love was his reward for his interest in them, which at their ages they accepted without looking for a reason behind it.

With the same unquestioning submission, George, completing the eighth grade in 1887, departed for St. Bartholomew's, an event of major significance in his father's Concern, and one that had taken a great deal of serious consideration. The school was now old enough to have graduated some thirty classes, members of which had gone on almost without exception to Harvard, Yale, Princeton, the University of Pennsylvania, Dartmouth, Williams, and the University of Virginia, or to theological seminaries. It was a church school, the church being the Episcopal, situated in Eastern Massachusetts, and except for a handful of Southern boys, the students came from cities and towns in Massachusetts, Rhode Island, Connecticut, New York, New Jersey, Pennsylvania, Maryland and Delaware. Although not themselves alumni, Harry Penn Downs and Morris Homestead were sending their sons to St. Bartholomew's. This fact, while influencing Abraham Lockwood, was of secondary importance in his consideration of suitable schools. Of major importance was the school's New England location and its graduates' records at the colleges—needless to say, their extra-curricular records. Abraham Lockwood had already decided upon Princeton for his sons, but he wanted them to have friends at Harvard, Yale, and Penn as well, and since the majority of St. Bartholomew's boys went to Harvard or Yale, the school provided the right opportunities for such friendships. Abraham Lockwood carefully avoided the appearance of imitating Downs and Homestead, and did not ask them for help in placing George at St. Bartholomew's. Instead he went about it through Gabriel Bromley, assistant rector of Trinity Church, Gibbsville, and Joe Calthorp, a classmate and Zeta Psi at the University, both personal friends of the rector-headmaster of St. Bartholomew's. Abraham Lockwood wisely decided not to attempt to impress the school with his modest claim to social correctness, but to underplay his Philadelphia trumps. In the course of his correspondence and his single interview with Arthur Francis Ferris he told the headmaster that he hoped to have his *sons* accepted at St. Bartholomew's because their background for a hundred years had been solid Pennsylvanian, on both sides of the family, and since he could afford it, he wanted them to have the benefit of New England education. He lightly mentioned New England origins, but candidly stated that neither he nor his father nor his grandfather had any personal acquaintance with those Lockwoods.

His strategy, he well knew, fitted in nicely with Arthur Francis Ferris's cautious, slow-moving plan to admit a few boys who were not quite the usual type of St. Bartholomew student. Ferris had accepted one boy from Chicago and one from Buffalo, in his hesitant program against what he called inbreeding; and while not committing the school to an acceptance of Penrose Lockwood, he took the older brother George. He had already satisfied himself that the financial present and future of the Lockwood family was safe, and any misgivings he may have had in regard to Abraham Lockwood were put at rest by Joe Calthorp and Gabriel Bromley, who assured him that Lockwood was being over-modest in his social and business attainments. Joe Calthorp, who had not been a member of The Ruffes, mentioned that organization to Ferris, and Ferris noticed approvingly that Abraham Lockwood never brought it up. Bromley reported to Ferris that Lockwood and father had built the Lutheran church in their home town, and here again Lockwood had been silent.

Abraham Lockwood, to be sure, had had the advantage of knowing that Arthur Francis Ferris had a Concern of his own—St. Bartholomew's School.

And so, in the autumn of '87, those old friends Morris Homestead, Harry Penn Downs, and Abraham Lockwood were together again on a sleeping car to Boston. The Homestead and Downs boys, meeting the Lockwood boy for the first time, drew closer together in blank hostility to the stranger, to the embarrassment of the three fathers. It was the first setback for Abraham Lockwood's Concern as well as the first time he had ever felt the rush of love and protective hatred that a parent experiences when his child is abused. For his son's stupid cruelty Harry Penn Downs was to pay with his life.

But in spite of the inauspicious beginning of his boarding-school career, George Lockwood was a delight to the Rector. The boy went rapidly into the lead in first-year algebra and Latin, and he was one of the best foot-racers in his class. His room was orderly, he kept his person clean, and his early homesickness lasted only until the masters gave public recognition to his excellence in his studies. Arthur Francis Ferris congratulated himself on his judgment; in spite of his misgivings about the boy's father, Arthur Francis Ferris had allowed the good of the program to prevail over prejudice, and his instinct was proving sound.

Every boy at St. Bartholomew's was given—for fifty cents, chargeable to his bill for books and incidentals—a small wooden box, 4″ deep by 12″ wide by 16″ long. The box had a hasp, and for an additional fifteen cents the boy was given a padlock and two keys. He retained one key, and the other key was held by the head prefect. But the privacy of the box was respected. No boy was supposed to open another boy's box, and no master was supposed to open the box without the boy's permission.

Every boy kept his own special treasures in his box: letters, pen-knives, candy (forbidden), extra collar and cuff buttons, shoelaces, family photographs, horse chestnuts, Indian arrowheads, medals for scholastic and athletic accomplishment, journal-diaries, watches and watch fobs, stamps, money (forbidden), locks of girls' hair, Sunday neckties. The boys had learned from handed-down information that the boxes were sometimes opened, in their absence, by masters in search of suspected pipes and tobacco and dirty pictures. Although candy and money were forbidden, punishment was not meted out for their possession; the illusion was maintained that the boxes were *not* opened by masters, and small sums of money—under a dollar—and bits of taffy were not considered serious contraband. Every boy had his own special hiding place for his key; some kept it around their necks on a string. And it was not considered bad form for a boy to go off by himself with his box rather than allow his roommates to see the contents; on the other hand, it was considered a fighting offense and violation of the boys' own code for one boy to force open another boy's box. Most boys had special places for their boxes, and a boy returning to his room would know immediately that the location of the box had been changed. "Who moved my box?" he would demand, and the question was the next thing to an outright accusation, was in itself often enough to touch off an argument that would lead to a fight. The supreme compliment was for one boy to show a friend the souvenirs and trinkets in his box, but two boys could be the best of friends all through school years without such a gesture. A boy carved or burned his name in the lid of his box, and even when he had nothing very interesting to disclose, the box was still his, private and secret and precious. Since there were no locks on any of the dormitory doors, a boy's box and the moments he had alone with it provided the only one way—short of a solitary walk around the pond—to get away from his schoolmates and the masters. A boy who opened another boy's box risked not only a fight with the offended one but a beating by the offended one's friends.

Originally intended as a container for such articles as shoe blacking and brushes, hair combs, handkerchiefs and such necessary items and possessions, the box was a St. Bartholomew's institution and tradition, and graduates of the school always took their boxes home with them, sometimes to use them all through college; and already there were boys at St. Bartholomew's who were using boxes originally owned by their fathers. Boys like Francis Homestead and Sterling Downs, sure enough of themselves on their own ground, got a quick lesson in humility by being reminded that they had *new* boxes, not their fathers'.

The contents—and sometimes the emptiness—of a boy's box were always examined with self-consciously penetrating care by the masters, especially by the newer, younger masters, who were readers of Arthur Conan Doyle. They could not, however, be present when a boy opened his box privately, in a far corner of the study-hall, when the boy, out of the needs of loneliness and unhappiness, would select one or two items to look at and fondle, rejecting all the rest. Nor could they know that some boys never reached that point where the box and its contents were preferable to human company. Some boys used their boxes just to keep things in.

George Bingham Lockwood's box, which had *G. B. Lockwood* burned in the lid by a poker from the common-room fireplace, may have been unique. Instead of being a catch-all, with numerous unrelated items in a scramble, it had four compartments, each containing its own more or less homogeneous articles. George had had slots cut in the inner lengthwise sides of the box to hold three little fences that made the four compartments. His silver watch-and-chain, collar and cuff buttons and safety pins were in one compartment; his handkerchiefs and neckties in another; his money and postage stamps in a third; his letters from home and his soap and eau de Cologne in the fourth. Except for the separating panels the box and its contents offered no strikingly unusual reward to the snooping masters. A few silver and copper pieces were the only contraband, and a curious master would close the box in short order.

But the box had more to offer: it had a false bottom. The little fences that formed the compartments also deceived the eye. The fences, or panels, could be slid out of their slots, the contents of the box dumped on a desk, the box turned upside down, and by gently tapping the exterior bottom of the box, George would cause the interior "floor" of the box to fall out, and with it his secret treasure, two five-dollar gold pieces and a ten-dollar banknote. The possession of so much cash could have led to his expulsion, since no explanation he could give would be satisfactory to the masters or to Arthur Francis Ferris.

George Lockwood—who went through four years at St. Bartholomew's without a nickname—had been given his box in the general distribution a week after his arrival at the school. For the first four months he used the box to protect the kind of personal possessions that roommates borrow—soap, hair combs, shoe blacking—and since George had no need to have recourse to the box for solace, and since he always knew without reexamination what was in the box, the only fun he had with it was in keeping it locked and unlocking it in private. Then, a few weeks after being given the box, he learned that masters sometimes opened the boxes without warning their owners, and this violation of privacy so angered him that he studied his box more intently, until he worked out a plan to defeat them. At Christmastime he took his box home with him and for fifty cents Mr. Dunkelberger, a Swedish Haven carpenter-and-joiner, fashioned the compartments and the false bottom. Mr. Dunkelberger was an artist in his line and had made many such hiding places in desks and bureaus and trunks, and he enjoyed the conspiratorial nature of George's commission. ("Vat you keep in it, Cheorchie? Luff letters, say?") George put his Christmas presents from his Hoffner grandparents—the gold pieces—and the ten-dollar bill from his father in the false bottom of the box, and returned to St. Bartholomew's with a gleefully defiant attitude toward the snooping masters. He would open his box once a week, and from time to time he could tell by the rearrangement of his possessions that a master had been going through the box, but Mr. Dunkelberger had done his work so skillfully that in all the four years George was at St. Bartholomew's the hidden money was never discovered.

It could be said that George Lockwood made no close friendships at St. Bartholomew's, or, with equal truth, that he had made many. He changed friends as often as he changed roommates. Only in the last year were the boys allowed to choose roommates, and George, permitted by the rules to choose two roommates, chose only one and left the selection of the other up to the head prefect. The one he chose, and who accepted his invitation, was Sterling Downs. In the beginning George had not liked Sterling any more than Sterling liked him; but in their second year at St. Bartholomew's they had got along somewhat better; and in their third year George felt sorry for Sterling Downs, as did all the boys in the school. In that year Sterling's father committed suicide.

The joint speculative account maintained by Harry Penn Downs and Abraham Lockwood had gone from the original $10,000 to as much as $600,000 in less than ten years, largely, but not entirely, through purchases and sales of stocks that Downs had studied. At unstated intervals Abraham Lockwood would suggest that they liquidate their holdings, and he would take his profits, reinvest them in other securities or real estate, and wait until Downs came to him again with a new proposition. Abraham Lockwood never refused to go in with Downs, but he did not always go in for the amount Downs asked; he demurred sometimes because he regarded the particular stock as too dangerously speculative, sometimes because his money was tied up in other ventures; but there was scarcely any doubt that Downs was a successful speculator. The figures $10,000 and $600,000 were basic; the larger figure did not nearly represent the sum that had been divided between the partners. In actuality they had each taken more than a million out of the stock market during their partnership, and $600,000 was the high point of the account as of the year 1889.

The two men had made money together from the start, but they had been making larger amounts of money during the latter years, when relations between them were less cordial than ever before. Downs knew no reason for his partner's attitude, since he could not have divined that his friend Locky had been offended by Sterling Downs's rudeness to George Lockwood. He attributed the coolness—when he thought about it—to Lockwood's preoccupation with his other business enterprises, and so long as Lockwood continued to put up 60 percent of the cash for their speculations, Downs was willing to dispense with the amenities. Not that Lockwood was overtly rude; but their meetings latterly had no social character, did not occur so much at mealtimes. At one point, briefly, Downs contemplated a gesture toward improving social relations: his wife had never met Adelaide Lockwood, and his only meeting with her had been at Adelaide's wedding. But Martha Sterling Downs was not the most gracious hostess, and she would be at her least gracious while entertaining for an upstate woman who had her trouble with her v's and w's and had probably never heard of the Philadelphia Assembly. Downs quickly dismissed the social idea, and went on meeting Lockwood at their offices in Philadelphia and Swedish Haven.

At these meetings Lockwood usually had an accurate estimate of the condition of their joint account. "You've made thirty thousand, I've made twenty," he would say. "Let's take our profit now." He seldom was insistent when Downs would urge their staying in a stock a little while longer, but there were exceptions to this amenability and Lockwood could be stubborn. When that occurred, Downs would yield, and there was no sharp difference between the partners until the spring of 1890.

They met in Downs's office, and Lockwood wasted no time. "Harry, let's sell our sugar stock," he said.

"Why? It looks pretty good to me. We're going to clean up in that, Locky. That's one of the best things we've ever had."

"Haven't I got any say in the matter?"

"Of course you have. But in this case you're making a mistake. Do you know anything about Havemeyer?"

"I don't know anything about Havemeyer. But I know about the Bank of America and those other banks failing, not to mention the life insurance company, also here in Philadelphia. I want to get out and stay out for a while. You can do what you please, but let me have my share now. It comes to a hundred and twenty thousand."

"I can't," said Harry Penn Downs.

"Why not?"

"I haven't got it."

"What's the matter, you haven't got it?"

"We have no sugar stock at all. I lied to you. I didn't buy any. This was the one time you shouldn't have asked me."

"It sounds like the one time I *should* have asked you."

"No. I've always been honest before, Locky, and I've made money for both of us."

"What did you do with the money?"

"Well, it's none of your damn business as long as I admit I'm a crook. But I'll tell you. I lost it playing poker."

"You lost $150,000 playing poker?"

"More than that."

"Where? Who with?"

"At the Union League, never mind who with, although I suppose you could find that out if you tried hard enough."

"Yes, I suppose I could. Even at the Union League they don't have many games as big as that. I didn't know you belonged to the Union League. I thought you were a Philadelphia Club member."

"I am in the Philadelphia Club, but I won't be much longer, I guess. Locky, I was cleaned out. I have my house and my job here, and that's about all I have."

"But a year ago you were worth well over a million."

"Indeed I was, and winning at poker. But I've had a run of bad cards, and I did the usual things. I stayed in with hands that I should have dropped."

"Why didn't you get them to play whist?"

"These men are poker players, not whist players."

"Do you mean to tell me that you've lost over a million dollars playing poker?"

"I mean to tell you exactly that."

"How could you do that? Well, you *could*, of course."

"I lost over $400,000 in one night. Then I went to New York to play with some of the same men, and I lost almost the same amount."

"Oh, *those* men! Why, you never had any right to be playing against *them*. They can keep playing till their luck changes."

"I had as much right to be playing poker against them as I had to be outguessing them in the stock market. And don't forget, for a while I was a winner."

"How long have you been playing for such high stakes?"

"About three years."

"You should have let me know."

"I didn't think so. As long as I was making money for you."

"Is this pretty well known in Philadelphia, that you've been losing all this money?"

"I guess so."

"Does your wife know?"

"She does now. The point is, Locky, what are you going to do? You can have me arrested, of course."

"I could, but that wouldn't get me my $120,000."

"No, it wouldn't."

"You're cleaned out, you say. But what about your house? I'll take your house."

"Oh, no you won't. I've given that to my wife, long since."

"My dear fellow, you'd be insulted if I gave your wife a house, but that's what you're suggesting I do."

"If that's the way you want to look at it."

"That's the only way, Harry. If it's so well known here that you've been losing so heavily, where would you be able to raise fifteen cents? Not in this town. These Quakers are going to be very silent when you try to borrow money."

"They have been."

" 'Thee has been dishonest, Harry.' But why should I lose $120,000 because *you've* been paying the money to multi-millionaires in New York City? They weren't friends of yours, or partners. The men I have in mind are older than we are, very rich, but it's your old friend and partner that takes the loss. Why should I give Martha Sterling a house? She wouldn't remember me if she came in this office. No, you've got to find another loser. I didn't even have the fun of looking at a hand."

"What if I still refuse?"

"Harry, you know that my father killed two men."

"Yes, I heard that. Are you going to kill me?"

"No, hardly that. But I've lived all my life under that cloud. Could I get into the Philadelphia Club?"

"No."

"Of course not. And not for something *I* did. You're in the Philadelphia Club, and the Assembly, and I never could be. Although my father was acquitted. And here you sit, having stolen money from me, a lot of money. I'll give you a month to find $60,000. That's half. We were in on a speculation, so I'll take that much of a loss."

"Well, I suppose you're being decent, Locky. As decent as I have any right to expect. But I won't ask Martha to give up the house, and I know damn well I can't raise $60,000."

"Take a month. Your luck may change. Won't your multi-millionaire friends take your I.O.U.?"

"No. The losers pay by cheque at the end of the evening. I can't write a cheque for $10,000 at this moment, and we start those games by buying $10,000 worth of chips."

"Take me to one of those games. I might win."

"I can't. They don't ask me to play any more."

"Well, then I guess we have nothing more to say to each other. A month from now I hope you'll have raised sixty thousand somehow. I *do*. You and I are through, but I hope you'll land on both feet again."

"Thank you, Locky. Sorry about this."

"Yes, it *is* too bad," said Abraham Lockwood rising. "Harry do you think I'm entitled to a truthful answer to one more question?"

"Maybe."

"You didn't lose all that money playing poker, did you?"

Downs stroked his chin. "No."

"You were also speculating in some things you didn't let me in on?"

"Yes."

"Were you doing that as a favor to me?" Keeping me out because you didn't want me to lose money?"

"How easy it would be for me to lie to you now. No, Locky, I wasn't protecting you. I often traded in stocks that I didn't think you were entitled to know about."

"Why wasn't I? It was my understanding that I was to be in on everything that looked good."

"Let's just say that I made a mental reservation."

"From the very beginning?"

"I suppose so. Go ahead and say it. I've been a crook all along."

"You saved me the trouble. Well, at last we do understand each other."

"No, not quite. I never did understand you, Locky. I've never known just what you wanted. Still don't. Something besides money, and it isn't social position."

"I'd tell you, but right now it doesn't seem like a very worthwhile ambition. In fact it seems very foolish. But I'm talking in riddles. Good day, Harry."

"So long, Locky. Will you shake hands?" Downs got to his feet.

"Harry, I can't. I wish you luck, but I can't shake your hand."

"Good. I understand. It's a very dirty hand. Filthy dirty."

"Good day, Harry."

On his way to the early evening train Abraham Lockwood distinguished the name "H. P. Downs" in the midst of the newsboys' gibberish. He bought a newspaper and felt the shock of confirmation without surprise upon reading that Harry had placed a pistol to his ear while seated at his office desk. The newspaper could not entirely leave out references to his stock market operations, but obviously an effort was being made to show no connection with the recent bank and insurance company collapses. On the homeward train Abraham Lockwood was glad to be headed for Swedish Haven, away, away from Philadelphia. He thought he knew precisely the degree of his guilt in Harry Penn Downs's suicide; he had given his partner and friend the final push. But before the homeward journey was over Abraham Lockwood was once again involved in his Concern. One human life could not be charged up against the Concern, but the unknowing victim had known what he was doing, and he had jeopardized the Concern itself—stealing from it—and threatened harm of a sort to one of the beneficiaries, George Lockwood.

The irony of George's subsequent invitation to Sterling Downs was not lost on Abraham Lockwood; having his son extend a kindness out of pity was very nearly laughable. But the irony interested Abraham Lockwood less than the fact that a Lockwood was now in the gracious position vis-à-vis a Sterling Penn Downs, and the other fact that a man had committed suicide as an indirect result of his interfering with the Concern. Somehow the Harry Penn Downs suicide and George Lockwood's invitation to Sterling Downs became, in Abraham Lockwood's mind, proof that the Concern had achieved the dignity of an establishment, the substance of an *établissement*. It was getting to be like one of those private banking firms that can maneuver a nation into war; or perhaps like a railway, a coal mine, a powder mill, in which human life must be counted among the production costs. Or—coming back to what the Concern really was—a man's suicide and a boy's gracious act belonged rightly in the general scheme of the building of a dynasty.

During those weeks that followed Harry's suicide Abraham Lockwood often wished he knew someone in whom he could confide the secret of the Concern. He had already dismissed Adelaide as a possible confidante. He had a wild, short-lived impulse to confide in old Peter Hofman, who as a man of power would understand some aspects of the Concern but as an unimaginative, conventional individual could not be expected to see very far into a future that for him had no reality. Morris Homestead, a member of a dynasty, would understand some aspects of the Concern but the dynasty of which Morris was a member was already in being, and nothing so new as the Lockwood Concern would hold as much interest for the present head of a dynasty already in its third century. Morris Homestead's placid acceptance of his inherited and continuing place in Pennsylvania history was an attitude that Abraham Lockwood viewed with admiring envy, and Morris served better as an unconscious model than as a contemporary confidant. And so, for the time being, the secret of Abraham Lockwood's Concern remained intact, having survived some vague suspicions on the part of Harry Penn Downs. It was, of course, much too early to explain the Concern to George Bingham Lockwood. The boy might not take kindly to the notion that his regimen was being ordered with his grandsons' and not his own life the beneficiary. George, his father knew, was an obedient boy, but not a subservient one and not an unimaginative one. The younger son, Penrose, was already in the habit of obedience to his father, his mother, and his older brother, and Abraham Lockwood was already sure that Penrose would go through his entire life always obeying someone, therefore would not be a hazard to the Concern so long as the right kind of person gave him the right kind of guidance. Abraham Lockwood looked forward to the time when George, married and with children of his own, could be apprised of the existence of the Concern in such a way as to make him a willing convert to it. That time, however, was not now.

(It was often remarked upon in Swedish Haven that Abraham Lockwood was a wonderful father to his sons.)

In his preoccupation with the Concern and his growing fortune, his motivated interest in other men, women and children, and money, Abraham Lockwood had little time or curiosity for what was happening to himself. The Concern, his own secret, was, to be sure, a personal matter comparable to a religious zeal, but in function the Concern dealt with the actions and postures and behavior of others than himself. Consequently Abraham Lockwood had not done much thinking about Abraham Lockwood, and he was taken by surprise when he discovered that the secrecy of the Concern and his reluctance to confide in Adelaide had altered his relationship with his wife. It was as though the Concern had become a mistress, whose existence was to be denied. So big an unshared secret, so integral a part of his thoughts and actions, daily and hourly, had grown insidiously from a precautionary measure to a conditioned attitude. At least every day of his life, and in many of his waking hours, Abraham Lockwood had to exclude Adelaide, until on no certain day, at no certain hour, but from one sleeping to one waking he was conscious of having entered into a different phase of his relationship as husband. He saw a mole on her shoulder that he had not noticed before; one breast was slightly lower than the other; her Pennsylvania Dutch accent was nearly gone; changes had been taking place, and his failure to have noticed them taking place was bewildering until he traced the reason: the Concern.

Abraham Lockwood was now forty-nine years old; in good health, rich, and consciously enjoying the respectful treatment he was earning by maintaining his position in the community. He had not taken stock of himself at any of the milestones—at, for instance, age forty or age forty-five—and he was far from ready to slow down now, with so much yet to be done. The man who slowed down, stopped. A Morris Homestead had never moved at a rapid pace, since there was no particular reason for him to do so; a Harry Penn Downs had moved at a rapid pace but he had slowed down, or been slowed down, because he had not had real staying power. Harry Penn Downs, in Abraham Lockwood's opinion, had resorted to dishonest practice because he was exhausted. He had consumed his legitimate energy, had then taken to desperate gambling and finally to plain theft. In any event, he had had to slow down, and slowing down, had stopped.

According to custom, there was no one but immediate family at the funeral of Harry Penn Downs, a suicide. But when a week had passed Abraham Lockwood wrote a note to Martha Sterling Downs and, at his request, she allowed him to pay her a call.

As he had said during his last meeting with Downs, Martha Downs would not have recognized him, but she was expecting him and was thus forewarned. She rose to greet him as he followed a maid into the library, and if he had vaguely expected a tearful, abject widow, he quickly conceded how wrong that was. "Good afternoon, Locky," she said. "It's very nice of you to call. You didn't bring your wife, I see."

"I never thought to. You didn't know each other, and this—"

"Wouldn't have been the right moment. You're right. Sit down, Locky. I call you Locky as if we were old friends. Do you mind that?"

"I like it."

"There'll be a cup of tea in a little while, but let's wait, shall we?"

"Yes."

"I know you're not a drinker, although if you'd like something?"

"No thanks."

"I'm very pleased that our sons are going to room together next year. It's nice to continue the association. Smoke, if you like. I do, so it doesn't bother me."

"I haven't got anything *to* smoke. I never carry cigarettes."

"Well, have one." She offered him her tiny silver case, and he lit their cigarettes. "I'm also pleased that we may be neighbors this summer. You have a cottage, or a boathouse, whatever they call them, at a place called The Run, haven't you?"

"Why, yes. For several years. Are you going to be there? That would be very good news."

"You must know the Westervelts? Well, Mr. Westervelt is a cousin of mine, and he very kindly offered to let us have his boathouse. We couldn't afford to go away otherwise. They're going abroad this summer, so it works out very nicely."

"They have one of the nicest boathouses at The Run. One of the few that you can live in. You know what The Run is? It's a reservoir, an artificial lake, owned by the coal company, and people like J. B. Westervelt get the very best boathouses. You'll enjoy it, if you don't mind bathing in cold water."

"I prefer it to ocean bathing. Is your wife a swimmer?"

"No. This will probably be our last summer at The Run. Adelaide wants to go to the seashore next year." He stopped talking and she continued to look at him until he became uneasy. "Is there something wrong, Martha?"

"She laughed. "Oh, no. No." She laughed again.

"What's funny?"

"I couldn't possibly tell you. Not possibly in a million years. It's funny, and you'd enjoy the humor of it, but quickly, let's find something else to talk about. I hadn't realized I was staring."

"It must be something good."

"Don't ask any more about it, please. Perhaps we'd better talk about Harry. Did you lose a lot of money, Locky?"

"Do you want to know how much? Actually although I lost some cash, my biggest loss might be called hypothetical. The profits on the cash Harry was supposed to invest for our account."

"Naturally I've never seen the woman, never laid eyes on her."

"What woman?"

"Oh, now don't pretend, Locky. I know all about it. In fact I've known about it for almost two years, so don't spare my feelings. Unfortunately, though, I'm told that there's no way to get any of the money back. Legally, it's hers. Or at least it would be so hard to prove what isn't hers. The lawyers say that the New York courts would never make her give anything back, and of course if the Pennsylvania courts decided in our favor, what good would that do? She'll never show her face in this State, and she has no money here. Have *you* met her?"

"No."

"One of the lawyers said she's totally unlike me, which he intended for a compliment. But then in the next breath told me how feminine she is. And of course beautiful. I wonder how many others there were. Harry spent a great deal of time talking about that sort of thing, but I thought it was to shock me. The way some husbands do because they think their wives like to be shocked. Well, I guess I did encourage him. Some of our conversations wouldn't bear repeating. Poor Harry. How I must have bored him when I thought I was being deliciously naughty, and all the time he had a beautiful mistress in New York. Beautiful, and feminine, and young. Twenty-five or -six. I guess there must have been others. Yes. Harry and I married too young, the month he graduated. I'm selling this house. You wouldn't like to buy it, would you?"

"It's a beautiful house, but a bit too far away from Swedish Haven."

"Buy it, and I'll be your mistress. Wouldn't you like to have a mistress to come to when you're in Philadelphia? Of course I'm not beautiful, or young. But I'm feminine. That lawyer infuriated me when he said that."

"Of course I'll buy the house, if you go with it."

"There, that makes up for Mr. Jonas Ripley's insulting remark."

"That's what you get for having Jonas Ripley as your lawyer. I knew him in my college days, and I've hardly ever seen him since, but I guess he hasn't changed much. The kind of lawyer that people go to because his name is Ripley."

"That's usually good enough reason, in Philadelphia."

"I haven't said anything to offend you?"

"No, no. I say much worse things about them than you'd ever think of saying. I never traveled much with the pack, didn't you know? No, I guess you didn't. All the years that you and Harry were in partnership together, I've never met your wife, and isn't this the first time you've ever been here?"

"I came here when I was at the University, but after the war I went back to Swedish Haven and stayed."

"You were wise."

"Why?"

"Well, unless you'd married a Philadelphia girl you'd have found that those college friendships haven't very much meaning. As soon as those boys graduate from college they come back here and start being Philadelphians again. The worst of them of course are those that never left, the ones that stayed here and went to the University instead of going to Harvard or Yale. All those boys that were in that whist club of yours. That one with the question mark for a stick-pin."

"The Ruffes. The club still exists."

"Oh, I'm sure it does, but I'm sure it has other reasons for existing besides whist." She smiled. "It used to."

"That's the very same smile you had on your face when you wouldn't tell me *why* you were smiling."

"Then we'll have to quickly change the subject again."

"The smile had something to do with The Ruffes. You were not supposed to know anything about The Ruffes. *My* wife doesn't."

"Then you're better at keeping secrets than Harry was. Some secrets, at least. I know *all* about The Ruffes, or I used to."

"Well, since you're in on our secrets, why not let me in on your secret? Why did you smile?"

She shook her head. "No, Locky. Not in a thousand years."

"Well, we're progressing. First you said a million years. Maybe I can get it down to a hundred before I leave."

"A million or a thousand, both mean never. When do you go to The Run place?"

"A week or two after school closes. Will you be there then?"

"Yes, just about the same time. I own this house, you know. It isn't part of Harry's jumbled estate. And I'm going to put it on the market in a week or two so that people can come and see it while I'm away."

"Oh, then you've decided not to sell to me?"

Her manner suddenly changed. "What if I took you seriously?"

"I took you seriously."

"No you didn't. But I have a reputation for speaking my mind, not always to my advantage, and if I offered myself as mistress to some of the men I know, it would be taken very seriously. And I'd mean it seriously. I'm not very young and I'm not very pretty, but there doesn't seem to be much else for me to do."

"You're certainly not serious now, although you sound it."

"Why not? I'd be better off as the mistress of some men I know. Men that have flirted with me and wanted to make love to me, and still would. I'll have nothing but this house, you know, or whatever I get for it in cash. That will be enough to finish the children's education, but where will that leave me ten years from now?"

"You *are* serious."

"It's the best thing that could happen to me."

"And the worst."

"Because people talk? They've talked already. They've always talked about me in Philadelphia, and when Harry shot himself the gossips got busy immediately. The women that didn't know he had a mistress thought that I must have had a lover. Well, I did. My first. A year ago. He ran like a deer, d, double-e, r, when the rumors started about Harry losing so much money. Oh, he ran! He's still running. Took a trip around the world, with his wife, of course. You don't hear Philadelphia gossip, but I do, even when it's me they're gossiping about. Although they never knew about my startled faun."

"I've always wondered where people like you would meet."

"What bed we'd use?" She pointed upward. "Mine. My own bed. Whenever Harry went to New York to see *his* light of love."

"But the children, and the servants."

"After they'd gone to bed. From ten o'clock on. I don't know how or where other women had their rendezvous, but that's the way mine were."

"And what about his wife?"

"Well, I don't know how much I can tell you without identifying them. But he had a very good excuse to spend the night in town quite frequently. On business, you might say."

"He was a doctor."

"I won't say."

"Why didn't she become suspicious?"

"She was too clever to show much suspicion. When a woman has those suspicions, and is married to a very rich man, she'd better not give vent to her suspicions unless she's prepared to risk an open break. In this case, the woman wasn't willing to risk anything. The husband could have told her the truth and she'd have acquiesced. I never thought much of her. She had no pride. All she wanted was a life of ease and luxury. A box of chocolates and a trashy novel. A tiara that Queen Victoria wouldn't wear. Footmen in knee breeches—oh, dear, I *shouldn't* have said *that*."

"I don't know anybody that has a footman in knee breeches."

"Yes you do. You've never happened to go to their houses."

"Excuse *me*."

"You know three or *four* men who have footmen in knee breeches."

"I guess I don't know them very well."

"No, but you probably thought you did. That's why you were wise not to live in Philadelphia after the War. I'm changing the subject deliberately."

"I'm looking forward to this summer."

"Are you changing the subject too?"

"No, I'm not."

"Oh. You're changing it back?"

"Yes."

"To me and my revenge on Harry?"

"Yes."

"I think we've exhausted that topic. It's curious how we ever got on it. I don't think I trust you, Locky, but I like you. Or maybe it's the other way round. It is. I trust you, even though I can't really say I like you."

"That's too bad, because I like you."

"Yes, I know you do. You're not in love with your wife, are you?"

"I don't think I am, any more. We've been married a long time."

"Happily?"

"Yes. Yes, I would say happily."

"This is the time when you'd better be very careful. A clever young thing could twist you around her little finger."

"I doubt it. I don't like clever young things. In fact, I guess I don't like cleverness in a woman at all. When I was a young man during the War I had my fill of clever young things. Some of the cleverest in the world, I guess. The women in the diplomatic corps in Washington. They were *too* clever for *me*. So I went home and married a Pennsylvania Dutch girl. Pretty. Intelligent. But not clever. A clever girl never would have fitted in with my—" He stopped abruptly on the verge of giving the first utterance to the Concern.

"With your what?"

"Oh, my life, the kind of life I preferred."

"That isn't what you were going to say."

"Isn't it? No, I guess it isn't."

"What *were* you going to say?"

He shook his head and smiled. "Not in a thousand years, Martha."

"Touché."

"Show me the rest of your house."

"You can come and see it when I'm not here."

"No, that wouldn't be the same."

"No."

"Then let's say, whenever you're ready."

"Are you that rich, Locky?"

"I think I am, but I'm not going to woo you with greenbacks. I couldn't buy what I want from you."

She looked at him quickly, slightly troubled. "I wonder how you meant that. It could be the greatest compliment I ever had in my life."

"What other way could I mean it?"

"I'm grateful to you for it, but I wish I hadn't heard it. I have other plans."

"Forget the other plans."

"No. I have to think."

"Well I'll be at The Run after the first of July."

She became his mistress during the first week of July. He took her for a spin in the naphtha launch, tied up the launch on the south shore of the dam where there were no boathouses but in full view of the boathouses on the north shore. They went into the woods, and when they were in deep enough he took her in his arms. She had not spoken during the ride across the dam, and she went with him into the woods as if in obedience to a command. She kissed him eagerly, pressing her hands at places on his shoulders and down his back, always bringing him close to her and turning her head from side to side while holding his lips with her kiss. She took off her skirt and made a rug of it on the ground and sat on it while he helped her with the rest of her underclothes. Then he stripped and there was no time for tenderness or discoveries or sensuality but only the demand of each to possess the other before the world came to an end. Nothing that one said was heard by the other, and not by intent but by the speed of urgency they reached quick, very nearly simultaneous climax.

Her dampened hair streaked down over her forehead and she kissed him many times while he was tired. Now they could hear voices, wafted from the opposite shore, some speeches quite distinctly. A rusty oar-lock in a passing rowboat very near their shore. The music puffing out of the carrousel in the casino at the eastern end of the dam. The bell on the large launch that was about to make its hourly tour of the dam. The air whistle on the electric railway car from Gibbsville echoing down the valley.

"I didn't hear anything before," she said.

"You'd better put your things on. You never can tell when there may be picnickers."

"Why didn't you think of that before?" she asked, not crossly.

"Why didn't you hear anything before?"

"I'd like to go in for a swim, just the way I am. And you with me. I'd love to swim all the way down to the breast and back. And then maybe we could lie here together."

"All right, let's."

"Don't tease me. I just might. Oh, that was lovely, Abraham Lockwood. Think how far away we are from the other side of the dam."

"A quarter of a mile."

"No! *No!* Turn your back to the other side and you'd walk all the way around the world before you got to it."

"All the way around the world, less a quarter of a mile."

"Exactly. I'm glad our first time was in the woods like this. The Garden of Eden."

"Speaking of the Garden of Eden, there are serpents over on this side. I don't mean picnickers, either."

"Why didn't you think of *that* before?"

"I can only think of one thing at a time."

"I wish there was more to see here. How many times are you going to be able to take me sightseeing?"

"Not many, I guess."

"Shall we pick some berries to take back to your wife?"

"No. I'll tell her we looked for some but saw a copperhead. Sometimes you do see a copperhead where there are huckleberries. Don't ever walk through these woods without a stick."

"I'm not afraid of snakes, I rather like them."

"Yes, but they don't know that, and don't try to convince them."

"Do you care what happens to me?"

"Yes."

"Do you know what has happened to me?"

"What?"

"Everything. I love you."

"I love you."

"Yes, in your way you do."

"Why is my way different from yours?"

"It's man's love. Mine is woman's love, and no other man will ever have me again, as long as I live. I swear it. You will have to go with your wife, but I'll never have to go with another man. You won't mind going with your wife, but I could never bear to have another man. I'm surprised, too. I didn't expect to feel this way. But I do. I began when we got in the launch. I didn't want you to talk, and you didn't. Anything you said might have been wrong, but you didn't say anything. As though you knew how much I wanted you. Oh, I'm chattering so nervously because I'm still shaking inside. Next week I must go to Philadelphia, and you and I can spend the night in my room. Would that be nice?"

"Yes," he said. "What were you smiling at that day, you wouldn't tell me."

"Oh. It's embarrassing to tell you, but I can't refuse you anything now, so I guess I'll have to tell you. When Harry and I were first married he told me a lot of things. And he told me about you. That you were known as the Stud Horse. I'm sorry, but I've never been able to look at you without thinking of that. Until today. I don't know why, but in the launch I never thought of it. If I had, I might have been afraid. And I wasn't afraid, was I?"

"No. But I'm nearly thirty years older than I was then. Some women have bigger teats than others, too. Some people have bigger noses, or ears. Adelaide never heard about me and never saw another man—well, she did, come to think of it—but she never seemed to think I was out of the ordinary. Did you ever stop to think of how many tiny little women are married to big men? And how many big women marry little men? I think the whole thing is exaggerated. It's a man and a woman getting together that counts."

"Well, now you know why I smiled," she said. "Why are *you* smiling?"

"I was thinking how quickly a million years can pass," he said.

Adelaide Lockwood had never seen her husband walk across the street with another woman; now, in a fortnight at The Run, he had twice gone off alone with Martha Downs, on the pretext of showing her about the resort; but with Adelaide Lockwood life was extremely simple, and a man who went off alone with a woman, a woman who went off alone with a man, and the two gone together for hours at a time—that man and that woman wanted to be together to the exclusion of all others, and if they desired no other company, they desired each other. Desiring each other, given the opportunity, they would have each other. Thus her reasoning.

"What is there between you and Mrs. Downs?" she said, in their third week at The Run.

"You know what there is between me and Mrs. Downs. Nothing. She's Harry's widow, and I've been showing her around."

"I don't believe you."

"Suit yourself."

"It stops, right now."

"You can't stop something that never began."

"Yes you can. You can stop something before it begins."

"She only has another week here."

"Then you don't have to show her around any more. She shouldn't have come here. This is no place for her kind."

"You're talking nonsense. George and her son are going to be roommates next year, and her husband was an old friend of mine, and partner."

"Such a friend you didn't need, that stole money from you and never invited you to his home. I don't want you to see this woman any more."

"Who's giving orders around here?"

"I never did, but I will now. I don't want my home broken up. You've been with this woman, it's no use lying to me. I can tell by looking at the both of you. And there's other ways to tell. I'm twenty years married to you, don't forget. Twenty years in the same bed with a man, a person isn't easy to fool."

"If that's all you have to go on, you're making a lot out of nothing. The first year we were married we did it every night."

"Ah, stop your lying. I can always tell that, too, when you're lying to me. I don't know many men, but I know two. You, and my father. These two I know."

Adelaide had not believed his lies and had left no doubt of her disbelief, so that in consequence her accusation stood undenied, the charge became the truth, accepted and in a sense acknowledged by them as the truth; the acceptance and the acknowledgement became a condition, and the condition was the cessation of their relations as man and wife. Although they had slept in the same bed throughout their married life, now after a few nights of the new coldness she put a cot on the porch and lay there. "Why did you do that?" he said.

"I don't want you in bed with me, wet from her."

"You want to let everybody know. The servants, the children."

"Before was when you should have thought of that," said Adelaide.

"Very well, then we'll never sleep in the same bed again."

"I the same as told you that, didn't I?"

"I guess you did."

"What if I have a man?"

"I'll divorce you. Have you got one?"

"No, but I wanted to hear what you'd say."

"Then you heard. Don't have a man, or I'll sue you for divorce."

"You won't always be here, Abraham. Think that over," she smiled in a way that was extremely unpleasant for the absence of unpleasantness in the smile.

"Who would you have?"

"It could be anybody, Abraham. Just as long as he had a cock to give me."

He slapped her.

"A cock to go in me," she repeated, and he slapped her again. "Hit me as much as you want to, but now I got you worried." She held her hands over her face to protect herself, but he did not again strike her.

"I'm not worried, but you'd better be," he said.

"All the same, I'm not. You're going to see how it feels for a change. Every time I talk to any man. Every time you go away. 'Who is she with?' you'll say to yourself. I know who *you're* with, but you'll never know. Friends of yours, or the grocery boy. I could be doing the same things to the grocery boy while you're with Mrs. Downs. If I go visit my father in Richterville, who am I with? You won't know. Maybe I'll be out in the back alley, Abraham. Do you remember me telling you about that? Maybe I'll be like your younger sister."

"You know where she died. In the crazy-house."

"Put me there, I dare you. You don't want any more disgrace. Disgrace you'd be afraid of. You started it, Abraham, but I know you. I know what you want. I know your weakness. The boys. The sons. Disgrace me, divorce me in the courthouse, but I'm not dumb, Abraham. You want everything for the sons, and that's why you'll never do anything else to me. Don't ever hit me again, either. You did that for the last time."

He went upstairs to their bedroom, where he kept his pistol in a locked drawer, but in the time it took to find the key his impulse to murder her subsided. To find the key, he had to think; and before he could think he had to regain some self-control. He sat on the edge of their bed, out of breath from fury and the dash up the stairs. He saw that his hand was shaking, making odd shadows on the floor under the weak light from the bracketed kerosene lamp. One of the sons—Penrose—was snoring in the boys' room, and down under the boat landing the bullfrogs were grunting. A woman laughed in a nearby boathouse and her laugh was answered by a dog at the far end of the dam. For the moment he forgot why he was in the bedroom, then remembered again when he became aware that he was gazing at a tintype of his father, made three-quarter face so that the mutilated ear would not show. Moses Lockwood, who had killed two men. Who had killed more than two men, but was remembered only for those two. Now Abraham Lockwood knew where he had hidden the key, hidden it so that his sons would not play with the pistol. He got the key from its hiding place behind his father's tintype, unlocked the drawer, unloaded the pistol, put the cartridges in a different drawer, locked both drawers and returned the key to its hiding place. A little delay had saved him once from committing murder; a longer delay might save him again. He blew out the lamp and lay in his bed. She had escaped death, she would never again be in danger of it from him, but she would never again delight him or be delighted by him, by touch, by word of mouth, by a smile of welcome understanding, by gladness seen or heard. Let her live that way; that could kill her, for her to deny love or for love to be denied her. She was not one to be sustained by hate. Let her waste, wither, die, and let her stay out of the way of The Concern.

They had put their sons on the train to Boston, and now, for a change, they could walk together publicly, for a few minutes, without causing suspicion. "I didn't realize you had such a handsome son," she said.

"You'd seen him before," he said.

"Barely, and not dressed up. At that age they don't look like anything till they've put on their best. Then you can begin to tell how they'll look when they're grown. He's going to be a ladies' man. Imagine wearing a buttonhole at his age."

"Why not?"

"No reason why not, but Sterling never would have thought to. George looks fully twenty years old. Sterling looks sixteen."

"I don't want him to grow up too fast."

"You can't stop it," she said. "We have all day to ourselves, but we can't go just anywhere. Would you like to meet a cousin of mine?"

"It's pretty hard not to, in Philadelphia."

"This one is very unusual. An odd bird called Alice Sterling. She has a salon. She's getting along in years, but she's still one of the most interesting women I know. She likes me because I'm almost as independent as she is."

"I've heard of her. She's the queen bee of a bunch of artists and bohemians, isn't she? I don't want to meet her."

"Very well, you won't have to, but take me to her house, please. That's my headquarters for the day. You're coming out tonight, aren't you?"

"Of course."

"Well, take me to Alice's now. I have some things to talk about that I don't want to put off."

They took a hansom to Alice Sterling's house near Rittenhouse Square. The sitting-room in this house that seemed so dark from the outside was made bright by the floor-to-ceiling windows, washed to a sparkle, and by dozens of small objects—statuettes, figurines, china, pictures and frames—that picked up the light and relayed it from one shiny thing to another. "A cheerful room," said Abraham Lockwood.

"She needs it. She's an unhappy woman."

"Where is she now?"

"In her room. She stays in bed all morning. The rest of the day she just steadily imbibes her whiskey, sip by sip."

"Why is she unhappy?"

"Too long a story. I'll go up and say hello to her and be right down. You don't want to stay for lunch? We can have it alone. She won't be coming down."

"No, I have a lot of things to attend to."

She was back in five minutes. "My cousin wants to know if you ever knew someone named Robert Millhouser, lives in your part of the world."

"It's a Lyons name. Nesquehela County. No, I don't know the party."

"Just as well. She didn't try to hide her distaste for Mr. Millhouser. Sit down, my dear, and don't kiss me. This is a sinful house, but not our kind. Here women kiss women and men kiss men."

"Do you know, I remember hearing that a long time ago. And this is such a cheerful room. Do you know where I heard it? In Washington, when I was a young army officer. That was one of the first times I heard of Mrs. Sterling. Is she your cousin, or her husband?"

"She's a double cousin, by blood and by marriage to another cousin."

"It won't be long before brothers and sisters marry in this town."

She laughed. "I don't know if they'll ever *marry,* but that explains why some of them never marry anyone else. Please sit down now and let's have our talk."

"Very well."

"We've avoided this, but I can't put it off any longer. Are you going to settle some money on me? Is that what you intend to do, or are you planning to give it to me quarterly? I really have to know."

"I didn't realize you were in difficulty. How much do you want?"

"That isn't answering my question, and I know you must have thought about it."

"I'd rather do it quarterly."

"How much can I count on?"

"Well—fifteen hundred a quarter? That's five hundred a month."

"Five hundred a month? Is that everything?"

"Don't you think that's a lot of money?"

"No. I wouldn't think so if it was over and above the upkeep of my house, the servants. Five hundred a *month*, my dear! I have children to educate, all sorts of expenses to meet. I could do it on a thousand a month."

"I thought you had a buyer for your house."

"I have, but that money doesn't come from you."

"Oddly enough, I consider that it does," he said. "But I won't go into that now."

"Do go into it," she said. "Let's be brutally frank."

"Well, I might have been able to take the house away from you. It was bought with money stolen from me."

"You know better than that. I've owned the house for years. How could you ever prove it was bought with your money?"

"I think it could be done, but since I don't intend to try, the question needn't come up."

"But it has come up." She paused. "I see. You consider the house a sort of a settlement. Well, I don't. Harry gave me the house, but on the other hand, I turned my money over to him to invest. Your claim would surely never take precedence over mine."

"It's a point of law that neither of us know much about. My impression is that if Harry had lived he'd have had to make restitution, and that if I could show that he had transferred title to you after he'd committed a crime, the transfer wouldn't be valid in court. But there's a question of ethics that should concern you."

"Ethics? What about your ethics toward your mistress? Whatever's gone before, my dear, I'm your mistress."

"Yes, but you could end that any time you felt like it."

"I can, and now I do. I warned you, my dear. I asked you if you could afford me. I said to you, in these exact words: 'Locky, are you that rich?' And you said you weren't going to court me with greenbacks. Woo me, I think you said. And you said you couldn't buy what you wanted from me. What did you mean by that? I was never certain."

"I don't know."

"I took it as a great compliment."

"That was how I meant it."

"Then what has changed? Your greenbacks couldn't woo me, but did you expect to have me as your mistress for nothing? What was your idea of a mistress? A woman that you hid away somewhere and went to bed with when you wanted to? There *are* those. Harry had one. But who will ever know how much money he spent on her? A lot more than five hundred a month. If I had your money and you were my fancy man, I'd give you more than five hundred a month. Oh, it's a good thing we had this conversation now."

"Yes, it is. I thought we loved each other."

"Of course we do, Locky my dear. And I thought I would never give myself to another man. But you're so frugal. Just because I'm a lady is no reason why I must live in Manayunk and do my own housework, send my children to the public schools. You don't seem to understand any of this. I didn't even marry Harry for love-in-a-cottage, you know, and I'm much too old and wise for that now. I'd rather give pleasure to some old man, and I know a few. Can't you give me a million dollars?"

"No."

"Oh, I thought you could. I always thought you could. I was so happy that day, that first time. A man who could make me want to give myself to him, and who was going to make me safe and secure. You misled me, Locky—but I forgive you. Fortunately I'm at an age when no one man can ruin my life, at least not because we've shared certain pleasures. I've always had a great curiosity about men, and they've always been attracted to me. Yes, it was a very good thing we had this conversation."

"You must be careful."

"Why?"

"Well, your curiosity. It could get you into trouble."

"My dear, I'm in mourning."

"What's that got to do with it?"

"A widow can see as many men as she pleases, until she starts seeing one too often. That's when the gossip starts . . . Oh, my friend is back from his trip around the world. I had a note from him."

"The doctor?"

"I never said he was a doctor. That was your guesswork. Truthfully, Locky, aren't you a little bit relieved that we can chat like this? We've been as intimate as two people can be, but now that it's over, isn't it a relief? I never did like you, remember. I trusted you, and I did love you, but this is the first time I ever felt that I liked you. There are two dear old people here in Philadelphia that have a wonderful friendship, and I've always heard that years ago they had a passionate love affair. Got over it, rode out the scandal, so to speak, and now they're just the dearest friends. You and I might be that kind of friends some day."

"No, I'll never think of you as a friend."

"Well, all right. I don't think our paths will cross much anyway, once I settle down."

"Settle down to what?"

"Settle down to the arrangement I thought I had with you. Well, I hear my cousin moving around and I think it would be polite if I went up and chatted with her. Goodbye, Locky dear. I'm sorry you won't stay to lunch."

He was eased out with such finesse that on the sidewalk he did not know which way to turn, and when he got his bearings and headed east he had a bewildering sense of having been the loser in a financial transaction, although his intelligence told him that the reverse was true. He had lunch alone in an oyster-house and later paid a call on Morris Homestead, with whom he was opening an account.

"I saw you at the station," said Morris Homestead. "You and Martha Downs and your boys. I had to leave my boy and hurry down here. No chance to stop for a chat. How is Martha? We haven't seen her."

"She seemed well. Bright in spirits."

"You can always count on that with Martha. And brighter than ever, now that a certain eminent physician has returned to town. No one has any illusions left about old Harry, but Martha has a few things to answer for too. Did she behave herself this summer? She was a neighbor of yours, wasn't she?"

"It's a very quiet, unfashionable place. No high life."

"Martha can supply it if it isn't there. I've always said about Martha that where there's so much smoke, there must be some fire, and I don't think Kingsland Rawson was the first to feel the, uh, glowing embers. I never trusted myself with her."

"Is that so, Morris?"

"Nothing you could put your finger on, but always that sly look, that *double-entendre*. Sometimes the *double-entendre* was put in such a way that I'd have a hard time remembering the innocent meaning. I don't know. One of these days Martha's going to go too far, and she'll find that things you say and do as a young woman aren't always very becoming in an older one. Her family aren't going to pick up after her forever."

"I guess I hardly know her well enough to comment."

"You don't, and you're fortunate. Now you take Alice Sterling. Do you know Alice Sterling? Cousin of Martha's? Cousin of mine, for that matter."

"I've only heard of her. Never been introduced to her."

"Alice is eccentric, we all know that. Drinks like a fish. Has some of the oddest birds for friends, that sponge off her in every way possible. And yet Alice through it all is a perfect lady, and she doesn't antagonize people as Martha does. Alice became a widow very young, and it wouldn't surprise me if she'd had a lover or two in her day. Out of loneliness, don't you know? Oh, nobody knows what goes on there, or what Alice really thinks. But everybody knows what Martha thinks. She says whatever comes into her head, cruel things, sometimes, and indiscreet when they're not cruel. I know I'd never trust Martha with any secret of mine, and poor old Harry had to take up with that woman in New York just to have someone to confide in, to *talk* to."

"There was more to it than that, though, wasn't there, Morris?"

"Well, of course I assume so. You mean the primrose path of dalliance. Yes. That, too. But poor old Harry was driven to it. Companionship that he never got from Martha, but could get from Mrs. What's Her Name in New York."

"Oh, I thought Harry and Martha were very companionable."

"If you got that impression you must have got it from Martha."

"I did."

"Not from Harry."

"Harry never mentioned Martha to me."

"Too much of a gentleman. He never mentioned her to me, either, but of course I could see for myself. Will you take a cigar, Locky?"

"Yes, I'd enjoy a cigar, thank you." He took a cigar out of the proffered humidor, ran it across his upper lip. "Ah, this isn't one of your toofers."

"Toofers?"

"Two for a nickel."

"Oh. Oh, no. Mr. Middleton keeps me supplied. I'll send you a box of them next month, if I may. Mr. Middleton gets a shipment of the leaf once a month, and these are made up to my special order. Hope you don't mind if the box has my name on it. Little personal touch, you know. Form of vanity, of course. Now then, down to business, Locky, eh?"

"Down to business. Nichols Sugar. I want to buy some."

"Nichols Sugar? Nichols Sugar. Oh, yes. Yes, I know of

it. Let me see what we have on it." He reached for a little silver bell, but Abraham Lockwood stayed his hand.

"I can tell you all about it. I've been studying it for quite some time. I meant to go into it last spring, but in the confusion of poor Harry's death I withdrew from trading, and that decision has cost me a nice potential profit in Nichols. Now I'm convinced that—"

"Excuse me, Locky. Didn't the court rule against the Havemeyers last spring?"

"Ah, you do know what's going on in sugar?"

"I was naturally interested in the court decision that dissolved the sugar trust. A very important decision to all of us. How would you have stood to make money then?"

"Nichols Sugar wasn't one of the companies in the trust, therefore not subject to the dissolution."

"Disillusion would be a better word for it. These law courts have taken over the management of all industry and commerce in this country. Where are they going to stop, is the question."

"Well, if I knew for sure I'd soon be a very rich man. As rich as you, Morris."

"I'm not so sure that you're not this very minute," said Morris Homestead. "Between us, just between us, I didn't *gain* anything by poor old Harry's manipulations. I'm sure that you lost some, but so did I, Locky. Never let friendship mix with business. I came to his rescue two years ago when you turned him down."

"When I turned him down? But I never did turn him down. I refused to go into one or two things with him, but I never turned him down for a loan, if that's what you mean. Did he tell you that I refused to come to his rescue?"

"Yes he did, and I took your part. But then I lent him a fair sum. Friendship. He had no right to expect you to do anything for him on that basis, and I told him so. My position was different. I was his closest friend, his oldest friend. You'd only known him as a classmate in college, not as boys together and so on. Now it appears that he lied to me."

"Yes, he lied to you, as he did to me and apparently to a great many others."

"We were victimized. Poor old Harry. A very good business man until he turned to evil ways, and then he didn't know how to be a crook."

"I came to the same conclusion, although in a roundabout way. No, I never refused Harry a loan. I would have, mind you, but he never asked me for one. Knew better, I guess."

"But why did he tell me that particular lie?"

"I think I know, Morris. He wanted to prove to you that old friends are best. He'd tried to get money from a new friend, me, but that new friend hadn't come through."

"Yes, that's it, Locky. A devil, wasn't he? Diabolically clever, to no good purpose. A bullet in the brain."

"Would you object to telling me how much you lent him?"

Morris Homestead hesitated. "If you'll treat this as confidential—seventy-five thousand dollars."

The impression Homestead had been giving was that he had lost a sizable chunk of the Homestead millions. "Seventy-five thousand," said Abraham Lockwood. "Well, that didn't hurt you much, did it?"

"Not judged as a sum of money, no. Not in relation to what I have left. But I've never experienced a total loss before, Locky. When I've been the loser I could always salvage *something.* I hate to lose money, that's why I never lend money unsecured. Never. Except to Harry, I did. And he proved the wisdom of my lifelong rule. Lend money unsecured, say goodbye to it then and there, all of it."

"You give away a lot of money."

"We do our share. But when we give away, let's say fifty thousand dollars, we know what the money's to be used for. We take a good long time before we decide, and the beneficiaries have to prove to us that the money isn't going to be wasted. So in a sense we retain control of the money, even when it's an outright gift. But if a man came to me for fifty thousand dollars, partly secured, I would refuse him. Unsecured, partly secured, or full secured, I seldom lend money, because money you *lend* becomes money that you relinquish control of. The borrower can do what he pleases with your money. And you might find that you'd lent a man money to destroy you. A man could borrow $50,000 from you, then use that money to, say, buy control of a company you were interested in."

"Has that ever happened to you?"

"Oh, no. It never has, but it could. It never will if I can help it. Money is power, Locky. You know that. But it's power that can be turned against you, even your money, if you don't control it. We've given money to charity in the form of securities, many times, but we always retain the voting rights. How easy it would be for some trustee to vote my stock against my best interest, and regrettably how many trustees there are that would do just that."

Abraham Lockwood was full of new admiration and respect for his old friend. It was a pleasant as well as a vaguely chilling surprise to discover that Morris Homestead *thought* about money; pleasant, because it put them on common ground; chilling, because in the thirty years he had known Morris Homestead, Abraham Lockwood might easily have antagonized Morris in some money matter, and they would not now be where they were, about to get together in a business venture. "You're a very shrewd man, Morris," said Abraham Lockwood.

"I have nothing else to do."

"Nothing else to do? Why, you're a sporting man, and an art collector. A philanthropist. All those things. A social leader."

"There are twenty-four hours in a day, Locky. Some of the activities I'm best known for take only a matter of minutes of my time. But uppermost in my mind is always—I've never talked about this. Well, I've said this much, I might as well finish. Our money, the family money, I've never thought of as my own, only my own. It came to me from both sides of my family, you know. When I was thirty-seven years old a very considerable sum was concentrated in my care. My capital was doubled, and it was no mean sum before. Until then you would have been right to say that I didn't care much for business affairs. I had more than ample means, more than enough for a man of my tastes and my few extravagances. But then I came into a second large inheritance, and the money ceased to be what it had been—the wherewithal to live as I liked to live. All that new money, that extra money, was a responsibility, and put together with the other money, the whole thing became responsibility, if you see what I mean. Until then, it was *my* fortune, that had come to me from my father. But when I inherited from my mother, the two fortunes becames one, and *all my* responsibility. Not only did I stop thinking of it as wherewithal, money to pay my bills. But it was suddenly not my money at all. I was only the custodian of it. There were my children to think of. The very least I could do was take care that that money went to them intact. Stewardship, they call it in the Bible." He smiled. "The first thing I did, the first thing that happened to me, soon after I came into the second inheritance—I became stingy. All my life I'd been given, or bought, the best of everything. I'd been raised, as they say, in the lap of luxury. But overnight I became stingy, and that lasted for a couple of years. Although I was twice as rich as I'd ever been, I didn't buy a new suit of clothes, a new pair of boots, a new hat, for two years. I went over household bills with a fine-tooth comb. Why was our meat bill so high last month? When did we drink all that wine? That sort of thing. We'd always paid our bills quarterly, but for two years I paid them annually so that I'd have the benefit of that interest. For almost two years I gave no money to any new charity, only charities that I'd been contributing to and that my mother had contributed to in her lifetime. It wasn't that I didn't want to be thought an easy mark. It was just that I couldn't bear to spend money.

"Then I began to see what the trouble was. I was afraid of that money. Afraid of money? No. Afraid of the responsibility. Afraid I would do something wrong or foolish. And then I realized that I had been doing something very foolish, if not exactly wrong. In my stingy period I had also been so timid that I hadn't been investing my income. One of my managers—I have several who managed various things for me—finally came to me and pleaded with me. Invest that cash, he said. Money that's not promptly reinvested is dead money. Dead. Dead. Dead, he kept repeating. And then he made me realize that instead of accepting my responsibility, I'd been shirking it. He proved to me that my timidity, my caution and stinginess, had cost me several hundred thousand dollars, at least. He knew what I'd been going through. A man named Leon Spruance, a very understanding fellow. 'Morris,' he said. He knows me well enough to call me by my first name. Worked for my father. 'Morris, it's time you did something constructive with this money.' And then he showed me that I not only had failed to make proper use of my income from my own point of view, but that I'd been retiring large sums of money from the general welfare of the country. That was some years after Cooke's failed, but greenbacks were still untrustworthy, and Spruance showed me that I was unpatriotic not to put my cash to work. Unpatriotic, and taking a risk with those greenbacks. Property, that was the thing. Property, not cash. Property, whether it was securities, real estate, mortgages. But property, not cash.

"Ever since then I've known what I want to do, and more or less how to do it. Reinvest, reinvest. No risky speculations, but keep putting the money back to work. I wouldn't go into Nichols Sugar with you, Locky. I can afford *not* to speculate, but I know you're not satisfied with what you have, so you must take some chances. Right?"

"Right."

"When you have as much as you want, the goal you've set for yourself, I might be able to let you in on some less speculative things that come our way now and then. But I think I'm correct in assuming that you haven't quite reached your goal. What is it? Five million?"

"A bull's eye," said Abraham Lockwood. His goal until that moment had been three million, but he was in a mood to flatter Morris Homestead.

"Meanwhile we'll be overjoyed to have you as a client. I always hoped you'd come with us some day," said Morris Homestead. "I'm going to make sure to send you those cigars."

The promise of the cigars was as shocking as a slap in the face. There were so many large and small things Morris Homestead could have offered Abraham Lockwood: a partnership in the Homestead firm, an invitation to join the Philadelphia Club, an invitation to his house for a weekend—all sorts of things. A box of cigars was exactly the present that Abraham Lockwood sent to the Swedish Haven police chief at Christmas. But on the way home the sting went out of the slap; Morris Homestead was Morris Homestead, and the bestowal of his confidences regarding money was, for Morris a high compliment; the box of cigars belonged in another context; and as for the partnership or the club membership or the weekend invitation, they would never be forthcoming, and now Abraham Lockwood knew it. The knowledge had an oddly satisfactory effect; it more firmly fixed his base in Swedish Haven. He was no longer a young man, and quite by accident he had been shown where he belonged for the rest of his life. He had reached the point of unprecedented intimacy with Morris Homestead, and he soon understood that Morris never would have guessed that his friend Locky was waiting to be asked to become a part of the Philadelphia life.

Abraham Lockwood never ceased to wonder at the thinking and even the feeling that he believed to be his own, only to be duplicated by Morris Homestead's thinking and feeling. Morris Homestead's Concern was a protective position over what he already had, while Abraham Lockwood recognized his Concern for an acquisitive enterprise; nevertheless in both cases there was this desire for money for more than its own sake. Abraham Lockwood could see, as at a distance but now at least faintly discernible, the established dynasty, the sons of George and Penrose who would possess the same feelings of responsibility and noblesse oblige that governed the actions of Morris Homestead. Abraham Lockwood could even look back upon himself from the vantage point of the second generation to come, and see himself recognized as the major architect and builder of the dynasty. (At least they would so recognize him if they had any sense.) What was now his Concern would be an accomplished fact two generations hence. Of that he was certain, although ten years earlier he had been less confident that the scheme could be accomplished in such a comparatively short time. The change toward optimism was a result of several developments; the world in general was moving faster than ever before; and as he contrasted himself with his father there was already progress at so rapid a rate that it was very nearly incredible. In sum, the Lockwoods in three or four generations would have achieved the position that the Homesteads had reached in more than two centuries.

Once again Abraham Lockwood saw the inevitability of his remaining in Swedish Haven. Several times he had been tempted by Philadelphia—or, more accurately, had weakened in his determination to remain in Swedish Haven. But some circumstance had always taken him back. A box of cigars, a grasping woman—these had redirected him homeward now. A small gesture of generosity became a kindly banishment; the demands of an exciting but expensive mistress had been a momentary threat to his fortune and thus to the welfare of the Concern, and he had retreated to Swedish Haven before the last syllable of "a million dollars" was out of her mouth.

When the cigars arrived Abraham Lockwood wrote a carefully courteous note of thanks, then, in a rare moment of ironic humor, gave the cigars to Schissler, the night constable. Morris Homestead was something of a constable, in his way.

"We don't see much of you these days," said Morris Homestead.

"No, Morris," said Martha Downs. "And I know you count the hours from one time to the next."

"Well, no, hardly that," said Morris Homestead. "But you do seem to have disappeared."

"I'm still in mourning," she said. "It's only seven months since Harry died. I've got five months to go."

"Of course. You don't consider this a party?"

"I consider it a bloody bore. Don't you? You must, or you wouldn't be driven to small talk with me."

"Well, it isn't intended to entertain us. It's for the young people."

"And it's a bloody bore. It is for you, and it is for me. Awkward, silly little girls. Pimply, ungainly boys. Except for that Lockwood boy. You know him, of course. Abraham

Lockwood's son. The most interesting boy here, and the only new blood."

"Why is he so interesting?" he said. "He's on the verge of handsome, but interesting? Why?"

"Why is anybody interesting? He's different. He's good-looking. He dances well."

"You haven't proved your point."

"I know. I'm just talking as a woman, looking at the new crop. You men do that. Perhaps *you* don't, Morris, but most men look at the young girls. Well, I look at the boys, in exactly the same way, with exactly the same thing in mind."

"And come to the conclusion that if you were thirty years younger you'd set your cap for George Lockwood?"

"My cap. My nightcap."

Very amusing, Martha. Luckily the boy is safe."

"Yes, from me. But not from those daughters and nieces and cousins of ours. He isn't safe from them, yet."

"Why not?"

"Because he's still young enough to be unspoiled. To do a nice thing on an impulse. Instinctively. And without counting on any reward. What he did for my Sterling."

"What did he do for your Sterling?"

"Hasn't his father boasted about it to you? I'd have thought Locky would have told you all about it."

"You don't like Locky?"

"I don't dislike Locky, but I know what he is, and so do you."

"Well—I suppose I do. But I've always liked Locky. What about the son?"

"As soon as he heard about Harry, he asked Sterling to be his roommate at St. Bartholomew's this year. The other boys may have wanted to be nice to Sterling, but George Lockwood was the one who did something."

"I hadn't known that. It's very difficult for boys to be nice to each other. They think it's a sign of weakness."

"Of course they do. But George Lockwood was a little bit better than that. And it wasn't because Sterling was one of his best friends. Sterling as a matter of fact had been stand-offish toward George. But he was so touched that when he told me about it he cried. The one boy that he'd least expected to be nice to him. George Lockwood."

"I had no idea," said Morris Homestead. "I also didn't know that it would matter so much to you."

"No, you didn't. I believe that. You've always known all about me, haven't you, Morris? What do you do when you find that people refuse to be pigeonholed."

"I don't know, Martha. What do you do?"

"That's a fine boy you have, Locky," said Morris Homestead. The men were having cigars and a moment of male privacy at the St. Bartholomew's commencement.

"Thank you, Morris. He *is* a good boy. I have high hopes for him."

"I know you'll want to see him a Zeta Psi, but I hope you don't mind if we try to pledge him."

"Thank you, Morris. But he's not going to be a Zeta Psi or St. Anthony either."

"What have you got against fraternities? I've always thought you were a very loyal Zete."

"I have nothing against them. But George is going to Princeton."

"To Princeton? By his choice, or yours?"

"Mine, originally, but now he wants to go there, too. Penn is inbred, Morris."

"I don't see how you can say that. You went there knowing nobody, and you made Zeta Psi and The Ruffes."

"I made Zeta Psi because they thought I was one of the other Lockwoods. I never denied it. I let them go on thinking it."

Morris Homestead laughed. "No. They let you go on thinking they were thinking it. *We* always knew you weren't one of those other Lockwoods. So Zeta Psi must have known it too."

"Are you sure? All these years?"

"I'm sure about us, and I'm almost sure about Zeta Psi. With us it was the first question that came up. 'Is he one of those Lockwoods?' All we had to do was to inquire, and we found out that—well, we found out too much, I guess."

"About my father?"

"Yes."

"You've known that all these years and never mentioned it to me?"

"Well, I shouldn't be mentioning it now, and I wouldn't if you hadn't first. I have never repeated anything that was said in The Hall."

"Zeta Psi took me in in spite of that. I'm very touched."

"So did The Ruffes."

"Did all the Ruffes know about my father?"

"Some of them did. Those that belonged to St. Anthony certainly did, and I imagine those that belonged to Zeta Psi. Does this change your wanting to send your boy to Princeton?"

"It would have, but it's too late now. The boy wants to go to Princeton and not to Penn."

"You never quite understood some things, Locky. Shall I speak frankly?"

"I wish you would. We have been."

"Then I shall. Some years ago I made a few very tentative inquiries about putting you up for the Philadelphia Club. I wasn't very hopeful, but I thought you might like to be a member there. Well, the answer was no, so I never mentioned it to you."

"Morris, will my boy make it?"

Morris Homestead spoke gently. "No, Locky, he won't. You can spare him that, at least. I'd be very glad to help him elsewhere, but if he ever mentions the Philadelphia Club, discourage him. Memories are too long. When *he* has a son, the son will stand a good chance. The old-timers will be dead and gone, but some of the same men that don't want you will still be around to oppose your son."

"You all knew about my father, all these years."

"Yes. It's so easy, you know, Locky. We know all about each other, so that when someone like you comes along our curiosity is aroused and in a very short time we pool our information. I'm sure the same thing happens in Swedish Haven and Gibbsville."

"Indeed it does. Well, thank you, Morris. I don't think I ever had any illusions about myself, but I could have embarrassed George."

"I'm very fond of the boy, Locky, and I wouldn't want to see him embittered over a thing like that. Too many good qualities."

"How do you know about his good qualities, Morris?"

"Well, I could say that I've seen him take all these prizes here today. And I've noticed that he has good manners. Nice-looking. But best of all I like what he did for Sterling Downs."

"You astonish me, the things you know. Where did you ever hear that?"

"Oh, Philadelphia gossip isn't always mean, Locky."

"But Sterling Downs will get in the Philadelphia Club, won't he? His father was a crook, a liar, and had a mistress in New York. My father—well, I guess I see it."

"Harry was a bad egg, but that's the way he turned out. That isn't the way he was born. If your father had been one of those other Lockwoods, we wouldn't be having this conversation. You do see that, don't you?"

"Yes."

"Furthermore, a lot of us liked Harry, and I was one of them. We don't like what he did, but we still like him. That's one of the nice things about Philadelphia. Some day your grandsons will benefit by that. Make haste slowly, Locky."

"Why did you say that?"

"Because you're right. We are inbred, and George or at least his son may furnish us some new blood."

"That is *not* what I have in mind for him, Morris."

"How interesting. Would you care to tell me more?"

"No."

"But there is a lot more. I feel sure of that."

"Indeed there is, my friend. Indeed there is."

"Well, good for you, Locky. Good for you."

It was as though all of Abraham Lockwood's plans were laid out on the lawn before them, the whole Concern exposed to view, and Morris Homestead was too much of a gentleman to steal a look.

"Adelaide is looking well," said Morris Homestead. "She must be very proud of George, too."

"Yes, she is looking well."

"Can't say the same for Martha, but then Adelaide's life and Martha's don't bear comparison."

"No, I guess not."

Morris Homestead smiled. "I should *hope* not. Martha's getting a little old for that sort of thing."

"What sort of thing?"

"She has an affinity, and everybody knows who it is but nobody will come right out and say it."

"Then how do they know?"

"That's the great mystery, how those things become known. My own theory is the way they sit together, and the way they avoid each other. An irregularity in conduct would cause talk, of course. Martha and her affinity would never go away together—on the same train, that is. But I've watched these two. At a party he'll never sit with her first, always with others first. Then when he does finally sit with her they're much too formal for two people that have known each other all their lives. When they're alone together at a party they seem to have nothing to talk about, but they have to sit together for a little while, because *not to* would be too obvious, too."

"I wouldn't know what to talk about with Martha."

"But you'd find something, and in any event I'd expect you to have to *make* conversation with Martha. Not so with those two, who've known each other for over forty years."

"How are her finances?"

"Why did you ask that? You've touched on the very thing."

"Just curious. Why?"

"Well, Martha's finances took a sudden upturn. That's how I happened to know about her and her affinity. It corroborated my other evidence, my observations. But I also happen to know that Martha has all the money she needs to meet her expenses."

"How much, for instance?"

"Well, I can only guess, but on her present scale of living, she must spend close to a thousand a month."

"Would the gentleman give her, say, a large settlement? Securities? Twelve thousand a year is two hundred thousand at six percent. Would he settle that much on her? Two hundred thousand?"

"He could. I don't know that he has. In our small world it might be wise to, instead of paying her by the quarter or semi-annually. A good-sized settlement, a quarter of a million, would be better than having to pay her bills several times a year. No use *reminding* people to be suspicious."

"What if she took that money and then told her affinity to go to hell?"

"Oh, never! He can do that to her, but she wouldn't dare do it to him. No one would ever speak to her if she did that. She'd have to move away, to New York. Harry was a crook, but we were and still are fond of him. But for Martha to do a thing like that would be unthinkable. Un*think*able. Not very practical, either."

"Oh, I don't know," said Abraham Lockwood.

"The bird in the hand? No, Locky. There may be more than two birds in that bush. What I'm implying is that she may stand to get more than twice two hundred thousand, eventually."

"He couldn't just put it in his will."

"Nothing as broad as that. But if the happy relationship continues, from year to year he can quietly take care of her."

"It's a doctor, you told me."

"Yes, but all his money didn't come from healing sick people. Oh, you'd recognize the name. If you gave a little thought to it you could probably guess."

"Isaac Wickersham."

"What a beautiful spring day. True, it's almost summer."

"And I hit the nail on the head, first try."

"Beautiful spring day."

"Oh, of course. Dr. Wickersham belongs to St. Anthony."

"Finished your cigar, Locky? We'd better be getting back to the women."

"All right, let's get back to the women. So that's who it is? I've been introduced to that old fart at least once a year for the last thirty. I used to think he was a Doctor of Divinity, he looked at me so disapprovingly."

"He's not so very old, Dr. Wickersham. Sixty. And they all live forever, that family. His father's still alive, which disproves the old wives' tale that port wine shortens your life. Comforting thought."

"A good screw never hurt a man, either."

"Why limit it to men? Well, here comes a man that could have had better luck. Arthur Francis Ferris. Wonder if he ever buggered any of our boys."

"You come out with the damnedest things."

"I know. It's being away, I guess. That, and feeling more at ease with you."

"You at ease with me? I was always the one that was ill at ease with you."

"I know. Isn't it a pity? Hello, there, Arthur. Very good show you put on today."

"Thank you, Morris. Good afternoon, Mr. Lockwood."

"Good afternoon, Father Ferris. Guess this place will seem very quiet and empty tomorrow."

"Ah, yes. But September will soon be around, and we have Penrose with us then. I hope he does as well as George. Quite a mark to shoot at."

"Don't expect too much of Penrose."

"I gather Penrose is more like my offspring," said Morris Homestead.

"Your boy wouldn't have given us any trouble if he'd been a little less like his father and a little more like his mother."

"That's the kind of thing you think fathers like to hear, Arthur. The fact of the matter is that I was always a very conscientious student, all through school and college, and you can go to hell."

"Have a little respect for my cloth, Morris. And besides, Mr. Lockwood may not understand."

"I delight in taking you down a few pegs, old boy. You're so confounded deistic, if that's the word I mean."

"It isn't. Proving what a conscientious student you were."

"Well, you're a dear old thing, and I wouldn't have your job for ten million dollars."

"Let's not speak of money, Morris. I'm saving that topic for luncheon, which is almost ready, by the way. I see you gentlemen have already had your cigars."

"Yes, we know only too well what we're going to get for

lunch. Chicken in library paste as usual, I suppose. Vary the menu next year, Arthur, and you may find us more generous."

"Be more generous, and I'll vary the menu," said Arthur Francis Ferris. "And now, Morris, run along, will you please? I'd like to have a word with Mr. Lockwood."

"Well, what's *he* done that the Rector has to take him aside?" Morris Homestead, genuinely mystified, left them.

"I thought I ought to speak to you beforehand, Mr. Lockwood. The fact is—your wife and Mrs. Downs have had words. My sister, Mrs. Haddon, is acting as hostess today, and she was there for part of it. Took place upstairs in the Rectory. Constance wouldn't tell me what was said, but apparently it was rather unpleasant. A rather unpleasant exchange, in fact. I'm telling you this now because I wanted you to understand why we've changed your places at table. George and Sterling Downs and their two families were scheduled to sit next door to each other, but we've separated you. I'm very sorry this had to happen today of all days, but I gather from what my sister told me that whatever the cause, it's been coming to a head for some time. So I thought it best to forewarn you. The boys are going to expect to be seated near each other, but you'll know why we've changed that."

"Very unfortunate," said Abraham Lockwood . . .

I went upstairs to use the toilet and she was just coming out. I didn't bother to say anything to her because I said good morning to her a couple of hours before, and I don't get any pleasure out of wasting words on her. The slut. But she took umbrage because I didn't speak to her, and she made a remark, an unladylike remark. Maybe I wasn't supposed to hear it, but I did. If you want to know what the remark was, all right, I'll tell you. She said she was glad she could use the toilet before me instead of after me. I let it pass. I didn't let on I heard it. I just went in, and when I came out she was still there in the room, waiting. I started to walk past her, but she stood in my way. "Please let me pass," I said to her. "Not before I give you a piece of my mind," she said. Maybe those weren't her exact words, but something like that. "Not before I give you a piece of my mind. Not before I say what I have to say." It was something to that effect. I wasn't listening to her very carefully. I just wanted to get out of the same room with her. I wanted to get a hundred miles away from her. And from everybody else here, for that matter. This is no place for me. I'm a Pennsylvania Dutchwoman from Richterville, Pennsylvania, where people like me and respect me, and treat me with politeness. Where I was born my folks are respected. Just let any of these New England Yankees or Philadelphia Quakers come and see us in Richterville, what people think of us. They'd soon find out that there's one part of the world where Adelaide Hoffner counts. That's how I was raised. I wasn't raised to think myself anyone's inferior, and no matter what's happened to me since I was a young girl, I never learned to think myself as anyone's inferior.

You go to Philadelphia, or come here to St. Bartholomew's, and anyone can tell that you feel their inferior. You pretend as if they were your chums, and some of them pretend it too, but you're not chums with them. They have their own chums, and you're not one of them. I had all these years to think about you, and I could have told you something about yourself a long, long time ago, but I thought you'd get over it. But you never have. The first time I ever knew you, at my sister's wedding, you were so handsome and such a conceited person. But I should have asked myself, "Who were you?" Abraham Lockwood from Swedish Haven was all you were, no better than the younger fellows at Barbara Shellenberger's. Just older . . .

Anyway, she stood in my road, this Martha Downs. "What do you mean, walking in here and ignoring me?" she said. "I spoke to you once, that's enough," I said. "I don't wish to speak to you any more, so please get out of my road," I said. "You talk like a bumpkin and you are," she said. "I'd rather be a respectable bumpkin than what you are," I said. "How do you know what I am—unless your husband told you?" she said. "Nobody had to tell me what you are," I said. "My husband didn't tell me anything. He didn't have to," I said. "Any wife knows when her husband's been with one of your kind." Oh, we said more than that, back and forth, till finally she said, "I think I'll take him away from you again." "Again?" I said. "I never took him back. What's been in you I don't want in me." Then this Mrs. Haddon came in and said, "Ladies, ladies," and I said, "Singular number. Don't put me in the plural with her," and then I came down here.

I want to leave this place right away. You can stay for the lunch, if that's what you want to do. But I'm going to hire a carriage and take the next train to Boston. Suit yourself, what you want to do. But George is coming with me. I asked him if he would, and he wants to. Stay if you want to, but you'll only be making a spectacle of yourself if you do. And I know this much about people, Abraham Lockwood. Your friends won't think any the more of you if you let your wife and son leave and you stay. For my part, I don't care if you stay for good. I only know you're a fool.

THE reader will do well to remind himself that the Lockwood Concern existed throughout the better part of a hundred years without ever being given a name. It was for that reason that George Bingham Lockwood always had difficulty in establishing the point at which his awareness of the Concern began. At first vaguely and then clearly he saw that his father had plans for him, that there was some sort of governing theme to his father's direction of his life; but where other boys were being influenced and urged and ordered to study this for the law, that for medicine, to train certain muscles for use in certain games, to cultivate alliiances with some contemporaries but not others, George Bingham Lockwood could find in his father's counsel only the recurring wish that George—and the younger brother Penrose—would always remember that home was Swedish Haven, Swedish Haven was home. Repetition of this wish, expressed in various forms, eventually resulted in George's recognition of Swedish Haven residence as his father's rather modest hope for his family's future, and this was not difficult to understand, since at St. Bartholomew's nearly every boy accepted—or was already rebelling against—the eventual return to some *place;* a city, a town, an estate, a plantation, from which he had come, and which was more than the middle-class idea of home. The place, whether it was a populous one or an isolated establishment in the country, had implications of family continuity and prestige, and even those boys who were already rebelling against returning showed by their rebelliousness an awareness of the formidable opposition they must encounter. This was as true of the city boys—New York, Boston, Philadelphia, Baltimore—as of those who were listed in the school roster as coming from Prides Crossing, Massachusetts; Towson, Maryland; Purchase, New York. The city boys invariably referred to some rural postoffice or estate name in a tone that was more meaningful than the manner in which they spoke of their town residences. It was never strange to them that George Lockwood should come from a place called Swedish Haven; the names of their own places were just as strange. (The boys from Chicago and Buffalo had a worse time of it in that respect; the Chicago boy was nicknamed Chicago, and the Buffalo boy, Buffalo—both nouns being considered sufficiently disparaging for prep school nicknames.)

His father's one wish seemed moderate enough and happened to conform with George's own intentions as of his final years at St. Bartholomew's and the beginning of his career at Princeton. He was still young enough to want very much to be home at Christmas; to visit his grandfather in Richterville, to collect the presents from his Richterville relatives, to go to the young people's dance in Gibbsville (his social stock in Gibbsville had jumped immediately upon his admittance to St. Bartholomew's, to which no Gibbsville parent had ever applied in behalf of a son), to eat the rich, heavy Pennsylvania Dutch sweetmeats, to go on sleighing parties for chicken-and-waffle suppers. The Philadelphia parties were fun, but less fun than the festivities closer to home. The Philadelphia parties were fun because George Lockwood knew that girls liked him; the Lantenengo County parties were fun because girls liked him and he did not have to be so careful about being too attentive to them; in Gibbsville everyone, without exception, knew who he was. The knowledge did not make for universal cordiality; some of the boys and some of their fathers were hostile or indifferent; but they knew who he was, and though he was young, he was old enough to like being recognized.

Life in Swedish Haven was pleasant quite apart from the festive occasions. At St. Bartholomew's the boys and their parents were discouraged by Arthur Francis Ferris from all ostentation. George Lockwood and everyone else could name the boys whose families actually owned ocean-going yachts and racing stables, but there were other boys whose families could afford yachts and great stables and chose not to. Consequently, in among the inconspicuous nonspenders who possessed great wealth were mixed the sons of those who could not be called wealthy. There was so much wealth at St. Bartholomew's that it was not fashionable, and any display of it was considered gauche. It was hardly a democratic school in its attitude toward candidates for admittance; social prestige, which was usually accompanied by more than adequate means, was the first requirement for entrance, and a George Lockwood never could have got in the school without the support of Morris Homestead and Harry Penn Downs, who vouched for Abraham Lockwood as an acceptable if not quite accepted man. No Jew, even of the Sephardic aristocracy, and no Roman Catholic, even of Maryland or Louisiana line, was admitted to the school during the Nineteenth Century. No native of the vast area between Charleston and New Orleans was able to satisfy Arthur Francis Ferris's social standards, nor would he let in any son of a brewer (distillers' sons were acceptable if they belonged to the landed gentry), a meat packer, a Baptist, a dentist, an Italian, a South American, or a grand opera singer male or female. A clergyman who wore gaiters had a better chance of getting his son into St. Bartholomew's than a minister of the gospel who wore a business suit, and a surgeon's son had a better chance than the boy whose father was a pill-doctor. The president of a country bank got his son on the St. Bartholomew's list a full generation ahead of the cashier of a large city bank. (None of this deterred Jews, Catholics, Alabamans, brewers, meat packers, Baptists, dentists, Italians, South Americans, tenors, Presbyterians, general practitioners or bank cashiers from trying to have exceptions made.) Nevertheless, Arthur Francis Ferris, having assembled a student body of the elite, thereupon made a conscientious effort to treat them all alike. He was a despot, but one who insisted on democratic practice among the boys. They dressed alike in a non-military uniform that was similar to the Etonians'; they made their own beds and washed out of tin basins; they formed ranks to march from classroom to classroom. Ferris's strictness in regard to the possession of cash made money illegal tender, and the richest boy in school at any given moment was the one who had earned the most privileges, which consisted of intangibles such as a boy's being allowed to study in his room instead of going to study-hall; leaving his light on after nine-thirty. Sometimes that boy had been George Lockwood, although he had never been elected Head Boy of his class or of the school, and the democratizing process had left him eagerly receptive toward the admiration, friendliness, obsequiousness, and adulation that awaited him in Swedish Haven, Richterville, and Gibbsville. The growing conviction that he was brighter, cleverer than his schoolmates, and the sense of his attractiveness to girls and older women, had together created an egotism that needed that which St. Bartholomew's had denied and which on his home ground was freely given. In such a state of mind he entered the freshman class at Princeton, already committed to one condition of the Lockwood Concern. He would never live anywhere but Swedish Haven.

At Princeton the slightly spurious democracy of St. Bartholomew's vanished immediately. Only one other boy—"Chicago"—had come down from St. Bartholomew's to Princeton; all their classmates had gone to Harvard, Yale, and—the Philadelphians—to Penn. But there were eight St. Bartholomew's boys in the sophomore, junior, and senior classes, and they had taken their proper place in the Princeton social hierarchy, thus easing the way for G. B. Lockwood and Anson "Chicago" Chatsworth. The formidable front presented by boys from Lawrenceville and The Hill made for a defensive unity among St. Bartholomew's boys that was not necessarily the case at Harvard or Yale. Old boys from St. Bartholomew's who had not been especially fond of Lockwood or Chatsworth in prep school now called on them and made a point of being seen publicly with them. These old boys had already made friends among the few graduates of Groton and St. Paul's at Princeton, and Lockwood and Chatsworth were tentatively absorbed into this smallish group. This cabal bypassed the boys from the New Jersey and Pennsylvania high schools and the lesser prep schools, and since their existence as an informal homogeneous unit always contained the threat of formal organization, they were always able to get themselves elected to one or two of the more fashionable eating-clubs. A club composed of their own number would automatically have become as prestigious as any in the university, with an inevitable loss of some prestige for the clubs already in being.

In his first week at Princeton George Bingham Lockwood discarded the notions of democracy that had been superimposed at St. Bartholomew's. It was ridiculously easy summarily to dismiss one-third of the freshman class on account of their clothes; but by the same token it was easy to be deceived by elegance: there were freshmen who dressed well whose good taste in clothes would never be enough to overcome handicaps that were not so readily apparent. In his first few days George Lockwood became friendly with a well-dressed classmate about whom he knew nothing except that he came from New York, obviously had money, and in spite of his blue eyes was of French extraction. The classmate's name was Edmund Auberne. It came as a jolting surprise to learn that the man's name was O'Byrne, that he was an Irish Catholic and a graduate of Fordham Prep. George Lockwood never had heard or seen the name O'Byrne, never had heard of Fordham Prep, and felt slightly tricked that he had not immediately recognized an Irish Catholic. As he saw more of O'Byrne and heard his quite deadly comments on undergraduates and faculty George Lockwood recovered his confidence in his judgments; if he could have heard the Irish name at the start of their friendship he would have known that such sardonic humor did not belong in the makeup of the kind of man O'Byrne had seemed to be. O'Byrne was sophisticated, witty, disrespectful, and apparently friendless. A second jolting surprise came with the early discovery that O'Byrne had an older brother who was a guard on the football team. (Football was not then played at St. Bartholomew's, and George Lockwood had never seen an intercollegiate game.) O'Byrne therefore was not quite so lonesome as George Lockwood had guessed him to be. O'Byrne, in fact, constantly upset George Lockwood's notions of him; he was an entirely new experience for George Lockwood, whose personal knowledge of the American Irish was limited to the laboring men who lived in Irishtown, on the mud flats of Swedish Haven, and to a few others who worked around horses as coachmen and hostlers. O'Byrne's father was a Dublin-educated doctor, presumably a successful one. Edmund, or Ned, had been abroad twice, and he spoke of Bourke Cockran, Chauncey Olcott and Agnes Repplier as visitors to the O'Byrne house in New York in an impressed way that prevented George Lockwood from confessing that he had never heard of *them*. Ned O'Byrne's whole attitude toward Princeton and the social system irritated George Lockwood, who did not believe his friend was in any position to be critical of a system that would automatically reject him. But when O'Byrne mentioned one day that his father was on a special train, touring the West with one of the Vanderbilts, George Lockwood once again was confused by this fellow who would not stay in a pigeonhole. O'Byrne was also a good card-player, who quite frankly expected to supplement his allowance while at Princeton with his winnings from the undergraduate body. (In the first semester of freshman year O'Byrne won more than five hundred dollars from Anson Chatsworth alone. "We must do everything we can to help him pass his examinations," O'Byrne told George Lockwood. "You help him with his math and I'll help him with his Latin. That chap is going to make up for my old man's stinginess, these next three years.")

George Lockwood was prepared to terminate his friendship with O'Byrne whenever it was expedient to do so, but he found that as he began to know the class as individuals and not merely as a group of young men with only the common tie of a hope to graduate in 1895, he would seek out the company of O'Byrne and two others. Those three were his choice, and finally O'Byrne was his choice of the three for two apparently contradictory reasons: he could relax with O'Byrne, and O'Byrne stimulated him. The other two of the three were Ezra Davenport and Jack Harbord.

Davenport was having a second try at freshman year, having flunked out on his first try, with the distinction of having failed his examinations in every subject. His indignant parents, unable to expend their wrath on Princeton University, put Davenport in a cramming school from February to August, and he was readmitted to college as a freshman. At nineteen he already had the look of a voluptuary, and he would grow into the look as time went on. He was a cigarette-fiend and affected the habit of speaking with a cigarette stuck on his lower lip, which bounced up and down as he spoke. He was constantly pushing back his forelocks, which constantly fell over his forehead. He cocked his head at an angle, to keep the cigarette smoke out of his eyes, and this habit made him appear to be attentive to conversations in a worldly-wise way. It took George Lockwood the better part of four years to realize that Ezra Davenport had attached himself to him, that Ezra had a weak stomach for alcoholic beverages and that his conquests of the female sex were largely, although not entirely, imaginary. Merely by flunking out of college in his first freshman year Ezra Davenport had established himself among the hellers of the campus and his prematurely dissolute appearance gave credibility to the role he had assumed. He was actually a meek little fellow, an only son of two good-sized fortunes, who was unequal to the demands put upon him by his father and mother. In other circumstances he might have become a hotel clerk or an ineffectual member of the clergy, but he too was a victim of a Concern.

Jack Harbord was as correct as Ezra Davenport was wrong. It was hard to believe that anyone could become so upright in the first nineteen years of his life, a little harder to believe than that Davenport had become so worldly in the same time. Harbord was a rich boy, well dressed, gentlemanly manners and all, but in his case the accouterments of wealth and upbringing were reassuring; Jack Harbord would never use his money or his personality for sinister purpose. He was a tall blond with a magnificent physique, and he was elected class president without opposition, almost entirely on a fixed smile and a seemingly inexhaustible willingness to be helpful and good. "A very good man, Harbord," said O'Byrne. "All good. No evil at all, not a bit. Doesn't need an ass-hole like you and me. I understand he was born with his second teeth all in place. A good, good man, our Jack."

"But that's what he is. Why are you sarcastic about him? You prefer him to Davenport, don't you?"

"He's not as trustworthy."

"As Davenport? You're crazy in the head."

"How can you trust a man that's so good? I can trust Davenport because you know what a bounder's going to do. A pious son of a bitch like Harbord, watch out for his kind. He'd hang me, given the chance, but you wouldn't understand that."

"Then explain it."

"Wait, and I won't have to explain it. He won't put a rope around my neck, but I'm not counting on his vote. I voted for him, by the way."

"Why?"

"Because I wanted to make it unanimous. Harbord knows how many are in the class, and one vote against him would have caused him loss of sleep. He'll be a strong class president, very good with the faculty. But he wouldn't have been quite as good if everybody didn't love him. At heart a despicable, cruel coward. The infant Jesus protect me from the like of him."

In due course Harbord cautioned George Lockwood against O'Byrne. "Just don't be seen with him too often, George. The clubs get the impression that you're not going to be a good club member if you have a close friend that's not going to make a club."

"Isn't O'Byrne going to make a club?"

"His brother's club, probably. But not any that you or I want to be in. Your father was a Zeta Psi. Well, that's what Ivy used to be. A word to the wise, George. After you're in, see as much of him as you feel like, but take my advice."

George Lockwood said nothing to O'Byrne, not so much

from a desire to spare O'Byrne's feelings as from a reluctance to concede that O'Byrne had been right about Harbord. O'Byrne's sardonic accuracy was not an endearing quality, and the friendship very nearly was terminated a few weeks after Harbord's conversation.

George Lockwood managed to see O'Byrne frequently, but he contrived to have their meetings less public. "Which is it going to be, George? Have you decided?"

"Decided what?"

"Just about the only thing we decide for ourselves here. Is it going to be Ivy, or one of the others?"

"That's something it's not good policy to talk about."

"I know, I keep hearing that. Everybody I've talked to says the same thing."

"If you go around talking about it, you're going to be left out in the cold."

"Oh, it's no problem for me. Either I ride in on my brother Kevin's broad shoulders or I don't ride in at all. Kevin's a wild man, you know. If I don't get invited to join his club he'll resign, not that he has a strong feeling of brotherly affection, mind you. No. But we have a younger brother that Kevin wants to go to Princeton, but Jerry thinks he'd like to go to Yale, and if Kevin's club spurns me, Jerry won't come here. So you might say I'm in the middle, with nothing to worry about. It's all up to Kevin. You have a different kind of a problem."

"Have I?"

"Oh, yes, but if you don't want to talk about it . . . I thought it would do you good to get it off your chest."

"I have a younger brother, too. At St. Bartholomew's."

"How old?"

"Four years younger."

"But four years at St. Bartholomew's, he may want to go to Yale or Harvard. Or Penn."

"No, he's coming here."

"Ivy or no Ivy?"

"No matter what."

"Hmm. You won't even mention the name. That's good form, George. You must have been taking lessons from Jack Harbord."

"Oh, go to hell."

"Very good form. It'll be Ivy for you, George. I think you can safely count on it. There's a poker game tonight. Chatsworth's room. Will you be playing?"

"No."

"Be glad to take your I.O.U."

"I'd be glad to take yours, but I have to study. Don't you ever study?"

"In the mornings, sometimes. I was a day scholar, so I'm used to getting up early. I'll never *like* it, but I'm used to it . . . Oh, I have a bit of friendly advice for you, chum."

"What?"

"Don't get too chummy with Davenport, at least till after the club elections. He doesn't pay his gambling debts. At least he doesn't pay me, and I've been given to understand that he still owes some from last year. That's going to come up during the club elections, and you don't want them thinking he's your bosom companion. As far as that goes, I'm no help to you either, George, but they'll never be able to say I renege on gambling debts."

To the eternal confusion of the undergraduate body, at club elections Ezra Davenport and Jack Harbord were taken into Ivy, George Lockwood and Ned O'Byrne into Orchard, and inoffensive Anson Chatsworth got nothing. George Lockwood did not receive an Ivy bid; Ned O'Byrne did not receive a bid from his brother's club. Lockwood and O'Byrne each had three other bids besides Orchard's. Davenport's only bid was from Ivy; Harbord had a bid from every club in the university. "I haven't seen Kevin," said O'Byrne. "But I hope he's holding his temper."

In George Lockwood's junior year the contingent of Eastern Pennsylvanians at Princeton were joined by a freshman named David Fenstermacher, from the town and county of Lebanon, and from Mercersburg Academy. George Lockwood did not notice Fenstermacher until they took the same northbound train from Philadelphia during the Christmas holidays. Fenstermacher was very young (but all freshmen looked young) and George Lockwood would not have noticed him even then had it not been for the Princeton-pennant sticker on Fenstermacher's valise, a bit of ostentation that had never appeared on George Lockwood's luggage.

The freshman and the junior were standing near each other, waiting for the train platform gate to be opened. Ordinarily George Lockwood would have ignored the younger man, but in the spirit of Christmas he opened the conversation: "I see you go to Princeton."

David Fenstermacher smiled. "Yes I do, Mr. Lockwood. I'm from Lebanon."

"I see. Then you change trains at Reading."

"Yes sir."

"Take the Fort Penn train there, I guess."

"Yes sir. I get off at the Outer Station and take the Fort Penn train and I'm home inside of an hour. I'll be glad to get home."

"Why? Don't you like Princeton?"

"Oh, I like it all right but I like home better. I haven't had a square meal since September."

"Well, we all have to go through that freshman year. You are a freshman, aren't you?"

"Yes sir."

"Where did you go before Princeton?"

"Mercersburg for two years, before that, Lebanon High."

"Oh, then you have a lot of friends at college. Mercersburg sends a lot of boys to Princeton."

"Yes. You're from Swedish Haven, aren't you?"

"Yes. How did you know?"

"You were pointed out to me by a friend of mine, a boy from Gibbsville. Alden Stokes. He was in my class at Mercersburg and I'm going to visit him during the holidays."

"You going to the Assembly?"

"We're going to some dance but I don't think it's called the Assembly."

"Oh, yes. The Young Peoples'. Alden Stokes is a cousin of a cousin of mine."

"I know."

"How did you know that?"

"He told me."

"Good Lord, you must have discussed me pretty thoroughly."

"Well, I guess we did."

"Good grief!"

"It was mostly very flattering. I guess you won't be in Swedish Haven much."

"Why do you guess that?"

"Oh, you're supposed to spend most of your vacation in Philly and New York. That's what I heard."

"You heard wrong. I may go to one or two parties in Philadelphia, but I don't enjoy them any more. I think a man ought to be home at Christmas. It's all right to visit friends. You going to Gibbsville. But I guess Gibbsville isn't very different from Lebanon. I've never been to Lebanon."

"Gibbsville is livelier. They have more parties than Lebanon. Our young people mostly go to Reading or Fort Penn for the big balls there."

"I'm supposed to go to a ball in Fort Penn on the 28th or 29th."

"Oh, yes. My uncle's on the committee. Did you ever hear of him? Roy Reichelderfer? He went to Yale."

"No."

"He's my uncle. A big fellow. Everybody likes him. The Reichelderfers are all big. My cousin Paul is over two hundred pounds and he's only fourteen."

"But you're not more than a hundred and fifty."

"I'm not a Reichelderfer. I'm a Fenstermacher."

"Oh."

"I guess I didn't tell you my name. David Fenstermacher."

"Oh. We have a lot of Fenstermachers in Lantenengo County. In fact, there are some in Swedish Haven. But I don't know any Reichelderfers, at least I don't think I do . . . Well, at last. Are you sitting in the Pullman?"

"No, only when I travel with my parents."

"Well, if I don't see you during vacation—back at Princeton."

"Goodbye, Mr. Lockwood. It was a pleasure to meet you."

This encounter became significant on New Year's Eve, at the Gibbsville Assembly. George Lockwood's "drag"—the girl he had invited to the dance—came down with an attack of boils on Christmas Eve, and he attended the function as a stag. He thus was free to keep his card as full or as empty as he wished, to have a cigar when he felt like it, and to visit the punchbowl. He was having a glass of punch when he was accosted by Red Phillips, a Gibbsville acquaintance. "I've been looking all over for you," said Phillips.

"Not in the right places."

"Listen, George, there's a girl here from Lebanon says she would like to meet you. You know her brother or somebody in the family. Are you free for the second waltz after intermission?"

"Let me look. Yes. What name?"

"Eulalie Fenstermacher."

"Oh. Her brother's a freshman. Is she pretty?"

"She's very pretty and a good talker."

At the second waltz after intermission George Lockwood presented himself, was introduced to Miss Eulalie Fenstermacher, and swept her out onto the dance floor. "You were very nice to my brother. Thank you."

"The pea-green freshman? Oh, he was a nice kid."

"You sound like Methuselah. You're going to wish you hadn't some day."

"Not I. It's girls that want to pretend they're younger, not men. Have you started to lie about your age, Miss Fenstermacher?"

"No, and I never intend to. I just won't tell anybody."

"You won't have to. You're either nineteen or twenty now, so I'll always know within one year how old you are."

"You're so clever, Mr. Lockwood."

"What's clever about that? It isn't hard to guess a girl's age. I can guess any woman's age, under thirty. Then it becomes more difficult, but under thirty it's pretty easy. Where do you go to school?"

"I graduated last June. From Oak Hill."

"Oh, that's not very far from Princeton. To think that you went to school near me—and Lebanon isn't so very far away either. Do you think it's a small world, Miss Fenstermacher?"

"That depends."

"On what?"

"On whose world you're talking about. Your world is small. You lived in the same college with my brother for three months, but you never saw him till last week. That's because your world is tiny. Therefore you make the world itself seem infinitely larger."

"I follow you so far, but I didn't know I was going to get into higher mathematics. Don't tell me you're a bluestocking, Miss Fenstermacher."

"Oh, I wouldn't try to tell a *Princeton* man *anything*."

"Why not? Just because it's so hard to educate your Lehigh friends? Don't give up so easily."

"At least Lehigh men are willing to learn."

"They'd better be. They have a lot to catch up on."

"I thought Red Phillips was a friend of yours."

"Well, he introduced me to you, I'll say *that* for the poor, unsophisticated piece of humanity. Did you go to the ball in Fort Penn the other night?"

"Yes, why?"

"Because now I wish I'd gone."

"My uncle was on the committee."

"Are you fending off a compliment? I said I wish I'd gone."

"I heard you. I didn't know whether you intended it as a compliment or because you wish you'd been there to tease me."

"Was Red at the ball?"

"Red Phillips? Heavens, Mr. Lockwood, I have other escorts besides Red Phillips."

"How many others?"

"How *many* others?"

"How—many—others? I want to know how many I have to contend with."

"I didn't know you planned to contend."

"Of course you didn't, but you know it now. You can put them out of their agony right away, and also make it much easier for me."

"Such self-confidence, I declare."

"Wouldn't it be more merciful to put them out of their agony now? When I arrive at your house I sincerely hope you will have got rid of the mandolin players, at least."

"How did you—"

"Oh, that's obvious. I'm sure the whole F. & M. glee club serenades you all summer."

"Did my brother tell you that?"

"Good Lord, no. That would be obvious too. Franklin and Marshall. Lebanon Valley. Muhlenberg. Lee-high. Lehigh, Lehigh, Gott verdammt sei."

"Mr. Lockwood! I think you've been sampling the punch."

"That's a good idea. Let's go over and have a glass of punch and we can stand behind the palms and then you stand your next partner up."

"You're a little Dutchy, aren't you?"

"My mother's name was Hoffner. Why not?"

"Oh, I know Hoffners. In Richterville."

"They're the ones. What do you say to my suggestion?"

"I say no. If you wish to dance with me again, you have to ask Red. I think my card is filled."

"Well, I gave you the opportunity of a lifetime. You can't say I didn't."

"I didn't say you couldn't come and see me in Lebanon."

"No, you didn't, did you? Well, when?"

"Spring vacation. My brother'd be only too glad to invite you, and we have plenty of room."

In August of that summer, his last college vacation, they reached an understanding. An understanding was an unofficial, unannounced engagement to be married, and had its own rules and conventions. Eulalie Fenstermacher told her mother that George Lockwood wanted to be engaged to her. "Have an understanding," said Mrs. Fenstermacher. "You can have an understanding till George graduates. That's always better." An understanding did not involve the young man's obtaining the consent of the girl's father, and the father remained out of the picture until the propitious moment. The custom of having an understanding, which in the lower classes was known as "going steady," offered most of the advantages without entailing the risk of a publicly announced and publicly broken engagement. Thus it could be said of a young couple, "They had an understanding, but they changed their minds," and neither party would be marked as jilted. During an understanding a young couple could be together a great deal, but their friends did not entertain specifically in their honor. Mainly what was implicit in an understanding was that the young man and the young woman were already forsaking all others, and only waiting for circumstances, such as time, to make the formal announcement feasible or desirable.

There was something more honorable in an understanding than in an engagement. Mutual trust and confidence was deeply involved. An engagement had the status of a quasi-legal agreement, and a young man was bound by public opinion to conform to the social laws governing engagements. Strictly speaking he was not so bound in an understanding, except by honor and decency and love, and he was technically freer than in an engagement. In many cases the formal engagement came as a relief to both parties, since the restrictions of an engagement were traditionally defined, and both parties knew what they could and could not do. During an understanding, for example, a young lady could be escorted home from a picnic by a young gentleman who was not her fiancé-to-be, provided that the fiancé-to-be was not at the picnic. But after the announcement of her engagement she would not *attend* a picnic without her young man. At a ball an engaged young lady deferred to her fiancé's wishes as to her dancing partners, and engagements had been broken for violations of such rules.

A total virginity enveloped Eulalie Fenstermacher during the months of her understanding with George Lockwood, and this was acceptable to George Lockwood. Their early kisses, which had led to the understanding, were now timed to the precise point where amorousness was about to proceed into eroticism. The young man and the young woman were now so enormously conscious of the implications of marriage that if Eulalie parted her lips, if George put his hand anywhere on the front or the lower part of her body, he or she would withdraw from the embrace. Nor could they permit themselves to have conversation that mentioned her bosom or her legs. George Lockwood was not a virgin. During his first year at Princeton his father had recommended an establishment in Philadelphia that was the present-day version of the Phoebe Adamson place. "It's where you'll be safe," Abraham Lockwood had said. "But always wash to be sure." It had not seemed strange to George that his father should know of such a place; most fathers knew of such places and many fathers made the preliminary arrangements for their sons, sometimes with the injunction that a boy of eighteen should stop "flogging the dummy" and when he felt horny to save it for a woman. Once on a visit to Ezra Davenport's house in northern New Jersey Mrs. Davenport's personal maid, a French woman, had taken off her clothes for Ezra and George and rather roughly disposed of Ezra and sent him out of the room while she gently but quickly attended to George. "This Ezra, pouf! Nothing. He only wish to see me with you," she said. But she was ugly with her clothes on, and on George's second visit to the Davenports she was no longer there. Once on a northbound train from Philadelphia a heavily perfumed woman wearing an ostrich-plumed hat sat beside George, looked him up and down several times, and put her hand on his thigh, kept it there, then slowly moved it upward and gently massaged him. "Open up honey so I can get inside." He undid his trousers and she brought him to orgasm. She said nothing more until the train was slowing down for Reading, when she handed him a calling card. "If you're in the neighborhood, honey. A high-class place, for gentlemen."

With so much experience in addition to the lore and legends he had absorbed at St. Bartholomew's and Princeton, George Lockwood was not ignorant of the female body or of the excitements and pleasures to be enjoyed in intimacy with it. He was moreover conscious of an effect he had on members of the opposite sex, conscious of it when frequently they were not. Bold women—the Davenports' maid, the woman on the train—seemed to recognize his special interest in them or at least to be aware of him as a comrade in a game. The girls in his own circle, the sisters and friends of his friends, might be less forthright or generous, or more obtuse, but within the restraints of the conventions they had always seemed to *like* him more than they did most of his contemporaries. His success with girls could not fairly or accurately be judged by the extent of his erotic experiences with them, since everything that could be done to deny privacy was being done. Ten minutes, five minutes completely alone with a girl was a rare occasion, even after Eulalie and George had reached their understanding. Girls were constantly watched by mothers, by sisters, by brothers, by servants, and especially by other girls. A maid would enter a room carrying a feather duster, a brother would come in to look for a book, and a girl's contemporaries would not even bother to make a feeble excuse. But the closest surveillance was that of the young lovers themselves, by their sharpened vigilance over their erotic impulses. There were times when George knew that Eulalie was *letting* him make the next, more intimate move, anticipating the hand on her breast, the creeping fingers inside her thigh. She would sit on the sofa, enjoying the liberties he would not take, letting him enjoy them with her until he would take his lips away from hers and they would sigh together as though only a kiss had ended. He could not be sure how far the suppressed excitement had taken her, or had not taken her, but nearly always at such times she would say, "I love you," in a way that was meant to be a reward, and a reward which indeed he had earned.

There was no doubt for George that he loved her. His curiosity made the familiar tests, and his feeling for her passed them all: wanting to be with her, needing to write her, looking forward to her letters, wanting to confide in her, to tell her unimportant things, using her as a standard of her sex, wanting to protect her, and imagining the riotous pleasures that awaited them, to be followed by tenderness immeasurable. Then there were manifestations that surprised him: he became fond of her brother, wanting only the best for him. He became jealous of a friend named Mildred Haynes, whom Eulalie saw every day. And always, always, he wanted to talk about her.

To alleviate this compulsion he chose the least likely, most obviously wrong, confidant—the sardonic Ned O'Byrne. But O'Byrne's ironic wit was one language; he also spoke another, that of sympathy (George now recalled how quickly O'Byrne had understood Ezra Davenport) and warmth. "I'm going to have my brother Penrose as best man, but I want you to be an usher," said George Lockwood in their senior year.

"Don't commit yourself, George. There'll be a lot of noses out of joint if you have me."

"Fuck them."

"Well, if you feel that strongly about it."

"I do. I'm not going to have anybody from St. Bartholomew's. Except my brother, of course. And nobody from Philadelphia. Nobody from Ivy."

"Not Ezra? He'll cry his eyes out."

"He can be ring-bearer. I might ask *one* boy from St. Bartholomew's."

"Chatsworth."

"Yes. How did you know?"

"I guess I was hoping you would. He got the shitty end of

the stick here, some day they're all going to be God damned sorry, because Chatsworth is a better man than most of them."

"Why do you think that, Ned? I agree with you, but we've never had much to say about him."

"Well, I don't know. Dignity. Anson Chatsworth was more entitled to a club bid than I was. More so than at least half of those that got in the best clubs. I think it was an accident that he was passed over. You know now how those things can happen. A fellow like Chatsworth, nothing to make him outstanding, and yet eligible for every club here. So by accident no club gives him a bid, because they all think he'll be in some other club. But he wasn't a crybaby, and he didn't resign from Princeton. The opposite of Ezra. I'm sure Ezra peed his pants when he made Ivy, and I've often wondered what possessed them. I'd give a lot to know how he made it. I think he had a great-great-grandfather that was a signer of the Declaration of Independence."

"Chatsworth had an ancestor that was president of Harvard."

"There, you see? If Chatsworth had gone to Harvard he'd have been in one of their best final clubs, but here he was left out in the cold. I wish we could get him in our club."

"He wouldn't come in now. And anyway, I'm going to have to work hard for my own candidate."

"Your future brother-in-law. You have your work cut out for you. Dave's a nice kid, but a wish-wash."

"No he isn't, not really. He'll improve with age."

"George, he's a wish-wash. He's a perfect example of a no-bid fellow. Don't get into a scuffle over Dave Fenstermacher. You're the only man in the club's going to be for him. He may get a bid to some place, but everybody in our crowd is going to think that you only want him because you're going to marry his sister. Another thing you ought to take into consideration, it won't break his heart if he doesn't make a club. He must know by this time where he stands."

"You never know, and you always keep hoping."

"Well, I'll grant you that. You do keep hoping." O'Byrne laughed. "When I got my bids, for about sixty seconds I thought maybe one of them would be Ivy."

"Would you have taken Ivy?"

"No. For one reason, and one reason only. I couldn't learn to stomach Jack Harbord. That mealy-mouthed hypocrite, there'll never be room on this earth for the two of us. If I heard he was at death's door I wouldn't blow my nose to save his life."

"Well, when we leave here we'll never have to see him again."

"I won't. You will. You'll never see me at a class reunion. The last Princeton thing I do will be to usher at your wedding, and then I'm going to disappear. I'm heading straight for the Kimberley, to make my fortune in the diamond fields."

"You never liked it here. Why did you stay? Family?"

"Why else would I stay? My father. I'm very fond of my old man. I understand him perfectly, you know. My mother was determined that at least one of us would become a Jesuit priest, but my father was just as determined we wouldn't. So he pushed Kevin and me into Princeton, away from the Jesuits, and then my younger brother into Yale. He's hoping that I'll follow Kevin into medical school, but he knows it's a forlorn hope."

"Why is he so much against the Jesuits? He's a Catholic."

"He's a Catholic, but in Ireland he went to the Brothers, the Christian Brothers, and the Jesuits try to make them feel that they're hoi polloi. And maybe they are. *I* think they are, but I'm a snob. Anyway, there's always some Jesuit having dinner at our house and my old man has been fed up with them for years, the way my mother worships them. I've observed on occasion that my old man is also a bit fed up with my mother, though he may try to hide it."

"I'll tell you something in strict confidence. I think my mother and father really hate each other. I've never said that to another human being."

"That's no rarity, George. The number of husbands and wives that hate each other must be appalling, appalling. It's one of the reasons why you never hear of me going out with a nice Catholic girl. I don't want to get married, but I'm soft-hearted and if I fell for a Catholic girl I'd hear myself proposing to her some moonlight night. Therefore, to be on the safe side, I bestow the privilege of my company on Protestant girls and now and then a pretty little Jewess. That should keep me a bachelor for a good many years. But don't let me discourage *you*, George."

"You don't. Lalie and I aren't like my father and mother."

"Your mother I take it was English extraction."

"No, she was Pennsylvania Dutch, the same as Lalie's family."

"Oh, but Lalie—nothing against your mother, mind you,

but in your mother's time girls weren't given much of an education."

"Well, my mother had the same amount of schooling as Lalie. In fact, my mother was pretty bright. Is, I should say She can read French and High German, as well as speak Pennsylvania Dutch."

"I see. You mean that you and your father are different."

"Yes. Very different."

"I only saw your father that one time when he stopped off to see you. I thought you were very much alike, but you can't tell much from such a short meeting. You didn't look very much like him, but you had some of the same mannerisms."

"He's all business."

"Well—you're not all monkey-shines, if it comes to that. When you set your mind to a thing—"

"Are you trying to tell me I'm like my father? I'm not. We're very different, outside and inside."

"I wouldn't argue that question. I don't know what you're like inside."

"Funny you should say that."

"Why?"

"My brother said that about my father. 'Nobody knows what Father's like inside.' The same words . . . So you're going to South Africa?"

"Unless I change my mind. You know. Last year I wanted to go to Oxford. I expect to be a citizen of the world, and I thought Oxford would give me the right polish. Not to mention the entree that being an Oxford man gives you. I forget why I gave that up. I guess I fell under the influence of Villon. But now I fully intend to make a great fortune in the Kimberley, buy a steam yacht and equip it with heavy guns and prey on British shipping. In other words, become a pirate. A freebooter. Then maybe be a sort of Patrick Sarsfield, raise hell in Ireland. Every so often we have to remind the English that they're trespassing."

"Do you really think you'll ever do any of this, Ned?"

"Well, it takes money."

"I meant go to South Africa."

"That takes money, too. I won't travel steerage. I may have to spend the rest of this year playing cards with Chatsworth and Davenport. I wish Harbord played cards, but he promised his mother. So he *says*. I don't believe him for a minute. He just doesn't want to gamble."

"How much money have you won from Chatsworth?"

"Altogether? I guess about three thousand, but that wasn't

all clear profit, as you well know. You took your share of it, and I don't want you to play in May and June, when I open my big final campaign on the Chatsworth bankroll. When you're in the game the others try to play like you, and it's a restraining influence on the betting. Davenport especially. Is your fiancée going to let you play cards?"

"*Let* me play cards? It's not up to her whether I play cards or not. I'd never ask a woman permission to do a thing like that. I'd just go and do it."

"Well, good for you, and the best of luck," said Ned O'Byrne.

In late winter, following conversations with Lalie and her mother, George arranged to meet Judge Fenstermacher to obtain his consent to the marriage. "You write a good letter, George. I like a good letter. It tells a lot about a man if he can express his thoughts without committing himself too much. But now you *want* to commit yourself, don't you?"

"Yes sir. I wish to ask for Eulalie's hand in marriage."

"Yes. Well, you've had this understanding for some time now and both of you have a level head on your shoulders. I'm going to give my consent. I've looked into your background, and I've observed you in my house. Yes, you may marry Eulalie, and I trust you'll both be very happy."

"Thank you sir."

"Mrs. Fenstermacher informs me that you wish to announce the engagement after you graduate."

"Yes sir."

"What do you plan to do for a living, George? I know your people are comfortable, but what do you expect to go into?"

"I haven't decided. My father and I've been talking, but I haven't decided."

"Well, it isn't as if you had to go right out and get a job. Your family are comfortable. You'll wish to make your home in Swedish Haven?"

"Oh, yes."

"Well, I'm in favor of that. We've always lived here, and I hope David will settle here when he graduates. I want him to study law at my college, Dickinson, and then settle here. Did you ever hear any of your family speak of William L. Lockwood?"

"No sir."

"Never heard of William L. Lockwood. Well, William L. Lockwood was one of the founders of my college fraternity. Sigma Chi."

"Is that so?"

"Thomas C. Bell, James P. Caldwell, Daniel W. Cooper, Benjamin P. Runkle, Franklin H. Scobey, Isaac M. Jordan, and William L. Lockwood. They were the founders of Sigma Chi, at Miami University out in Ohio, the year 1855. They were all members of Deke with the exception of Lockwood. I had to memorize all that when I was initiated."

"Is that so?"

"Be nice if you could trace some connection with William L. Lockwood. That would make you and me fraternity brothers, so to speak. I wish they had Sigma Chi at Princeton. They did have, but then Princeton did away with fraternities. I would have liked David to be a Sigma Chi. Is your father a Mason, George?"

"No sir. He's a Zeta Psi."

"Well, you don't mention the two together."

"Oh, I thought *you* mentioned Sigma Chi and the Masons."

"Not exactly together, though. I guess you did think I was coupling one with the other, so that's my fault, but that's neither here nor there. Your Grandfather Hoffner's a Mason, that I do know."

"Is he?"

"You didn't know that, George? Yes, you have very good Masonic connections on your mother's side. We'll have to speak about this again sometime. Just now I'm a little worried about David at Princeton. You have these clubs at Princeton, so it isn't as if I could write to the Sigma Chi chapter, but David's told me he doesn't expect to join a club. George, now that you're coming in the family, I wish you'd have a talk with David, make him see how important it is to mix with people."

"It's a ticklish subject, Judge."

"Ticklish subject? How so?"

"Well, I belong to a club—"

"I know you do. One of the best, I'm told."

"Thank you. But if I talk to David about the advantages of joining a club, he may get it in his head that I'm trying to get him to join *my* club."

"Well, what if he does? I'd be satisfied to have my son and my son-in-law in the same club. If you can't both be Sigma Chi's . . ."

"But I don't speak for my club, Judge. I don't decide who gets invited to join. I can blackball somebody, but that doesn't mean I can invite somebody. You know how these things work."

"Of course I do. But this club you belong to is only a club, not a secret organization like Sigma Chi, or the Masons. It's just a club."

"We have secrets, just the same as if we were Alpha Beta Gamma Delta."

"Then what David's been trying to tell me is that you're not going to invite him. It isn't that he doesn't *want* to join. Do you realize what you're doing to the boy? Do you realize that three of his friends from Mercersburg are sure to be invited to clubs, and he isn't?"

"They can't be sure, his friends. They won't know till the last minute."

Judge Fenstermacher tapped his heel on the carpet, ran his fingers around his neck between skin and collar. He got up and walked to the window, then came back and stood before George Lockwood. "Let me hear it from you in plain language. You ask permission to marry my daughter, but you're doing nothing to help her young brother."

"Judge, I've done all I could to help David."

"All you could? What have you done? Sat idly by while other young pipsqueaks keep him out of your own club. Do you think any member of my family would ever set foot in such a place after that? Do you think Eulalie would visit your club? Or I? Or Mrs. Fenstermacher?"

"I'm sorry, Judge. I don't know. I only know that I've been trying for nearly a year to get David invited to our club. But I'm not the one that decides. It's a committee."

"Damn your committee!"

"He may be invited to join some place else."

"I don't want him to join some place else. I want to know whether my prospective son-in-law has any standing with his friends. If not, then I don't want him for a son-in-law."

"Well, then I guess that's that."

"What do you mean, that's that?"

"I'll have to tell Lalie that you've turned me down."

The meeting had taken longer than was expected by Lalie and her mother, who were waiting in the sitting-room, and when George Lockwood joined them their nervously expectant smiles vanished. "What happened?" said Lalie.

"He says to wait? Is that it?" said Mrs. Fenstermacher.

"He thinks I should have got David into my club."

"Oh, dear me. I was hoping that wouldn't come up. David understands, but I knew Judge wouldn't. Oh, dear."

Lalie went into his outstretched arms. "Don't cry," he said. He turned to her mother. "I'm over twenty-one, Mrs. Fenstermacher. You know that. And Lalie will soon be."

"Yes, but don't do anything—rash."

"It won't be rash," said George Lockwood. "I can support her. I'm very well off."

"It isn't that, George. Let me deal with Judge."

It was a Sunday. They had all been to church, but they had not yet sat down to the large Sunday dinner that always followed attendance at divine service. Now they heard the judge's deep voice. "Bessie, come here," he was calling.

"You two stay here," said Bessie Fenstermacher.

George Lockwood never knew what was said between the judge and his wife. He sat with Lalie in the sitting-room for fifteen minutes behind the rarely closed doors. They comforted each other with the words and sentences of love, with kisses and tears and the common anger. Then there was a knock on the door, the door was opened, and Bessie Fenstermacher, half-smiling, said to them: "It's all right. Just say nothing. Pretend like nothing happened. Dinner's ready."

"Mama, what did you tell him?" said Lalie.

"I talked to him. Don't ask me any more questions. Dinner's ready," said Bessie Fenstermacher. She rested her hand on George's arm. "You have sense, George."

"All right, Mrs. Fenstermacher."

"He's a judge, remember. He has to be right, so don't put him in the wrong. Be polite, like nothing happened."

"I'll do my best."

There were only the four of them for dinner. The judge stood up while carving the roast chicken, which gave him something to do. "George, can I give you light or dark?"

"I like the white," said George Lockwood.

"I see you have plenty of sweet marjoram in the filling, Bessie," said the judge. "Maybe George doesn't like so much sweet marjoram?"

"Yes, I do. I like it.

"Well, that's lucky. Lalie, you pass George his plate please. And George, help yourself to the mashed and sweets. The gravy's there in front of you. Lalie, you want the second joint?"

The conversation at the beginning was on the topic of food, always a reliable and inexhaustible topic among the Pennsylvania Dutch. The meal consisted of the large main course and dessert of hot mince pie and ice cream. George and the judge drank coffee with their meal, the women drank water. But though there were only the two courses, the amount of food was prodigious. Meat, candied sweet potatoes, mashed white potatoes, red beets, stewed corn, mashed turnips, creamed onions, and endive in olive oil, with side dishes of cranberries and a slaw. Thought was put away while the two men and two women concentrated on emptying their platters, and conversation never got far from the principal topic, the business at hand. Distracting talk was never encouraged at a Pennsylvania Dutch table, and silences were not embarrassing. (Prattling children would be asked, "Did you come to eat or did you come to gabble?" and it was within the rules for a talky child to lose a piece of pie to a non-talking neighbor. "That'll teach you not to talk so much," the parents would say.)

After dinner the men went to the judge's den for cigars. "When do you have to go back to Princeton?" said the judge.

"On the 3:10."

"Change at Reading, and then change at Philadelphia? What time does that get you there? Around supper, I guess?"

"It'll be after supper."

"Well, we better pack a box for you to eat on the train."

"Oh, I'll be all right, thank you. I'll manage."

"On a Sunday it won't be easy, but that's up to you. You won't get to see your folks this trip? All day Sunday on one train after another, it seems a shame."

"It was worth it to me, sir."

"Well, I hope so. We had our angry words, but now it's all over and done with."

"But there's something I want to say, Judge."

"Is it about that other subject? My son?"

"Yes sir."

"Then don't say it. I consider the matter closed and I don't wish to talk about it, now or ever again. I gave a promise."

"Very well, sir."

"Some day you'll have a son of your own—no, I won't say any more. You make Lalie happy and I'll be satisfied . . Well, George, I think there's the team to take you to the depot. Yes, there's the barouche. Is your valise all packed? Oh, you didn't have one, of course. All day on the train."

"Since seven o'clock this morning. Well, thank you, Judge."

"No hard feelings on either side, George."

"No sir."

But back at Princeton, away from Lalie's pretty face and miserable tears, George Lockwood had his first doubts, and he found that curiously, perversely, they were centered on Bessie Fenstermacher. Until this too-eventful day he had regarded her as a round, meek woman who obeyed her husband and kept house for him, who was still obeyed by her children but would soon yield even that authority. But on this day, in a quarter of an hour, she had created another picture of herself; and as George Lockwood thought about it, he recalled that it was Bessie Fenstermacher who had made the decision to have an understanding instead of an engagement. And now he thought back upon the scene in the sitting-room, with Lalie in tears of disappointment. Tears of disappointment, indeed, but whose disappointment? It came to him now that Lalie had immediately looked at her mother and had kept looking at her, that her unhappiness was as much due to her mother's disappointment as her own. And then, he recalled vividly, the words Bessie Fenstermacher had spoken: "I was hoping that wouldn't come up. David understands, but I knew Judge wouldn't . . . Let me deal with Judge." The round, meek woman had anticipated possible trouble, had apparently discussed the club problem with David—and was fully confident of her ability to deal with the judge. The round, meek little woman, who dominated her family's lives, and who so often reminded George Lockwood of Lalie.

It was natural enough for a mother to remind you of her daughter, for a daughter to remind you of her mother.

George Lockwood went for a walk, but he knew as he left the dormitory that he would be looking to see if Ned O'Byrne's light was on. He knew that he hoped O'Byrne's light would be on, and it was.

O'Byrne, who roomed alone, was sitting in his easy chair, with his carpet-slippered feet propped up on a hassock. He was in a shabby wool bathrobe, smoking a calabash pipe. He held up a book. "I was just thinking about you."

"What are you reading?"

"It's *Missionary Travels in South Africa,* by David Livingstone. You remember, 'Dr. Livingstone, I presume?' I presume?"

"Why would that make you think of me, for the Lord's sake?"

"Because I'm doing my homework, getting ready to go to Africa. And you've been spending the day in Lebanon, P-A, doing *your* homework. So you're back, eh? Sit down and tell me about it. There's a cigar in the top drawer there. I was saving it for after breakfast, but *you* smoke it. That way I'll have to smoke me pipe, which I'm trying to break in but with very little success."

"I have a cigar, thanks, if you'll give me a match."

"There's a match in the match-safe, to your right on the desk. What went wrong, man? Something did, I can tell."

George Lockwood related the incidents of the day, but withheld the newly forming doubts.

"Well," said Ned O'Byrne.

"Is that all you have to say?"

"Oh, no. 'Ay me! For aught that ever I could read,/ could ever hear by tale or history,/ the course of true love never did run smooth;/ but, either it was different in blood,—/ or else misgraffed in respect of years,—/or else it stood upon the choice of friends,—/ or, if there were a sympathy in choice,/ war, death, or sickness did lay siege to it,/ making it momentany as a sound,/ swift as a shadow, short as any dream,/ brief as the lightning in the collied night,—' "

"All right."

"Shut up. 'Lightning in the collied night,/ that, in a spleen, unfolds both heaven and earth,/ and ere a man hath power to say, 'Behold!'/ the jaws of darkness do devour it up:/ so quick bright things come to confusion.' I'm finished, but I gave you the whole damned thing instead of just the usual course-of-true-love."

"Thank you very much, it was heart-rending."

"The mother seems to exert a great deal of authority, George. I'd keep on the right side of her if I were you. She'll come in handy some day, and it's plain as day she's all for you. There's one person I'm glad I'm not tonight."

"Who's that? The judge?"

"The girl. Lalie."

"Why?"

"Oh—it's hard for me to say."

"Haven't you got some quotation from Shakespeare that covers it?"

"I'm sure there is one, but I'm not showing off now. I'm just thinking of a young girl that's had a pretty bad day, all in all. You'll want to hit me in the mouth for this, George, but I don't think you love her."

"I don't want to hit you in the mouth."

"Then for God's sake tell her—no, don't."

"Tell her what?"

"Is this freeze you had today, is it going to last? Maybe better give it a couple of days, but you haven't been talking like a man in love, and the fair, honest thing is to put an end to it before more harm is done. I wish you hadn't come here tonight, I swear to Christ I do. I nearly always take the woman's side, in spite of knowing that they damn well can take care of themselves. All right, then I'll take *your* side."

"Don't take any side."

"I'll take your side, if I like. My heart goes out to this girl, but they're wiser and smarter than we are in these things. So look at it from our point of view. Supposing you did break it off. If you don't love her, you're doing her a favor. If it turns out you do love her, which I doubt, you're the principal loser. Why aren't you arguing with me, protesting that you do love her? You know why, George. You can't make yourself lie to yourself."

"I don't know what I think, or what I want to do."

"Write her a letter tonight and sleep on it. Pour it all out and see how much of it you believe in the morning. You know we have one thing in the Catholic Church that I'd like to hold on to. Confession. I stopped going when I came here, but I think it helps a lot of poor souls to go on living. They pour it all out once a week or once a month, and they come out of the box feeling that they have a new start. *Absolvo te,* the man says, and for fifteen minutes it's a new world. Till you bump up against a pretty ass in the trolley car, but then your impure thoughts and desires are on a new slate, not the old one. Very comforting, and I miss it."

"You're all a bunch of hypocrites."

"I don't doubt it for a second, but the purest of angels for fifteen minutes or so. Not a worry in the world, not the slightest concern. Will you write the letter, George? You may learn something about yourself."

"What?"

"I don't know. It's you learning about you. You may find out that you love this girl much more deeply than you realized. I consider myself a very wise fellow, but it's my own belly-button that fascinates me the most. By the way, Chatsworth's in trouble. He was looking for you this afternoon, and I told him you were away for the day."

"A woman?"

"A girl in New Brunswick. He told her he was from Rutgers but her old man tracked him down to here. She's knocked up. They want a thousand dollars, and the most Chat could raise was around four hundred. He has till tomorrow night to raise the full amount."

"Well, let's go over and see him. I can let him have the money."

"I gave him two hundred, that was all I had. I'll win it back. Do you want to go over now?"

"Sure."

"He wants to get the money in secrecy. There were only a few he wanted to ask. You can write a cheque for six or seven hundred, and get it cashed?"

"Yes. Or more, if necessary."

"Well, then let's go over and see Chat. Is it cold out?"

"It's gotten colder. You'll need a coat. How long has he been screwing this girl?"

"Since last fall, he told me."

"I can go to the bank in the morning. Is Chat taking the full responsibility? How does he know he's the one?"

"We talked about that. He said the father honestly didn't want to make trouble. The girl wasn't virtue itself. But she's knocked up and the father's a poor man and wants Chat to pay for the kid. He says he won't blackmail Chat."

"That's what he says, but what's he doing?"

"Well, he knows Chat's graduating in June and he may never see Chat again. Oh, Chat takes the blame. He doesn't deny anything. But there'll be hell to pay in Chicago, and if the faculty finds out, Chat's through here."

"Yes. Well, get a wiggle on."

"I'm ready."

There was a light on in Chatsworth's room. They went up the two flights and knocked on his door, but there was no answer.

"Fell asleep," said O'Byrne. He opened the door gently. "No one here."

"Wait a minute," said George Lockwood. "The wardrobe."

Both doors of the wardrobe were open, all the suits and coats that belonged in it were on chairs and on the cot. Ned O'Byrne and George Lockwood went in, and now they saw Anson Chatsworth. There was a noose of dirty clothesline about his neck and tied to the thick cross-bar of the wardrobe. He was wearing trousers and a shirt without a collar.

"Mother of God," said O'Byrne.

"Jesus," said George Lockwood. "How did he do it?"

"Cut him down, George," said O'Byrne. He stood over the wastebasket and vomited.

"I haven't got a knife. He's dead, isn't he?"

"Yes, he's dead. That you can be sure of." O'Byrne wiped his mouth with his handkerchief. "We can't leave him like that."

"Don't we have to? For the police?"

"Ah, fuck the police. What a way to talk, in the presence of . . ." He did not finish the thought. "I want to untie him, but I can't." He suddenly was forced to vomit again. "George, I'll go for the police, if you can stand to be alone."

"You go, and I'll wait in the hall."

"You sure you don't mind? I'll do this again if I don't get some fresh air."

"Go on, Ned. I'll stay out in the hall. You're sure he's dead?"

"I know he is. I saw one once before." He departed, and George Lockwood stood in the hall to wait. Then quite slowly he began to cry, and he put his head on his arm and rested his arm against the wall and cried freely.

"Hey, Lockwood? Are you drunk?"

George Lockwood did not turn to face his questioner.

"George? What's the matter?" the voice asked.

George Lockwood shook his head, and the unknown student put his hand on his shoulder. "George? Can I help you? What is it, old fellow? Don't cry, George. Tell me what it is."

"Chat," said George Lockwood.

"What? *Chat*, did you say?"

"He's dead. *Don't go in,*" said George Lockwood.

"Chatsworth is dead? You mean he's dead in there?"

George Lockwood stopped crying. "Oh, hello, Bender. Have you seen O'Byrne?"

"I saw him downstairs, he was in a hurry."

"Yes. Chat hung himself. He's dead. We found him."

"Chatsworth? I saw him after supper. He's dead? You mean he committed suicide?"

"Yes. Don't go in, Benson. I mean Bender. I always get you mixed up with Benson, I'm sorry."

"That's all right, George. Come on down to my room and wait there. Do you want me to get you a glass of water?"

"No thanks. *Yes!* Will you get me a glass of water? Please? I didn't know I was thirsty. I would like a glass of water. You don't have any whiskey or anything like that, have you?"

"No, I don't drink. At first I thought you were drunk, though."

"I know."

"I'll get you the water and maybe you'll feel better."

"Thanks very much, Bender."

Bender with his tumbler of water and O'Byrne with a constable arrived together.

"Are you all right, George?" said O'Byrne. "We sent for a doctor, too, but I know it's no use."

Students were now forming a group in the hall, some half dressed, some in nightshirts, some in bathrobes. They heard the constable say, "He's dead, all right. Where's the two boys that found him?"

"He wants you, George. You and O'Byrne," said Bender.

The constable was trying to control his own agitation.

"You're both here at the college, ain't you? I seen you before. What's your names?"

"O'Byrne."

"Lockwood."

"Lockwood and O'Burns? The senior class?"

"Yes sir," said George Lockwood. "We're both seniors."

"And this poor fellow's name you say is Chatworth?"

"Chatsworth. Anson Chatsworth. He comes from Chicago, Illinois," said George Lockwood.

"And the two of you come in and found him hanging here. What time was that about?"

"Less than an hour ago," said George Lockwood.

"Less than an hour ago," said the constable. He did not know what question to ask next. "Are you his roommates or— no, there's only the one cot. You're friends of his?"

"Yes sir," said O'Byrne.

"Uh-huh. There was no sign of life when you seen him?"

"They wouldn't have let him hang, you damned fool," said a voice in the growing crowd.

"Who said that? I'll run you in," said the constable.

"Can't we cut him down?" said O'Byrne. "Is there any reason why you should leave him like that?"

Action was something the constable understood. "Yes, I guess it's all right to cut him down. You. O'Burns. Give me a hand."

"Not me!"

"You're the one wants him cut down," said the constable.

"I don't want to touch him."

"Make way, please." A voice with authority was heard. A middle-aged man—Professor Raymond Revercomb, of the English-teaching staff. "Go to your own rooms, fellows. Disperse. You're only in the way here," he said, but having said it made no further effort in that regard, and no one left. "O'Byrne. Lockwood. You discovered him?"

"Yes sir."

Revercomb entered the room. "Good God, let's get him down. In the name of decency, let's get him down. This is grotesque. Constable, can't you cut that rope?"

"I was just getting ready to, but I need help with the corpse."

"Well, I'll help. Lockwood, you stand on his left side and I'll stand on his right. Constable, you cut the rope, and Lockwood, you and I carry him to the cot. Good God. Good God."

George Lockwood shivered upon touching his dead friend, but he did as he was told and they put Chatsworth on the cot.

"Cover him," said Revercomb. "Somebody's been sick in here."

"Me," said O'Byrne.

"Well, I don't blame you, but let's open a window. What do we do now, Constable? I mean the legalities."

"I sent somebody for Doc Perry."

"He can take as long as he likes," said Revercomb. "He'll do no good here, or any other doctor."

"Well, I guess if I write down some more witnesses the next thing is send for the undertaker."

"O'Byrne and I, and Bender," said George Lockwood. "We were the first here."

"As far as you *know,*" said the constable.

"Listen to him!" said a student.

" 'As far as you know.' "

"I warned you before, I'll run you in," said the constable.

"Shut up, whoever said that," said Revercomb. "Show some respect, please. And you, Constable, bear in mind that you're on University property."

"You bear in mind that I was sent for, Professor."

"Oh, all right, all right," said Revercomb. "What shall we do? Lock this room till the undertaker gets here? You fellows didn't find a note or a letter, did you?"

"I never thought to look," said George Lockwood.

"Neither did I," said O'Byrne.

"Yes, there ought to be some kind of a letter," said the constable. "They usually leave a letter. Though not always. The women are more apt to leave a letter, those that can read and write. If anybody finds a letter, or a note, turn it right over to me."

"You mean now?" said George Lockwood.

"Of course, now. I'll look in his pants pockets, and Professor, you go through his desk."

The four searched, but no letter was found.

"Lockwood, O'Byrne, there's no use your hanging around here any longer. Go on back to your rooms and try to get some sleep. The authorities will notify us if they want you. Inquest, I suppose. I'll stay here till the undertaker comes, and that's about all we can do tonight."

"What about his family, Professor?" said O'Byrne.

"I'll attend to that. We will. We'll get off a telegram as soon as we have more details. Goodnight, now, boys."

"Goodnight, sir," they said.

Out in the cold air the friends of Anson Chatsworth walked aimlessly in the shadows of the bare elms. "Do you want to come back to my room?" said O'Byrne.

"All right," said George Lockwood. He had two roommates, Lewis and Loomis, but they were not his close friends; propinquity had not created intimacy. "I don't think I'll sleep, do you?"

"Well, you can stretch out in the Morris chair. You ought to get *some* sleep, George. You've had a Christ's-own of an exhausting day."

In O'Byrne's room George Lockwood said, "Would you ever do that, Ned?"

"Meaning what Chat did? I've thought about it. I'd never hang myself. That's because Judas Iscariot hanged himself, I guess."

"I had a friend at St. Bartholomew's, his father was a friend of my father's. He shot himself in the head. I think I'd shoot myself in the heart, or take poison. I wouldn't hang myself, either. Especially after tonight. He shouldn't have looked that way."

"He wasn't thinking about how he'd look."

"But I would. Wouldn't you? A bullet in the brain they say—"

"I know, I know."

"I'd care about how I looked, and I'd care about the shock to people that saw me."

"I guess I would too, and I guess for that reason you or I won't ever do it. Chat was a pretty simple sort of a fellow."

"Not stupid."

"No, of course not stupid. But not used to worrying, not used to thinking about things the way you and I are all the time. He wasn't used to trouble, and this thing he got into was too much for him."

"I guess that was it."

"Hear the bell."

"Uh-huh. The end of the day. Now it's Monday. The new week is starting. But not for Chat."

"No, not for Chat. It's all over for Chat."

"Jesus, I'm tired."

"Go to sleep. Don't fight it. Sleep, George."

"Think maybe I will." He was asleep before O'Byrne put the blanket over him.

Their testimony at the inquest was brief, and they were treated with consideration. George was therefore surprised when O'Byrne, on leaving the borough hall, said: "God, I'm glad to get out of there!"

"It wasn't as bad as I thought it'd be."

O'Byrne looked behind them and said: "I got this in the mail, Tuesday after Chat died. With it was $200, the same money I gave him that Saturday. Read it."

Ned:—It's no use. Even if I get the money that will only be the beginning of my troubles. I could not face my family after bringing this disgrace on them. Thank you for being a true and loyal friend. This is goodbye.
A.C.

They had stopped under a street lamp so that George Lockwood could read the note. He handed it back to O'Byrne.

"I don't know whether to keep it or burn it. In a way it's evidence," said O'Byrne.

"Yes, but they gave a verdict, the only one they could give. Chat hung himself while of unsound mind, or whatever the wording was. You did the right thing, Ned. If you'd shown them the note they would have asked a lot of questions. It's better to let the whole thing die down."

"If the girl's father keeps quiet."

"No use making trouble now."

"With Chat's family."

"Chicago's a long way from New Brunswick. I just don't think he'll make any more trouble. What would be the use? Even if he went to Chicago Chat's family wouldn't have to believe him. It would never hold up in court, I don't think."

"I wish I knew the girl's name," said O'Byrne.

"What would you do?"

"I probably wouldn't do anything, but it doesn't seem right. You realize that you and I are probably the only ones here that really knew why he did it."

"That's a blessing. Let's keep it that way."

"All right. Shall we take an oath? I solemnly swear that I will never reveal or divulge what I know about the death of Anson Chatsworth."

"I solemnly swear the same thing," said George Lockwood.

Their oath was tested on the following day. Each of them was called into Revercomb's office on the campus. "Lockwood, Mr. Chatsworth is coming here in the next few days and he'll want to know all there is to know. Is there anything you would care to tell me?"

"No sir."

"Nothing at all you want to tell me? You know more than you told at the inquest, of that I'm sure."

"Why are you sure, sir?"

"Don't answer me with a question. You know why Anson took his life."

"I have nothing to say, sir."

"Well, I'm not going to make any threats. But you were under oath at the inquest."

"All they asked me was to describe what I saw."

"And to tell the whole truth, et cetera. You're fencing with me, Lockwood."

"You're entitled to your opinion, sir. But I was away all day Sunday, in Lebanon, Pennsylvania. The last time I saw Chatsworth was the Friday before he died."

"Don't start building up a big alibi, Lockwood. All I care about now is whether you have anything to tell me that might be of some comfort to Chatsworth family."

"No sir, I haven't."

"By inference, of course, you know something that would *not* be a comfort. Well, all right. You may go."

"Thank you, Professor." George Lockwood got to his feet, took a few steps toward the door.

"Lockwood," said Revercomb.

"Sir?"

"I had a visitor last week. A man from New Brunswick."

"Did you sir? From Rutgers?"

"You know he wasn't from Rutgers, not this visitor. He was a nice man. A working-man, and he spent his own money to come here. He told me that he'd been to see Chatsworth. He even told me why."

"He did?"

"Yes. I want you and O'Byrne to know that when Mr. Chatsworth comes here, I'm going to tell him about my visitor, and after that it's up to him, Mr. Chatsworth. We're not taking any official position in the matter. Chatsworth is dead. But I want you and O'Byrne to know that personally, not officially, but speaking for myself, I can't help admiring your loyalty to your friend. Carry that into the world when you leave Princeton."

"I'll try sir. Thank you."

George Lockwood and Ned O'Byrne compared their experiences they had had in Professor Revercomb's office. They were very nearly identical. "I asked him to tell me the name of the man from New Brunswick," said O'Byrne.

"And?"

"He said it was none of my business. He was right, too."

"I'd just as soon not know," said George Lockwood.

"On thinking it over, me too."

The death of Anson Chatsworth had served to divert the young lovers from the distressing effects of George's scene with the judge. Lalie was eagerly and perhaps excessively sympathetic; her thrice weekly letters in the fortnight following Chat's suicide made no mention of her father, her brother, or of the anguish she had been caused by her father's outburst. Instead she wrote of the sadness of death, the mystery of suicide, the advent of spring and new life and hope. The first of these letters was welcomed; the others seemed forced, insincere, strategic, and for a stretch of five days George could not bring himself to answer her. His silence disturbed her; she sent one of her rare telegrams:

MISS YOUR LETTERS HOPE ALL IS WELL LOVE.

He showed the telegram and explained the circumstances to O'Byrne.

O'Byrne shook his head. "I'm sorry, George. I don't want to say anything."

"I don't want advice," said George Lockwood.

"Yes you do, and I'm not giving any."

"I just want to talk about it."

"You want to get me talking about it. Please don't ask me to, because whatever I say will be wrong. It's your problem. Write a letter. Write several letters. Write a half a dozen. And don't show them to me. Pick out the one that says what you think, what you feel, and send it off by special delivery mail. The few pennies extra won't break you."

"Are you inferring that I'm stingy?"

"The word is implying, as you should know from your St. Bartholomew's Latin."

"Implying, then. Are you implying that I'm stingy?"

"I haven't seen you light your cigars with ten-dollar notes, not lately."

"I haven't seen you with a ten-dollar note since Chat died."

O'Byrne jumped to his feet, but even with that much warning George Lockwood was not quick enough to ward off the blow, a punch to mouth and nose that blinded him.

"Only a bastard would say a thing like that," said O'Byrne. "Put up your fists."

"I can lick you, O'Byrne. But I shouldn't have said that."

"You're only bigger. You can't fight better. I want to fight you for that."

"No." George Lockwood, taller and at least as strong, pinioned O'Byrne's arms to his sides and shoved him to his cot. Then he left the room, and there was blood from his nose on his handkerchief. An hour later he heard O'Byrne's voice through the open window.

"Lockwood? I want to talk to you."

"Go on down and talk to him. We're trying to study," said Lewis, one of the roommates.

O'Byrne was standing in the light from the entryway lamp. "I brought you your telegram. And my apologies."

"Nobody behaved very well," said George Lockwood.

"The fact of the matter is that you hit a sore spot, and I didn't know it was there."

"Do you need money?"

"No. Let's walk, and I'll tell you." They set out in the direction of Kingston, marching silently in step for the first few minutes. "I hit you because the truth hurts. I'm not broke. But I was counting on my winnings to take me to Africa. I ought to know better than to count on winnings."

"There's still Davenport."

"There's Davenport and a rich sophomore that transferred from Ohio State. But I no longer want to play. There's a game tonight I could come out winners, I'm sure. There I go again, but I could. But I've lost interest. Ever since Chat died I haven't wanted to play. I used to like to play with him. I took his money, he had plenty of it, and we always had a jolly good evening."

"Do you blame yourself because he didn't have enough money that time?"

"No. It isn't that. You had money in the bank and we were on our way to give it to him."

"True."

"No, I don't blame myself that way. It's just that the fun's gone out of it. If I sit down and see a deck of cards and a stack of chips, I'm afraid it'd be too much for me, I don't think I'll ever want to play cards again. Gambling—yes. That's too much a part of me to give that up. But not cards. The irony is that cards are the only gambling I'm good at."

"How much do you need to go to Africa?"

O'Byrne shook his head. "No thanks, George. I'll never go to Africa, either. That was part of it, don't you see? Chat. Poker. Africa. All part of the same get-rich-quick scheme."

"Yes, I can see how that would be."

"Did you ever stop to think of these things, George? Chat went up to New Brunswick. Met a young woman that took his fancy. Gave her one too many cockloads, and now she's bearing him a child that will grow up a bastard. The terrible thing that happened to Chat, the grieving his mother and father are left with, forever asking themselves why, why, why. And of considerably less importance, one Edmund O'Byrne, Class of 1895 Princeton University, is unable to conquer the diamond fields of Africa. Take a look at that bluish ball up there, hanging in the sky, and think of all we know about it. The argument is that the Intelligence that created it wasn't concerned with you and me and the like of us. But the great complications and all the inevitability of them George, the things that do happen to you and me—to me they're better proof of that intelligence than the big big bluish ball. The argument is that we're too infinitesimally small, George, but it seems to me the smaller we are, the greater the proof of that Intelligence. Who short of God could make so much trouble? This is the kind of talk my mother's Jesuits blame on Princeton."

"Well, you certainly didn't learn it here. As far as I know, God is supposed to be so big, so powerful that it's no problem for Him to invent, I mean create, the moon *and* you and me."

"My friend, that's another argument, but it doesn't *argue* anything. That's just a statement of faith. I'd rather put one theory up against another instead of making one theory into a great universal truth. You'll never get any fun out of your intellect if you don't argue with yourself. And you'll never argue with yourself if you take what the theologians give you, all wrapped up in ribbons. Red for the Sacred College of Cardinals. Orange and Black for Princeton. Blue for the moon and Yale."

"You never saw a Yale-blue moon."

"And please God, I never want to. I like this God damn place. After four years of throwing horse turds at it I find that I'm getting reluctant to leave. I feel the same way about Ireland, except that I *know* I'll go back *there*."

"You'll come back here."

"No. And even if I do? Ireland is forever. Princeton is only four years of my life, and Princeton means nothing to me *but* four years of my life. Princeton without the four years of my life doesn't mean anything to me. Ireland does mean something, would if I'd never been there. Ireland is instead of the church that I gave up, my mother that bores me, the songs I never wrote but had going in my head."

"I wish I had something like that."

"Maybe you have, and don't know it."

"No. My father may have it, a little. But I haven't."

"Well, you can live without it—although I wouldn't want to. You have something else, I guess, to take its place."

"You don't really believe I have, do you, Ned?"

"You cried for Chat. That much I know. Poor old Bender, he'll never get over seeing you cry. His eyes well up when he thinks about it."

"O'Byrne?"

"What, Lockwood?"

"My grandfather killed two men. He was tried for manslaughter for the one."

"Now I never knew that."

"I know you didn't. But I'm not what you think I am."

"Not the true gentry?"

"No."

"That explains a few things."

"What things, for instance?"

"Well—certain hesitancies."

"Like what?"

"I'd be hard put to give you examples, but since you've told me this, I'll confess that I noticed you're not always as sure of yourself as you ought to be. Most of the time, yes. But not always. Much as I dislike Harbord, he's always sure that what he's doing is the right thing. He's doing it, therefore it's the right thing. If you have a son, he'll probably be as sure of himself as Harbord is. You're more sure of yourself than your father is, aren't you?"

"Oh, yes. Much more."

"What about your grandfather, the killer?"

"Very sure of himself, I think."

"Yes. No doubt he didn't care."

"Not a bit."

"Virile stock, and you're used to having money. Your son will be an aristocrat. Then you ought to have him marry an Italian or a Spaniard before the inbreeding starts."

"Maybe I ought to marry an Italian."

"Time to turn around, George."

"Yes, I guess so."

Now they could laugh, and they did.

Harvey Fenstermacher—Harvey Stonebraker Fenstermacher, to give him his full name—prided himself on two things: he was a man of his word, and he was not a hypocrite. He also prided himself on being a good Christian, a good Mason, a good Sigma Chi, a member of an old Lebanon Valley family, an honest judge, a Godfearing member of the Reformed Church, a better than average shot, a prudent banker, a knowing farmer, a fancier of fine Holstein stock, a good judge of trotters, a pleasing baritone, and a real family man. Now, however, he was disturbed by his deviations from excellence in the matter of keeping his word, in his sincerity, and in his role as family man.

He did not feel right about the way things were turning out with regard to his daughter Lalie and George Lockwood. There were often times when he found it hard to believe that Lalie was made the same way as her mother; that she was a female woman. Bessie Fenstermacher was female woman, all right, and not only did they have the children to prove it, but Bessie, in the long years of their marriage, had been quite surprising in her demands on his masculinity. That had not been the Bessie he married; she was just like all the other girls of good family—at first—but she certainly had learned quickly. Harvey Fenstermacher supposed that that was the same thing that would happen to Lalie; that she was a female woman and, once married, would probably behave the way her mother behaved. But Harvey Fenstermacher did not like to think about that, and so he didn't very much. He preferred to think of Lalie as she looked at, say, fifteen, with her hair plaited and hanging down her back and wearing a girl's version of a sailor suit, and not bothering about or bothered by boys. No, not fifteen. Twelve. At fifteen Bess Fenstermacher had reported, Lalie had already started mensing, had been mensing for over a year. Why did they have to grow up and all? Well, they did, and it was nature.

Harvey Fenstermacher put up no serious objections when Bessie favored an understanding between Lalie and George Lockwood. As far as he was concerned, an understanding could go on forever—though he knew better—or it could end in a few weeks. Understandings were harmless if the parents exercised a little extra vigilance, and he could count on Bess to take care of that. But then after Christmas Harvey Fenstermacher was unexpectedly reminded of the other, permanent and final possibilities that an understanding could imply. In his professional life he could have managed postponements and given his law clerk some investigative work to do; but now Bess was prevailing upon him to give his quick consent to an engagement. She wanted Lalie to marry this Lockwood boy, and she wanted no interference from Harvey Fenstermacher. "We don't know so much about him," said Harvey.

"Maybe *we* don't, but *I* do. I made inquiries, and you can bet your boots he's as good as there is in Lebanon, or better. The father is worth up in the millions, the mother was one of those Hoffners from Richterville. You stay out of this, Harvey, and don't ruin Lalie's chances."

"I don't have anything against the boy, but what's the hurry yet?"

"The hurry is there is no hurry," said Bess. "The hurry was last summer when I made them have an understanding. Now the understanding time is over and the engagement time starts. You don't go out in the yard and shake a George Lockwood out of the pear tree. You should hear David on how lucky Lalie is. David considers himself honored if George Lockwood gives him the time of day, that's what David thinks of him."

"Is he that friendly with David? Maybe he'd do something for the boy."

"This isn't your politics, Harvey. Don't monkey around. Let's get Lalie engaged and married."

If that was how Bess felt about it, Harvey Fenstermacher was not going to oppose her. She was pretty sharp in some things, and if Lalie was ready to get married, let her mother take the full responsibility. In a way he had said goodbye to Lalie when she was fifteen. Or twelve. He did not really know this female woman who said she was in love with this Lockwood boy. Let her marry and go away, and then bring him some grandchildren. It would be nice to have some grandchildren. Cute little buggers they'd be.

So it rested until the day of George Lockwood's formal request for Lalie's hand. Harvey Fenstermacher tried to be agreeable, tried his best, but Lockwood rubbed him the wrong way. The fellow did not talk like a Pennsylvanian, he dressed too old for a college senior, he had artificial manners. He was like one of those out-of-town lawyers that came into Harvey Fenstermacher's court for Iron Company cases. They were over-prepared, insolently polite, and if they lost they always appealed. They treated his court like a way-station on the Fort Penn, Richterville & Lantenengo. Lawyer in his court or suitor in his home, George Lockwood rubbed Harvey Fenstermacher the wrong way, and the quarrel which happened to be over son David and the club situation at Princeton was inevitable; they might just as easily have quarreled over something else, and honestly admitting this to himself, Harvey Fenstermacher was troubled.

He had pretended all was well, but he felt hypocritical, miserable. If it was possible to justify what he was about to do, he would justify it, but justified or not, he was determined to keep Lockwood from marrying Lalie.

Within two weeks from the time of the Sunday quarrel Harvey Fenstermacher had all the justification he needed, and there was sweet triumph over Bess to make the justification more than complete. Ironically, she had furnished him with one of his leads; conveniently, right in Lebanon.

On the way home from the court house Harvey Fenstermacher always passed Vic Hoffner's ice cream parlor-candy store, occasionally stopping to pick up a brick of ice cream or a box of candy. Vic was a prosperous merchant, a good Mason, a Godfearing member of the Reformed Church, although not ever a visitor to the Fenstermacher residence.

"Afternoon, Vic."

"Afternoon, Judge. Half a pound of jordan almonds, pound of chocolate nougats. A day early this week. Must of had company Sunday, say?"

"Uh-huh. Company. If you got a half a minute, Vic?" said Harvey Fenstermacher. It was not unusual for the two men to speak in private on lodge and church matters. They seated themselves on bentwire chairs in the rear of the establishment.

"All right, we're private," said Hoffner.

"You're related to a family named Lockwood over in Lantenengo County," said Fenstermacher.

"Distantly. Only distantly. I know the family you mean. That's the young fellow come in here with Lalie. Well, his mother was a Richterville Hoffner, and me and her father are first cousins. She was, uh, uh, Adelaide Hoffner and married this Abraham Lockwood. I was to the wedding. They's married back, oh, I don't know, twenty-five-so years ago."

"Tell me all you can."

"Well, you mean about the Lockwood side? Swedish Haven is their town. Very well-to-do. I heard he was a millionaire, Abraham Lockwood, and I wouldn't doubt it. You want everything, Harvey?"

"All you can tell me."

"Well, Levi Hoffner, my cousin, he had these six daughters and he was well-off, too. But I don't remember him being too pleased with Adelaide marrying Lockwood, rich or no rich. Now I have to think a minute . . . Ah, yes. Abraham Lockwood had a father, and where he come from I'm not reliable. I did know, but I forgot. Anyhow, the father of Abraham Lockwood murdered a fellow in broad daylight."

"Murdered a fellow?"

"Well, he shot him dead and he stood trial for it. They

must have the records of it in Gibbsville. Isn't Gibbsville the county seat over in Lantenengo?"

"Yes, and it doesn't surprise me, anything that happens over there."

"Me either. Some of those mining villages, they have a murder every payday. Irish Mollie Maguires, they call them."

"Oh, sure. I remember *them* very well."

"Well, Lockwood got off free, but then he killed another fellow. No! No, it was the other way around. He killed one fellow first, and they couldn't prove it. I think that was what Levi said. Then the second time he killed a fellow, they hauled him into court. But he went free."

"This was the father of Abraham Lockwood? The grandfather of the young fellow that's been in here with Lalie?"

"You have right. But there's more yet. This they didn't find out till Adelaide was married. Now let me think a little . . . Ah, yes. Lockwood, Abraham, was all right in the head, but his mother not and his sisters not. The sisters they had to put away. Oh, yes! Now I remember! The one sister was in the crazy-house and the other they didn't put her in till the wedding was over."

"And the mother?"

"You'll have to ask, Harvey. Here my memory is not so good on. But she was wheely. You know, going around in her head the wheels. Slang."

Harvey Fenstermacher nodded. "Does your wife know all this?"

"No. I wasn't a married man then and I never said nothing to her about any Lockwood."

"Well, she got this far without hearing it . . ."

"I'm not a talker, Harvey. Don't you worry."

To obtain court records from Lantenengo County would take some time, and Harvey Fenstermacher was not even sure that he liked having his confidential law clerk acquire so much information about a prospective son-in-law. And what was the use? He did not want legal documentation; what he had got from Vic Hoffner was enough for his purpose. He took the train to Reading and from there to Swedish Haven.

Abraham Lockwood's offices were in a small one-story brick building in the business district of Swedish Haven. There was a brass plate on the front door, and there were dark green curtains on rings that slid on a brass rail, shutting off pedestrians' view of the interior. The legend on the brass plate was Lockwood & Company, Est. 1835. It was a substantial-looking place, and just inside the door there was a polished walnut fence as a reminder to visitors that they were not free to proceed unannounced.

"I wish to see Mr. Abraham Lockwood," said Harvey Fenstermacher. "Here is my card."

A middle-aged woman in a shirtwaist and skirt, wearing a fleur-de-lis watch and oilcloth sleeve covers, said: "Judge Harvey Fenstermacher, Lebanon, Pennsylvania. So? Will you kindly take a seat, Judge?"

"I'd rather stand, thank you."

The woman went back to a private office, and Harvey Fenstermacher saw a man at a roll-top desk take the card, look up, and look out toward the visitor. The man signaled to Harvey Fenstermacher to come back to his office.

"Good morning, Judge Fenstermacher," said Abraham Lockwood. He was a tall thin fellow and a bit of a dude; the cut of his suit was not unusual, but it was light grey and had satin facing on the lapels, and he wore a gold question mark as a stickpin in his Ascot. He had a Greek-letter fraternity pin on his waistcoat. Lockwood kept a hand on the doorknob and waved Fenstermacher to a chair with the other hand. Accidentally or by design he was not offering to shake hands.

"Good morning to you, sir," said Fenstermacher. He waited for Lockwood to sit down, observing the manner in which Lockwood flicked aside the skirt of his coat.

"Offer you a cigar, Judge?"

"Not this early in the day, thank you."

"In town for the day? Of course I've heard about you from my son George."

"George is what I came to see you about."

"Well, that doesn't surprise me, Judge. I guess matters have proceeded pretty fast with our young people. Mrs. Lockwood had a letter from George day before yesterday."

"Saying?"

"Saying that he'd proposed to your daughter and been accepted."

"Is that the first you heard of it?"

"The first I knew that it had gotten to that stage. The young people today seem to take things into their own hands more than we ever did."

"Some do, some don't."

"Yes, I guess that's true. George does. I always encouraged George to be self-reliant, and he is. That makes it easier for me, in a way. Because when I pull in the reins he knows I mean it, and we have no arguments about it. I don't often have to speak to him twice."

"I see. Then maybe that makes things easier all around. My daughter was taught to obey but we didn't do it the same way you did. We gave her her orders every day of her life."

"Well, that was your way, and we had ours, and both ways work," said Lockwood. He suddenly leaned forward. "The question is, Judge, what is it that's made easier all around?"

"Uh-huh. You're a clever man, Mr. Lockwood."

"A busy member of the bar doesn't just accidentally pay a call on a business man sixty miles away. Clever? Well, I inherited some horse sense from my father."

"What else? I don't mean money."

"What else did I inherit? Is that what you came to see me about?"

"Partly."

Abraham Lockwood got up and stood at the window. "You don't like clever men, do you, Judge?"

"No, I don't."

"Very well, since you've already called me clever, I have nothing to lose, so I'll be clever. You want to stop this marriage because you've been digging into our family history." He turned around and faced Fenstermacher. "All right. I'll stop it."

"How?"

"That's none of your damn business, Judge. Your business is to go back to your little pile of shit in Lebanon and crow like a rooster."

"Don't you talk to me like that, you—"

"What will you do? Fine me for contempt of court? Get out before I kick you out, you dumb Dutch bastard. And keep your distance or I'll brain you with this poker." Lockwood balanced the poker from his fireplace.

"You got already two murders in your family," said Harvey Fenstermacher. "I found out what I want to know." He shook his fist at Abraham Lockwood. "Set foot in Lebanon County once, Mister," he said, and left.

"You'll never get the truth out of your old man," said Ned O'Byrne. "Neither will Lalie out of her old man. But it stands to reason that Judge Fenstermacher went there with a chip on his shoulder. He's the one that went to Swedish Haven, not your old man to Lebanon."

"My father's pretty clever sometimes. He could outfox the judge, if he wanted to. But I wonder if he wanted to."

"Oh. You think your old man was against this marriage?" said O'Byrne. "Why?"

"Ah, that's where he's clever, my father," said George Lockwood. "He never lets anybody know what he's thinking, or why he does anything."

O'Byrne looked quickly at his friend; it was the first time in their four years' acquaintance that he had heard George Lockwood speak of anyone in such tones of innocent admiration. It silenced O'Byrne's ready irreverence.

Agnes Wynne was not a member of the main, Thomas Wynne line, but as a second cousin and the only living female of her generation she partook of the benefits and protection that went with the name. Her father was always taken care of with some job in the Wynne Coal Company that did not require a technical knowledge of coal mining. He was paymaster at one colliery, purchasing agent at another, assistant superintendent in charge of outside—surface—work at two of the larger operations. Before he was thirty years old he realized that the name Wynne, that had got him his jobs, also kept him from enjoying the complete trust of the men he worked with. The company spy was to be found in all grades of coal mining personnel, and while the employes he dealt with were not actively hostile to this gentle, amiable man, they never could forget that he was a Wynne. This, of course, was understandable when the jobs he held kept him in daily contact with the men who worked with their hands, but conditions did not greatly change when he became assistant superintendent. A superintendent always had his eye on the colliery next above, and the superintendents of the largest collieries were ambitious for general managerships and vice-presidencies. Every superintendent's secretary always knew more about a colliery than Assistant Superintendent Theron B. Wynne, the cousin of Old Tom. But there was no place else to go, and Theron Wynne knew it, and so he went fishing at the company dams and wherever he could find an unpolluted stream; he painted his pictures of the breakers and the culm banks, and once or twice a year he would be off to Wilkes-Barre or Gibbsville for a three-day drunk. One advantage of being a Wynne was that he could tell his boss beforehand that he was taking a few days off on private business, and since he was not indispensable, no questions were asked. On his return he would always have nice presents for his wife and for Agnes, and Bessie Wynne would thank God that no harm had come to this defeated man, with his frail body and his awkward efforts to make people fond of him. He could tell Bessie, and no one else, that in college he had wanted to become a missionary, but his older cousin was footing the bills for his education and expected him to go to work for the Wynne Coal Company. He had failed Cousin Tom while still in college, when a physician said he could never work inside a mine and should therefore abandon the thought of studying to be a civil engineer specializing in mining. The defeat of Theron Wynne was accomplished early in life, for he had also failed himself for the same reason, health, that prevented his fulfilling his secret ambition to bring Christianity and the Presbyterian doctrines to the black man in Africa. Sometimes, watching the men quitting the mine at the end of a shift, Theron Wynne sardonically observed that the faces and hands of the miners were blackened as dark as any he would have preached to in the jungles; their faces were as black and their resistance to his preaching would have been as firm; but Theron Wynne made no attempt to convert the Irish and Lithuanians and Poles. His own faith was shaky, as frail as his body. As the years passed and he did not die, he discovered that his constitution had acquired the habit of staying alive and become equal to the few demands he put upon it. He could walk many miles through the woods if he did not hurry, and his semi-annual debauches in Wilkes-Barre and Gibbsville seemed to exact no more than a temporary distress. Even his conscience ceased to trouble him two days after he got home and was once again in the routine of respectability. He loved Bessie and was gratefully fascinated by her love for him and for her having made him a fully functioning man. But his love for Bessie was not comparable to the love he breathed for his daughter.

The mystery of Agnes Wynne had no beginning; he accepted as fact the evidence that by making love to Bessie he had started a life that grew until it was ready to be expelled from Bessie's body, but from his first sight of this thing that was his child he understood that the changes in himself had already begun; he did not know when. Nor care. In a little while his first sight of her was also lost in the past, as had been the love-making, as had been Bessie's uncertainty and then conviction that she was carrying a child. The presence of his daughter in his life enabled him to admit that he had not wanted a son; he had been ashamed to admit that even to himself while Bessie was carrying Agnes, but he could confess to himself after Agnes was born that he had been *afraid* his child would be a boy. When a boy grew up he would expect his father to be strong and forceful and talented in ways that Theron B. Wynne was not. That boy would have been embarrassed by his father. The possibility that a second child would be a male was less frightening to Theron Wynne; Agnes would be there to stand between her father and the critical, disappointed glances of her brother. But the breeding capacities of Bessie and Theron Wynne were exhausted in Agnes, and she remained unique in her father's experience.

Bessie Wynne did all the hard things that were necessary to the raising of the child; the disciplining, the punishments. But Bessie in her wisdom and contentment was satisfied to have Theron appear to be benevolent, provident, loving, as though in his place as father and husband he were above the hard things. He in turn conceded nearly all authority to Bessie. "It's no use going to your father," she would say to the child. "He's as strict as I am." The child was taught not to test her father's strictness, and the myth became in a practical sense a reality: Agnes believed that her father was the true source of strength in the family, and his favors and amiability were made to seem like rewards.

It was a quiet household, wherever they happened to be living, in whatever Company house they inhabited. Until Theron was an assistant superintendent the Wynnes had no hired girl; once a week they had a woman in to do the washing, and Agnes was brought up to help with the household chores. Later there was always a hired girl as well as a Monday-and-Tuesday woman for the washing and ironing Theron paid no rent in the Company houses, and nearly everything he needed for himself and his family could be bought wholesale through the Company stores—food, clothing, their Chickering upright piano, his fishing tackle, his art supplies. Coal for their stove and furnace was delivered free of charge, and Theron Wynne had the use of a horse and buggy or cutter as a privilege of his rank. The social standing of the family was doubly automatic; they were Wynnes, and Theron Wynne's jobs were always considered office jobs.

Agnes was sixteen before her second cousin Tom Wynne got what he called a real good look at her, and what he saw he liked. "Theron, you know who this girl looks like? She looks like Aunt Agnes."

"Well, that's who we named her after, Cousin Tom."

"You look like your grandmother, girl. Pity you never saw her. You remember Theron's mother, Bessie?"

"I sure do, Cousin Tom. But I don't want you to spoil this one telling her she resembled Grandmother Wynne. Don't want to turn her head."

"They won't turn this one's head, will they, girl? You look

to me like a pretty sensible young lady Where you got her in school, Bessie?"

"Here. Hilltop High School."

"Uh-huh. What are you taking, girl?"

"Which course? The four-year. I'm a junior."

"I'm in favor of that. You intend to give her a year away at boarding school, Theron?"

"After she finishes High, we might."

"You didn't say what subjects you're taking, girl."

"The regular four-year course. This year I'm taking geometry. Plane geometry. Latin—Cicero, that is English First-year French. High School Civics. And drawing."

"Keep you busy? You passing everything?"

"Yes sir," said the girl.

"*Tell* Cousin Tom," said Theron Wynne. "She has the highest marks of any girl in her class, and the best of anybody, boys or girls, in Latin and French."

"Conduct? I guess I don't have to ask that."

"Oh—all right, I guess," said the girl.

"*Tell* him, he wants to know," said Theron Wynne. "She has the highest mark in Deportment, too. That's Conduct. She never had anything but 'A,' all through High."

"I knew it. You can tell by looking at her. Theron, I recommend you and Bessie don't wait till she finishes Hilltop High. Send her to boarding school. Young lady, will you excuse yourself while your father and mother and I have a talk?"

"Yes sir. Excuse me," said Agnes, leaving them.

"Do you realize this is the only female Wynne of her age? Her generation. I'm going to do something for this girl. I like the cut of her jib. Good manners. Neat and clean. And I had no idea she was so smart. You pick out a good school, and I'll foot the bills."

"Oh, Cousin Tom . . ." Bessie Wynne began to cry.

"Hell, I put her father through Lafayette and he didn't disappoint me the way some other relations have. You know who I'm talking about. My own son, yet to do an honest day's work. The money he cost me, I'd like to see my money do some good for a change. You pick out a good school and we'll sit down and figure out the cost and I'll put that money in the Hilltop bank, in case some Union hooligan takes a shot at me."

"Oh, they wouldn't do that, Cousin Tom," said Bessie Wynne.

"They wouldn't, eh? You must think the Mollies are a thing of the past. Maybe you don't hear about them so much any more, but I never go anywhere without a pistol in my pocket, let me tell you. The Molly Maguires had big families, don't forget, and my brother Albert helped to hang some of them . . . Anyhow, you pick out a school for Agnes, and Theron, you write me a letter." He brought his voice down to a whisper. "Don't want her to get interested in boys. Hilltop High School. Boys, Wrong ideas. Calf-love. Marry some Schwakie."

"I know," said Bessie Wynne.

"Well, you decide," said Cousin Tom. "And Theron, I'll hear from you in a day of two."

"You bet, Cousin Tom," said Theron Wynne. "And I wish I knew how to—"

"Good, sensible girl. And has looks, into the bargain," said Cousin Tom Wynne. "I have to be going."

Agnes was taken out of Hilltop High after junior year and enrolled at Miss Dawson's in Overbrook, where, like herself, most of the boarders were girls who had had a year or two in a public high school. The day pupils were the daughters of nearby Overbrook, Chestnut Hill, and Germantown families, and many of them would be leaving Miss Dawson's for New England and Southern boarding schools for the final two years. As a result there was a constant turnover in the student body that made life interesting for the girls but did not make for efficiency among the teachers. The good ones did not stay long. "This place is like the Broad Street Station," said one teacher in parting. But to Agnes Wynne and her parents and to the citizens of Hilltop and the other coal towns Miss Dawson's was a fashionable finishing school that put the finishing school stamp on its girls and set them apart from the girls who were going to Wilson and Goucher and Hood and Bryn Mawr, the bluestockings, who went to college because they wanted to go into competition with men.

Cousin Tom Wynne, for all his admiration of Agnes's brains, did not volunteer to continue her education, although she graduated from Miss Dawson's at the head of her class. She had made good, and it was time for her to come home and wait for a suitable husband. Cousin Tom Wynne sponsored her by giving a dance at his house, to which were invited all the coal and lumber and beer and whiskey and legal and medical plutocracy of the area.

George Lockwood was not invited to the dance. Swedish Haven, although it was only a few miles from Gibbsville, was not considered to belong to the coal region. It was the last Pennsylvania Dutch town on the way northward, and Gibbsville was the first coal town. It made no difference that George Lockwood was only half Pennsylvania Dutch; he belonged to Swedish Haven, whatever his name. In Swedish Haven you heard Pennsylvania Dutch spoken more than English; in Gibbsville even the families of German ancestry were letting the patois die, while they adapted themselves to the New England Yankee influence that had always prevailed. George Lockwood, of Swedish Haven, got to the Thomas Wynne dance because he was a Princeton man who was in the Wynneville neighborhood for a Princeton wedding.

It was the year after the breaking of his engagement to Lalie Fenstermacher. He was living at home, getting started on the task of taking over his father's business interests. Abraham Lockwood systematically acquainted George with the real estate holdings in the town and the farm properties in the rural area; the bank, the distillery, the coal-dredging operations in the river—and the portfolio of shares in distant enterprises. Instead of a liberal allowance Abraham Lockwood put his son on the Lockwood payroll and gave him a desk in the Lockwood & Company office. Father and son walked to work together every day and had noon dinner together at their table in the Exchange Hotel. By degrees Abraham Lockwood transferred responsibility and then ownership of minor properties to his son, and in a year's time George Lockwood was already a well-to-do man in his own right. He was also, without realizing it, becoming more and more involved in the affairs of Lockwood & Company and in the advancement of the Lockwood Concern. He was a beloved son, in whom his father was well pleased. His mother could not stand the sight of him; he was replicating the original Abraham Lockwood with an eager innocence that she found as distasteful as though he had set out to taunt her. Adelaide Lockwood was sickened and then sick as she watched her son adopt his father's mannerisms and try to overtake him, sometimes successfully, in cleverness. Abraham Lockwood was delighted and proud when George produced schemes to save money or make it; he would overlook the unsuccessful ones and overpraise the effectual. And always the father consciously and the mother vaguely were observing the son's seduction by the Concern. This thing, whatever it was, that Abraham was trying to engineer was no longer resisted by Adelaide. She had given up on George, and she was only half-hearted in her attempts to hold on to Penrose. The younger son, now a freshman at Princeton, would succumb to George's influence as George had succumbed to his father's, and Adelaide Lockwood caught one cold after another until a particularly heavy congestion developed into pleurisy and death. She could look back and find only one triumph over the Lockwoods: she had made her father-in-law take down that wall.

Not a man or woman in Swedish Haven knew that it was not pus in the chest that had caused her death. There was no diagnosis of hatred or chagrin or frustration, and of the three tall men who stood at Adelaide's graveside the younger two seemed grieved and baffled. The oldest man seemed only grieved, but then he *was* older and the aging learn to accept the inevitable. A nice stained glass window eventually was installed in the Lutheran Church in Adelaide's memory. Pastor Bollinger was secretly grateful that Abraham Lockwood wanted no special ceremony dedicating the window; Bollinger had his doubts about how many parishioners would attend a dedication, and what could you say about a woman who would never be missed?

The widower and the bereaved son made a handsome pair on their marches between home and office, and with the departure of Adelaide Lockwood from the local scene, the all-male Lockwood establishment created less resentment than hitherto had been the case. Abraham and his son George kept pretty much to themselves, as the Lockwoods had always done, but the citizens were beginning to look upon Abraham and George Lockwood as something more than individuals; they represented, or George represented, the family's third generation in the town; three generations of money, two generations of money with style, higher education, military service, imposing connections in Gibbsville and Philadelphia, and a continuity of residence in the town and of increasing earning power. The two men walking together, father and son, were now being spoken of in not altogether unfavorable tones as "our aristocracy." Bigger towns had their aristocracy, and now Swedish Haven discovered it had one of its own. The aloofness that had been resented during Adelaide's lifetime was now permissible and even admirable in the all-male Lockwood family. The Concern had been expedited by the departure of the female member of the family, and now Abraham Lockwood was ready to proceed to the next phase.

The Fenstermacher fiasco, he decided, was a lucky accident. A union with the Lebanon County Fenstermachers, headed by a judge, had at first glance offered some advantages; but from his own experience Abraham Lockwood became convinced that the Concern would be better served if George could find a suitable wife who was not Pennsylvania Dutch. The Pennsylvania Dutch knew how to hold on to their money and to make more, and they were extremely respectable when they got rich; but they were stodgy. They were middle-class Germans and with few exceptions they so remained, generation after generation. Adelaide and her family had pre-Revolutionary roots, and had been rich for more than a century; but no one even in jesting tones had ever called them aristocratic. They had shown no disposition to capitalize on their long American history or their generations of wealth. The first member of Adelaide's family to have the look of an aristocrat was her son George, and it had taken Lockwood blood to achieve that. If George went to the Pennsylvania Dutch for a wife, his children might turn out to be Hoffners, and the Lockwood Concern would be dissolved in a single generation. Abraham Lockwood was determined that next time he would be more vigilant from the beginning when George took an interest in a young woman. Meanwhile he would consolidate his position in the boy's esteem, which he would do by companionability, sensible generosity, and tokens of respect for his son's judgment, and at the same time exercising early caution in the control of George's relations with young women. The boy was concupiscent and susceptible, his father knew, and obviously attractive. He had to be watched. Fortunately he had gone through college without becoming a boozer.

Abraham Lockwood was careful not to turn into a bore. At the office he kept the boy busy and on many days they would have no conversation from eight-thirty until noon, so that the dinner hour was a recess for both. "How would you like to go to the crew races next week?"

"Next week? I'm sorry, Father, but that's the week I'm going to that wedding," said George.

"What wedding is that? Who's getting married?"

"A fellow in my club, a fellow named Lassiter, is marrying a girl whose name I forget. They both live near Hazleton "

"Franklin M. Lassiter's son?"

"Yes. Coal-mining."

"Oh, I know that. The Lassiters. The Wynnes. Well, you ought to have a good time up there. Those coal millionaires know how to spend their money."

"Yes, I'm catching a train here, stopping just for me. A special train that starts in Philadelphia, picks up fellows along the way. Sleeping cars, a diner, and a chair car. We use the train as a hotel while we're up there."

"There was no such luxury when I was your age Well, I'm sorry you'll miss the crew races but you'll have a better time where you're going."

"See what you missed by not going to Princeton?"

"It might surprise you to know that when I was at the University we used to feel sorry for the Princeton fellows. We were in a city, don't forget."

"Yes, I'll bet you were a gay blade."

"On that subject, silence is golden, my boy. I prefer you to have some illusions about your father."

"All right, if you have yours about me."

"None. Absolutely none. But have your good time now."

At the last minute Thomas Wynne extended a blanket invitation to the young gentlemen in town for the Lassiter-Powell wedding, and they were conveyed to the Wynne estate in mule-drawn buses. The Wynne gardens were lit by Japanese lanterns and a special pavilion had been erected for the dancing. The pavilion, in approximately the shape of a Chinese pagoda, was assembled on a slope just below the Wynne mansion and thus offered a view of the Company-owned Lake Wynne and of Lawyer—originally Loire—Valley. The location was remarkable, and visitors always exclaimed at its beauty. "You know *why* it's so pretty," Tom Wynne would reply. "All around here, to the east and the west and the south, are coal mines. No matter how you come here, by train or by team, you have to go through the mining patches. Then you get up here and you don't see a single breaker, no culm banks anywhere. That takes you by surprise, and that's the way I want it to be. Some day after I'm dead and gone they'll sink a shaft there where you see that little village, they'll start cutting timber. But as long as I have any say it stays this way."

In the twilight before Agnes Wynne's dance George Lockwood listened to the old man's set speech. "You might say it's a very expensive view," said George Lockwood.

Thomas Wynne turned to him. "Yes, if you want to reckon it in dollars and cents it is, young man. You're Mr. Phillips?"

"No sir, this is Mr. Phillips. My name is Lockwood. This is Phillips, this is McCormick, this is—"

"Uh-huh, uh-huh, uh-huh," interrupted the old man. "I knew the others, I didn't know Phillips and you. Lockwood. Are you in business, or you still studying?"

"I'm in business with my father."

"Would that be Abraham Lockwood? Over in Swedish Haven?"

"Yes sir."

"I know the name," said Tom Wynne. "Well, gentlemen, I trust you enjoy yourselves." He left the group to mingle with other guests before the serving of dinner.

The evening was well along before George Lockwood's turn to dance with the guest of honor came, and she was beginning to run out of small talk. More accurately, she was tiring of repeating the same small talk to so many strangers ". . . And you're with the wedding?" she said, wearily. "Mary was such a pretty bride."

"She was no such thing, but as long as Pudge thinks so," said George Lockwood.

"I don't think that's a very nice thing to say about your friend's fiancée. Wife."

"Well, if you'd said Pudge was a handsome bridegroom I wouldn't have agreed with that, either. He's a good fellow, but you must admit, not an Adonis."

"I look for more than that in my friends," said Agnes.

"I know. Fortunately *they* don't *have* to look for more than that in you."

"Is that a compliment, or are you implying that they wouldn't find any more?"

"It was meant as a compliment. I wouldn't say anything uncomplimentary at this stage of the game."

"At this stage of the game? What makes you think there'll ever be any other stage of the *game*, as you call it?"

"I withdraw that, Miss Wynne. I don't suppose I'll ever see you again after this evening. Your grandfather didn't like me, either, by the way."

"My grandfather? Where did you ever know my grandfather? And which one? They're both dead."

"I thought that was your grandfather, the man that's giving this ball."

"He's my cousin. My father's first cousin. Why didn't he like you? What did you say to him?"

"To be truthful, I think it was my father he doesn't like. As soon as I mentioned my father's name, Mr. Wynne ended the conversation. Although it could have been me, of course I'm not famous for buttering people up."

"No, I shouldn't think you were. Not that buttering people up is very commendable."

"But I can make enemies without saying a word."

"But you don't leave it to chance, do you? You do say a word, don't you? I think you want people to dislike you. What you said about Mary was unnecessary. And what you said about Pudge."

"Why would I want people to dislike me? You, for instance. You're the belle of the ball, besides being the guest of honor. And I gave you one sincere compliment that you twisted around. You didn't have to do that."

"I don't like to get personal on such short acquaintance."

"I'm humbly apologetic, Miss Wynne, and I trust you'll forget the whole incident." The waltz ended here, Agnes took his arm, and he escorted her to a group of young people. During the remainder of the evening he saw her glancing at him from time to time, neither smiling nor with hostility, but unquestionably conscious of him.

There was a picnic next day at the Lake Wynne boathouse, the concluding event of the wedding and ball festivities. The guests were all young people, chaperoned by Theron and Bessie Wynne, the nominal host and hostess. The water was very cold, and no one went bathing, but most of the guests took turns in the rowboats. Thus George Lockwood found himself alone with Theron and Bessie Wynne at a picnic table.

"Well, I guess you'll all be glad to get home and get some sleep," said Theron Wynne. "How far do you have to go, Mr. Lockwood?"

"I'm getting off at the second stop, Swedish Haven. First stop Gibbsville, then Swedish Haven."

"Oh, yes. Swedish Haven. I've never been there. I've gone through it on the train, many times, but never got off. Isn't that where my friend Jacob Bollinger is? The minister? My friend—I haven't seen Jake in years, but we were friends in college."

"Pastor of the Lutheran Church, yes."

"I used to love to hear him talk. When he came to college you could hardly understand him, he was so Dutch."

"Still is."

"Do you speak Pennsylvania Dutch?"

"A few words, and I can count in it. My mother was Pennsylvania Dutch. Richterville."

"Oh, yes. That's in Lebanon County?"

"No, it's still in Lantenengo, but just over the line."

"The last time I saw Jake Bollinger he'd just been called to the Lutheran Church in Swedish Haven, and I asked him if he expected to find a lot of sinful people there. He said no, but there was one family that the head of it had committed two murders, and got off scot-free. I didn't think such things happened among the Pennsylvania Dutch. That sounded more like us in the coal regions."

George Lockwood rose. "The next time you see Reverend Bollinger you must get him to tell you the name of that family."

"Oh, then it's true? I thought Jake might have been pulling my leg. He had a peculiar sense of humor for a preacher. Sly little jokes."

"I know the family very well. Will you excuse me? I'm in the next boat."

Theron Wynne's letter arrived a week later.

Dear Mr. Lockwood:

I am writing to offer my deepest apologies for the unfortunate remarks I made Sunday last at the picnic at Lake Wynne. I cannot find words to tell you how sorry I am that my blundering, loose tongue could have inflicted such pain. To make matters worse, your gentlemanly restraint in the face of such stupid scandal-mongering set an example to me, although you are the younger man whereas I am more than old enough to be your father. I would give anything I possess to be able to make amends or to in some way wipe out all recollection of my words. In conclusion I can only say that never in my life have I been so abject in my apologies and expression of my regret. I trust you will find it in your heart to in time forgive my blunder. I remain,

Yours very truly,
Theron B. Wynne

George Lockwood read the letter twice and tossed it in the wastebasket. A week passed, and he got another letter from Hilltop, Pa.

Dear Mr. Lockwood:

I take the liberty of writing to you because whatever my father said to you at the picnic, he did not mean it. I know that he has written you a letter of apology but he is still upset by what he said. He will not tell me what it was because he said it was so "awful." My mother also refuses to discuss it with me as my father has forbidden her to repeat what he said to you. Whatever he said, I have never seen him so upset and I know it is preying on his mind. I would be extremely grateful if you would accept his apology (if you can do so) and write him a note to that effect. You don't know my father but I assure you that in all his life he has never intentionally caused anyone harm, he is too gentle and kind to hurt anyone.

Sincerely yours,
Agnes Wynne

He was rereading her letter in his office when his father came to leave for the noon meal. "Feminine stationery," said Abraham Lockwood. "Did you make a conquest?"

"Maybe, maybe not," said George Lockwood.

Theron Wynne's letter had if anything annoyed George Lockwood more than the blunder; George Lockwood had been annoyed, irritated, angered, but that had passed, and the letter only served to remind him of the blunder and repeat the annoyance. It was, moreover, undignified of a middle-aged man to be, as he said, so abject, and George Lockwood failed to answer the letter because he felt Theron Wynne did not deserve an answer. But the letter from Agnes Wynne was from Agnes Wynne. Until her letter there had been no reason or excuse or opportunity to see her again. Now that was changed.

Dear Mr. Wynne:
I wish to thank you for your letter. I assure you that I bear no "hard feelings" as to the things that were said at the picnic, knowing that no harm was intended. I have often been in the same predicament myself. I am planning to visit Wilkes-Barre and Hilltop on business in the near future and trust that I may have the pleasure of seeing Mrs. Wynne and yourself and charming daughter. I remain,

Sincerely yours,
George Lockwood

It made no difference that George Lockwood had no business to transact in Wilkes-Barre or Hilltop. Three days after he mailed his letter he was urgently invited to break his journey with an overnight stop at Lake Wynne, where the Theron Wynnes had a summer cottage.

The foolishly pathetic joy of the forgiven bungler was all over Theron Wynne's pinched little face, and Bessie Wynne was pleased because her husband was pleased. They seemed to think he had come to see them, and he was not left alone with Agnes until after supper. "I have to be at the colliery at seven A.M., so I hope you'll excuse me if I go to bed with the chickens."

"It's nice being here at the cottage, but the only objection is Mr. Wynne has to get up an hour earlier," said Mrs. Wynne.

"Yes. I'd like to sit up and talk, but ha' past four comes early."

Mr. and Mrs. Wynne at last retired.

"You might have answered my letter, too," said Agnes.

"I wondered what was making you so stand-offish. So that was it? If you want the honest truth, I wouldn't be here if it hadn't been for your letter. That's my answer. I would have stayed on the outs with your father, but not with you."

"*I* wouldn't have *apologized.*"

"You wouldn't?"

"No. If you didn't have the good sense to know that what

he said wasn't deliberate. I mean if I'd said it. Or anyone. Nobody makes that kind of a faux pas intentionally."

"Nobody makes any faux pas intentionally. That's what a faux pas is, if I remember correctly. But people ought to be more careful what they say and who they say it to."

"Are you always that careful?"

"I thought you didn't know what your father said."

"I found out. He was so upset he finally told me," she said. "May I ask you a personal question? Did you ever know your grandfather?"

"Of course I knew him. I knew him very well. He used to tell me about the War. He was wounded at Bull Run."

"Was he *always* going around shooting people?"

"I could take umbrage at that."

"I can't help it. He sounds so different from the only man I really know well, my father."

"Oh, come now, Miss Wynne. The only man? I saw you at your ball, don't forget."

"Half of them I didn't know any better than I know you."

"You will, though."

"Don't know as I care to."

"Have you ever been kissed?"

"Certainly not."

"What's the matter with the local swains in this part of the world?"

"Nothing the matter with them. They know how to respect a lady, as gentlemen do everywhere."

"If I asked you for a kiss would you call for help?"

"No. But that's what your answer would be—no."

"Then if I *stole* a kiss?"

"Is that the real reason why you came here, Mr. Lockwood?"

"You're catching on. Yes."

"Then it's a good thing you're not staying long. I'd hate to think of you wasting your valuable time. I've heard that about Princeton men, that they have a very high opinion of themselves as heartbreakers. Dear me, to think that I should be so honored."

"Dishonored, don't you mean? You sound as though a harmless little kiss was the next thing to a seduction."

"Really, Mr. Lockwood. This is going too far."

"At least I see you know the meaning of the word."

"You can know the meanings of words without—I know what surgery means, too, but I don't care to undergo an operation."

"I wish I'd brought my chloroform."

"Your chloroform? I don't get your meaning."

"You mentioned surgery. Maybe if I had some chloroform with me I could put you to sleep and then I could kiss you."

"What an unpleasant thought. Your mind must be in the gutter, to have ideas like that."

"My mind is often in the gutter, but at least I'm willing to admit it."

"Anyone can tell that, just by listening to your conversation."

"When you get into your little bed tonight, think of me in my bed and only a thin wall separating us."

"*Good-night,* Mr. Lockwood." She was gone, but in a minute or so she came back, still angry. "Are you staying up, because otherwise I have to blow out the lamps."

"I'll blow them out. Will it bother you if I leave mine on in my bedroom? Will you be able to sleep?"

"I'm sure I'll be able to sleep, thank you."

For an hour after he went to bed he tapped his fingernail intermittently on the thin, varnished wall. At breakfast Bessie Wynne said, "Did you sleep well, Mr. Lockwood? Sometimes the first night in the woods people have a hard time getting to sleep."

"Slept like a top. Did you sleep well, Miss Wynne?"

"Me? Not very. I thought I heard a mouse or a rat."

"But you're not afraid of them," said her mother. "Some of the houses we've lived in when Mr. Wynne and I were first married."

"Oh, I'm not afraid of them but they keep me awake."

"Mr. Wynne said to say goodbye and tell you how nice it was to have you with us. And if you're coming up this way again, we wouldn't think of letting you stay in the hotel. At least not the one in Hilltop."

"Well, now I may take you up on that, Mrs. Wynne. I have to pay several visits around here this summer. My father makes me do most of the traveling now that he's getting on a bit."

"You must be a great help to your father," said Bessie Wynne.

"Thank you. And you'll be here all summer?"

"Yes, we have the cottage till the middle of September, then Cousin Tom Wynne keeps it open for his friends that go gunning. He has friends come from New York and Philadelphia and they stay till they all get a deer. One brought down a bear five or six years ago."

George Lockwood's undefined hope that Agnes Wynne

might show her gratitude—"extremely grateful," she had said in her letter—in an extreme gesture was, he now realized, foolishly romantic thinking on his part. Extremely and grateful were words without meaning to her; she might more truthfully have said, "I will thank you very much." But she was a puzzling girl, therefore an unusual one, and he had developed a theory (that had not, it is true, been tested) that an unusual girl could be seduced without matrimonial obligations. So far in his experience he had not achieved a seduction of a girl of good family. They were too well protected from seducers and from their own instincts. Lalie Fenstermacher had several times been only minutes away from giving in, and he had heard of one case of a Princeton acquaintance who had seduced a girl with the connivance of her brother. But when George Lockwood saw the girl in the flesh he ceased to regard his acquaintance as either a dashing or a lucky man, but rather as a fellow with a strong stomach. It was not then merely a question of seducing a girl of good family, but an attractive girl of good family. And Agnes Wynne was all of that. She was desirable, and it would be a real triumph to seduce her and then to abandon her to her rather haughty, somewhat intellectual independence.

Agnes was nineteen years old, notably slender among her contemporaries, so much so that George Lockwood would not ordinarily have singled her out for seduction. Her lack of voluptuousness in fact indicated to him that the eventual possession of her body was not the only pleasure he anticipated. He wanted to take her down a few pegs. He had found out her exact position in the Wynne dynasty, which would discourage fortune-hunters, but he had also seen that his own contemporaries liked her, enjoyed her company, and actually competed for her approval, and so at nineteen she probably would not stay single very long. As to her position among the Wynnes, although it was discouraging to the more impatient fortune-hunters, he had heard that she was the favorite female relative of old Tom Wynne and consequently had some prospects. On the other hand, there were many young men whom he had seen being attentive to Agnes and who would not have to marry for money. Any one of them might marry her in a year or two, and George Lockwood was not interested in being second. Love was nowhere in his arrangements.

Luck had provided the excuse and opportunity for his renewal of acquaintance with her, but now he would not trust to luck. It was not necessary. The invitation to revisit the cottage on the lake had come spontaneously from Theron and Bessie Wynne, and George Lockwood guessed that Agnes would not oppose her parents. Family cordiality existed, but not equality; it would have been unthinkable for her seriously to assert herself by that kind of independence—and he suspected that all her independence really amounted to nothing more than some originality of thinking. She was not deep, but only a little different from the others, as a Southern girl's accent made her seem different at a party in the North. He argued for and against her unusualness; was fascinated by it and repelled by it and denied its existence. But he found that whether she was deep or not, different or unusual or not, she occupied his thoughts as no girl had been able to since the parting with Lalie.

On his second overnight visit to the cottage on the lake she pointedly had taken off to visit friends in the northern part of the Commonwealth, near the New York line. He revealed no annoyance, but made himself charming with her father and mother and improved the shining hours by tapping Theron Wynne for information on the Wynne Company coal and timber resources. Coal leases and the mining of coal required special knowledge and considerable financial resources, and neither George Lockwood nor Abraham had any intention of investing in anthracite, but Lockwood & Company owned two small lumber and planing mills and their timber leases would soon be worthless, when the stands of timber were exhausted. New land would have to be found, and if there was no available acreage, the next best thing was to get a good price for the milling equipment. The visit was also an opportunity to collect information on the status of the Hofmans and Stokeses. Mostly by implication Abraham Lockwood had indoctrinated his elder son to be ready to take full advantage of any situation that would be profitable to the Lockwoods and costly to the Hofmans and Stokeses. There was nothing he could put his finger on, but George Lockwood accepted it as fact that his father hated his Gibbsville cousins. On George's part the feeling was not so intense, but when Theron Wynne, unaware of the kinship, remarked that the Stokes boys were somewhat less shrewd than Old Man Hofman, George Lockwood had an unprejudiced opinion that might some day be useful.

He timed his next visit for a month later, correctly assuming that Theron and Bessie Wynne would insist on Agnes's presence in order to avoid the appearance of rudeness. Transparently, as a protection, she had invited another girl to be a house guest. Ruth Hagenbeck was not a good choice for Agnes Wynne's purpose; she promptly developed a crush on George Lockwood, blushed when he spoke directly to her, and made non-sequitur interjections in the general conversation when she was at the table. At supper, for instance, Theron Wynne was saying: ". . . and the next year we moved to Hilltop."

"I think so too," said Ruth Hagenbeck.

"Beg pardon, Ruth?" said Theron Wynne.

Ruth Hagenbeck was staring at George Lockwood.

"*What* did you think, Miss Hagenbeck?" said George Lockwood.

"Oh, she wasn't thinking. She just wanted to have something to say," said Agnes Wynne.

"I don't think that's very nice, Agnes," said Bessie Wynne.

"Well, if she had something to say, nobody's stopping her. What were you going to say, Ruth?" said Agnes.

"Just for that I won't tell you," said Ruth Hagenbeck.

Theron Wynne resumed his story, and without warning Ruth got up and left the table.

"You hurt her feelings, Agnes. You go right in and tell her you're sorry," said Bessie Wynne.

Agnes Wynne was gone more than ten minutes. When she returned she said, "Ruth asks to be excused. She has a headache."

"From not eating, no wonder she has a headache," said Theron Wynne. "Take her in something on a tray, Agnes. Maybe some chicken broth."

"She wants to be left alone, Father."

"Oh. Well, too bad," said Theron Wynne.

"I'll go in see how she is after supper," said Bessie Wynne. She did so, and reported that Ruth was sound asleep and that it was likewise bedtime for herself and her husband. Once again Agnes was left alone with George Lockwood.

"You'd never be like Miss Hagenbeck, would you?"

"If you're going to say anything against her, she's one of my closest friends."

"I'm not going to say anything against *her*. It's against *you*. You're such a cold fish that you'd never get all flustered the way she did."

"I don't know what you mean by all flustered, and as far as your personal remarks are concerned, Mr. Lockwood, the less said the better."

"Miss Hagenbeck was very sweet. Very young and unsophisticated—"

"We're both the same age," said Agnes. "In fact she's nearly a year older than I am, if you must know."

"And she's flustered because I'm here."

"Weh-hell, I've never *heard* such egotism—that takes the cake, I must say."

"You're just as flustered as she is, only you show it in a different way. Such as going to Scranton when you heard I was coming."

"If you're referring to the time I went to Montrose, you had nothing to do with it."

"Would you swear that on the Bible? Here, here's the Bible. Put your hand on it and swear."

"Do no such thing. And what if I did go away because you were coming? I shouldn't think that's any proof that I was flustered by the great, charming, handsome Mr. George Lockwood. Quite the opposite, in fact. All that talk about stealing kisses, and worse."

"Worse? Oh, yes. Seduction."

"I just hope the rest of the younger men in Swedish Haven aren't like the one I've met. If you're any criterion, Mr. Lockwood, I feel sorry for any lady that has to live in that town."

"Be careful what you say. You may be living there some day."

"I'd rather die. I'd rather die. I'd sooner marry one of the hunkies than be married to you."

"Just for that I'm going to make you marry me."

"Not for all the money in Pennsylvania. The world."

"I haven't got all the money in Pennsylvania, but I'm going to wait till you marry me, I don't care how long it takes. And I forbid you to marry anyone else. I forbid you to give yourself to any other man but me. You're going to be my wife and nobody else's."

Home again he realized that in his anger he had said many things that he did not believe and would not have said except in anger. But having said them, having heard himself say them, he believed them. He began to believe, too, that his angry commitment was the right thing, and that the absence of love in the entire transaction made it a better thing, stronger and more sensible and unconfused by emotion. For the next few months she was constantly in his mind. There would be times when he found himself clenching and opening fists, and discovering that half his thoughts were on Agnes Wynne when he had not been aware he was thinking of her at all. His work did not suffer; on the contrary, he became more engrossed in it than hitherto, but Abraham Lockwood wondered.

That autumn both Presidential candidates were younger men than Abraham Lockwood, Bryan so much younger that biologically he could almost have been Abraham Lockwood's son; McKinley enough younger so that he could have been a pea-green freshman when Abraham Lockwood was a grand old senior. The outgoing President, Stephen Grover Cleveland, was Abraham Lockwood's age, and that seemed appropriate too, for Abraham Lockwood was tired and he was quitting. The task of acquainting George with details of the family holdings had been a stimulating one and a timely one; temporarily it had regenerated his own active interest in the Company, and almost daily some call had been made on his memory for details of the various family enterprises. But several times he had caught himself in errors, lapses that he did not confess to George. It was easier to let the errors cost a little money, if that had to be, or to lie to George. ("But Father, you told me thus-and-so." "No, George, quite the opposite. You got confused. I think I may be going too fast for you. No harm done, son. We all make mistakes, and you can't be expected to learn everything overnight.") Abraham Lockwood was not worried about money; there was now so much of it that both sons would be millionaires when he died. There was no one family or no conceivable alliance of Swedish Haven families that would challenge the Lockwood position. Abraham Lockwood's Concern now was financially secure, and on looking back he saw that it had been contemptibly easy to make the money that was the prime essential to the success of the Concern. The recurring fear that he would not live to see the human continuity of the Concern began to bother him seriously, the more so because he knew that George was not to be hurried in such matters—if in any matter.

It was a relief then to discover that George was interested in a young woman of the Wynne family. The discovery was made because of as well as in spite of George's silence on the subject: George had made several unexplained trips to the coal region, and had come back in a mood that in a young man explained itself. "Find out for me who your brother is enamored of," Abraham Lockwood wrote in a letter to Penrose Lockwood. "I am convinced there is someone, but his 'suit' is not meeting with success. Naturally I do not wish you to be blunt in your questioning or to reveal to him that I have expressed curiosity." Penrose was unimaginatively obedient, and the desired information was soon forthcoming.

"You were talking last summer about getting some timber leases," said Abraham Lockwood to George."

"Last fall, I believe it was."

"Yes, I believe it was. Well, has anything come of it?

There's a big future in lumber. The population's increasing. In the 1880 census we only had about fifty million. The 1890, only ten years later, it was over sixty million. A million a year. If that keeps up, George . . ."

"I haven't looked into it lately."

"Well, maybe you ought to, before they grab everything in sight."

"Who is they?"

"The big mills, the mining companies. Speculators like us."

"We could never do it on as big a scale as those people out in Minnesota."

"No, but we could cut timber here, in a modest way, and supply the local needs without paying those high freight rates from the Northwest. We could compete."

"Well, if you want me to, I'll have another look."

"Otherwise we'll soon have to sell our mills, and at a loss."

"What made you think of timber all of a sudden?"

"Whenever I go to a funeral I think of timber, George. I'm not getting any younger."

"Oh, Father, you'll live to be a hundred."

"I wish I thought so, son. But I buried three college classmates in the last year. Three in one year. We're dropping off fast . . . Have another look around and get some prices on timberland. Would you like me to go along with you?"

"No use you going to that trouble."

"Suppose I made some inquiries? Or would you rather I didn't? This was your idea, so I don't want to interfere."

"I'll look around some more," said George Lockwood.

His father had no excuse to invade the Wynne country, but he had fortified George Lockwood with an excuse to revisit the region on his own. The rapidity with which George availed himself of the opportunity told Abraham Lockwood what he wanted to know: that George wanted to see the Wynne girl again and needed only an excuse.

George Lockwood went to Hilltop, registered at the miserably uncomfortable hotel, and hired a rig with a driver, a garrulous Irishman named Kane. (George Lockwood was totally ignorant of the fact that his father had maneuvered him into a repetition of combining business with romance, as Abraham Lockwood had done with Adelaide Hoffner.) "Is it a sort of a surveyor you might be?" said Kane.

"You might say that," said George Lockwood.

"Is it moining properties then that—"

"No, not mining properties."

"Because I was about to say, not that I don't need the extra piece of change, mind you, but me conscience would never permit me to take your money under false *pre*tenses. The truth of the matter being, to all intents and purposes, Mr. Lockwood, you won't find a square acre for miles around that the mineral rights ain't spoken for be old Tom Wynne, God damn his murderous black heart."

"Murderous?"

"You're a stranger, so you wouldn't be up on the misfortunate slaughter of seven innocent men some twenty years back. The Wynnes and the like of them seen to it that seven innocent men were condemned to be hung."

"The Mollie Maguires?"

"Then you heard of them?"

"I never heard they were innocent."

"And you never will, if you listen to the Wynnes and them. But you never heard of the handprint on the wall of the Carbon County jail? I daresay you wouldn't of heard of that."

"No."

"No. Well there's the mark of a hand on the wall of a cell in Mauch Chunk prison, and how it got there is a story in itself. One of the condemned men, the morning of the execution, he placed his hand on the wall of his cell and solemnly declared, 'As God is me judge I'm innocent, and the mark of me hand on this wall will attest to me innocence.' Well, the mark remains to this day. To this day, and no matter how many times they scrape it off and whitewash it, they can't erase the imprint of that innocent man's right hand."

"Oh, you've seen it?"

"Seen it? No, I haven't seen it. I've never had occasion to be on the inside of the county prison, but it's a well-known fact to Protestants as well as Catholics. No, I haven't seen it, and I'm sure neither has old Tom Wynne seen it either. But I'll wager you I sleep better nights than old Tom Wynne and them, that can't whitewash or scrape or paint out the proof of their guilt."

As he anticipated, George Lockwood inevitably encountered Theron Wynne on a Hilltop street. "You didn't let us know you were here," said Theron Wynne.

"I was afraid you'd think I was hinting for lodgings," said George Lockwood. "And I'm only going to be here a day or two."

"Important business, no doubt. I don't know what else would bring you to Hilltop in the cold weather."

"Business. I don't know how important. I trust Mrs. Wynne is well, and your daughter Agnes?"

"Mrs. Wynne was down with a touch of rheumatism, every year about this time she complains. But she's up and about again, thank you. Agnes is substituting at the kindergarten, and we're all getting ready for Christmas. Agnes won't be here much through the holidays, but I'm glad of that for her sake. There isn't much in the way of a nice social life in Hilltop, for a girl that's been away at school. Come and take supper with us tomorrow? I'd ask you for tonight, but Mrs. Wynne wouldn't like to be caught unprepared."

"I'm going back tomorrow, unfortunately, but thank you, and please remember me to them both."

"A cup of tea. Come in for a cup of tea this afternoon," said Theron Wynne. "They often have a cup of tea, Mrs. Wynne and Agnes."

"Well—if you're sure it wouldn't inconvenience Mrs. Wynne."

"It'll give her an excuse to display her good tea set."

George Lockwood was surprised to find a florist in Hilltop, and he took a dozen hothouse roses to Bessie Wynne. They served as a conversation piece. "You must have got these from Jimmy MacGregor," said Bessie Wynne. "I know Jimmy's roses."

"Why? Is there more than one florist in Hilltop?"

"There are three," said Agnes Wynne.

"That's two more than we have in Swedish Haven," said George Lockwood. "Three florists, and I frankly didn't expect to find any."

"Oh, don't be deceived by the surroundings," said Bessie Wynne. "In the spring and summer the backyards are full of flowers. Even if it's only a sunflower, the miners—at least the English and the Welsh—"

"And the Scotch and the Irish," said Theron Wynne.

"Yes. The hunkies don't plant many flowers, but all the others do. They may have a space no larger than this table, but in the evening you'll see the men cultivating their little gardens. And of course they all try to grow vegetables, even the hunkies. Cabbage. Beets. But the women grow the vegetables mostly."

"Amazing. I suppose they want to brighten their lives," said George Lockwood. "A bit of bright color. I don't know much about flowers. My grandfather did. Trees, too. He should have been with me on this trip. I'm looking for timberland, for our mills."

"You won't find any for sale, I'm afraid," said Theron Wynne.

"Oh, everything is for sale, isn't it? If you want to go high enough?" said George Lockwood.

"Yes, that's true. But as a business proposition you

wouldn't want to buy any of the timberland in this section. My cousin's Company wouldn't sell, and I doubt if the other companies would either. What's more, some of those Pennsylvania Dutchmen from down around Allentown have been here ahead of you and tied up what was left."

"I found that out today."

"You'll have to go farther north, and even there you'll find that a few families own the best land. Some of that land got for two or three dollars an acre, I'm told. That may be an exaggeration. Up around the west branch of the Nesquehela, some of the Holland Dutch from York State bought that land from the Indians, as far back as a hundred years ago. Some of it they never cut, but now I understand they're pretty busy with logging operations."

"What will happen when you've mined all the coal out of this section?"

"Two hundred years from now?"

"Is there that much coal still to be mined?"

"So they say," said Theron Wynne. "Two hundred years of prosperity. If you have any money to invest, buy stock in any of the big coal companies. No matter how much you pay for it, it's going to be worth more. This country, the United States, that is—is going to buy more and more anthracite coal."

"And in two hundred years this place won't be fit to live in. It's ugly enough now, but think of two centuries of culm banks piling up," said Agnes Wynne.

"In two centuries, Agnes, the culm banks will be covered with mountain laurel. And in any case you and I will be covered with—I guess culm. Agnes doesn't realize that industry and prosperity take their toll."

"Yes, I do, Father. I can remember when the coal dirt at Number Twelve was only as high as this house. Now it's a mountain."

"Not quite a mountain, Agnes," said her father.

"I confess I wouldn't like to live in the coal region," said George Lockwood.

"But you have to admit you'd be willing to profit from coal mining. And if you got hold of your timberland, I don't know which is uglier. A culm bank, or a hundred acres of stumps after the loggers get through with their work." Theron Wynne was petulantly defensive.

"Maybe we'd better change the subject," said Bessie Wynne.

"I agree," said George Lockwood. "Mr. Wynne doesn't like what industry does to the landscape, and neither does Miss Wynne. But neither do I. Nobody does. Nobody likes to hear the squeals from a slaughterhouse, either, but we all like scrapple for breakfast."

"Ugh. I hate scrapple," said Agnes Wynne.

"Well, do you like steak? A cow doesn't make as much noise as a pig, but if you want to have steak, the cow has to be hit on the head first. Your shoes are made of leather, Miss Wynne."

"Thank you for telling me."

"Some religions won't allow you to wear shoes, or buttons that are made of horn—" said George Lockwood.

"No, *not* religion," said Bessie Wynne. "Business is bad enough, but if we start talking about religion we'll spoil our tea party."

"Mrs. Wynne is referring to the discussions Agnes and I have about religion, not to anything you might say, Mr. Lockwood."

"Oh, Mr. Lockwood understood that, didn't you?" said Bessie Wynne.

"Of course," said George Lockwood. "There's one thing I must say, if you promise not to think me forward. But every time I have a conversation with this family, it's stimulating. What you said about my grandfather last summer, Mr. Wynne—"

"Oh, dear," said Theron Wynne.

"Well, it was true, and I don't think we ever get anywhere by not facing the truth about ourselves. *I* didn't shoot two men. That was done before I was born. Before my father was born, I think. But in those days—I'm not making excuses for my grandfather—but in those days they lived more primitively, you might say. Men carried guns all the time because they had to. We have farmers that had grandfathers who wouldn't think of going out to plough a field unless they had their rifles with them. Really. I don't know about up here, but there were Indians living in the woods during my father's boyhood days, and sometimes they'd kill a farmer and make off with his wife and children."

"They were desperate, those Indians," said Theron Wynne, the man who had wanted to be a missionary.

"Desperate or not, you know it's true, Mr. Wynne."

"Yes, I've heard tell of Indians still living in the woods over in Nesquehela County."

"And white men, too. Not only in Nesquehela, but in Lantenengo County. In the Blue Mountains there are families living there that don't even speak Pennsylvania Dutch. They speak High German, same as they did a hundred years ago. They live like Indians, never come to town. I know that for a fact. The farmers know about them and they're deathly afraid of them because they're wild. They even look peculiar —you know why."

"Why?" said Agnes.

"Never mind why, Agnes," said Bessie Wynne.

"I shouldn't have said that. I'm sorry."

"Oh. Inbreeding," said Agnes.

"*Agnes!*" said Bessie Wynne. "We don't speak of such things in polite society."

"It was my fault," said George Lockwood. "Anyway, I was saying if we don't face the truth about ourselves, how can we learn about other people? For instance, knowing about my grandfather. If I didn't know that, I'd be liable to think your cousin was a terrible villain."

"Cousin Tom Wynne?" said Theron Wynne.

"I don't know if it's true or not, but the Irish think he had a hand in hanging those Mollie Maguires."

"The Irish are notorious liars, Mr. Lockwood," said Theron Wynne. "How could they be otherwise? They confess their sins and promise to mend their ways, but the drunkards among them go right back to their drinking, the brawlers to their brawling, and so forth and so on. They're like children, naughty children, and you can't reason with them because when you try to they look at you with that half smile as though *they* considered *you* hopelessly—what's that French word, Agnes?"

"Naïve."

"Naïve. I've tried to be patient with them, the way you would be with a child, and I used to be very fond of them. For instance, you can leave money lying around and they'll never touch a cent of it. And when we've had illness in the family they've been just as worried and attentive as they would be about one of their own."

"Mrs. Ryan when Agnes had that croup," said Bessie Wynne.

"I remember Mrs. Ryan. She wrapped a flannel thing around my neck, and covered my chest with some sticky stuff."

"Now how on earth do you remember that? You were only three years old," said Bessie Wynne.

"It smelled like oatmeal."

"I think it *was* oatmeal," said Bessie Wynne. "An oatmeal poultice."

"At times like that they can be kindness itself," said Theron Wynne. "But we were young then, and not much better off than they were. As soon as I began to get somewhere with the Company—how could anybody in his right mind blame Cousin Tom for hanging those desperadoes? They were tried in a court of law, and convicted."

"I don't know," said George Lockwood. "But I wasn't shocked. I mean, even if your cousin did have them hanged, from all I've ever heard about the Mollie Maguires they deserved it. I'm sure my grandfather would have given them just as good as they sent. You have to protect what's yours or people like that will take it away from you."

"I see what you're aiming at," said Theron Wynne. "Cousin Tom Wynne and your grandfather, the similarity. Well—we'll never know. Cousin Tom never shot anyone that I know of, but he always goes armed."

"You used to too, Father," said Agnes Wynne.

"When I was in the paymaster's office."

"Would you have shot a holdup man?" said Agnes Wynne.

"In self-defense."

"In defense of the payroll?" said George Lockwood.

Theron Wynne smiled. "You know, every time we took a pay to one of the collieries I'd ask myself that question. We had these heavy tin boxes with the cash in them, bills and coins, nothing larger than a twenty-dollar bill, of course, and not many of *them,* I assure you. So it was quite a lot of cash money, as much as $3000 in one pay, and very inviting to a bandit, I should think. We'd go by train to the larger collieries and stay in the pay car, which had iron bars on the doors and windows. But when we were paying one of the smaller collieries we'd be met at the station by a mule team drawing the colliery ambulance and we'd get in that and ride to the colliery office. There'd be three, four, five of us, depending on the size of the payroll, and we'd all have shotguns. And I'd sit there with my sawed-off shotgun across my lap and wonder what I'd do if we were held up. I guess I would have done whatever the other men did. It would have been a dreadful thing to shoot a man with one of those shotguns. There wouldn't have been much left of him at close range, and I guess that's what kept them from trying to rob us. You didn't have to take aim with one of those guns. Just point the gun in their direction and pull the trigger. I don't know, I guess I'd have shot a highwayman. And answering your question, yes. In defense of the payroll. In self-defense, but also in defense of the payroll, because in that case it would have been one and the same. A bandit wouldn't be attacking the payroll. He'd be attacking me to get at the payroll, so whether I defended myself or the money in those tin boxes, who's to say? In either case the man would have been just as dead whether I was defending myself or the Company funds. I was glad when I was taken off the pay crew."

"So was I," said Bessie Wynne.

"Were you, my dear? You never said anything."

"Didn't want you to know how worried I'd been, because after all they might have put you back on the pay crew."

"Well, now isn't that strange, that you had a secret worry that I never knew about till this minute?"

"I was never worried," said Agnes Wynne.

"You weren't?" said her father.

"No, I thought the gun was just there for show. I never for a minute thought you'd have to shoot anyone. And I certainly never thought anyone would shoot *you*."

"We have several payrolls, none as large as $3000, but I'd shoot a holdup man if he didn't shoot me first. Not that I ever do the actual paying, but the payrolls are all kept in our office. We have one main office for all of my father's business ventures, and our bookkeepers handle all our accounting there. Now that I think of it, we often do have $3000 in the vault, and it's in small bills and coins. I have a revolver in my desk drawer, and so does my father, and I wouldn't hesitate to shoot a man that tried to rob us. Neither would my father. Of course you might say it's in the blood." He smiled wryly, defiantly.

"I would never shoot a man over $3000," said Agnes Wynne. "I'd tell him to take the money and be gone."

"Would you send for the police?" said George Lockwood.

"Of course I'd send for the police."

"Then I don't see what the difference is, really. The difference is shooting the man yourself or getting the police to do it for you. But philosophically there's no difference at all, is there, Mr. Wynne?"

"Philosophically? No, I suppose not. But we mustn't argue philosophically with the fair sex."

"Oh, come now, Theron," said Bessie Wynne.

"Yes, Father, you don't have to treat us like bird-brains," said Agnes Wynne.

"There's nothing wrong with your brains, ladies. In some respects you're the equal or even the superior of men when it comes to brainwork," said Theron Wynne. "However, you do allow your emotions and sentiment to confuse the issue sometimes, don't you agree, Mr. Lockwood?"

"I'm afraid to answer that truthfully, I've had such an enjoyable visit. And I have to go now, and I don't want to leave an unfavorable impression. Thank you very much, Mrs. Wynne. Miss Wynne. Mr. Wynne tells me you're going to be away through the holidays. By any good fortune are you planning to attend the Gibbsville Assembly?"

"How did you know? Yes, I am."

"Delightful. This is my first year as a full-fledged member, and that makes me, in a manner of speaking, your host, or one of them."

George Lockwood went away pleased with the outcome of the visit to the Wynnes'. If the conversation had been spirited, to the point of controversy, they had always managed to get back on safe ground before animosity took over. He was sure that Agnes Wynne was more taken with him than she had ever been before; she had actually smiled in an intelligent and friendly fashion when he left.

As a full-fledged member of the Gibbsville Assembly he was expected to pay his share of the deficit, if any, and to serve on the floor committee for the first two years. The deficit never had amounted to more than twelve dollars per member, and the ball usually made a small profit which was applied to the next year's fund. As a floor committeeman he was expected to wear a purple band across his bosom and to see to it that none of the older ladies was left sitting alone. Floor committeemen did not take their duties seriously after the supper intermission, when the party took on a younger character, partly because the very old went home, and partly because the gentlemen by custom would go to the cloakroom for a nip of whiskey or brandy, neat. Inevitably a few gentlemen went back for more, and by one o'clock the ball was lively, with an hour of music and dancing remaining.

George Lockwood had some acquaintance with nearly all the Gibbsville Assembly list, and out-of-town guests immediately stood out. He saw Agnes Wynne immediately on her arrival, and he knew from an earlier inspection of the list that she would be on the arm of Robert Leeds. Leeds was a career man in the mining industry; he belonged to the Wilkes-Barre-Scranton area, at the other end of the anthracite coal fields, but for the time being he was learning the business in Gibbsville, where his family's prestige would not interfere with his training. He was a personable fellow, quite bald at twenty-eight or so, a product of Andover and Yale, and so conscious of the Gibbsville mothers' (and fathers') approval that he had carefully imported an out-of-town girl as a protective measure. To invite a young woman to the Assembly was a very serious matter in Gibbsville, but it was somehow less serious for a Scranton Leeds to invite a Hilltop Wynne.

The hopeful Gibbsville parents at least could go on hoping so long as Robert Leeds remained uncommitted locally.

George Lockwood made no attempt to dance with Agnes Wynne until after the intermission, when all the dances became "extras," not booked well in advance. "Bob, are you going to let me have the second extra?" said George Lockwood.

Leeds looked at his card. "No, but you can have the third."

"The third it is," said George Lockwood.

"Slave market," said Agnes Wynne. "Some day the day will come when the gentleman has to ask the lady."

"Never," said Leeds. "Do you know why? Because the unpopular girls would be left out in the cold. They're the ones that wouldn't stand for it. The men would only dance with the prettier girls. Right, George?"

"Except the floor committee. I don't know if you noticed some of the ladies I plodded around with tonight, but now I think I'll take off this ribbon and end my servitude. Miss Wynne, would you care for a purple ribbon, with my compliments? It would go well with your blue-green eyes. No? Bob, would you like a purple ribbon? Entitles you to a dance with old Mrs. Stokes."

"Thank you, I have had that pleasure. Not tonight, but on other occasions."

"Mrs. Stokes happens to be my hostess and my chaperone, and she's not as ancient as all that."

"I only wanted to differentiate between her and young Mrs. Stokes, who happens to be a cousin of mine," said George Lockwood.

Later, when he was dancing with Agnes, he said, "It always seems as though we had to not exactly quarrel, but disagree."

"Yes."

"Have you ever wondered why?"

"I don't think I have."

"Truly you haven't?"

"Here we go, we're on the verge this very second. You doubt my word. You think I *have* wondered why."

"Yes, I do, Agnes." He felt her stiffen to his touch. "You have such very positive reactions to me that anyone as intelligent as you are must wonder about them. *I* know the reason. You don't like me, you don't think you ought to like me, and you don't want to like me. But something happens when we're together that goes much deeper than liking or not liking."

"You were engaged to be married, weren't you?"

"Not quite. An understanding."

"And the understanding led to a misunderstanding?"

"If you want me to tell you all about it, I will. *All* about it."

"I was told that the girl's family were cross because you wouldn't help her brother get into a club. If that's what it was, I'm on your side—for a change."

"I'm glad to have you on my side, but in all fairness there were other reasons. But the principal reason, it took me some time to realize, was that we weren't suited to each other. If we had been, the other reasons wouldn't have mattered."

"I believe that. I believe that whole-heartedly."

"So do I. And it was very fortunate that we broke off, whatever the reason. Because I'd have been married less than a year when I first met you."

"Would you?"

"Less than a year, a newlywed. And she would have known that I'd fallen head over heels in love with someone else. I'm told women do know that."

"You will never fall head over heels in love with anyone, George Lockwood."

"How do you know?"

"You don't deny that. You only ask me how I know. You'd never let yourself, that's why."

"I'm afraid you're right," he said. "And yet as soon as I said that I suddenly feel that I'm in love for the first time in my life. Can you understand that?"

"Yes, I can. Because this one true confession sweeps away half truths and insincerity. Yes, I can understand that."

"Let's both be truthful with each other, Agnes."

"What do you want me to say?"

"That we're in love."

"All right. I'll say it. We're in love."

"And that's the truth?"

"Don't start out by doubting me. And let's not talk any more. Let's dance. I love to dance!"

One of the rare sentimental impulses in the lifetime of George Lockwood was to ask Robert Leeds to be an usher at his wedding to Agnes Wynne, and Leeds's elaborately polite refusal nearly led to the breaking of the engagement.

"He's a damned, filthy snob," said George Lockwood.

"No," said Agnes Wynne. "Bob isn't a snob the way you mean it."

"I wonder how far back they can go, the Leeds family, before they come across something they'd rather hide."

"I can tell you exactly how far. Bob's uncle, at one time a minister of the gospel, but now dear knows what he is, living out West. Left his wife and three children and an important pastorate in Schenectady. Just disappeared. Although there may have been reasons that were hushed up. No, Bob isn't what you say."

"These coal barons. They're all alike, every one of them. Your father doesn't want us to get married because your cousin doesn't approve of the Lockwoods. What right has he? My grandfather killed two men, but how many others did he kill fighting with the Union army? Do they hold that against him? No. They never mention that, because the Wynnes all stayed out of the army. They stayed home and got rich."

"George, it wasn't so much what your grandfather did that worries Cousin Tom."

"Cousin Tom, Cousin Tom."

"Please—let me say this. You *must* listen."

"I'm listening."

"You've always thought people held your grandfather against you, and it's true, some people do. But that isn't what has Cousin Tom worried. Oh, I wish I didn't have to say this."

"Say it, say it."

"Do you know about your father's two sisters? Your aunts?"

"Of course I do. They died of consumption, but my father's healthy, and I never showed any signs of it, or my brother or anyone else in our family."

"They didn't die of consumption, George."

"They died of consumption in the county hospital."

"In the county hospital, but it was something else."

"Of drink?"

"No. Brain fever."

"Brain fever? Who made *that* up? That's a damned lie. They were only—I don't know how old they were, but they had galloping consumption and died of it very young."

"Ask your father."

"I don't have to ask my father. How else did I know?"

"Ask him again. Make him tell you the truth. I'm not afraid of the truth, I'm willing to marry you. But it's not fair to have other people know this and keep you in the dark."

"You're *willing* to marry me? After this accusation maybe I'm not willing to marry you."

He left her house and returned to the Hilltop Hotel, although it was early evening. Now that they were engaged to be married it was unthinkable that he would spend the night in the Wynne house, and his visits to her, involving two train rides at awkward hours each way, and a night in the grubby hotel, were a test of his devotion. He was angry at her and at his father, and the next morning, having had to shave in cold water after very little sleep, and to ride in a slow combination freight-and-passenger train to Gibbsville and wait over for the next train to Swedish Haven, he was impatient to attack his father.

He went directly from the depot to the Lockwood office, and the morning was almost gone. "Did you have an enjoyable trip?" said Abraham Lockwood.

"I've got something I want to talk about. Now." He closed the door of his father's office.

"Talk away," said Abraham Lockwood. "Although you might have the politeness to say good-morning. I'm not used to having people storm in my office like a bull in a china shop."

George Lockwood dropped his satchel on the floor. "What did my aunts die of? My Lockwood aunts."

"Oh. Somebody's been putting a bug in your ear. Very well, I'll tell you. Your Aunt Rhoda died of the quinsy. Your Aunt Daphne died of obstruction of the intestine."

"You always said they died of consumption."

"They often say that about people that die in the county hospital. They both died there."

"Why are you lying to me? How can you sit there and tell these bland lies when you know I know better?"

"Well, what *do* you know?"

"They were both crazy in the head and they didn't have consumption. They were in the *In*sane, not with the consumptives."

"All right. They were. I suppose Agnes has broken your engagement."

"I wouldn't blame her if she did, the things I said last night. But if you'd ever told me the truth I wouldn't have said those things."

Abraham Lockwood was gathering strength, and now he began to fight back. "Sit down, you contemptible pup, and listen to *me* for a minute. Who are you to come in here and show disrespect to your father? I'll tell you something about yourself. For years you've believed that my sisters, your aunts, died of consumption. Consumption. An incurable disease. You've always known that about your aunts, but twice you've gone ahead and proposed marriage in spite of believing there was consumption in the family. Did you tell that girl in Lebanon that you had two aunts die of consumption? I'll just bet you didn't. And Agnes Wynne—did you tell her? No. But you were willing to marry those girls without telling them. Now all of a sudden you hear that they didn't die of consumption but were put away for being out of their heads. Which is worse? Consumption, or being mentally unbalanced? Consumption is, and any doctor will tell you. People get over nervous breakdowns, and I could name you ten people right here in town that had them and got over them. But consumption is in the blood."

"So is insanity."

"Prove it. Prove to me that it's inherited. Do you know how people go insane? They have a certain disease and they go insane. Syphilis. They get scarlet fever and sometimes they go insane. They get overexposed to the sun and they get softening of the brain. *Or*—they aren't delivered right, at birth, and the mother or the midwife or the doctor does something to the skull while it's still soft. There's any number of ways, such as being hit on the head in an accident or thrown from a horse. But it's always either some kind of a pressure on the skull or else some fever sickness."

"Then are you going to tell me your sisters caught the syphilis?" said George Lockwood. "Or they both got thrown from their ponies?"

Abraham Lockwood now told one of his safest lies. "Your aunts caught the scarlet fever, Rhoda caught it from Daphne, and they never got over it. That happened so long ago, it was before I even married your mother. They nearly died of it, and they would have been better off if they had. They changed overnight from bright healthy children to weak and sickly children. They couldn't keep anything on their stomachs and my mother and father had to watch them wasting away, and not only that, but the girls got so they didn't recognize their own parents. Then the next thing was they had to be put away or they'd have done away with themselves. Anything would have been better than what they went through, not to mention my father and mother suffering along with them and unable to do a thing for them. Every doctor we had said the same thing. Brain fever from the scarlet fever, and no hope of a cure. But they both lived for several years, till Rhoda got the quinsy, and Daphne an obstruction of the intestine. You can find proof of that in their death certificates, in the court house, and not a word about brain fever. And if they'd died of brain fever it would have said so, but they didn't. If they'd died of consumption it would have said consumption, too. If the Wynne family want to make an issue of it, you can't deny it that your aunts had brain fever. But it was caused by scarlet fever, and brain fever wasn't the cause of their deaths. Now you can go home and think things over, and I hope when you get through thinking you'll come to the conclusion that a boy owes his father more respect. Go on,

George. You've hurt me inside, and I don't feel like eating any dinner today."

"I'm sorry, Father. I apologize."

George Lockwood carried his father's lie back to Theron Wynne, who could be counted on to relay it to Tom Wynne; and such candor on George's part, which implicitly included candor on the part of Abraham Lockwood, effectively disarmed Tom Wynne. He withdrew his objections to the marriage, and gained a new respect for the Lockwoods. At his insistence (over no strong protests by Theron and Bessie Wynne) the wedding took place at Lake Wynne, and it was a tremendous social event. Not a man in the entire coal industry of the rank of superintendent and above was left off the invitation list, regardless of corporate affiliation. Coal men, railroad men, lumber and powder men, financial men and lawyers, the higher Protestant clergy, two Protestant bishops, one Roman Catholic bishop and two of the monsignori, the governor of the Commonwealth, three state senators and one United States senator, were among the men on Tom Wynne's list. It was tacitly understood that this might be the last opportunity to pay homage to Tom Wynne during his lifetime, and the invitations had the force of a command. On the evening before the wedding there were nine private or chartered Pullman cars in the yards near Lake Wynne, and on the day of the wedding all Wynne workmen, from breaker-boys to colliery superintendents, were given the day off with pay. Nothing to compare with it had ever been seen in the coal region, and Tom Wynne was making certain that any future social event would have Agnes Wynne's wedding to contend with. It was somewhat confusing to the guests on the Lockwood family list to discover, individually, that the elderly, square-jawed, iron-faced gentleman who greeted everyone was not Theron Wynne, the bride's father; but they quickly found out what was what and who was who. If the bride's father could not afford such a display, at least he, or his daughter, stood in well enough with the money branch, and that was the next best thing.

"Do you wish we were being married in the church in Hilltop, without all this fuss?" said George Lockwood the day before the wedding.

"Truthfully, no. He has all that money, Cousin Tom, and all the fuss doesn't bother me. I feel as thought I were just *going* to a big wedding, instead of being the bride."

"You don't feel like a bride?"

"No. Tomorrow I will, I'll have to act the part and I'm not very good at acting. He'll want me to be pretty, and modest, all the things the bride should be. But all this other business might as well be happening to someone else. How do *you* feel?"

"Probably like your father must feel. That we have to be here, but only out of courtesy. Not to you, but to your cousin. The one that's most pleased, next to Mr. Wynne, is my father. He and my mother had a big wedding, too, for those times."

"I wish your mother could have been here."

"Yes," said George Lockwood, but in truth he had not previously given any thought to his mother.

The Presbyterian Wynnes and the Lutheran Lockwoods agreed that the only nearby churches—the Methodist of the Welsh and the Roman Catholic of the Irish—were not suitable, and Tom Wynne's wish to have the religious ceremony in his house was complied with more or less automatically. The decision limited the number of persons who could attend the ceremony, but in Tom Wynne's words, it meant fewer weeping women. It also restricted the number of young people in the bridal party, a fact which Abraham Lockwood did not find to his liking. "I wish you could have had more ushers," he told his son.

"Why? Four's enough, with Pen."

"Oh, it's nice to have a lot of ushers," said Abraham Lockwood, thinking of the Lockwood Concern.

"Why?" said George Lockwood. "It'd be different if it were a big church wedding, but with so few at the ceremony it'd be ostentatious of me to surround myself with ten or fifteen friends of mine."

"Ostentatious. You are quite right," said Abraham Lockwood. The boy pleased him; he was that much more alert to the rules of good form, thus already habituated to one of the essentials of the Concern.

The bride and groom marched and stood and waltzed through the ceremonies, religious and secular; briefly touching and being touched by a thousand men and women; saying a word, uttering a name, smiling when they did not know or could not remember a face in the brigade of guests. Late in the reception there was a shower of rain, and in the confusion of guests hurrying from tent to tent, George and Agnes Lockwood sneaked up to the mansion and changed into their traveling clothes. Inexplicably the cry, "They're leaving," went around and became a solid chorus, and the crowd pushed inside the mansion and blocked the main stairway. Standing on the first landing, Agnes looked down at the crowd and then in dismay at George.

"They'll let us through, don't worry," he said.

"Where's your bouquet? You haven't thrown your bouquet!" someone called to her.

"I don't know what I did with it," said Agnes to her husband.

"Never mind," he said, and then, to the crowd: "Will you let us through, please?"

"Your bouquet! Your bouquet!" It became a chant, and now for the first time Agnes lost her poise. The mass of humanity, the half but only half humorous demand for her bouquet, and then, at the far edge of the crowd, the sight of her father helpless to reach her to say goodbye—were all too much for her. "I'm frightened," she said to her husband, and seized his arm.

"Nobody's going to hurt you," he said, roughly. "They'll throw a little rice, that's all."

"I can't go down these stairs. I can't move. Take me around the back stairs," she said. *"Please!"*

"Oh, Christ. All right."

A Brewster landau with a pair of cobs and Tom Wynne's coachman on the box was waiting as a decoy at the foot of the porch steps. Its purpose was to mislead the guests while the bride and groom slipped out a side door and eluded the more exuberant merrymakers by riding off in a mule-drawn ambulance.

"We can go out the kitchen door and make a run for it," said George Lockwood.

The maneuver was successful, and the bride and groom drove away unnoticed while the clamor continued inside the mansion and on the porch and lawn. They sat on folded blankets inside the meatwagon, as the miners called it, and the mules proceeded at a dainty trot to the railway siding. It was about three miles from the mansion to the waiting locomotive and coach that would take them to Mauch Chunk. Agnes was still shaking and out of breath when they reached the siding.

"Now don't have hysterics," said George Lockwood.

"That's what I've been fighting. I'm sorry, but I haven't been able to say a word."

"That's all right. Just try to calm down."

They were alone in the coach. "Nobody's going to bother you now," said George Lockwood. "We'll be at Mauch Chunk in plenty of time for the New York train, and nobody's going to know us. We'll be in New York City before eleven o'clock."

Once aboard the New York train Agnes Wynne Lockwood relaxed with an audible sigh. "Everything went well right up to the end, and then something happened to me. I did everything wrong. I never said goodbye to Cousin Tom. I didn't throw my bouquet, and Ruth Hagenbeck was so counting on it. And then those people packed in there, and poor Father. You didn't see him, did you?"

"No."

"I'll never forget his face. Trying to smile to me, but hemmed in, crushed, and unable to move in or out. Mother was there to help me change, but poor Father. I know he wanted to give me one last kiss."

"Really, Agnes. I'm not planning to drop you into the Hudson River."

"Poor George. I wouldn't blame you if you did."

"Would you mind if I went out and smoked a cigarette?"

"Not at all. I wish I had something like a cigarette, but you go ahead and maybe I'll collapse for a few minutes."

They had a suite in the hotel, and Agnes immediately declared she was hungry. "You must be, too," she said. "We haven't really had anything all day."

"Shall we have champagne?"

"Do you mind if we don't? I never want to taste it again. All I want is something like scrambled eggs and some tea."

"All right. Scrambled eggs for two. Pot of tea. Pot of coffee, and a split of champagne."

"Very good sir," said the waiter. "In about twenty minutes, sir?"

Agnes unpacked, hung things in the wardrobe and put other things in the bureau drawers, gazed out the window at the midnight activity in Herald Square, but did not succeed in using up the half hour that passed before the supper arrived. She was wearing a shirtwaist and skirt, part of her going-away outfit. "I wish you'd say something," she said.

"What would you like me to say?"

"Well, we're usually so talkative."

"I know we are, but circumstances are different now."

"That's why I wish you'd talk."

"They affect me, too, Agnes. The circumstances."

"Oh. I guess I didn't think of that. I didn't think of your side of it. Purely selfish on my part. Well, I'm glad you're nervous, too. Mothers tell their daughters *some* things, but I never heard of a mother yet that advised her daughter on how to make conversation on the wedding night."

"There's all the time in the world for conversation."

"All the same, I wish I had something to talk about for five minutes now."

"You're talking. Keep on."

"But you're not helping. Ah, our supper."

The tactful waiter had brought two champagne glasses, and when he left, George Lockwood raised his glass. "To you, Agnes, I hope you'll be happy."

"Of course I'll be happy, George. We have something together that maybe I don't altogether understand it, but it's us." They touched glasses, sipped the wine, and began their first conjugal meal.

"I wasn't so hungry after all," said Agnes. She got up and went to the bedroom, closing the door behind her. Fifteen, twenty minutes later he opened the bedroom door. The room was in darkness and Agnes was in bed.

"Are you awake?" he said.

"Heavens, yes," she said. "I've never been so awake in all my life."

He undressed and got into bed beside her, immediately discovering that she was completely nude. He had not touched a woman's body in a year's time, and in the frenzy of first holding her to him he moved his hand everywhere, and she put her arms around his neck. But after the first minute his hand returned to her hard nipples and found no softness behind them. From the waist up she was almost a boy, and he had so much and for so long wanted a woman. He opened her legs and entered her, and she came back at him like a woman in pleasure and some pain, and that much she knew how to do. She brought him quickly to climax and held on to him while trying to reach it herself, but he slid out of her and she was a long time in realizing that for now she must give up. They had not spoken a word, but now she said, "You'll teach me, won't you?"

"Yes," he said. But he could not teach her to be Lalie Fenstermacher.

On the death of Tom Wynne, a year after her marriage to George Lockwood and five months after her first miscarriage, Agnes Lockwood inherited $100,000 outright and $50,000 in a trust fund for her children, if any, the same to become hers if after ten years she had no living children. It was small money in comparison with George Lockwood's personal fortune and his prospective inheritance from Abraham Lockwood; but it was hers. The trust fund for the children was being administered by a Wilkes-Barre bank—seventy miles removed from Swedish Haven. The $100,000 was in the form of stocks and bonds of the Wynne Coal Company, which she could not dispose of without first offering to sell back to the Company. "It's nice to be independent," said George Lockwood.

"Well, it is," said Agnes Lockwood. "Now I don't have to ask you for money all the time."

"I haven't noticed that you ask me all the time."

"Every time I need it."

"Have I ever refused you? Have I ever even questioned you?"

"No, you're very generous. But it's always been your money. Now I have a little of my own, and if I buy you something, you won't be paying for it. It's nice to be able to give things, George."

"Yes. It gets a bit tiresome you'll find. To be always on the giving end, I mean."

"Well, hereafter you can be on the receiving end, too."

"It'll be a novelty, I assure you."

"I, on the other hand, have never been able to give as many things as I wanted to."

"You were never poor, Agnes."

"Not exactly, but money was always scarce. We paid no rent, we bought things wholesale at the Company store. We got passes on the railroad when we traveled. But Father never had much cash, and Mother's family had to watch every penny."

"Well, your father's well fixed now. What's he going to do with his hundred thousand?"

"Take Mother on a trip to Egypt, first. Then he wants to write a book."

"About Egypt?"

"Oh, no. A sort of history of the Wynne family in the United States, but mostly about Cousin Tom Wynne. And he'd like to get in a lot of things about the woods and streams that he loves to roam around. Father was never meant to be cooped up in an office."

"I just wonder who'd buy a book about Tom Wynne and the woods up that way. I know I'd read a book about my grandfather, but not one about Tom Wynne. Unless of course your father intends to expose some family secret. But knowing him, I don't expect that."

"You're always so sure that Cousin Tom had some guilty secrets to expose."

"I'm convinced that any man that has over $5000 has some guilty secrets."

"Does that include the Lockwood family?"

"Good Lord, I could *begin* with the Lockwood family."

"But you're honest, and your father's honest."

"Till proven otherwise."

"George, you always like to pose as semi-rascal. Why?"

"It's not a pose, Agnes," he said.

"I think you want to be like your father."

"You don't think my father's a rascal, or a semi-rascal, surely?"

"He's much closer to it than you are. As old as he is, and even if he is my father-in-law, he can make me feel as if I didn't have any clothes on, just the way he looks at me sometimes."

"Don't I make you feel that way too?"

"It isn't the same. All you have to do is ask me, or not even ask me. We're husband and wife, and we have that relation. Those relations. But your father is my father-in-law, and he shouldn't be thinking those things."

"You can't hang a man for his thoughts."

"No. Not for his thoughts."

"The way you say that—has there ever been more than thoughts?"

"Not with me."

"With someone else? My father and someone else? Someone in particular?"

"Maybe it only happened once."

"Really? What?"

"Something I saw. Last Friday. He was sitting in the summer house, in his rocker, and there was a woman there sitting beside him. I could see she had her hand in his trousers, fondling him."

"Who was the woman?"

"I didn't know her. I'd never seen her before. But she had her hand all the way in."

"I'll be damned. Right out in the open? Where were you?"

"In the bay window, the second-story bay window. I didn't know he was expecting company, and I was surprised to see he had someone with him."

"Is that all she did?"

"All I saw, but I watched them for at least five minutes and they went right on talking while she fondled him."

"He do anything to her?"

"No, not a thing. She wasn't a young woman, by any means. But she was stylishly dressed. It could have been someone he'd known a long time ago, but I never knew people that old carried on that way."

"I didn't think they could."

"Well, it was quite a shock to me, to see those two old people laughing and talking and the woman with her hand in your father's trousers."

"I wonder who it could have been. And yet I don't suppose

I'll ever know. Unless she comes back. Would you recognize her if you saw her again?"

"Oh, I think I would," said Agnes Wynne.

"My father *is* an old rascal, and no semi about it."

"And you're tickled to death. You're so proud of him."

"I'll sing you a song we used to sing in college. It's very naughty, mind you."

"That shouldn't stop you," she said.

"Here goes: 'I dreamt that I tickled my grandfather's balls/with a little sweet-oil and a feather/but the thing that tickled the old man the most/was rubbing his two balls together.' "

" 'I dreamt that I dwelt in marble halls,' " said Agnes. "It's from an opera, I think. Such pretty music and what a nasty thing to do with it."

"Oh, don't be a prude, Agnes. It's no more than what you've been telling me, made into a song."

"You don't understand, George, honestly you don't. What I've been telling you about your father—the way he affects me, and the thing I saw—they don't shock me. Well, they do shock me. But I'm only shocked because . . . I guess I don't know why. Or I know why but I can't explain it."

"If it happened to *your* father—"

"Exactly! I couldn't in a hundred years imagine my father having that effect on a girl. And as for the other! What shocks me is that I can't think of any of that in connection with fathers, mine or yours. And I've gotten to know your father, the past year. He's old, and not very well, and dignified. And it's so undignified to sit in a rocking chair and enjoy a woman fondling your private parts. You must admit that."

"Undignified, but I give the old boy credit for having some spark left. I hope I do at his age."

"How old *is* he?"

"He's about sixty, I guess. They never tell you their age, parents."

"Well, when *I'm* sixty I hope I can keep my hands to myself. It doesn't really matter what men do."

"It does to men. And your father—"

"I'd rather we didn't talk about my father."

"I don't mind talking about mine."

"Because you're proud of him, gloating over it. And you do want to be like him when you're old. Well, you probably will be, if that's what you want. And you can find some woman to entertain you."

"Why shouldn't that woman be you?"

"That wasn't your mother with your father in the summer house. That was some woman out of his past."

"I have no women in my past."

"Don't lie to me, George. That's such a foolish lie, too."

"Well, they're all forgotten, Agnes. All forgotten, all in the dim distant past."

"I sincerely hope they are."

Agnes Lockwood had not protested when she found that Abraham Lockwood was to continue to live in the house. It was a big house, with servants and a big yard. On the second story there were five bedrooms and a sitting-sewing room, and a bathroom at one end of the hall. On his own initiative Abraham Lockwood had the bedroom adjoining his converted into a second bathroom, thus giving him—and them—as much privacy as they needed. The old man (as he referred to himself and as he was referred to behind his back) had his breakfast tea in his bedroom every morning at seven o'clock, but it took him a long while to shave and dress, and now George Lockwood went to the office without him. On some days Abraham Lockwood did not arrive at the office until shortly before noon; on some days he did not go to the office at all. He had no diagnosed illness, he had not been to see a physician, and he did not complain of any localized pain. But he was tired, physically tired, and he informed George that it was going to be up to him to instruct Penrose in the complexities of the business when the young brother graduated from Princeton. "I have to rest," he would say after noon dinner, having rested all morning. George Lockwood had full power of attorney, and in a few months after his marriage he was recognized by the business community as the *de facto* head of Lockwood & Company. Older men in the business community saw in George an unpredictable combination of the characteristics of Moses Lockwood's secretiveness and Abraham Lockwood's ostensible approachability. In the latter case they had been deceived by the contrast between Moses Lockwood's methods and those of his son, but the deception—or self-deception—had become a fixed belief and as good as a fact. They never knew that Moses Lockwood was candor itself compared to the intricate secretiveness of his son; that Moses Lockwood was forced by his record of violent anti-social acts into a life of unsociability, or that Abraham, with his dedication to the Lockwood Concern, calculated the efficacy of all his human contacts in the perspective of the Concern.

Agnes Lockwood became accustomed to the presence of her father-in-law in the morning hours, when she would be busy with her household duties but never so busy that she could not take the time to exchange small talk with him. Her fear of him, which was self-consciousness on her part, vanished and with the growth of self-confidence she found that curiosity had taken the place of fear. He was tired, undoubtedly; his physical resources had diminished, but his mind was fully active and even in brief exchanges his conversation was entertaining, as though he were deliberately setting out to be good company for her. Here she saw a similarity to her husband's strange charm, which finally had attracted her more than it repelled her and that consisted—when she thought of it—of making his personality felt and remembered. Primarily it did not matter if the personality of the charm created hostility; the basic motive was to be felt and remembered, and this, of course, was a highly complimentary strategy.

Thus Agnes Lockwood progressed in her relationship with her father-in-law, so that in the second year of her marriage and once again pregnant, she got closer not only to him but to the secret of the Lockwood Concern. Abraham Lockwood could say to her, as he did one morning, "Agnes, are you expecting again?"

"Why—yes. Does it show?"

"Not in your tummy, but in your eyes."

"My eyes?"

"Yes. Your color eyes change a lot more than brown do. Brown stay the same, but blue change to grey, or deeper blue. All depending on how the person feels. You show anger and pleasure by the color of your eyes, from one minute to another, sometimes. You can't keep any secrets, Agnes, and this one is one I don't want you to keep from me. George knows, of course."

"Of course. George, and Dr. Schwab. That's all for the time being. I haven't written to my parents yet. They'd want to come home from their trip and I wouldn't want that. They'll be home in plenty of time."

"This means a lot to me, this baby. To you and George, of course, and your father and mother. But if possible more to me than to anyone else."

"You said that before I lost my first."

"This one means just that much more. I'm getting on, and it isn't only wanting to see a grandchild. I look far beyond that, Agnes. To a time I'll never see, when this grandchild has grandchildren."

"I guess everybody does, don't they?"

"I doubt if they give as much thought to it as I do. All my

life I've looked ahead to four generations beyond my own."

"*Four* generations! Why four?"

"That would be my grandchildren's grandchildren."

"But you'll never see them. Why do you care so much? You don't have to worry about a royal family."

"Don't I? I guess not."

"And why stop at four generations? Why not six?"

"Because four generations from now, plus my generation and my father's, that'll be six generations. A span of two centuries of our family in this town."

"I wouldn't count on their wanting to live here fifty years from now. Penrose doesn't want to live here *now,* and heaven knows what my children will want to do."

"Make them stay here. If you promise me that I'll leave you a million dollars, Agnes."

"I couldn't promise that, Mr. Lockwood."

"You're going to have a strong influence on your children, Agnes, and if you can persuade one son to stay here, it's worth it to me."

"I couldn't promise that. I couldn't even promise to influence them. My father wanted to be a missionary, and instead of that he spent his whole life in the coal-mining business."

"And he's been very happy."

"No. You're not happy going through life never doing the one thing you wanted to do. That's what kept my father back from higher promotion in the Wynne Company. He didn't care enough. He did his work, a full day's work for a full day's pay, but that was to support his family."

"He might not have enjoyed the life of a missionary."

"But he never had a chance to find out, one way or the other. You've been happy here, George is happy here, but if I have a son how do I know he'll be happy here? Swedish Haven is a pretty little town, especially after some of the places I've lived in, but the Lockwoods weren't even the founders of the town."

"Quite true, but it's where our branch started to amount to something, beginning with my father. And it's our town now, Agnes. We own it, to all intents and purposes."

"Then it is a sort of royal family you have in mind."

"We don't believe in royalty in this country."

"No, but—an aristocracy. Is that what you want, Mr. Lockwood?"

"Everything you say about it, every time you give it a name, you make it sound an unworthy ambition. But believe me, it isn't. The Wynne family were headed in the same direction, but your cousin didn't look beyond. You mustn't take this personally, Agnes, but you know as well as I do that Tom Wynne got rich by taking coal out of the ground and making the countryside ugly. Forests laid bare. That's not what we want to do. Make money, yes, and we have. But some day, maybe in your own husband's time, we may own the whole stretch between here and Richterville. Nice clean little towns, prosperous farmers getting their fair share, and us at the head of it. You and George, or your children. Lockwoods, living right here in town, not J. P. Morgans living in New York City, or Drexels in Philadelphia."

"Then after Richterville? Why not Gibbsville, for instance? That could stand some improvement."

"It's too late to do anything about Gibbsville. The Morgans and the Drexels have the control up there. Richterville is where my wife came from, so your husband has some rights there. It sounds like a great deal, to own eleven miles of farmland and two little villages on the way, but we could do it now if we didn't have our money at work on more profitable enterprises. One of these days George will get hold of the Richterville bank, and with it most of the farms to the east of Richterville for a distance of five miles. Since we already own the bank here, we hold the paper from here west."

"Gracious! A principality."

"Nothing wrong about it, Agnes. There are ranches out West that take in forty or fifty miles in one direction. And some of the old Spanish families owned whole states. Nobody can do that in the East. It's too built up, and the railroads are too big. And I wouldn't want to do it. All I hope for is this town and the town my wife came from and the land in between."

"And what about to the east and the south of here?"

"We have a few properties to the south, but the rest I never took any interest in. The Coal & Iron owns the timberland and the big dams. J. P. Morgan. And the farm land to the south is too hilly to cultivate. You have to go twenty miles to the south before you get good farm land, and that's Reading and Lebanon Dutchmen's territory. I'm Lutheran, and half Pennsylvania Dutch, but I'll never be one of those people and I don't want to be."

The will to live, to see his first grandson, was not as strong in Abraham Lockwood as Agnes Lockwood's will to give birth to the child. Abraham Lockwood died of double pneumonia in the seventh month of Agnes Lockwood's pregnancy. The town, and the southern part of the county, gave Abraham Lockwood a nice send-off; formal and large, with every funeral cab in Gibbsville and Swedish Haven spoken for, and the streets of the town, the railroad stations, some private residences and the Exchange Hotel crowded with very respectable-looking strangers. Agnes Lockwood, big with child, was somewhat surprised by the size of the crowds, but the occasion would be noteworthy in her recollection for two things: on the night of Abraham Lockwood's death she saw her husband weep for the first and only time; and, secondly, on the afternoon of the funeral, upon returning home after the interment, they encountered a woman in the downstairs hall. She came up to George Lockwood and held out her hand. "You don't remember me, George, but I knew you when you were a boy. I'm Sterling Downs's mother."

"Of course I remember you, Mrs. Downs. You were very nice to come."

"It isn't Mrs. Downs any more. It's Mrs. Wickersham."

"I beg your pardon," said George Lockwood. "I'd like you to meet my wife. Agnes, this is Mrs. Wickersham. I went to school with her son, and do you remember the summer you spent at the Run, Mrs. Wickersham?"

"I'll never forget it. That's where I really got to know your father and mother. I just had to wait and see you, George, but now I must catch the train." She released George Lockwood's hand, smiled at him and at Agnes, and hurried out.

"All the way from Philadelphia," said George Lockwood.

"And was in love with your father."

"I don't know."

"*I* do," said Agnes Lockwood. She was the woman that day in the summer house. She's prettier, close to."

"Good Lord, I wonder how long that had been going on," said George Lockwood. "Now get some rest, Agnes. Don't try to see any more people. You've done your part."

She smiled. "I'll do my part in about six more weeks."

George Lockwood's gratitude to Martha Downs Wickersham was of a special kind, having nothing to do with her last respects to his father, and actually having little to do with her. She had revealed, inadvertently and unawares, that his father had had at least one mistress during the life of Adelaide Lockwood, and George Lockwood needed that fact to justify his own affair with Lalie Fenstermacher Brauer.

Lalie's marriage to Karl Brauer, a Reading lawyer, was quick and ostentatious, to make everyone forget about George Lockwood. The Fenstermachers did not even send George Lockwood a post-nuptial announcement of the marriage, but he read about it in the Reading *Eagle* and two Philadelphia newspapers. The *Eagle* provided the Karl Brauers' home address on North Fifth Street, and George Lockwood paid a call one morning when he returned from his wedding trip. "I wish to see Mrs. Brauer," he told the maid.

"Mrs. Brauer, or Mr. Brauer? If you want him, he's at the office down Penn Street."

"No, this is a matter that concerns Mrs. Brauer."

"I'll tell her. Just step inside."

In a few minutes Lalie came downstairs. "Good morning, Mrs. Brauer," he said quickly, for the benefit of the maid. "I'm from Wanamakers."

She was startled, but the maid, hovering in the hall, could not see her face. "Oh, from Wanamakers. Well, come in here and we can talk."

He followed her into the front parlor, a long narrow room that had only one entrance. "Did you bring the samples?" she said.

"I have them here in my pocket," he said.

She lowered her voice. "Are you out of your head? Make it quick, whatever you want to say, and don't ever come here again."

"I won't stay long."

"You got married," she said.

"Yes, just the same as you. I got married. And I wish I hadn't. Not only for my sake, but for hers."

"Why tell me your troubles?"

"You're part of my troubles. I want you."

"You're too late for that, George. I'm a married woman now and with a good husband."

"I have a good wife, but I still want you. And I've found out what I want to know. You still want me."

"No."

"Yes."

"Go away," she said.

"It's too soon to go away. I'm supposed to be showing you some samples."

"You must be out of your head."

"In certain ways I am. *The blue will cost a little more than the green, Mrs. Brauer.*"

"The blue is more expensive? I didn't know that. She's on her way to the basement now, but you go, hear?"

"I'll go, but I'll be back."

"I won't let you in. I'll leave word, you're not to be let in."

"Stop this talk, Lalie! We're not children, and I'm serious. I'm leaving now, but I'm not giving up. When you're ready to meet me, send me a note to the Gibbsville Club."

"Meet you? Meet you where?"

"Anywhere. Here, when Brauer goes away. He has to go away sometime."

"Here? In this house? That woman has a room here, she never goes out."

"Discharge her and hire somebody that goes home at night."

"Go away, George. You've gone clean out of your mind. Karl wold kill the two of us. He loves me."

"Don't you think *I* love you?"

"No! No! If you did you'd leave me alone."

"If I don't hear from you in two weeks I'm coming back."

"Please, George. Don't ever come back."

He left her and walked quickly down Fifth Street to the Square, exulting in her weakness and the restoration of his confidence. In eight days there was a note from her: "Nine o'clock Thursday night. Alley gate back of house. Do not come by 5th Street.—L."

There was still some daylight at nine o'clock, and he thought as he made his way to her house that it would have been wiser to enter the house from the tree-darkened street than from an alley where there would be no trees. But he obeyed her instructions, such as they were, and boldly opened the gate in the alley fence, walked up the brick path toward the back porch, and, not to his surprise, as he put a foot on the porch step the door swung open. Now, however, he was in for a surprise: the timid, nervously excited girl he expected on this first rendezvous was all in his imagination. Lalie closed the door and embraced him, held her mouth up to be kissed, and clung to him for a moment in a way that guaranteed that this would not be one of their frustrate raptures of the past. Once she had made up her mind to meet him in these circumstances, she had committed herself to the full. "We go upstairs," she said, her first words, and she led him by the hand.

The bed was turned down, there was light from a gas fixture on the wall. She pulled open his cravat and undid the top buttons of his white linen waistcoat. "I can do that much more quickly than you can," he said.

"Do it, then," she said. She sat in a straight chair and watched him. "Almost as much clothes as a woman. I'm nearer ready than you are."

"I kind of guessed that," he said.

"Now me," she said, and stood up and unbuttoned her gingham dress, all she was wearing. They embraced again, and he was made frantic by her directness, the pressures of her fingers. "I think we better get in," she said. She lay in the bed and cupped her breasts in her hands, as though she were aiming them at him. "Be like a baby," she said.

"I was going to," he said.

She put her hands on the top of his head for a little while, and then some thought, some limit of nervous control, made her abandon tender sensuality. "You. Give it to me. Get in, get in," she said. He moved quickly, but he was barely inside her when she screeched. The words were not words, unless they were German, and his own orgasm was not much later than hers, but he had a distant thought and it was how lucky they had been not to attempt complete lovemaking in the Fenstermacher parlor in Lebanon. Climax did not end it for her. She now kissed him, his mouth, his eyes, his hands, his body, with loving tenderness. "Oh, I love you so, I love you so much," she said.

"I love you, Lalie," he said, and it was true.

They lay in peace for a while. "I've never seen you with your hair down," he said. "It's very pretty."

"It covers my boobies. You don't have any hair. Karl is like he was wearing a coat." She smiled.

"What are you thinking?"

"You got me ready for Karl, but then Karl got me ready for you."

"Yes, I suppose so."

"You don't want to talk about Karl so you don't have to talk about *her*."

"Why do we have to talk about them?"

"She isn't enough for you, say?"

"*Don't* talk about them, Lalie."

"You're chealous of Karl."

"Yes."

"Me too, of her," she said. "All over him is black hair, even his back. But he isn't enough for me, either, George. He loves me, but he hates me."

"Why does he hate you? Someone else besides me?"

"No, no, no, no. Never. Only you. I tell him, have patience. Have patience. Downstairs he wants to do it and I go upstairs with him, but if I'm not ready right away, he can't."

"Well, he seems to have."

"Oh, we do it. But I have to be in bed first. If I'm in bed, he comes home from work and sometimes he'll do it with his clothes on. Just take it out and put it in me. I tell him have patience, everybody's different. It's because he's like a bull, and he wants to be a bull. The men ask him when he's going to have a baby, and he comes home angry. He wants to blame me, but he knows he can't blame me, and that's why he hates me often. If the men would shut up."

"Yes."

"Why did you come to me, George?"

"I missed you."

"Yes, I missed you, too. But maybe you better have some patience, too, George."

"With her?"

"Yes."

"It won't keep me from loving you, Lalie."

"She's cold?"

"No, it isn't that. She just isn't right for me."

"Is she afraid of you? Of a man?"

"No, it isn't that, either."

"Well, tell me. I told you."

"I don't want to say it, Lalie. Don't make me."

"Could anybody make you do something you didn't want to do? I doubt that."

"I'm selfish? Yes, I guess I am."

"I don't have any right to call anybody selfish. I was selfish to tell you to come tonight."

"You're not selfish, Lalie. Nobody could ever say that about you."

"I sacked a hired girl because I wanted to go with you. I had to tell a big lie to Karl. I told him the woman was lazy, and she wasn't lazy. She was a good worker, and jobs like this are scarce. But it was the only way I could meet you. Karl don't like for me to be alone at night, George."

"Meaning that you're going to hire another woman to live in?"

"Karl has money. He says I can have two women live in."

"How will we meet?"

"Maybe we don't. Reading isn't so big. If they saw me come out of a hotel."

"Why didn't you marry a poor man? Then I could have taken a room here, a boarder."

"Jokes don't help. Karl would kill a man, you know. Me, also. His friends make jokes with him, but he comes home and tells me, and I wouldn't be some of those men if he ever loses his temper."

"What if I gave Karl some law business? Would he invite me to stay here when I came to Reading?"

"You're crazy in the head."

"Crazy ideas work sometimes, but I guess that one's too crazy. Are there any rooms for rent near here?"

"To board? Around the corner I see signs in the windows, but that's crazy too."

"I know! An office. I'll rent an office. I have business in Reading every now and then."

"An office with a bed in it?"

"A sofa. I'll put in a desk and chairs, and a sofa. We have a sofa in our office for my father to take a nap. I'll look around, shall I?"

"Not in this neighborhood, though. And I could never go there at night, wherever you picked. We have the phone now, and Karl can always ring up if he's out for the evening."

"One friend. If you had one friend you could trust."

"I have friends I can trust, but not for this kind of a business, George. They wouldn't like me any more. They'd turn against me sooner or later, and even if it was ten years from now Karl mustn't know. You can come here this summer, then rent your office."

"I'll rent it now and they can get used to me coming and going at odd times, and by autumn they won't notice."

"Is that the way we're going to go on the rest of our lives, George?"

"No, Lalie. This won't last forever. One of these days you'll send me away for good. I know that, don't you?"

"Yes, but it's a good thing you said it. I didn't want you to tell me a lie. Sure, I know it."

"But when you send me away it won't be for someone else?"

"No. Only Karl. I married Karl."

She was his mistress for three years and they met in many places. Hazardously in second-rate hotels in Gibbsville and Philadelphia, more safely at the office George Lockwood rented, for quick erotic exchanges in the front parlor of her house, and once by accident when George and Agnes Lockwood and Karl and Lalie Brauer were stopping at the same hotel in Atlantic City. The two couples did not meet, but George went to Lalie's room while Karl was at a Turkish bath. "You're out of your head," said Lalie to George Lockwood.

"Don't ever say no to me, Lalie."

But for Lalie it was the beginning of the end. His selfishness had become arrogant recklessness, and though she went through with the assignation, her parting words that afternoon prepared him for the final break. "I *like* your wife," she said. "She's head and shoulders above you, just by looking at her."

"I never expected you to dislike her, Lalie. But I was sure I wouldn't like Brauer, and I don't."

In a year of haphazard infidelity George Lockwood made no mistake that Agnes Lockwood could fix upon, and the events of that first year, of changing from the protective affection of her virginal life with her parents to that of wifehood with George Lockwood, filled her thoughts to the exclusion of suspicion. It was a radically new way of life, which nothing she had been told or read could prepare her for. It had to be experienced by her before it became of any value or before she was truly the better or the worse for it. At night she would submit to George's ways of making love and she learned to take pleasure in them—or she would sometimes lie untouched and expectant for nights on end, but that too was part of learning. In the daytime hours she had the household duties, her own servants, menus and accounts, storekeepers and clerks, the restricted social life that was largely with Gibbsville families. She had her father-in-law, to learn about and to adjust to. And she had her abortive pregnancy all to herself. She had her home, that she was encouraged to regard as her own home, but that for most of that year was not her home but a place out in the cold, cold world. Her loneliness was relieved during her pregnancy by a desire to protect the pitiable life within her, that was hers and not hers and then was nothing but a shapeless mess on her bedsheet. Now home could never again be the place she had known with Theron and Bessie Wynne. There was no going back to that refuge or even to that way of life or to that earlier person. She had made a failure of her function, but it was a failure that established her maturity just as irrevocably as though it had been a success. Indeed, in some respects the miscarriage had advanced her maturity in that her function had achieved both of the terminal truths of life and death. It was a year for learning and some of it was harsh, but at least for that year there was so much that was new that for the present it could only qualify as information. Sagacity, good judgment, wisdom, prejudice, a philosophy, would have to wait their turns. Agnes Lockwood was going by a phrase she had heard—the phrase, a good wife—and all the information she collected in that year was in some way related to the phrase and to her eagerness to qualify for the designation. Milk turned sour in a thunderstorm; Krafft's was the best grocery store in Swedish Haven; the best morning train for Philadelphia left Swedish Haven at 8:45; all Lockwoods gave a dollar bill to the plate collection on Sunday; Abraham Lockwood liked unsalted butter on his breakfast toast; George Lockwood would not make love unless the room was pitch dark; there had once been a high brick wall around the Lockwood property; Protestant farmers did not work on the Catholic feast of the Ascension; scrapple was more edible if fried to a crisp; Miss Nellie Shoop was the best dressmaker in Gibbsville; Yock Miller was the same as Jacob Miller, but Ock Mueller was Oscar Mueller, and they both worked at the bank; no one laundered lace curtains as beautifully as the nuns in Gibbsville, but they certainly knew how to charge for their work; Moses Lockwood lost the lower half of his ear at the battle of Bull Run; Mr. Heimbach, the clockmaker who also tuned pianos, was allowed in the front door but other tradesmen had to come in through the kitchen; Penrose Lockwood was nice but not very bright in his studies.

Emotional experience, family lore, household chores, the familiarization of faces that a year ago had not existed for her—and then she was in the second year of her marriage. The second year was more of the same, but more of other things as well. She could, for instance, go to Krafft's in the morning and the people on the street would not point her out or stare at her; she was conscious of the difference between the earlier half-hostile politeness and the casual respect she was given as Abraham Lockwood's daughter-in-law. They were getting used to her, and she to them. It had been a crowded year, never again would a year seem so crowded, and she began to do many things by habit and thus have more time to notice things, but more than things she noticed people, persons, individual human beings with individual characteristics. Notably and inevitably she began to observe George Lockwood, and quite undramatically, without reason, in her mind she convicted him of infidelity.

In the first year he was all men in one man, and what he did and did not do was all she knew of the ways of men. Whatever he did was what men did, and it took that first year of marriage to separate George Lockwood from the mass of Man and to disperse other men from the vicinity of George Lockwood. As an only child she had wished for but learned to do without a confidante and to work things out for herself, and if the method did not make life easier, it had the virtue of accustoming her to introspection and inner debate. Likewise, in her case, it had sharpened if not quickened her judgment and her self-reliance. It gave her confidence in her judgment and her own resources. Something was wrong in George Lockwood's behavior, and since it was she who was suspecting that something was wrong, the something surely had to do with other women.

But as the months went by he continued to give her no reason to be suspicious. It became not so much a question of catching him in a slip as in catching herself in a false silent accusation. With nothing to go on, she had to give him the benefit of a doubt that she did not honestly feel. Then as time passed and she accepted the fact that he was too clever for her, she found that she was becoming reconciled to an offense that she had not been able to charge him with. And at that point she began to be afraid of him because she admitted to herself that fear of him—and of being in error; the two were interchangeable—had kept her from giving utterance to her suspicions. She had always been afraid of him, always from the very beginning, and yet as soon as she acknowledged this truth her fear of him was less distressing. Her loneliness, for example, had been caused by her fear of him. She wondered if fear of him had not caused her to lose her first child.

But fear of him, why? Other women might have reason to fear a husband's beatings, drunkenness, stinginess, or whatever, but from George Lockwood she feared none of those cruelties. More time passed before she discovered that what she feared, what she had been fearing, was the very thing she suspected: his infidelity, his desire for other women, the horrible fear that she would lose him to another woman, and the knowledge that she could no longer live without him. At last she discovered the dominant, pervasive truth: she loved him. It was not a good love, not the love she believed existed and had always hoped for, but Agnes Lockwood, secretly proud of her individuality, knew that this was the love for her. Opportunity had come and gone, but the other sweet and dear love had not stayed with her, and this love had stayed. Thereafter she was invulnerable to assault by George Lockwood's infidelity, and when she no longer needed additional proof, when he ceased to be too clever for her, she was on the verge of laughing in his face. Love born of fear, fear born of love. It didn't matter very much. Sweet and dear love would not last anyway with a woman who could love George Lockwood. Here lay a great and important truth for Agnes Lockwood: the fact that *she* could love George Lockwood and did love him established her individuality. She had always believed in her individuality, that she was perhaps a bit brighter than other girls, that she did not think the way they did (echoing the thoughts they had heard from their parents and teachers), that she did not like all of the same things they liked. And now she had a husband who would not be the man she would choose for her sister, if she had had one, but she had married him and she was content —if often far from serene. He was her partner in the full experience of life, and if he was selfish and neglectful, he was her partner nonetheless. He gave almost nothing of himself, but the discovery that this was so in his relations with her came after her discovery that it was so in his relations with everyone else. He was not, in other words, making any cruel distinction in his treatment of her. He was that way with everybody. As the months and years rolled on she became convinced that the only cruel distinction he made was in his treatment of his other women, whoever they were. Agnes Lockwood acquired an extra sense that informed her that one woman was gone and a new one was taking over; but none of them really took over. She was the continuing one, his wife, and one day she was able to face her jealousy, to admit to it retroactively because it was gone.

She was pregnant, in her seventh month, and the doctor had told her it would be safer to suspend sexual relations with her husband. "How long is this going to be?" said George Lockwood.

"Well—the doctor says three months, anyway," said Agnes.

"Three months!"

"Maybe four."

"It's due in two."

"But I don't know how soon we can start after it's born. The doctor says not so soon if we want to have more children. I can make you feel good without."

"That's not the same."

"It's all I can do for a while. I'm sorry, George," she said. "I want to, too, you know, but my bust is so sensitive."

"I hope they stay the way they are—I don't mean sensitive, but the size they are."

"I don't know," she said. "Do you want to go with another woman?"

"What other woman?"

"Oh, there are that kind of women."

"You mean whores?"

"Yes, but not just the kind the farm boys go to. There must be places in Reading and Philadelphia. I know there are. I wasn't born yesterday."

"What if I went to one of those places? What would you say afterwards?"

"You wouldn't have to tell me," she said.

"Oh. Then as long as you didn't know, you wouldn't mind so much?"

"I'd know, but you wouldn't have to tell me."

"You'd know? How could you tell?"

"You wouldn't be so restless."

"Restless. Is that the way I get?"

"Yes," she said. She knew he was thinking, wondering whether his restlessness ever had betrayed him, but in the dark she could not see his face.

"Why don't you say something? Are you asleep?" he said.

"I was waiting for you to say something," she said.

"I was thinking. You wouldn't mind if I went with another woman, and paid her?"

"I'd mind, but I wouldn't want to talk about it. I'd consider it something you had to do, because you're a man. That's why there *are* that kind of women, because men are so weak."

"Men are weak?"

"Morally weak, yes. Governed by their appetites, willing to cheapen themselves, just to feel good for a few minutes. You wouldn't want to be *seen* with that kind of woman, but did you ever stop to think what those women think of the men? The lowest kind of woman, I don't care how much you pay her, and the men are willing to get undressed and put their hard things into them. But how do you feel after you come in a woman like that? You don't love her, I'm sure."

"Me?"

"You've been with those women. You told me that."

"Oh, you mean when I was in college."

"How *could* a man be so intimate with a woman he never wanted to be seen with? The most private thing a man can do, and doing it with a woman that does it with dear knows how many other men. For money. Disgusting. But if you have to have that pleasure, go right ahead, George. I get pleasure, too. You know that. But if I can't have the pleasure with my husband, I do without it. You tried to make me want to do it before we were married."

"You didn't know it was pleasure then."

"How wrong you are. A woman always knows it's going to be pleasure. Much more so than men. It isn't over so soon for a woman, if she cares about the man. And if she doesn't, she's no better than one of your whores. I've never said that word before, but I don't mind saying it now."

"I do. I don't like you to talk that way. It's unladylike."

"Is it gentlemanly for you to say it? Or do you believe that you can talk and act in ungentlemanly fashion when you feel like it? I must get some sleep now, George. The doctor says I need all the sleep I can get."

"*I* won't sleep."

"Well, I'm sorry about that. Goodnight."

In the course of the conversation she had convinced herself of the low status of his other women, and had made them contemptible in his eyes without ever getting down to cases. During the next three months she was not certain of his fidelity, but it mattered very little. He would remember all she had said, and she had spoiled it for him, if only until she could once again have him for herself.

In all possible ways George Lockwood had been well and thoroughly prepared for his position as head of the family, manager of the family enterprises, and heir to the duties of master of the Lockwood Concern; in all possible ways, that is, save one: his father had never defined the Concern or given it a name. George Lockwood consequently was in the anomalous situation of advancing an undertaking whose existence he knew nothing about. It had no title, no motto, no slogan, no set rules. George Lockwood was vaguely conscious of a purpose behind his father's careful training in business matters, in the advantages and desirability of staying put in Swedish Haven, in the cultivation of an attitude to guide him in his relations with his social and business contacts. His father's latter-day comments on the comparative ease with which money was to be made had sometimes puzzled George Lockwood; but George, who was developing a mind of his own that was not merely a reflection of his father's, came to believe that the old man was attempting to give him confidence. If it was emphasized that to acquire money was not a formidable task for a man of superior intelligence, the man could proceed in a relaxed fashion, at a pace that suited him . . .

Now it was not true that such had been Abraham Lockwood's intention. His purpose had been to train George in a gentlemanly view of money-making; to decelerate, as it were, the son's aptitude. A few of George's schemes had come off surprisingly well, and this pleased his father. It was reassuring to know that the boy had a business head on his shoulders. But the ability to make money, once it had been demonstrated, was no longer the most vital subject in the boy's training. There was money enough, and Abraham Lockwood believed that the fortune would grow untended, in the course of the normal growth of the nation and with the protection provided by a good diversification of investments. The boy liked business, Abraham saw, and therefore could be depended on to make more money than he lost, to increase the size of the fortune so that it would remain outstanding in the neighborhood. With that worry out of the way, Abraham Lockwood could encourage other interests that would be of benefit to the Concern. There was the establishment of a family, there was an infusion of pride in the family position. As to the first, George had obligingly married into the Wynne connection, which would be helpful when his and Agnes's children were older; and as to the second, an awareness of the Lockwood position in Swedish Haven and even in Gibbsville had been helped rather than harmed by Moses Lockwood's record of violent behavior. The country was getting older, but it was still young and raw, and in many living memories a man of action was deeply admired. The war against the Confederates was far from forgotten, the frontiersmen of the Far West were more picturesque than the builders of the railroads, Little Big Horn was only two decades past, and at least Moses Lockwood had not killed in a quarrel over a woman, like Ed Stokes and Jim Fisk. The chief threat to family pride had been the resurrection of the Lockwood sisters, Rhoda and Daphne, and Abraham Lockwood died hating them because their untimely reappearance had made it impossible to be truthful with George. Given time, Abraham Lockwood could have told a mature George the secret of the sisters and advised him on how to dispose of the secret; but there had not been time in which to restore the good relationship of father and son, and without that good relationship Abraham Lockwood could not find the right moment to confide in George the unnamed dream of the Lockwood Concern.

. . . Nevertheless George Lockwood acted in accordance with the requirements of the mythical Concern and its dead author. Abraham Lockwood had done his job well. "I sometimes think that my father wished he'd stayed in the army," said George Lockwood to Agnes one evening at home.

"No, I don't think so. I think he wanted to be a baron."

"A baron?"

"To have a feudal estate, like an English duke."

"Oh, I know what you're thinking of. I know all about that. The land from here to Richterville? He had a plan for that. We worked on that together, but I didn't know you knew about it."

"In a burst of confidence one time, he told me."

"Really? That must have been toward the end," said George Lockwood. "He wasn't given to talking much about things like that."

"He seemed to want to tell me about it," said Agnes Lockwood.

"Oh, I'm sure he did. He liked you, and not only because you were my wife."

"I don't think he particularly liked me, but I was your wife—and having a baby. Go on, tell me about your father wanting to stay in the army."

"Well, he used to tell me about those days. Meeting so many interesting people, foreigners, ambassadors and their wives. He was cut out for that sort of life and I'm sure he was good at it. And yet he chose to come back here to Swedish Haven. Once in a while some festive occasion in Philadelphia. But it must have seemed very humdrum after those years in the capital. It may have had something to do with my grandfather. He was getting on in years and his health. The strange thing is that my father didn't start out to be the kind of man you'd expect to take over responsibilities. He was a gay dog at the University. Mixed with a very fast set."

"That's not unusual, for a young man to sow his wild oats and then settle down to responsibilities."

"No, I guess not. I seem to've done the same thing. But I always wanted to come back here to live. Always did. I hated New York and I can't say I liked Philadelphia much better. My friends there, in both places, think of me as living on the outskirts of civilization, but to tell you the truth, I think of them—well, when I go to one of the big cities I know just what I want to do, and it's always either to make some money or to spend some."

"Sometimes both."

"Yes, sometimes both. But always money, in some manner or fashion. Here I walk to and from the office with only a few coppers in my pocket in case I'm accosted by a beggar. But in the big cities money's always on my mind—and in my pocket. The pleasures the cities have to offer are all for sale, can be bought, and that isn't a very nice thought to have in mind when you're visiting. When we visit a friend's house I don't plan ahead on how much it's going to cost me, how much I ought to take with me."

"I never thought of it that way, but of course it's all true."

"Oh, yes," said George Lockwood.

"You're very deep, George."

"Well, if I am, I get it from my father. And my grandfather, too, for that matter, although Grandfather wasn't at all like my father. My father didn't often show his true nature to outsiders, but underneath he *was* very deep. *Very* deep. True, he had the advantages of a good education and he was never poor. He was more polished, and knew how to get along with people. And yet he'd never let anyone take advantage of him, or become forward with him. He could be very cutting when someone overstepped the bounds. He was a remarkable man. The glass of fashion, even though some people thought it was wasted on Swedish Haven. But he didn't do it for Swedish Haven. To be well groomed, well turned out, fine linen and all that—he did that for himself, his own satisfaction. And always keeping something back. A good appearance, letting people believe that what they saw was all there really was. But always keeping something back, and what he kept back was the real him. So that finally he died without any of us ever knowing him."

"You could be talking about yourself," she said. "You have no idea how often, when you talk about your father, you might as well be talking about yourself."

"Nonsense," he said.

"In fact, sometimes I think of you as—let me begin over again. Sometimes when I think of you and your father, I see you as a later edition of him. Like a book that the author wasn't satisfied with the first time, and years later made a lot of changes, but kept the same book essentially."

"What author? Did I change my father, or did my father change me as I got older? You're talking nonsense," he said.

"No, I'm not. The trouble with comparisons is we carry them too far. The thing we compare things to doesn't have to be exactly the same as the original thing."

"If anybody heard you, they'd think you'd been drinking," he said.

"Be fair. You don't like it when I see similarities between you and your father, so you deliberately confuse me. All the same, you are both alike. And the big difference is that you had him to model yourself after, and make improvements. Or anyway changes. I don't necessarily believe they were improvements. Although you do. You are your father all over again, one generation later."

"And I suppose he was his father, one generation later," he said.

"Not a bit, not from everything I know," she said. "Your grandfather had to struggle. He had to live day-to-day. He didn't have much time to do anything else. But he made it possible for your father to have leisure to plan a life, a position in the community for himself and his family. And you've continued what he started. It's nothing new. I've seen it happen in the coal regions. In the coal regions there are families that are now in the third generation of money, just like yours, here in Swedish Haven. And look at Philadelphia and New England. It's nothing new. But it's new to you because you're doing it. And it's new to me because I'm playing a part in it."

"Oh, really," he said.

"I am. I know that. Why did you marry me instead of some Swedish Haven girl with more money? Because even though I didn't have a rich father, I was well connected. Why didn't you marry one of the Gibbsville girls? There are lots of rich girls there, and you could have married one of them. But a Gibbsville marriage didn't suit your purpose either."

"I wanted to marry *you*, that's why," he said.

"I know you did. But whoever you married, George, you were never going to marry just the girl herself. Your father didn't, and you didn't either."

"Are you saying that my father didn't love my mother, and that I didn't love you?"

"That isn't what I meant to say, but I guess it's what I believe. I'm not what you want."

"What do I want, if you know so much?"

"Oh, you want *me*," she said. "I'm a ladv, and a very good housekeeper, and whenever you want to impress other people with the sort of wife you have, I'm satisfactory. But it's finally begun to dawn on me, George, that I was more *useful* than anything else."

"And when did that begin to dawn on you?" he said.

"When? I suppose it must have been about the same time that I began to realize that I had deceived myself about you."

"How?"

"Well—you were a handsome, worldly-wise man. Rather evil, I thought at first. That was because of the effect you had on me, which was to stir up emotions inside me that either I didn't know I had or else I was keeping hidden from myself. Doing what most girls do, who had the same kind of upbringing. And so I thought of you as a rather evil young man, but evil can be attractive, because there's something warm about evil people. Warm and human. And the very nicest girls think they can turn the evil into good without sacrificing the warm and human qualities. Don't forget, my father wanted to be a missionary."

"So he said."

"He believed it, and so did I, about myself. But after we'd been married I began to realize that you were not evil. You were cold and calculating, but not evil. And heaven knows, I've never been right for you in certain matters. I know you'd rather not discuss that, and I don't care to either. But I expected you to make me love you the way you wanted to be loved. You knew everything and I knew nothing. You had a lot of experience and I'd had none. But you lost patience with me, and that was really how I discovered that you didn't love me. If you had loved me, we would have—"

"We sleep together, and we have intercourse."

"Yes, we have intercourse, but I'm not right for you. I'm there, and that's all. It's not me you want, only the place where you put yourself inside of me."

"You get pleasure," he said.

"Now I do. Because I learned how to. But you didn't show me. It has nothing at all to do with loving each other. And if we can't have love then, no wonder it's missing everywhere else."

"Often you're the one that wants it."

"Yes, nearly always. Seldom it's you. And what do you think that tells me?"

"I don't know. What does it tell you?" he said.

"Things that are too humiliating to put into words. I never thought it would be this way. I never thought I would be this way. I've found out how women can cheapen themselves and call it love. I never used to think it could be done without love, and finding out that it can ruined my self-respect."

"I hadn't noticed that," he said. "You have a large supply of self-respect, it seems to me."

"What anything seems to you, George, is only that and nothing more."

" 'Quoth the raven,' " he said.

" 'Quoth the raven,' " she said.

The revelations in their conversation had the curious effect of making her seem, briefly, wantonly possessed, and he attacked her with a renewed vigor. But he as well as she was unaware of the rise and fall, irregularity and unpredictability of her sexual needs, and a night of unprecedented pleasure, as though between two erotically-minded strangers, was followed in the same week by a fiasco of dry pain for her and angry forced climax for him. They had talked too much without having created the tenderness that was essential to candor.

Although she was a woman of spunk, who believed she was

(and was) guided by a set of simple principles accumulated from her parents, Agnes was a woman whose physical resources were not equal to the demands put upon them by her spirit. She was anaemic. The blood that came out of her at menstruation was watery, and she was frequently constipated, a condition that was aggravated by hard and difficult bowel movements. She was not one to go to a doctor for relief from minor pains and aches, and during her life in Swedish Haven she acquired no confidante among the town women. Her position—or more precisely, the position of her husband—made it unthinkable to reveal to another woman the kind of intimate details that the other women shared among themselves. For lack of opportunity the other women were unable to offer the confidences that would invite an exchange on her part. Invitations of any kind were seldom issued by Agnes. On rare occasions they attended the more important social functions in Gibbsville—the Assemblies, wedding receptions, the garden parties in the spring of the year—at which the people of substance felt obliged to appear. But private dinner parties in private houses were infrequent in Gibbsville and almost unheard of in Swedish Haven. In both towns women saw the inside of other women's houses only at whist and "500" parties in the afternoon. Casual conversations were conducted in the grocery stores and meat markets, but they were likely to be interspersed with the clerks' recommendations of some nice eggplant or spring lamb. The fashionable Gibbsville women would also meet at the women's shops and milliners', but Agnes employed a dressmaker, who came to her house two or three times a year with patterns and materials. Mrs. Colby would make the trip by train from Wilkes-Barre and stay two or three days, occupying the spare room on the second floor back. She had news and gossip of Wilkes-Barre and Scranton, but as the persons involved were hardly more than familiar names from Agnes's girlhood, her visits were professional and industrious.

Wherever she went in the two towns Agnes was recognized and treated with the right degree of cordiality or obsequiousness, which was determined by the nature of her husband's relationship with the other husbands rather than by her own personality. In all her years in Swedish Haven that was to be the case; she was always the wife of George Lockwood, so much so that in the two towns there were not a dozen women and not a man who called her by her first name. She had a large, well-staffed house to live in and a splendid pair of bobtailed cobs to take her wherever she wanted to go, a Hudson seal coat with hat and muff to match to keep her warm, and people got out of her way when she entered a store.

But when she died there was not much that could be said about her, and nothing much was said. Even her daughter Ernestine was so repressed by the absence of grief at the funeral that her own grief became a formal, tearless performance. The distress that other mourners saw in her face was in truth anxiety for her brother, who had not answered her telegram informing him of their mother's death. When the last visitors had rushed away from the formalities Ernestine said to her father, "I'm worried about Bing. I can't understand not hearing from him."

"The last straw," said her father. "The last straw."

She saw then that her father too had his substitute for grief, and it made her understand him—and herself—a little better.

BOOK 2

□

■

GEORGE LOCKWOOD'S first impulse was to refuse—politely, of course—to see the young man from St. Bartholomew's. It could be done reasonably, properly, legitimately. He could say he had just finished his new house and was not yet settled in; he could plead the pressure of a new business venture (without revealing that it was to be in the confectionery line, a vaguely undignified enterprise); or he could invent an excuse. George knew full well that the only reason the young man wanted to call on him was to ask for a large sum of money for the old school. Penrose Lockwood had received an identically worded letter from the young man, whose name was Preston Hibbard, St. Bartholomew's '17, Harvard '21, M. B. A. Harvard '23. The class identifications followed Hibbard's name in the Alumni Directory, where he was listed as Acting Bursar. At St. Bartholomew's the young man had been a classmate of Bing Lockwood's, but George Lockwood had never heard Bing speak of him. The Alumni Directory listed eleven Hibbards through the years, all from Eastern Massachusetts.

"Did you get a letter from somebody named Hibbard at St. Bartholomew's?" said George to his brother.

"Yes, he wanted to come and see me," said Pen. "You know what it's about, don't you?"

"Money, I imagine," said George.

"Money, and lots *of* it," said Pen. "Murray Dickinson told me they're sending this guy around first to, uh, reconnoiter.

Find out how much the traffic will bear before they announce the drive."

"He picked the wrong time for me," said George. "My spare cash is in the candy business."

"You have to see him," said Pen. "He's going to call on every living alumnus. I don't know the kid, but his father was there when I was. John Hibbard. Boston banker. The Hibbards could write a cheque for the whole amount if they wanted to. They've had money since it was called wampum. Somerset Club. Wharf Rats. A hundred percent Porcellian all the way down the line. You might as well see the kid and get it over with, because those people don't take no for an answer."

"What are you giving?" said George.

"Oh, you know how those things are. You both feel around and somehow or other you find out what they have you down for, and then you cut it in half and you arrive at a sum. I'm seeing him a week from Tuesday, taking him to lunch, as a matter of fact."

"Then I guess there's no use stalling him off," said George.

"No, there's no use stalling him off, Compared to the Hibbard family the Lockwoods are rank amateurs when it comes to money."

"What does St. Bartholomew's want the money for?" said George.

"Oh, somebody just gave a lot of money to Groton, and our trustees see their chance. Pride in the old school. We'll show those God damn Grotties," said Pen.

Young Mr. Preston Hibbard arrived in Swedish Haven in a black Dodge coupe with disc wheels, except for the Massachusetts license plates a car that was indistinguishable from six doctors' coupes that at that very moment were likely to be parked at any hospital. With a green felt bag hanging from a cord in one hand and wearing a very old brown fedora that sat on the top of his head, Hibbard was being turned away by the uniformed Lockwood maid when George intervened.

"You're very punctual," said George. "Half past twelve just struck. Come in. Would you like to wash, and what can I offer you to drink?"

"I'll have whiskey and water, or a cocktail, if I may," said Hibbard. "And yes, I'd like to use the Peter." He employed the St. Bartholomew's nickname for the toilet.

He came back from the lavatory rubbing his fingers together. "You're the fourth St. Bartholomew's Lockwood I've had the pleasure of seeing in the last five weeks."

"The fourth? I knew you were seeing my brother."

"Yes, I had lunch with Mr. Penrose Lockwood last week. He took me to the Recess Club. The day after that I saw Mr. Francis Lockwood, who I believe is no relation."

"No relation. In fact, I've never met him. He came after my brother and I. Lives in Chicago?"

"Lake Forest, near Chicago," said Hibbard.

"And who was the fourth of this distinguished name?"

"None other than my old friend and classmate, your son Bing. I stayed with him and his wife overnight when I was in California. They have a very comfortable place, a ranch I suppose you call it. Bing was in great shape. I shouldn't be surprised if he turns out to be the outstanding man in our class."

"You don't say?" said George.

"All the signs and portents. I spoke to fifteen of the nineteen St. Bartholomew's boys that live in California, and every single one of them seemed to go out of his way to say something complimentary about Bing. The coming man in California."

"That's good to hear," said George.

"I'm not going to pretend that I'm not aware of some differences you and he have had, but I thought you'd be pleased to know he's doing so well. Financially, of course, he's doing very well."

"May I ask what he gave you?"

"Well, it will come out eventually. He pledged fifty thousand dollars."

"Fifty thousand? Oh, but you say pledged," said George.

"Yes, but half of it right away, and the other twenty-five thousand will be announced next Commencement. There's no question about his having it to give. I understand he's giving the same amount to Princeton."

"To *Princeton?*"

"Giving it, or has given it already."

"You're full of news, Mr. Hibbard. Tell me some more."

"Be glad to tell you anything I know. I gather that Bing went out there and went right to work for this man King and made a distinctly good impression from the start. Wasn't afraid to get his hands dirty, they said. Well, they're covered with liquid black gold now, metaphorically speaking. King had a son, a friend of Bing's, who was killed in an airplane accident, flying his own plane, and after that Mr. King treated Bing as if he were his own father."

"Hardly that," said George.

"Well, that isn't quite what I meant to say, under the circumstances, but in a manner of speaking," said Hibbard. "Do you realize that those people out there have oil derricks out in the ocean? That's the new thing out there. I've seen them. Perfectly amazing to see one of those towers a hundred yards offshore, with the thing pumping up and down. They don't miss a trick, those people."

"So my son has made his pile before he's thirty. Good for him," said George.

"With some help from you, I gather."

"No, the money he had to invest came from his grandfather. My father. I can tell you neither one of us would have put a penny in oil wells. I still wouldn't."

"Well, I have. On Bing's recommendation I've bought some San Marco stock. For myself, not for St. Bartholomew's. Our friends at St. Mark's School would be amused by that. San Marco's, St.

"I got it almost immediately," said George. "From what you've told me, though, my son is giving you cash and not stock. The school, that is."

"Oh, yes indeed. He made me promise not to invest any of the school money in San Marco stock. It's very risky at the moment, he said, because they're prospecting elsewhere. He didn't say where, but he said the whole thing could blow right up in their faces."

"But you put some of your own money in it."

"Yes, after I caught some of Bing's enthusiasm. I'm not in for a great deal, but these things pay off when they pay off, as witness the money Bing has made. You ought to see him, with hobnail boots and a Stetson hat, an old corduroy coat, driving around in a Rolls-Royce."

"A *what?*"

"He has a grey Rolls-Royce touring car that I don't suppose has been washed since he bought it. On the floor in the back are all kinds of tools and metal tubes containing blueprints and so forth. I asked him, why a Rolls instead of a tin lizzie, and his answer was so typical of those people. He wanted a car that he could fill with gas and oil and drive hell out of it without stopping for little things like a broken radius rod. When it wears out he plans to push it over a cliff and get a new one. I don't know how long it's been since you last saw Bing, but he's nothing like the Princeton snake in the Norfolk suit that I remembered. Still plays tennis, he and his wife. She's pretty good, too. I guess they all are, in California. They have a court made of some composition, much faster than anything I'd ever played on. She beat me, as a matter of fact. We played one set of singles and she took me 9-7, or 8-6.

Ran me ragged, and I've never been beaten by a girl before that didn't have a national ranking."

"I take it you liked her."

"Very much. There's no horse-shit about her. That may seem a strange thing to say about a girl, a young woman, but it's what came to mind. I don't mean that she isn't a lady, or unfeminine. Nor is she like the girls that I grew up with, who play pretty good tennis and can handle small boats. It begins I guess with the way she speaks. A low voice, and a Western accent that makes her chew her r's. She says core instead of car, dawler instead of dollar. And that accent is more masculine than feminine. But for instance when we played tennis, she was wearing a pair of blue jeans, Levis, and high-heeled boots. She just kicked off the boots and put on a pair of sneakers and was ready to play. She shot a snake while I was there. Just went in the house and got a big revolver and came out and killed this rattlesnake that I hadn't even seen, hiding in the bushes near the tennis court. She said they were entitled to roam around in the hills; but they had to stay off her property, on account of the children. She asked me not to tell Bing she'd killed a rattler, because he'd get a gun and go around looking for the mate and probably be shooting snakes till it was time for dinner."

"Did you see the children?"

"Oh, my yes. Stevie, named after Mr. King's son, and Agnes. The boy is about four, and the little girl is two. The little boy never says a word, just looks at you. And of course the little girl hasn't really learned to talk yet. There must be something to that climate. I have nieces and nephews the same age, and my young relatives don't seem nearly as robust. Bing and Rita aren't particularly gigantic, and I've met you and Mr. Penrose Lockwood and the late Mrs. Lockwood, Bing's mother. And I also saw briefly Rita's father and mother, Mr. and Mrs. Collins?"

"Collier."

"Thank you. But Bing's children are Mennen's Food babies. The boy is a towhead, and has a permanent tan, I guess. The little girl toddles around all over the place, which is why Rita is so vigilant about snakes, she told me. Personally, I wouldn't live there for anything, but I refuse to go to Squam Lake because they have rattlesnakes in New Hampshire."

They had proceeded from cocktails through the meat course, and the entree dishes were being taken away. "Excellent chops, Mr. Lockwood."

"Could you eat another? Only take a few minutes."

"I could, but I have to drive to Scranton this afternoon."

"Bob Mackie and Bayard Donaldson?"

"Yes. I've been warned not to expect much from Bayard Donaldson."

"I suppose not. The miners are out on strike. That may affect Bob Mackie's generosity, too," said George.

"Well, yes. But Mr. Mackie I believe has other irons in the fire, too."

"You really do your homework, don't you?"

"Oh, yes. There are only about seven hundred alumni, you know. Six hundred and eighty-eight, to be exact."

"And you're calling on every one of them?"

"Not every single one, separately. Some of the older men can't have visitors, and there are a few eccentrics who wax indignant if they're asked for money. We stay away from them. In the Boston and New York area, where most of our people are concentrated, we have small luncheons, especially for the alumni that haven't been out of college very long. But I expect to have seen, individually, close to four hundred men by the time I get through. It's been a very interesting experience, and I've learned a lot about the country, driving around."

"You drive? Did you drive to California?"

"And back. We have two alumni in Arizona, who I found out don't speak to each other. And two in Colorado. Denver and Colorado Springs. So I went out the Southern route and came back the Northern."

"How much have you got me down for?" said George. "I of course know what my brother has in mind. Don't count on me for that much."

"No? Then you're not going to come anywhere near Bing's pledge?"

"I'm afraid not, Mr. Hibbard. He has a son that in ten years will be ready to enter St. Bartholomew's. That problem is over, for me."

"Well, there's the question of your daughter, for instance. When she gets married, she may want to have her sons go to the old school. She may even marry a St. Bartholomew's boy."

"She may. She may also marry an Old Etonian or an unfrocked priest. I haven't considered her offspring."

"Well, could I put you down—tentatively—for twenty thousand?"

"You may put me down, finally, for ten thousand. Frankly, I don't see the necessity for this campaign. I've been told that it all started because some old Grottie gave his school a big fat sum, and our people are copycatting."

"That is true, as far as it goes, Mr. Lockwood. It's contagious. And a lot of our alumni say we don't need any more money, and that is *not* true. Costs are going up. For instance, it costs just three times as much to feed a boy as it did when you were there. And we've had to start paying our teachers decent salaries. We can't count on getting teachers who have independent incomes. For our best men we often have to compete with the universities, because of tenure and the prestige involved. We lost, as you know, two of our old reliables, one by death and one by retirement. Judson Heminway died last summer, and we had to look around for a new head of the mathematics department. We got a good one, but he didn't come cheaply. Man named Vollmer, from Penn Charter, in Philadelphia. We had to pay through the nose, because we were counting on Heminway to last at least another five years. In the case of old Socrates Barbour, he was due for retirement, so we were prepared for that. Excuse me just a moment, please." He got up from the table and picked up his green felt bag, which was lying on the sideboard.

"Why don't we move to my study and have our coffee in there?" said George. "Unless you'd like some more lemon meringue."

"That's a good idea. Moving to the study, not the lemon meringue. I've put on twelve pounds on this trip. I must say the old boys are hospitable. They must remember the rather Spartan diet we have at school, and I like to eat."

They moved to the study. "See you've got your old diploma on display," said Hibbard. "Lost mine in a fire two years ago."

"At school?"

"No, I had it in a little flat I keep in Boston. Bachelor digs on Chestnut Street."

"You're not married?"

"No self-respecting young lady would have me," said Hibbard.

"That's one way of putting it," said George Lockwood. "I suspect that you're still enjoying your freedom."

"Well, that too. Belonging to the administrative staff, I'm not required to stay at school weekends, so I'm in Boston a great deal, Friday afternoon to Sunday evening or sometimes Monday morning. Someone left a cigarette burning in my flat, and I lost a lot of personal stuff. My St. Bartholomew's and Harvard College diplomas. A couple of tennis trophies, and all my Spy pictures. An original Beerbohm, that I got the old boy to sign. God damn careless person."

"She must have been."

"I didn't say *she*, Mr. Lockwood."

"You didn't have to," said George.

"Well, I gave myself away, although I don't know how."

"If it had been a man you'd have said so, but you said 'God damn careless *person*.' "

"I'll watch that," said Hibbard. "This bag contains a lot of data that I compiled that I think has the answer to any questions that I may be asked. For instance, starting with what we intend to do with the money after it's invested. What we'll do with the income from one million, if we get it. What we'll do with the income from a million and a half, if we get that. What we'll do with the income from two million, and so on, up to five million. If we raise six million, we'll be slightly embarrassed, but only slightly and only temporarily, I assure you. None of the money, by the way, is going into physical plant. It is all earmarked for salary and pension and various and sundry insurance programs covering life and accident and disability. Would you care to have a look?"

"No thank you. My small donation doesn't entitle me to a look."

"Of course it does, but these things can be a bore. However, I brought along some snapshots that I don't think will be a bore. Have a look at these." He handed George an envelope. "All taken with a Brownie Number 2, and don't worry. No views of the Grand Canyon."

George examined the snapshots, two dozen pictures taken at Bing's ranch. Bing. His wife. The children. The ranchhouse. The Rolls-Royce. Oil derricks. The men were silent as George studied the photographs, put them back in the envelope and held it out to Hibbard.

"They're for you," said Hibbard.

"Oh—thank you. You really know your business, don't you, Mr. Hibbard?"

"That isn't why I took them."

"Then why *did* you take them?"

"Because in some ways I'm a Christer," said Hibbard.

"Explain that, please," said George.

"I have a brother who never sees my father. He's artistic, as they say in Boston. Henry won't have anything to do with the rest of us. I can't talk about him without making him sound like a wet smack, and in some ways he is. But he isn't, *really*. He quit Harvard, went to Paris, and is now living in Mexico. He apparently paints pretty well. He was given a show in Boston last year and he came back for it, but he never got in touch with my father or mother, never sent them an invitation to the show, and he borrowed my flat. He had a woman with him he said was Mexican, but she was no more

Mexican than Jack Johnson, and they left the place like a pigsty."

"I would say that your father was well off," said George.

"He doesn't think so. Henry was his favorite of all of us, and I never knew why. Got away with stuff we could never get away with. A spoiled brat, and to this day goes out of his way to make my parents unhappy. Wrote a letter to the *Transcript* over this Sacco and Vanzetti business, and signed his name. Oh, all sorts of things. My father's had one stroke, and I know the one thing he'd like best is to have Henry come home and behave like a decent human being. None of this resembles the falling-out that you and Bing have had, and yet it does."

"How?" said George.

"Well, I know that Henry would make it up with my father if he knew how. And from the way Bing spoke of you, there are no hard feelings on his part."

"It's possible there may be some on mine."

"Yes, but I didn't think so after seeing you look at those pictures. Actually of course I don't know what the bone of contention was between you."

"The bone of contention?" said George. "There was no bone of contention. A bone of contention is something two dogs fight over, and that wasn't the sort of thing we quarreled over. We had a difference of opinion that was irreconcilable at the time, and it seems to have turned out to my son's advantage. Very well. If he had ever needed my help, he only had to ask for it. But he hasn't needed it, and now he never will."

"More and more like the situation between my brother and my father."

"No doubt. Those things are inclined to fall into the same categories, you might say. Father and son dissensions. In our case, my son's success in California makes it very unlikely that we will ever be reconciled."

"Why?"

"None of your business," said George.

"None of my business unless I make it my business."

"It's still none of your business, and why should you make it your business?"

"Because, as I said before, I have a little of the Christer in me."

"I'm not familiar with that term. Does it mean what I think it means? A, uh, missionary? I've had some experience with a disappointed missionary. That's a career with very little future in it, Mr. Hibbard."

"My career isn't headed in that direction, Mr. Lockwood. My plans are all made. I have a pretty good idea where I'll be and what I'll be doing twenty years from now."

"That's good."

"Or even forty years from now."

"You arouse my curiosity," said George.

"I'll satisfy it. Do you know anything about my family? I wouldn't assume you did if it weren't for the fact that you've been to St. Bartholomew's and you're a business man."

"I know your family are extremely well-to-do, if that's what you mean."

"They are filthy rich, that's what they are. The family fortunes are well up in eight figures, to the left-hand side of the decimal point. And it gets bigger all the time. That embarrasses my brother, but not me. He got some Socialistic ideas at Harvard, and he doesn't want to be known as a rich dilettante. I'm not an artist, and I don't believe that the possession of good common stocks and so on is a sin. I like money, and I'm not a bit ashamed of it."

"Very sensible," said George.

"On the other hand, I have no desire to make more for myself. I don't want to live anywhere but Boston, or live in style. I pay sixty-three dollars for my suits, off the rack at Brooks Brothers, and I have five of them. Blue serge and grey worsted for winter, blue flannel and grey flannel for summer. And a tan gabardine for sporting events. Baseball games and such. I have a Dodge coupe that's good for another fifteen thousand miles. I don't spend ten thousand a year on myself, and that's taking care of club dues and my bootlegger, and thus and so. My only extravagance is tennis balls. I refuse to play with balls that the life's gone out of. I use at least a dozen a week, sometimes more when I'm playing on grass, during summer vacation. We still have clay courts at school. Well, I have *one* other extravagance. My pipe tobacco is my own mixture, costs me about seventy dollars a year. Blue Boar used to cost me about fifteen dollars a year, so that *is* an extravagance."

"Alarming," said George.

Hibbard smiled. "Well, it is, you know. It represented a drastic change in my ways, switching from Blue Boar to Mr. Preston Hibbard Special. I bought a pouch, so my friends wouldn't notice that I'd gone high-hat on them. My mother almost spilled the beans. She noticed the aroma and commented on it, so I had to take her into my confidence. By the way, why am I suddenly so lacking in reticence? I don't as a rule run off at the mouth this way."

"I said more to you about my son than I've said to anyone since he left here," said George. "Whatever the reason, I like it. I like hearing what you have to say. You started to tell me about your plans."

"Yes. Well, I expect to serve on a lot of boards. Boards of trustees, boards of visitors, et cetera. My father and both grandfathers did, and so will I. Some men, or most men, haven't got the time to devote to that work. They accept the directorates, and attend the regular stated meetings, but they have other work to do. There are a few men in a position to make that kind of work their career, and I'm one of them. The only job I've ever had is my present one, acting bursar. It's a lot of detail work and very good training. My next step will be to take over some of my father's trusteeships. Harvard. Two hospitals, and four or five corporations, two banks. I expect to have a very busy life, in work that I like, with the kind of men I like to be with. It's by no means all drudgery. A lot of pleasant social activity goes along with it. Luncheons. Dinners. Junkets. And the feeling that you're doing something worthwhile."

"Now that's very interesting," said George. "It corresponds to certain plans my father had for me, and I had for *my* son till he stormed out of here—not this house, but the one we used to live in. My plans, and my father's before me, were localized, and not so much confined to trusteeships and so on. I still have to go on making money, and I've just recently gone into a business venture that may be every bit as risky as oil speculations and won't offer the same fantastic returns. I go into a lot of things because they interest me, and stay out of others because they don't. When you don't have to actually earn your living, I see no point in engaging in business unless you get some other satisfaction out of it besides the making of money. That seems to be the way you feel about it too."

"Very much so."

"However, I'm afraid charity and welfare work doesn't appeal to me as it does to you. Perhaps because we haven't had our money that long, or as much of it. If my plan had worked out, perhaps this towheaded young grandson of mine eventually would have reached the stage where you are now. I would have been delighted with that." He paused. "The news you brought me today, about my son and his finances, means the end to my plan and my father's plan, and it's going to be hard to get used to."

"I'm sorry to be the bearer of bad tidings," said Hibbard.

"I'd rather hear it from you, this way, than less directly, from total strangers. You see, Mr. Hibbard, my plan required the presence here of my son and his family. It meant their living in Swedish Haven. My son knew nothing about business or money when he left here, and I was sure that in time he'd have to come back. Now he never will."

"Frankly, I don't think he will. He as much as said so. I don't think he has much use for the East, at least as a place to live. And neither has Rita. They love California, and I doubt if there's anything in the world that will move them out of there. I was about to say, short of an earthquake, but as a matter of fact they've even had minor ones of those. No, he's dug in."

"All the expense of St. Bartholomew's and Princeton to produce a Californian."

"My brother's background was St. Bartholomew's and Harvard, and Eastern Massachusetts since the Seventeenth Century, but now he considers himself a Mexican! I suppose the parents of the first American Hibbard said pretty much the same thing."

"They came here because of religious persecution," said George.

"Not the first John Hibbard. He wasn't one of the Pilgrims. He came later, to seek his fortune in hides and tallow. Actually a great-uncle of mine was in the shoe business when he died, and that more or less ended the family connection with hides. No one left to carry on the business, and his widow sold out just in time to miss out on supplying shoes to the Union army. Someone else made a fortune. In fact, a classmate of yours. Allan Ames."

"Is *that* where his money came from?"

Hibbard nodded. "That particular Ames money doesn't go back as far as some Ames money."

"I never knew that."

"Well, there are a lot of Adamses in Massachusetts, too. A lot of Warrens and Bradfords. Hibbards, too, for that matter. Not all the Lowells in the Boston phone book are related to Larry. In fact, not all the Lowells are Lowells, especially around Newton."

"That's true," said George. "A George Lockwood answered one time when I was being paged. He was quite insistent that he was as much George Lockwood as I. 'All right,' I said, 'but I happen to know it's my brother that's paging me. Does your brother call himself Lockwood too, or did he take something fancier?' Another time I traveled from Philadelphia to Boston, on the sleeper, with George Lockwood as my porter. Not a very unusual name, I've found. Not quite Smith or Brown, but not Saltonstall, either."

"There are quite a few of them where I come from," said Hibbard.

"But around here, you see, the only Lockwoods are my Lockwoods, our Lockwoods." He stopped abruptly, on the verge of confiding in this young man the full details of his plans for his family, now suddenly abandoned. The young man exuded no warmth; it was not the warmth of sympathy that seemed to invite such candor as they had allowed themselves and each other in this interview. Nevertheless George Lockwood, a cerebrating man always, was busily wondering why he was attracted to Hibbard and why Hibbard was attracted to him. George Lockwood theorized, and postponed for later consideration, as to the possibility that Hibbard recognized in him a new but authentic member of the class to which Hibbard belonged.

"It seems a pity that future generations of Lockwoods aren't going to occupy this house," said Hibbard. "Although perhaps they will. Who know? Bing's son may want to live in the East. It's of course much too early to tell, one way or the other."

"I'm not very hopeful of that," said George. "You've given me a very convincing picture of a permanent California family. I'll have to think about what to do with this place. My brother wouldn't take it. He's a New Yorker now, and who else *is* there?"

"Yes, I see how you could be discouraged. It's a fine piece of property, built to stay. It'll be here two hundred years from now. Anyone with half an eye can see that a great deal of careful planning went into it, and no expense spared, inside or out." He stood up.

"Would you care to have a look around?" said George.

"I should have been on my way before this, but yes, I would like to snoop a bit," said Hibbard. He smiled. "Those gargoyles, on the mantelpiece, evil-looking little rascals, aren't they? But amusing."

"I wonder if I could trust you with a secret. I believe I can. You belong to the Porcellian Club, don't you?"

"I do."

"And I suppose other organizations that don't tell everything that goes on."

"Oh, yes."

"Would you be interested in acquiring a secret that only two people would know—you and I?"

"If you're sure it'd be safe with me. I'm very good at keeping secrets, but you have no way of knowing that."

"Except my instinct," said George Lockwood. He went to

the study door and turned the key in the lock. "Now, if you'll put your hand on the second gargoyle from the right."

"Second from the right," said Hibbard.

"Turn it as though you were opening a door by the knob."

"Yes, it turns very easily," said Hibbard. "Now what happens?"

"Nothing, *unless* you push the gargoyle."

"Is that what you want me to do? Push it?"

"Yes," said George Lockwood.

Hibbard did as instructed and the wall panel rose, revealing the entrance to the hidden stairway. "Great!" said Hibbard. "Where does this go?"

"Upstairs, to a closet in my bedroom, or down to the cellar."

"Oh, what fun! And nobody knows about it? What about your carpenters?"

"Italians, expert craftsmen imported from New York. They had to know, but it isn't information that will ever do them any good."

"Ideally, of course, you would have had them murdered and their bodies sewed up in a sock and dropped in the Grand Canal."

"Ideally, but our local canal wouldn't be suitable."

"And other objections, too. What do you use the stairway for?"

"I haven't found any use for it as yet. I'm not even sure why I had it put in."

"Your servants don't know about it, of course?"

"Not even my wife knows about it."

"But now I do," said Hibbard. "Can you close the panel from the inside?"

"Oh, yes. And the gargoyle turns back to normal position."

"Do you know what it makes me think of?" said Hibbard.

"What?"

"Our boxes at St. Bartholomew's."

"That's exactly where the idea started. When I was at school, I had a box, just like everyone else. But my box was different. I had an old Pennsylvania Dutch carpenter put a false bottom in my box. I kept money in it."

"Against all rules," said Hibbard.

"Yes. But I had cash all the time I was at St. Bartholomew's. As you see, I've always been of a very secretive nature."

"Well, now I'll tell you something, Mr. Lockwood. I did the same thing. That is, I had a cache of cash all the time I was at school. Not in my box. When you were there, you weren't allowed to have any money at all. They of course relaxed that rule somewhat, but we were never allowed more than a dollar and a half a week. I didn't like that rule, so I disobeyed it for six years."

"Where did you hide yours?"

"I changed hiding places. One year I had twenty one-dollar bills in old bound volumes of the Congressional Record. Another time I kept my money in a bird-house, in a tree back of the old boilerhouse. I tacked wire screen on the hole to make sure no birds would take up residence in it. Another time I put the money in a Prince Albert tobacco tin and hid it behind the bulletin board in the boathouse, but someone found it. Twenty-five dollars. Then my master stroke. The cleverest bit of deception I ever accomplished. I put the money in an envelope, sealed the envelope, no name on the outside, and just left it in my pigeonhole in the mailbox. Anybody could have taken it away, but nobody ever did. It never aroused anybody's curiosity. Just a plain, cheap envelope. If it had had my name on it, or any name, it probably would have been a temptation. But it was so uninteresting that nobody ever took it. At least that's the way I doped it out."

"Was clever," said George Lockwood. "Why do you suppose we went to so much trouble? There was nothing to spend the money on, without becoming conspicuous, even in your day."

"Oh, I know why I did it. It may not be your reason, but mine was to outsmart everybody, the masters and my schoolmates."

George nodded. "That was mine."

"Our boxes satisfied our need for privacy. But some of us needed more than privacy."

"What did we need? What did you need?" said George.

"Privacy beyond privacy. Some boys had a hard time taking a leak when other boys were present. That was never my trouble. But I always had to have something that was particularly, especially my own. At school, it was my hidden treasure."

"And at college?"

"My flat, the same one I have now. The difference being that at Harvard my family never knew I had it. Now, of course, they do, but it's still mine. There's not one thing in it belongs to anyone else or that was given me by someone else. When I go there, I can shut out the rest of the world."

"Not that you always do," said George.

"No. It's had a lot of visitors, but they all have to go away. I lent it to my brother and his lady friend, and I felt they desecrated it. But then the careless young lady left a cigarette burning and somehow or other the evil spirits were exorcised. I bought the building a year or two ago and my next move will be to buy the houses on either side."

"So you don't have to lease the apartments to anyone you don't know."

"On the contrary. I don't lease to anyone I do know. Socially, that is. My tenants are all strangers, and naturally they don't know I'm the owner. That's the way it's going to stay."

"A kingdom of your own, on Beacon Hill," said George.

"Eventually, when I buy the houses in back of mine, so that nobody'll be able to see in," said Hibbard. "But I have no secret passageway. You've given me an idea."

"My little secret is modest compared to yours," said George. "I daresay you'll eventually own a whole city block."

"Possibly. But it isn't the size of the secret. Your passageway does as much for you as my houses will for me."

George nodded. "Yes," he said. "I've gotten very fond of this house in a very short time. It already has a character that most houses take years acquiring. I stayed with it every step of the way, when I was building it, and just before we were ready to move in, there was a fatal accident here." He told briefly the story of the boy impaled on the stone wall.

"I'm glad to see you're not superstitious about it," said Hibbard.

"Not in the least," said George. "Unless you consider an omen superstitious. Perhaps it is."

"What is the omen?"

"The omen is this: I built that wall to keep people out, just as my grandfather once did to protect himself from people who had threatened his life. That's too long a story to go into now, but he was threatened. So the idea of a wall around a Lockwood house, *my* Lockwood house, was by way of being a family tradition. My wall was no more popular than my grandfather's was in his time, by the way. In fact, this entire establishment was unpopular. I bought a farm, for instance, from a fellow whose family had farmed here for over a century, and I tore down everything. House, barns, et cetera, and the farmer moved out of the county. Then I put up my wall, more or less to serve notice on my neighbors and the people in town, and put the spikes in the wall. The first time we had a trespasser, he lost his life. How do you, as a Christer, feel about that?"

"That's hard to say. You had nothing to do with the boy's being killed."

"I ordered the spikes in the wall," said George.

"Well, I'm not in any position to criticize. I'm going to some lengths to keep people out of my life, aren't I? And I've always liked the idea of having a moat around a castle. I know a very religious man who has a small island in Maine, and I can just hear him piously criticizing you for putting spikes in your wall. But he gets his privacy by surrounding himself with the Atlantic Ocean. It'd take a very good swimmer to get there from the mainland. In fact, not everybody can get there by boat. I'll have to withhold any moral judgment on your wall. As long as you're not too critical of my little kingdom on Beacon Hill."

"How would you like to postpone your visit to Bayard Donaldson and spend the night here?" said George.

"Thank you, sir. I wish I could. I truly wish I could. Unfortunately it's not Mr. Donaldson but Mr. Mackie who's going to be my host tonight, and he's sailing for Europe the day after tomorrow. He stretched a point to see me tonight."

"In that case, you can't get out of it."

"Duty first," said Hibbard.

"Oh, he's a very entertaining fellow, Mackie. You'll be brought up to date on the latest dirty limericks, and those Scranton people go in for strenuous hospitality. Where do you go from there?"

"Tomorrow night I'll be at the Fort Orange Club in Albany, a small dinner for the alumni in that region. Driving home the next day, and putting my car in the shop for a complete overhaul. When this is over I'll need one myself."

"I should think so," said George. "What will you do to recuperate?"

"As a matter of fact, I'm going to sequester myself in my flat in Chestnut Street. Take a week off and see no one."

"I was hoping you'd say that," said George. "The human race can be much too companionable. I wish I had a greater fondness for animals, but they can be a bore, too."

"Well, I've enjoyed our misanthropic luncheon, Mr. Lockwood. It's been one of the bright spots on my tour."

"I hope you mean that," said George.

"Oh, I do. Mark my words, when I say thank-you, I mean thank-you, but when I say I've enjoyed myself I mean a great deal more."

"Say that again," said George.

"Why?"

"I just wanted to hear that rich Boston accent pronouncing 'mark my words.' "

"Mark my words? Get a State of Maine native to pronounce 'Hershey bar.' Mark my words, the Hershey bars at the Parker House can't be beat. How was that?"

"It takes me back to St. Bartholomew's."

"Speaking of which, I am putting you down for ten thousand. You'll be getting a pledge card in due course. Is that satisfactory?"

"Pending the latest developments from Groton. Before you go I'd like to have you meet my wife," said George. He went to the house telephone on the wall, pushed one of the buttons, and spoke. "My dear, Mr. Hibbard is just about to leave. Can you come down and say hello? . . . Thank you. . . She'll be right down."

Geraldine Lockwood appeared in a Fortuny gown. "I was sure you gentlemen wanted to be left alone," she said.

"Now I'll never forgive Mr. Lockwood for keeping you out of sight. Isn't that a Fortuny gown?"

"Yes, it is," said Geraldine.

"How the devil would you know that?" said George.

"Oh, I have other sides to me," said Hibbard. "As a matter of fact, I picked up that information from my sister-in-law. She wears them all the time. Different ones."

"Yes, they're nice for wearing at home," said Geraldine.

"Well, I hate to interrupt this fashion discussion, but if you're driving to Scranton, I understand there's a long detour between Hazleton and Wilkes-Barre, and you're not going to make very good time. Will you let me know if you're ever in this neighborhood again, and we can put you up for the night," said George.

"I most certainly will," said Hibbard.

George Lockwood helped him on with his topcoat. The men shook hands. Hibbard picked up his green felt bag. The Lockwoods saw him to his car and he was off.

"A charming, very attractive young man," said George. "Didn't you think so?"

"I didn't see him long enough to get any impression," said Geraldine.

"Oh, really? Watching the two of you, I thought I detected a spark of something or other."

"If there was any, you misinterpreted it," she said. "At least on my part. I was the opposite of attracted to him."

"Repelled?"

"Maybe not as strong as that, but I wasn't attracted to him."

"Why not?"

"He's a sneak," she said.

"A *sneak?* How on earth could you tell that? That's a preposterous thing to say, when you weren't in his company five minutes."

"I'm telling you what I thought," she said.

"Did I miss something? My back was only turned for a few seconds."

"He didn't pinch me, if that's what you mean. But he would. He has that look. Maybe that's what you called a spark. But I'll bet I know how he dances."

"This is monstrous, Geraldine," said George. "In two hours the better I got to know him, the more I began to believe that he and I had a lot in common."

"Well, I know how you dance," she said.

"If my partner happens to like to dance that way," he said.

"It's easy to blame the woman," she said. "Well, I have some letters to write."

"Who to?"

"What?"

"These letters you have to write. Whom are they to? You always use that excuse, letters to write, but you don't mail two letters a week."

"How do you know I don't smuggle them out and post them in town?"

"Well, you could, of course. But do you?"

"I'm going to let you worry about that. It'll give you something to occupy your busy mind."

He smiled faintly. "Mark my words, I shall do that very thing. All right, go write your mythical letters. I'm driving in to town. Is there anything you want?"

"From town? No. Unless you'd care to stop in at Mrs. Mohler's and ask her if my embroidery hoops have arrived."

"Embroidery hoops?"

"I've taken it up," she said.

"Have you really? Mrs. Mohler teaching you?"

"She said she would."

"I'd rather not, if you don't mind. You do as you please but I don't care to set foot in Mrs. Mohler's shop. She's a gossip, a busybody. She had a lot to say about Agnes and me when Agnes was sick."

"Yes, I suppose she did," said Geraldine.

"Oh, you knew that?"

"I surmised it."

"Surmised it from what?"

"Does it matter? She promised to teach me embroidery, and I'm told she's the best in town. I don't encourage her gossip but I must have *something* to do."

"How many times have I heard that?" said George.

"You'll go on hearing it till I find something," she said.

He had got his hat and topcoat out of a closet. Now he sat

down and folded the coat over his lap and dangled the hat in his thumb and forefinger. "Before you go upstairs to write those pressing letters, could you spare a minute?"

She replied by taking a chair.

"When you were married to Buckmaster, you did a lot of entertaining. You did a certain amount of traveling, and visiting your friends, having them visit you. But since you've been married to me you haven't made any effort to do more than the absolute minimum of entertaining. Granted there's nobody much in Swedish Haven, but there's plenty of activity in Gibbsville, as much as anyone could want. You dismiss the Gibbsville people as small-town hicks, and you pick out the ones that are hicks to bolster your argument. But you know full well that the town has more than its share of men and women that went to the best schools and have as good social connections as the people you and Buckmaster used to see. Gibbsville has its Rotarians, but it also has its Ivy Club people and whatever else you want to name. It isn't Long Island, it isn't the Philadelphia Main Line, but I don't seem to recall that you and Buckmaster cut a very fancy figure in those circles. Hardly anybody in Gibbsville goes to Palm Beach, but they do go to Orlando, and in the summer to Fisher's Island and Mount Desert, by preference. In London they stay at Brown's Hotel, by preference and by habit. So your argument that they're small-town hicks doesn't stand up. It's just that you aren't willing to make the effort."

"*You* never did, with Agnes," she said.

"Not very much, but Agnes had never been socially inclined, and you had. Also, Agnes was a full-fledged member of the coal region hierarchy, and you came here a stranger. You had to make some effort, and you refused to. You won't play golf, you won't even play bridge, and when you've been invited to play golf or bridge you've acted as though you'd been asked to join the ladies auxiliary of one of the fire companies. Those people are better than that, and they're *not* your inferiors, Geraldine. Some of them have more money than I have or Buckmaster had, and most of them come from families that go back two or three hundred years. Old Pennsylvania towns named for their ancestors. Old New England towns, too, because not all of them are old Pennsylvania. A hundred years ago or more a lot of them came down from Connecticut and Massachusetts. You don't know anything about the local history, because you don't care to."

"I'm not interested in any history," she said.

"Well, then, tell me what you *are,* interested in? If you showed any interest in anything, I'd encourage it. You bought two expensive vases that caught your eye, and I was rather hopeful that at last I had some clue to the sort of thing you were interested in. But no. You pass them fifty times a day and never look at them. You've never mentioned them since they were put in place. In fact, a couple of months ago I changed their places. They don't match exactly, and I wanted to see if you'd become aware of that, but you hadn't."

"I was told they did match," she said.

"They're a pair, but one of the dragons faces to the right and the dragon on the other vase faces to the left."

"Oh, I knew that for heaven's sake," she said.

"But you didn't know I'd changed their position," he said.

"Well, what if I didn't? Good Lord, I have other things to think about."

"What?" he said.

"I knew I shouldn't have said that."

"Well, you did say it, and I've asked you what the things are that you have to think about? And don't tell me Mrs. Mohler's embroidery lessons."

"I won't," she said.

"All right, what?"

"I think about you," she said.

"Tenderly, of course."

"Not any more," she said. She sat up straight. "I'm afraid of you."

"Afraid of me?"

"Not physically. But I've become afraid of what you're doing to me. Mentally I'm not your equal, and I've always known that. I knew I had a better mind than Howard's—"

"You had a mind, therefore it had to be better than whatever he has that passes for a mind."

"But one of the things that attracted me to you was your mind. From the very beginning you were able to exert some kind of a mental control over me. The other men I've known were attracted to *me*. Not for my mind, of course. Anything but. But when I met you, conditions were reversed. The physical attraction was there, but secondary. No man had ever twisted around everything I said, even the simplest things. First it was a sort of teasing me, making little jokes about things I said. But then you began to change my whole mental outlook."

"Allow me to correct you. You had no mental outlook. I may have encouraged you to create one."

"Well, why did you?" she said.

"Because I was attracted to you physically."

"Oh, I knew that, but why did you have to—"

"I didn't *have* to. I *wanted* to," he said. "I was determined to marry you, not just to have an affair with you. At my age a man ought to know what he wants in a woman. Casual affairs at my age can be had with young girls, and should be. But if you find a woman that's physically attractive, a mature woman, you ought to have the good sense to get more out of her than two or three nights in bed with her. You can know all about a young girl in two or three nights, if only because she is a young girl and has so little else to offer. But a reasonably mature woman, who's been going to bed with a man or men for twenty years, more or less, she's gone beyond the kindergarten stage and the nervous self-consciousness of the young."

"Tell me about Agnes," said Geraldine.

"No, I *won't* tell you about Agnes," he said. "All right, I *will* tell you about Agnes, enough for the purpose of this discussion. She had a first-rate mind, but she thought fucking was a sin. She was a hot little piece, but it was all for herself. She believed that the less pleasure you gave the man, the less sinful she was."

"How do you know that?"

"From the hundreds of times she made me rape her."

"Hundreds of times?"

"Every time. She wasn't very voluptuous. She wasn't at all voluptuous. Two little swellings instead of breasts, that she was ashamed of. So that when I went to bed with her she wanted no preliminaries. Force it into her as far as it would go, and get it over with. Then when I was through it was just the beginning for her. I hated her. And she hated me."

"Why didn't you get a divorce?"

"I didn't want a divorce. Instead of that, I had other women."

"You would have anyway," said Geraldine.

"Undoubtedly. At least Agnes kept me from ever having a guilty conscience, I'll say that for her."

"I begin to understand something about you and me," she said.

"Pray tell me, what is that?"

"You said that Agnes had a first-rate mind."

"She had," he said.

"Then what you wanted from me was a mind that you could have control over. The mature woman with the kindergarten mind."

"You're over-modest, my dear," he said.

"There you're wrong, George. I haven't got a first-rate mind, and I know it. But I am that mature woman, and I want to tell you something. My second-rate mind sees through you. I know a lot about men. Men give themselves away in bed."

"Do I? Yes, I'm sure I do," he said.

"Everywhere else, your mind makes you my superior. But not when you take your clothes off."

"No? Then does that mean you've stopped being afraid of me?"

"No, I'm still afraid of what you can do to me the rest of the time."

"What do you think I want to do to you?"

"Get even with women for what Agnes did to you," she said.

"That, my dear, is brilliant. You haven't been reading any books on sex, have you?"

"I don't have to read books on sex. The ones I did read didn't tell me anything I hadn't found out for myself. From men. Old stuff, as the kids say nowadays."

"Old stuff, except when it happens to you," said George. "You may have read about kissing when you were a little girl, but the first time a boy really kissed you, it wasn't old stuff, was it?"

"The first time I was really kissed it wasn't a boy. It was a grown man, and he had his hand up my leg."

"Oh, everything all at once," he said.

"Not everything. I was still a virgin when I married Howard. But I knew what to expect."

"Did he?"

"He was quite surprised."

"How?"

"That I was a virgin."

"And was he pleased?"

"Of course he was pleased."

"Yes, we all are," said George. "And I wonder why. After all, a gentleman doesn't return from his honeymoon and rush to his club and say to the fellows, 'Guess what! Susie had her cherry.' "

"You're only speaking of gentlemen," she said.

"Well, why speak of the others? You've certainly found out by this time that I'm a complete snob. I have to be. My grandson won't have to be, but I do."

"Your grandson but not your son?"

"My son is dead."

"What?"

"Don't take me so literally. He's very much alive and already a millionaire, according to young Hibbard. But he's out of my life and apparently never coming back into it. He's nouveau-riche. A self-made man, with a Rolls-Royce car and hobnail boots. He can go fuck himself, the little prick."

"What's happened? I've never heard you carry on like this," she said.

"Oh, go to hell," said George Lockwood. He rose suddenly and left the house, and in a moment she heard the Packard's deep hum in the driveway and the slag of the roadbed being spattered against the wall. George Lockwood was not himself.

George Lockwood believed that the secret of getting the most out of life was in getting the most out of people, and the secret of getting the most out of people was not to spend too much time with any individual at a stretch. No man or woman could be stimulating for days on end. Women, with their power to provide the most stimulating experience in life, were prevented by the physical nature of the male from maintaining their power after passion was spent. The male was obliged to retire until his vitality was replenished, a condition that sometimes had been speeded up by changing to another female.

In any case he had been with Geraldine too long. He returned from Swedish Haven in a better mood which, however, was created by his decision to get away for a few days and not by the mere passing of his irritability. After all, the irritability had been brought on by thoughts of his son more than by impatience with Geraldine. Nevertheless Geraldine had annoyed him, and it would be a relief to spend a few days in New York without her. In Swedish Haven therefore he went to the telephone booth in the railway station and made a long-distance call to his brother in New York. "I have no time to talk to you now, but I want you to call me at home at seven o'clock this evening," he said.

"Is there anything wrong?" said Penrose Lockwood.

"Nothing wrong. Just call me at seven, when I'll have more time to talk."

Promptly at seven, as George and Geraldine were on their way in to dinner, the maid told George that Mr. Penrose Lockwood was on the wire and wished to speak to him.

"Oh, Christ," said George. "Well, you go on in, Geraldine. I'll be with you in a minute."

"Your soup'll get cold," said Geraldine.

"There must be *some* way to keep it warm," said George.

"Oh, all right," she said.

George took the call in his study, leaving the door wide open if Geraldine cared to listen. "Yes, Pen. We were just sitting down to dinner."

"What did you want to talk to me about?" said Pen.

"About the candy business. Those advertising people, eh?"

"You're talking gibberish," said Pen.

"I'm quite aware of that. All right, then. I'll take the sleeper and I'll see you at the office in the morning. Give my love to Wilma. Thank you for calling."

He hung up and went to the diningroom. "I have to go to New York tonight. The advertising people have left a lot of stuff at the office, and you know Pen. He always wants to do the right thing. Didn't know whether the stuff was important or not, although as a matter of fact in this case it is. Sent his love."

"I imagine he has a lot to spare, married to Wilma."

"Would you mind driving me to the station? Ten o'clock," said George.

"Oh, really, now. Andrew hasn't had anything to do all day."

"Thought you might like some fresh air."

"I don't like to drive alone at night. Change my clothes to go out, and back again when I get home. And that's when I begin to get good reception on the radio. Why inconvenience me?"

"Please forget all about it," said George. It rather pleased him that he could leave in a mood of righteous disappointment. His mind was already made up as to the purpose of his trip to New York, but Geraldine's refusal to take him to the train set him free. He busied himself alone until train time, and when Andrew brought the car around, George called his goodbye upstairs to Geraldine, who was having trouble getting Cincinnati on the Atwater Kent. If she responded to his farewell, he did not hear her.

The sleeper ended its journey at Jersey City and he took the ferry across the river and went directly to his office. It was too early for Pen to be there, but the members of the office staff were reporting for work. To George's surprise, one of the early arrivals was Marian Strademyer. She was the real reason for his trip to the city, but he had half expected that she might take advantage of her relationship with Pen to assume certain small privileges, such as coming in late. She looked fresh and crisp, suitably businesslike and yet wholly feminine, and her femininity convinced him that he had obeyed an impulse that was timely in Swedish Haven and going to be timely in New York. She was wearing a dress made of a material that resembled blue serge, with a narrow leather belt at the waist and a white collar. It had almost the severity of a nun's habit; a string of beads could have dangled from the leather belt, and the white collar could have been stretched into one of those starched bibs that nuns wore. But George Lockwood had never looked upon nuns as sexless women. That brothel in Paris where the inmates wore nuns' habits had always seemed to George to require a degree of self-deception that was beneath his dignity; on the other hand, he had occasionally seen a genuine young nun whose complacent innocence he would gladly have investigated.

"We weren't expecting you till the 29th," said Marian Strademyer.

"No, something came up, and I came in on the sleeper."

"Have you had breakfast? Could I send down to the Savarin?"

"Had breakfast in the station restaurant, thanks. Had a shave over there, too. The train gets in awfully early. How have you been?"

"Oh, just about as usual, I guess," she said.

"Are you happy? You seem so," he said.

"Happy? That's something I never ask myself, especially at half past nine in the morning," she said.

"Well, if you give the impression of being happy at that hour, then you must be," said George.

"Oh, I guess that's because I'm healthy."

"Healthy, and young."

"Don't talk as if you were some eighty-year-old invalid," she said.

"Oh, but I just came from the barbershop. The man's beauty parlor," he said. "What time do you expect my brother?"

"Usually a little after ten, and he didn't say anything when he left last night, so I guess he'll be in in about a half an hour or so."

"Then I'll wait for him. I expect to be in and out of here all day."

"Will you need someone to take dictation? I can do it, or if you're going to need someone all day, I'll give you one of the other girls. We weren't expecting you till the 29th."

"Let's see how it works out. I'll need someone tomorrow, but possibly not today."

"Very well," she said, and left; but as she was leaving, with her back turned toward him, there was a hesitancy in her step that he took for a sign of reluctance to leave. Their relationship, he knew, had been replenished; his impulse had been based on sure instinct.

He filled in the time with some telephone calls to Charley Bohm, to Ringwall at the advertising agency, to the Carstairs for a room reservation. He was talking to the hotel when Pen entered his office.

"Hello, brother," said George.

"Good morning," said Pen. "What's all the mystery about?"

"Sit down," said George. "I just decided I wanted to get away from Geraldine for a few days."

"You're the damnedest man I ever heard of. You couldn't just pack a bag and come to New York, the way any normal human being would."

"There are subtleties that you don't understand. How is Wilma?"

"Oh, she's all right."

"But *not* all right. How are you?"

"How am I? What do you mean, how am I?"

"Well, that answer tells me that things aren't going very well for you."

"We're making money. If everything was as easy as that," said Pen.

"You're having trouble with your girl."

"I'd rather talk about that some other time—if I have to talk about it at all, which I suppose I do."

"Talk about it now, for Christ's sake."

"Let me go have a look at the ticker first. I want to see what something opened at. This is something of mine, a tip I got a couple of days ago." He went out to the large office and stood at the stock ticker, with the tape resting on his hand. George could see him nod and drop the tape into the tall basket.

"Okay?" said George.

Pen nodded more vigorously. "As predicted. You don't want to know what it is, do you? I'll tell you if you want to know, but you have to stay out of it."

"You're speaking of a stock, and not your personal life."

"Speaking of a stock, although you're right, I could have meant either one," said Pen.

"You could only have meant one, but it could have been taken either way. No, I'm not interested in your stock speculation, but I am in your love life."

"Wilma has taken up with some fairy. That is; I think of him as a fairy. Half the men I know don't seem to mind if their wives have some fairy around to dance attendance on them, and I wouldn't mind either. But this fellow may not be a fairy. His name is Eugene Hyme, H, y, m, e. He's a young Jew about thirty or so, related to some of those prominent Jewish families. Interested in music and all that stuff, but has a job downtown too, in the foreign exchange department of Glassman Brothers."

"You don't sound very worried about him," said George.

"Well, I am and I'm not," said Pen. "In the first place, he looks like such a long drink of water that a good screw would shake him to pieces. I could be wrong about that, too, but I don't think he and Wilma go to bed together. In the second place, I don't know what he sees in Wilma beyond the fact that through her he gets invited to houses that he'd never get invited to otherwise. In that respect he resembles me, except that after twenty years they've gotten sort of used to me. Wilma's old New York society connections. So much for Mr. Hyme."

"So much for Mr. Hyme," said George.

"I'll have to come back to him in a minute," said Pen. "I had a couple of talks with Wilma, and wish I'd been more like you. I'm not as good as you at these things. I tried to sound her out on the question of getting a divorce."

"Oh, Christ," said George.

"Oh, I wasn't as clumsy as all that. I didn't say divorce. But I put it to her that she seemed restless and unhappy, and I asked her if there was someone else."

"You trying to be clever! You're a blundering fool, Pen."

"I know. But I had to find out how she would feel about a divorce because I wanted one. I've gone back with my girl, and I want to marry her. It isn't fair to keep her from getting married if I'm not willing to marry her. She's entitled to a great deal more than she's getting under the present arrangement. In fact, she's entitled to marriage, to be my wife. Wilma has everything and gives nothing in return, whereas my girl gives me the only happiness I've known in years and gets practically nothing. At least in a material way. So I wanted to find out what it would cost me to be free to marry her."

"And you didn't find out," said George.

"Wrong. I found out that Wilma has no intention of divorcing me now or ever. It seems that after our first conversation, she confided in Mr. Hyme, and he guessed right away that I wanted the divorce, that I was restless and unhappy. And that I had a lady friend. And that's about where the matter stands."

"Wilma told you all that?"

"Yes. The next time I brought the matter up she talked as if she had a lawyer sitting in the room with us. She didn't sound a bit like herself, and I ought to know. She told me to have an affair, or as many affairs as I liked, but not to expect her to give me cause to divorce her. She came right out with it. She said that money was no consideration, but then in the next breath she said that if she took half and I kept half, we'd both be that much poorer. Each of us would only be worth half of what there is now."

"And she's quite right. Mr. Hyme has a great deal of common sense, it seems to me. And it is Mr. Hyme, I'm sure. Wilma would never have figured that out all by herself. So to get back to Mr. Hyme, your problem is why does he want to preserve the status quo? My guess is that Mr. Hyme wants to have a good friend in New York society, possibly for the rest of his days. Sooner or later Wilma's old friends will come to realize that it was Mr. Hyme who advised her to preserve her marriage. Therefore he is a very dependable man, not at all the gigolo type who could just as easily have persuaded Wilma to divorce you and marry him. Mr. Hyme is a dangerous man, the more so because he doesn't seem to be a bit dangerous."

"Yes," said Pen.

"And where does that leave you and your mistress?"

"I haven't had the courage to tell her the truth."

"I more or less gathered that. But why has she been so patient? Have you asked yourself that?"

"No," said Pen. "It never occurred to me."

"You're not giving her credit for very much intelligence. Haven't you stopped to consider the matter from her point of view? She surely must know that you're stalling her off. And this is the second time, if I'm not mistaken. You broke off with her once before, and then you went back. This time she must have thought you meant business."

"Yes. I told her it might take a while," said Pen.

"What is a while? A year? Two years? Two months? Actually how long has it been that you've been stalling her off?"

"Almost six months, I guess," said Pen.

"Pen, if you insist on being so damned honorable about all this, you ought to give her up. Why are you afraid to?"

"Who said I'm afraid to?"

"I do," said George. "Why don't you fire her?"

"You know who it is," said Pen.

"Yes, and I've known for a long time. Do you want me to fire her?"

"Certainly not. I don't want her to know that you know. If she has to leave the office, I'll be the one to tell her."

"And then what? She goes on being your mistress?"

"If she will be. But I want you to keep out of it. If you insist on her leaving the office, you can think up some excuse for firing her. But I'll be the one to tell her, and you keep out of the whole thing."

"Why don't we have her in here right now and both tell her? The time has come for putting all our cards on the table."

"If you do that, I'll never speak to you again as long as I live. The only life I have is with her, having her near me in the office, and the times we can be alone. I can see why you want to get her out of the office. But I'm not going to have you do anything that will interfere with the other times I see her."

"Pen, when you get fed up with her, you're going to wish you'd let me handle this."

"I'm not you," said Pen. "We're not a bit alike. I could never imagine going to all that trouble just to get away from my wife for a few days. Calling me long distance, making up some story about advertising, taking the sleeper. Christ Almighty, what a way to go through life!"

"Show me how your way is better."

"No better, maybe, but it's my way, not yours. You've never even seen your own grandchildren, that's where your way has gotten you. You never will see them, either, till they're old enough to be safe from you."

"Is that what young Hibbard told you?"

"It doesn't make any difference who told me. It's true," said Pen. "Your own son doesn't want you anywhere near his kids. You have a hell of a lot to answer for, my friend."

"To whom?"

"To God, maybe."

"Oh, dear me. Did you get that information from Hibbard, too? Or is that something you thought up all by yourself? You and Mr. Hibbard must have a lot to say to each other."

"Hibbard doesn't have to be afraid of you."

"Do you?"

"Not of you, but of what you might do to someone I love. But if you hurt her, George, you can start being afraid of me, I mean that."

George tapped his fingertips together and looked out the window. "What your friend Mr. Hyme said about your marriage applies here as well. If you feel so strongly that I'm the arch-villain of the piece, then we ought to call in the lawyers. But as Mr. Hyme said, if you take your half and I take mine, we'd both be that much poorer. What do you want to do?"

"I'll have to think it over," said Pen.

"That's right. Don't do anything impulsive. I'm here on an impulse, and a half an hour ago I was sure it was a good one. However, we shall see. I've come all this way. You think it over. I'll be in and out of here most of the day, and at the Carstairs tonight. Now if you'll excuse me, I want to run over and see Charley Bohm. Oh, and are you planning to tell Miss

Strademyer about this conversation? She offered to take some dictation, but that could be very awkward if you spill the beans."

"I'll spare her that," said Pen.

"You're such a good man, Pen. Such a good example to your older brother."

"Go fuck yourself," said Pen.

"Nope," said George.

The unsuspected duplicity of young Preston Hibbard would have to be dealt with, but first there was Marian Strademyer, Marian Strademyer and that reluctance of hers to leave this office. He rang for her.

"I came to New York for one special reason," said George.

"Oh, really? What was that?" she said.

"I'll tell you later."

"How much later?"

"Oh—say, six o'clock? At your apartment?"

She shook her head. "Can't be done," she said.

"Well, that's too bad. My trip is wasted."

"You could have phoned me yesterday," she said.

"No, this was on the spur of the moment. You wouldn't have been here."

She paused. "I'll see what I can do. You'll be back here this afternoon?"

"Yes, after lunch."

"I'll see what I can do," she said. He was tempted to say he knew what she could do, but it was a temptation he resisted. At least her part in the impulse he had followed remained sound. Indeed, as he quickly thought it over, his obedience to the impulse, though it encountered minor aggravation by Geraldine and possibly serious difficulty with Pen, continued to promise the relaxation he needed. A venture that went too smoothly was not stimulating. Even his displeasure over young Hibbard's double-dealing made Hibbard more stimulating than he might have been as a conventional Boston eccentric. Boston was full of conventional eccentrics.

The lunch club where he was meeting Charley Bohm was a dull place in one of the older skyscrapers, and Charley Bohm was a dull man; but there had been enough excitement for one morning, and George was pleased that for the next hour and a half there would be no demands on his mental energy. "We are coming along fine," said Charley, after they had ordered their lunch.

"Yes, I read all your letters, and I had a chat with Ringwall."

"There's a clever fellow, Ringwall. Clever enough to realize that this could mean a lot to him."

"We must emphasize that," said George.

"How do you mean, George?"

"At this stage of the game, we need one man's entire enthusiasm, all he can muster. You have other things to do, so have I. Other irons in other fires. My original enthusiasm has begun to dwindle, hasn't yours?"

"Well, maybe to some extent. Neither one of us are in the candy business. As far as I'm concerned, it could be the fertilizer business, just as long as I saw money in it."

"Exactly. But Ringwall mustn't be allowed to have such treasonable thoughts. I've been wondering whether we ought not to dangle a few carrots in front of his nose. Incentives."

"I'd wait a while before we do that. So far we don't have to," said Charley.

"Well, you see him much more than I do, but don't wait till he needs it. Try to anticipate the lessening of enthusiasm."

"What were you thinking of offering him?"

"What does he make?"

"I'd guess around twenty thousand a year," said Charley.

"Well, when we have our own advertising manager, won't we pay him twenty-five, and various extras based on production?"

"I don't know. Will we?"

"We'd better," said George. "Our advertising manager is going to have to be the hardest-working man we have. Anybody can make candy. Fill a vat with fudge and sprinkle a few raisins in it, and there's a product. But you have to give it a name, and get people to buy it. That's the advertising man's job. Incidentally, that wouldn't be a bad candy, a fudge with a few raisins in it. We might try it later. It might turn out to be better than what we have."

"Did you just think of it?"

"Just this minute."

"I can pretty nearly taste it," said Charley.

"Not bad, is it? Who knows, we may expand before we sell our first piece of candy. Then we'll need some financing. What do you know about Glassman Brothers?"

"Probably no more than you do. Not in the same category with Julie Bache and Otto Kahn, but one of the older Jewish houses. But why do you want to let the Jews in on it? I never heard of them going out of their way to make us rich."

"True, but I was thinking 'way ahead and I happened to

hear their name this morning. Do you know a fellow there named Hyme?"

"Oh, I know Leonard Hyme. He's a great old fellow, but he retired a couple years ago and lives in Europe. Vienna. I think he was born there. Why do you ask about him?"

"Oh, somebody mentioned his name, and I'd never heard of him."

"He has two sons in the firm, but I'm not acquainted with them. They're members here, but I wouldn't know one from the other. Oh, we won't have trouble raising money in the present market, especially if we get off to a halfway decent start. They'll come around and try to buy us out, but if we have another candy that we haven't even put on the market, we'll be sitting pretty."

"How much are you worth, Charley?"

Charley burst out laughing. "I'll be a son of a bitch! You know you're the first guy ever asked me that? All the years I've been in business, nobody ever asked me point-blank. All right, how much do you think I'm worth?"

"Three million," said George.

"More."

"Ten million," said George.

"Less."

"Between three and ten."

"That's as close as I'll let you get. But why did you ask?"

"I'm always curious," said George.

"Huh. I know fellows would give you a punch right in the nose if you asked them that question. That's a pretty personal question, George."

"They're the only kind worth asking."

"All the same, you're supposed to be a gentleman," said Charley.

"I have a little way to go yet, so I'm not bound by gentlemen's rules."

"Well, I always understood you to be a gentleman, you and Pen."

"Pen may be. He's four years younger than I, and that may have been just long enough. A very interesting notion, you know. Just those extra four years may have made the difference. Yes, I believe Pen is a gentleman, the first one under the wire."

"I'm sure I don't know what the hell you're talking about," said Charley.

George redirected the conversation into channels more familiar to Charley Bohm. They agreed to meet again on the 30th of the month, for the purpose of dangling a carrot or two in front of Ringwall. What had promised to be no more than a dull lunch with a dull man at a dull club turned out to produce an interesting theory: that four years of Lockwood family history had benefited Pen. Pen was a gentleman because there had been their grandfather, their father, George himself, and those four years to make him one. Four less years of their rough-diamond grandfather's influence could have made some difference; and there was no doubt at all that at a place like St. Bartholomew's a boy whose older brother and father had been there before him was more acceptable, therefore unperturbed by the need to fit in that tortured boys at school and college. Rivalry often existed between brothers, but George now saw that if there had been any rivalry it had been inconsequential and confined to small envy on Pen's side, envy of his older brother and not a lack of assurance of his position in the school community. Some day, when they were older, when they could look back on their lives and their relationship calmly, George would question Pen about that. It was quite possible that Pen was so stupid that he would be unable to recall his boyhood emotions, but it would be worth a try. Pen *was* stupid; gentlemen often were.

George returned to the office to pick up his suitcase. Neither Pen nor Marian Strademyer was back from lunch, and he left word with the girl at the switchboard that he was on his way to the Carstairs. He took a taxi uptown, checked in at the hotel, and took a long, hot bath. "To pretty myself for Miss Strademyer," he muttered. "I'm sure she intends to do the same for me." At four o'clock he telephoned her at the office.

"Are you at your own desk?" he said.

"Yes I am," she said.

"Good, then you won't be overheard. Shall we say six o'-clock at your apartment?"

"Make it half past," she said.

"Seven, if you'd rather."

"That would be better. I've had trouble getting out of my previous engagement."

"Oh, I'm sorry to hear that," he said.

"I'll tell you all about it," she said.

"Don't let it upset you. I'll see you at seven," said George.

Trouble getting out of her previous engagement, hence her and Pen's late return from lunch. George wondered where they went for lunch when they lunched together. But the city was so full of speakeasies that they could be a fifteen-minute taxi ride away from a Chelsea meeting-place and avoid acquaintances from the financial district.

With almost three hours to kill, George dressed slowly and walked to the Racquet Club. He watched, then played in, several games of bottle pool with some men who always seemed to be there. He had one light Scotch and water, which he nursed along until it was time to leave and at five past seven he mounted the steps of the Murray Hill house in which Marian Strademyer had her apartment.

She took the chain latch off the door and let him in. She had changed from her nun's habit to a print dress.

"You've done things to this place since I was here last," said George.

"Yes, I have, and it's done things to me, too," she said.

"What kind of things?" he said.

"Very bad things," she said. "Made me realize what fun it would be to spend a lot of money. A lot."

"Nobody could hold that against you," said George. "I've seldom enjoyed anything as much as building my house. Not that I'd ever want to do that again, but it was an experience worth having."

"Will you have a cocktail, or what?"

"Have you had anything?"

"Yes, I had a Martini."

"Then that's what I'll have. Are there any left?"

"Oh, my yes. I only had one. That's all I had time for," she said. "The shaker's practically full."

They filled their glasses and sat down in facing chairs in front of the fireplace.

"The phone is going to start ringing any minute and I'm not going to pay any attention to it," she said.

"Leave it off the hook," he said.

"No, I want him to think I'm out," she said. "If I take it off the hook the operator will report that it's off, and he'll know I'm here. Also, he might ask her to turn the howler on. He's very angry with me."

"He's in a difficult frame of mind," said George.

"Well, the hell with him. What were you going to tell me?"

"The real reason why I came to New York? Finish your drink and have another."

"Is it that bad?"

"I don't think there's anything bad about it, but on three Martinis you'll be more understanding."

"All right," she said. She refilled her glass and his, and drank hers quickly. "Okay. I'm ready. How about you?"

"Of course," he said, and held up his glass.

"Now I'm full of understanding," she said.

"Well, late yesterday afternoon I was sitting in my study

and I became conscious of the fact that I had the God-damnedest erection I've had in I don't know how long. It was there, that's all."

"Where was your wife?" said Marian.

"In the house, but this had nothing to do with her."

"But she might have appreciated it."

"It was not for her. At first I didn't know who it *was* for."

"If you had said it was for me, I'd have called you a liar," she said.

"Wait a minute before you call me a liar. I'm trying to be as truthful as possible. This wasn't for anybody, you or my wife or anyone else. But when I began to think about what I wanted to do about it, *then* I thought of you. You've heard the old story about Lord Droolingtool and the butler? 'Your Lordship has a big one today, shall I send for her Ladyship?' and Droolingtool replies, 'To hell with the old bag, I'm taking this up to London.' "

"You told me that story," she said.

"Well, this isn't London, but here I am."

"You're a son of a bitch. When I think of how different you are than your brother. He loves me, but all I am to you is part of a risqué story."

"Not all, Marian. I am, as you said, a very different person from my brother, and the proof of it is that I told you the story. Or re-told it. I've been accused before of not being romantic, but I show you a great deal more respect by being completely candid. You and I are very much alike, you know."

"Do you think so?"

"Yes, I do. Will you be as truthful with me?"

"I don't know," she said.

"This morning you were in my office, we chatted a few minutes and then you started to leave."

"Yes."

"You hesitated," he said.

"Did I?"

"You don't remember that?"

"I just remember feeling that you were looking at me. Staring at me, in fact. Almost as if you were making a pass at me.

"I've been making a pass at you for the last twenty-five hours."

"I've been making one at you for the last—nine, I guess it is."

"What if that telephone starts ringing?"

"I'll close the bedroom door. We'll hear it, but it won't be as loud."

"We may not even hear it," he said.

They stood up simultaneously and he held her in his arms and kissed her mouth. "I don't know whether it's the Martinis, but I don't know why we're standing here with our clothes on. Do you?"

"No," he said.

"Especially with the present you brought me all the way from Pennsylvania. You bastard, George Lockwood. I ought to hate you. I do, too."

"I know you do," he said.

She put her hand between his legs. "My present," she said. "Come on, let's open my present."

They were undressed and sitting on the edge of the bed when the telephone began to ring. "There he is," she said. "He picked a bad time."

"Pay no attention to it."

"But I will pay attention to it. I almost forgot about him, and now I want to do all the things he never wants to do. Oh, such a nice present, George, and all for me. Will you give me another on my birthday?"

"Or Christmas. Whichever comes first."

"Don't *you*," she said. "By this time he would have, but don't you. The Lockwood Brothers. You ought to make me a member of the firm. The silent partner. Oh, but I'm not going to be silent any more. George! Oh, you bastard. Oh, you wonderful bastard!"

"You bitch!"

"Say it again."

"You bitch in heat. You whore."

Once again the telephone began its ringing, but now they lay quiet and listened to it, her head resting on his arm, his hand gently pressing her breast. "What does he want?" said George.

"Oh, Christ, I don't know what he wants, and neither does he."

"What did you tell him?"

"I told him I wanted to be alone tonight."

"Is he here every afternoon?"

"Just about."

"Has he got a key?"

"Oh, sure. Sometimes he's here before I am. We don't always screw. Sometimes we don't even talk very much. He just wants to be here. Some days he has to leave as soon as I get here. I told him once that he was queer for the furniture."

"Is he queer?"

"The only way he's queer is by not being queer at all. Everybody does something, but not him. That's one thing that would make me a little afraid to marry him. I want the money, and not having to work for a living. But if he ever found out I had another man, he could be mean. He's terribly jealous."

"He is?"

"His kind are. He knows I've done everything. I've told him, trying to get him to relax more. But he's the one that's changing me. But then every once in a while I have to do it with somebody like you. You were right, you know. This morning in your office I got the shivers. If you'd come near me I'd have done anything you said, right then and there and I wouldn't have cared who was watching."

"I take it you have somebody like me."

"He's not like you, but he's not like Penrose. He's an actor and he lives around the corner on 37th Street. Oh, God, once he got out of here just in time. He and Penrose passed each other on the stairs, one Sunday afternoon. He was here all Saturday night and Sunday morning, and Penrose was supposed to drop in around four o'clock, but he got here around two. That's when I found out how jealous he could be. All I can say is, it's a good thing he didn't get here Sunday morning. There were four of us. Daisy chain. Everything. All Saturday night and Sunday morning. About once a year I have to let go, all my inhibitions. I wish you could stay all night, but he's going to keep on telephoning, and if I don't answer it by ten o'clock, he's just liable to show up, and that wouldn't be so good. He's sore at you, he won't tell me why, and I guess you won't either, but right now you're in his bad books. I'll cook you some dinner, then you'll have to leave. You could come back, though. Say around midnight, and stay. Even if he came here at ten o'clock, he never stays all night. He's being very careful about his wife. She has some pansy boy friend that tells her what to do, and Penrose doesn't want them to get anything on him."

"Suppose I leave now and you phone me at the hotel, say twelve o'clock."

"That might be safer. There's really no telling what he'll do, and I'd better get something to eat or I might just fall asleep and not hear the phone. Yes, you go now and I'll phone you as soon after ten as I can. You're at the Carstairs, as usual."

She was a bit shaky from the Martinis as she put on a negligee, and when he was leaving she took his hand and led it over her body. "That's so you'll come back, with another present for me. I wish you didn't have to leave, but this makes more sense. And you know me, I'm a sensible girl." They were the last words he was to hear from her lips. She kissed him, and gently pushed him through the door, and he heard the chain lock being replaced.

He had dinner in his room at the Carstairs after a bath and a change into pajamas and dressing-gown. He fell asleep on the counterpane while trying to give his attention to a novel called *Arrowsmith,* by the author of *Main Street* and *Babbitt*, books which he had rather liked. He awoke with a stiff neck, saw by his watch that it was five past eleven, and got up and washed his face. He ordered a pot of coffee from room service, and wondered how long he would have to wait for Marian Strademyer's call. The soreness in his neck disappeared as he moved about and his blood circulated more freely, and he found that the nap had refreshed him. Immediate desire for the pleasures that might await him with Marian was in the form of curiosity. In her mood, and in his, extreme vigor would not be essential. As he sipped his coffee and became wider awake he permitted himself only vague anticipation of the plans she had been making for the remainder of the night. On the other hand, he was willing to consider in some detail the position she might occupy in his future. He would remove her from the office and from the life of his brother, but he felt he could persuade her to become his own mistress. With Geraldine as his wife he had a definite need of a mistress; and since he had been given such a candid look at Marian's life, an understanding based on money and mutual tolerance would surely be acceptable to her. Pen's mistake with Marian was in making demands that were unreasonable when love was one-sided. Between Marian and George love was not present. Love? George Lockwood wondered if he had ever loved anyone but Eulalie Fenstermacher. Preposterous name. But had anyone else ever loved him? "I must be getting old," he muttered. An amusing thought after his performance earlier in the evening and his readiness for what was to come. Aging, yes, but not old. The Lockwood men did not get old that way; he recalled the scene that had been witnessed by Agnes when his father was visited by Mrs. Downs. Men who drank too much, who did not take proper care of themselves, lost their powers and got old at fifty. George was proud of his father. "Think of the old rascal," he muttered. And almost the best part of it was that Mrs. Downs would still want to do that to him. Mrs. Downs must have been quite a woman herself.

The night sounds of midtown East Side New York had changed, and the clock in the wall and his watch agreed that midnight had passed. Any minute now she would telephone. He put on his shoes and socks and his underwear, laid out his shirt and necktie. A delicate relationship between him and the silent telephone had come into being. He could almost *see* her voice coming out of the mouthpiece, although in actuality the sound of her voice would come out of the receiver. Exactly what would she say? Would she be terse and eager, languidly humorous, or very angry at Pen for delaying her? There was now no doubt that Pen had gone to her apartment, little doubt that he had made a scene. The scene may very well have been dramatic and messy, with things said that were bound to have unpleasant consequences. George was thinking of the scene in the past tense, but it very well might still be going on. The only thing he could not do was telephone her and make matters worse. Why did a man like Pen get himself into such situations?

The reading matter in the room consisted of the Gideon Bible and the Sinclair Lewis novel, and George Lockwood was not interested in the words of the prophets or in medical intrigue. He grew unreasonably angry at the Carstairs breakfast menu, which only served to remind him that he expected to have breakfast in an apartment on Murray Hill, prepared by a voluptuous young woman who wanted to please him.

And then the damned thing rang.

He lifted the receiver and took a deep breath so as not to show his impatience. "Hello?" he said.

"George! Oh, thank goodness you're there." The voice was Geraldine's.

"Of course I'm here. Why are you calling me at this hour?"

"You haven't heard. I was sure you hadn't. Oh, George, a terrible, terrible thing has happened. A *terrible* thing. It's Pen your brother Pen and some woman in your office."

"Make sense, woman, for God's sake."

"I'm *trying* to," she said. "Pen killed her, shot her with a pistol and then killed himself. Your nice brother. It's so awful, George, and I'm here alone."

"Where did you hear this?"

"From Wilma. Wilma phoned you here about, about fifteen minutes ago. The police are there and you've got to go to her. What shall I do? Shall I have Andrew drive me to New York? There are no trains."

"Stay where you are. Now let me get this straight. Wilma telephoned you, or telephoned me, and got you on the phone."

"The police went to her house and told her that her husband had killed a woman and committed suicide. Some woman in your office. Not his secretary but the woman with the German name."

"Miss Strademyer?"

"That's the name, yes."

"When did this happen? Tonight, of course," said George.

"It must have been around ten o'clock. Wilma didn't want to talk to me, she wanted to talk to you. You must go up there right away, George. She's in a state of I don't know what?"

"Did they both die right away?"

"How would I know that? They were both dead when the police got there. All that you can find out when you talk to Wilma. You don't want me to wake up Andrew—"

"Stay where you are till I get in touch with you. Where is Ernestine?"

"Ernestine? She's either in Rome or on her way there. Her last letter said she planned to be in Rome I think just about now. I'll have to find her letter and check on that."

"All right, do that tonight before you go to bed. Then get Arthur McHenry on the phone."

"Tonight?"

"Well, first thing in the morning."

"What will we need a lawyer for?" said Geraldine.

"Not as a lawyer, but a man who makes good sense. Don't do anything or talk to anybody without asking Arthur. If he's out of town get Joe Chapin, but try Arthur first. I don't suppose you know what they did with the body?"

"Yes, it's at the morgue. Both bodies, Wilma did say that."

"Wilma seems to have made more sense than you're making."

"I can't help it, George. I was just listening to the radio when she phoned. First I was afraid something had happened to you."

"Thank you, but nothing's going to happen to me."

"Well, who'd ever think a terrible thing like this would happen to Pen? I can't believe it. Did you know anything about this? Was he having an affair with this woman?"

"Do you think he'd murder somebody and kill himself if he wasn't?"

"Pen might. If she refused him, he was so repressed. I always thought he was too much within himself, never let himself go. But I never for a minute thought he could be leading a double life."

"Nobody leads a double life. One life is all anyone leads, good, bad or indifferent."

"Well, you never stop thinking, that busy mind of yours."

"Isn't it a good thing there's someone to do some thinking

now? You look up Ernestine's itinerary, and telephone Arthur the very first thing in the morning. Have you got a pencil there?"

"Yes."

"Write down this name. Solon Schissler. That's S, o, l, o, n, Solon. Schissler. S, c, h, i, s, s, l, e, r. He's the Swedish Haven undertaker. Have Arthur call him and tell him to be ready for a call from me."

"Are you going to have the funeral here?"

"Where else? Under the circumstances I doubt very much if Wilma will want him in her family plot, wherever that is. He belongs here, with the Lockwoods. So you tell Arthur to notify Schissler."

"Will it be a big funeral? A lot of people here?"

"Certainly not. When the New York authorities give their permission I'll have Pen brought back to Swedish Haven and go direct to the cemetery. Everything will be strictly private."

"Are you going up to see Wilma now?"

"As soon as I put some clothes on. You'd better take a bromide and get some sleep."

"All right, dear, I think I will. Goodnight, and I'm terribly sorry. I know you were terribly fond of Pen."

"Goodnight, Geraldine," he said. He hung up.

"I was," he muttered. "I was very fond of him. I don't think I ever knew that before."

He had the taxi halt at the 51st Street subway station. Without getting out of the cab, and reading upside down, he could see the front page of the *Daily News*: 2 DIE IN LOVE NEST. George bought copies of the *Times, World, American, News* and *Mirror*. Only the *News* and the *Mirror* had the story, and their accounts were virtually identical.

"You know you read them fuckin' papers, there's more shooting goes on in them love nests than there is humpin'," said the driver. "What the hell's a guy want to kill a woman for? The way I look at it, if you catch her humpin' some other guy, all right give her a punch in the nose for luck. But what the hell's use of taking a chance of frying for it? A cunt's a cunt, and there's two million of them right here in this city alone. Everybody wouldn't agree with me, but that's the way I feel about it. And I like it, I get plenty. Me and the wife are separated on account of that very reason. So I guess she's gettin' hers. But would I shoot her for that? I wouldn't give her the satisfaction. Or you take now this poor son of a bitch Gray, Judd Gray. She talks him into hittin' Snyder over the head with a sashweight. And now the two of them hate one another. So they'll both fry. You drive one of these hacks around New York City on the night side, that's an education in itself. Women! I tell you, Mister. That'll be forty-five cents."

"Very instructive," said George.

"I'll say," said the man.

At least the hackie had been as informative as the newspapers, which contained little that George did not already know. The skimpy accounts, hurriedly written, revealed that neighbors had heard the four shots, the three which Pen fired into Marian's negligee-clad body and the single shot he fired into his own temple. The shooting had occurred shortly after ten P.M. Neighbors described the Strademyer woman as an attractive person who dressed conservatively and played classsical music on the piano. Several times there had been complaints to the superintendent about all-night parties, but these had not been frequent. She was believed to have been a divorcée. Penrose Lockwood, Social Registerite, millionaire partner in a private investment firm, member of fashionable clubs, was a graduate of tony St. Bartholomew's School and Princeton University. He had been married for twenty-three years to the former Miss Wilma Rainsler, daugher of the late Mr. and Mrs. J. Killyan Rainsler, who were members of the old Knickerbocker families. There were no children.

The light was on in the vestibule of Pen's house. George rang the doorbell and was admitted by Norman Bunn, who had been the Penrose Lockwoods' butler through most of their married life. Norman had grown stout and red-nosed in their service and his eyes were now even more watery than usual. He had probably been interrupted earlier in the midst of a quiet session with a bottle of Pen's port. "Good evening, sir," he said. "May I say, sir, it's difficult to find words."

"Yes, thank you, Norman," said George, "Will you get rid of these for me, please? I bought them on the way up. They don't tell us very much."

"I've already seen the article in the *News*, sir. The policeman on the beat gave me a copy."

"Now, what about Mrs. Lockwood? How is she bearing up?"

"I'd say she was bearing up well, sir. She has a friend with her. Mrs. James. Mrs. Sherwood James, married to a cousin of Mrs. Lockwood's. She only lives around the corner, sir. She's been with Mrs. Lockwood over an hour, so she's had someone here most of the time."

"Anyone else?"

"Not now, sir. Mr. Hyme was here, briefly, but he didn't stop very long. The telephone has been *very* busy, as might be expected. And I had to ask my policeman friend for help in keeping out the press. One particularly obnoxious fellow represented himself as the assistant to the district attorney, but something told me not to let him in. And I didn't. A redheaded Irishman. The police knew him. Then there was a mousy young woman tried to pass herself off as a trained nurse, but we hadn't sent for a trained nurse. She was of the press, too. Her name is signed to the article in the *News*. Gladys Roberts."

"That's using your head, Norman," said George.

They climbed a short flight of stairs to the library. Wilma rose to greet him, and they embraced silently. He held her for a moment, and Dorothy James left them, saying she would be in the next room.

"I'm so glad you weren't far away," said Wilma. "I hated to disturb Geraldine, but you were the first person I wanted to turn to. Did you know anything about this, George?"

"No, it wasn't the kind of thing Pen would have confided in anyone, not even me."

"It apparently had been going on for quite some time," she said. She hesitated. "*I* knew about it."

"Oh, you did?"

"Oh, you mustn't blame me, George. I was sure it would pass. Things hadn't been going very well between us. Even the best of marriages get a little rusty, and we were at the age. I'll be truthful. I took a lover. If Pen could have a mistress, I could have someone too. We could both look the other way until you might say we came to our senses. But Pen became too deeply involved, and I suppose this woman wasn't going to miss this opportunity. Pen asked me for a divorce."

"He did?"

"I refused. Suddenly I was terrified. I'm not young, but I think I still have twenty-five or thirty years ahead of me, and the thought of living it out alone just terrified me. There were all sorts of reasons why I couldn't marry my lover. First of all, he was too much younger than I. He *could* be my son, as far as age is concerned, and it never would have worked out for the other reasons, too. Pen and I could have continued the arrangement, but he wanted too much. Or *she* wanted too much, which amounted to the same thing. Now, thanks to her, nobody has anything. Nothing but the kind of mess you read about in the tabloids."

"Wilma, you're quite a remarkable woman," said George. "I was dreading this."

"Did you think I'd be hysterical? Well, I was, before you got here. Or nearly hysterical. Hysterical for me. I'd gone to bed early and was half asleep when Norman knocked on my door and said there were detectives downstairs. Detectives downstairs and police out in front of the house. Those first few minutes I don't remember very well. I couldn't tell you which detective told me about Pen, or what I said, or did, or anything. Poor Norman, he's not used to that sort of thing either, and I'm sure he'd been having a quiet nip. Estelle, my maid, had the night off to visit her sister in the Bronx. The chambermaid stayed out of sight, and I'm going to fire her. My cook was no help either, but she's slightly deaf and every night when she's finished her work she retires to her room. She's very religious. Has a little altar in her room and spends a great deal of her time in prayer. She goes to the Mass every morning, every single morning."

"Fortunately you had Dorothy James in the neighborhood."

She hesitated. "A godsend, Dorothy. But I had to have a man to help me, and the only person I could think of was my financial adviser."

"I didn't even know you had one. I suppose I took for granted that Pen handled those matters for you."

"He did, for the most part, but I've been playing the stock market, just like everyone else," she said.

"Oh, I see," said George.

She looked at him. "You can stare me down, George."

"I wasn't trying to, Wilma."

"He's not my financial adviser. He's my lover. He lives at Seventy-seventh and Park, and he came right over. He was the one that told me to get in touch with you. He was also the one that calmed me down. Probably saved you a lot of trouble."

"Someone did. There's nothing hysterical about you now," said George.

"They took Pen to the morgue. I won't have to identify him, will I?"

"I think we can have someone from Stratford, Kersey and Stratford do that."

"He shot himself in the temple," she said. "She was shot in the heart. Why did he have to shoot himself in the head?"

"Well, he never had any vanity about his looks, alive. I doubt if he gave much thought to how he would look dead," said George. "Now, Wilma, some things to discuss with you. I have seen two of the tabloids, the *Daily News* and the *Daily Mirror*. The other one, the *Daily Graphic,* won't be out until today sometime, and the *New York Journal,* the Hearst paper, will be out about the same time. The *Post* and the *Sun* will try not to be sensational, but I know damn well the others will have a field day. It's the kind of story that was just made for them."

"Dorothy was talking about that. She had seen the *News* or the other one."

"I suggest that you let Dorothy take you away. There's no earthly reason why you should subject yourself to photographers and reporters."

"Dorothy has already offered to do that. Their house in Manchester, Vermont. I said no."

"I will arrange to have Pen's body sent back to Swedish Haven. Private funeral ceremony at the grave, where all the Lockwoods are buried beginning with our grandfather."

"I know about it. I saw it when Agnes died. And I expect to be buried there when my time comes. Pen and I spent half our lives together and we were still married when this thing happened. I wouldn't like myself very much if I wasn't there when he's buried. He was a good man, and he was good to me, for almost twenty-five years. He was so good that he had no ability to cope with evil. And what a disgusting hypocrite I would be, to publicly desert him now. No, George. Thank you for your good intentions, but Pen's entitled to that much respect. And love. I loved him. Not always. Not passionately. Not romantically. But the love you have for someone like him. All innocence. Great kindness. Gentleness. That's really it, gentleness. And of course the insanity in your family."

"Is that why you never had children?"

"Heavens, no. I'd have had them, in spite of the insanity in my family *and* yours. I never used a pessary in my life. We tried but we never had any results. The wrong mixture, I guess. You wouldn't call Sherwood James's father sane, but he invented almost as many things as Mr. Edison. And he had the same kind of gentleness Pen had. I'll be there when Pen is buried, just as he would have been for me. Unless—no."

"Unless what?"

"Unless my being there would embarrass you."

"How could it?"

"Oh—the extra notoriety, perhaps. One never knows about you, George. Everything you do is always so well thought out in advance. You never seem to do anything impulsive."

"When I do, it doesn't turn out very well," said George Lockwood.

"Just the opposite for poor Pen."

"I think we've left Dorothy alone too long," he said.

"She's spending the night," said Wilma. "If you'd like to, there's plenty of room."

"Thanks, but I'll be more efficient if I go back to the Carstairs. I'll be very busy on the telephone tomorrow—today, it is, of course. And they have a switchboard and they know me there. I'm going to have them give me another room, besides the one I'm in. That will give me two telephones. I'll register the extra room under the name of—James Sherwood. You ought to be able to remember that, in case you want to call."

"Sherwood James, James Sherwood," said Wilma. "Who will they get to identify her, the woman?"

"I don't know. I should imagine some member of her family will turn up. Why?"

"I just wondered. I just happened to think of her down there. Somehow it's worse for a woman."

"Why?"

"I don't *know* why, but it is. Probably for no better reason than because I'm a woman myself. Or do you suppose they're keeping them together?"

"No, my impression is that they have them all in separate boxes, that open like bureau drawers. Don't dwell on it, Wilma, and don't drink any more coffee. I'm going to ask Dorothy to put you to bed."

"I wish you were someone else. Anyone else."

"Well, I'm not, am I?"

"No, and I shouldn't have said that to you, should I? But I'll blame it on Nature. Life has to go on, and—oh, I don't have to explain such thoughts to you. Just hold me close for a minute, George."

"That would be a great mistake, Wilma, with Dorothy in the next room."

"Then go, please go. I'll be all right as soon as you've gone."

"Goodnight," he said.

All the large bills he had paid, all the good tips he had given through his years of patronage of the Carstairs now paid off: when he returned to the hotel from Wilma's house the night auditor, who also functioned as night room clerk, said merely, "The whole staff want to express our sympathy, Mr. Lockwood." The elevator man, an arthritic Irishman, said, "We're sorry for your trouble, sir." In his room, he had barely had time to hang up his topcoat when the telephone rang. It was DeBorio, the manager, who obviously had left word to be called immediately on George's return. "If the press should find out you're here, we can't keep them out of the lobby," said DeBorio. "But you can avoid them by using the service elevator and going in and out the employes' entrance. That's two doors away, and they won't notice you. Or, if you like, I can call a friend of mine at another hotel and guarantee you complete privacy." DeBorio was transformed from a fussy little man, permanently encased in a cutaway, with a dubious ribbon in his lapel, to a sentinel, and an alert one at that. "We also have certain political connections, Mr. Lockwood. Tammany Hall, if that could be useful. I know the mayor personally, and I even have his private phone number. The Biltmore isn't the only hotel they patronize."

From this totally unexpected source George Lockwood got at least the promise of aid and comfort that he needed. It was not so much a matter of availing himself of DeBorio's assistance as the knowledge that at this hour of the morning, when most of the city was asleep, he too could lie down and rest, with his vigilance relaxed and no danger from intruders. Wilma and others might turn to him, but whom could he turn to? This, he now realized, had been worrying him since Geraldine's telephone call—and the answer was provided by an Italian Swiss who wished to show his appreciation for an annual box of Upmann cigars. In return for those Christmas presents, George Lockwood could now compose himself for the sleep that his mind and body were beginning to demand.

He undressed and got into bed, confident that the moment he turned out the light his weariness would be a narcotic. But only his body retired. He lay in a position that had the formality of death, his arms straight down at his sides, his legs stretched full length, inescapably reminiscent of cadavers in a morgue. He had reached middle age with little first-hand knowledge of death. In the war he had gone from first lieutenant to captain at the same desk in the Embarkation Officer's headquarters in Manhattan. He had never witnessed violent death nor been present at a peaceful deathbed. Anson Chatsworth's suicide was a ghastly joke in the category of students' pranks; the Zehner kid, impaled on the spikes of George's wall, had never even been a face to remember. Agnes Lockwood had not invited him to her final farewell, and he had not wished to intrude. And yet he had some traffic with death. He had always fully sympathized with his grandfather in the killing of the two men who threatened him. In those times, with the same provocation, he would have killed. During the years with Agnes he had wished her dead and she came to know it, so that he had in effect trafficked with her death. He had never been able to fake pity for the weak, and he was not going to fake it now of all times, when his brother, through weakness, had unnecessarily murdered a woman because she was his weakness and his strength. That was it. Pen's act had been the extreme, the final, the inevitable act of a weakling, who had gone through life using good will as a disguise for his weakness, trading good will with the world in exchange for the world's bargain not to judge him too harshly—not to judge him at all. Nothing in Pen's life, nor Pen's life as a whole, could now bring on real sadness. In the next few days there would be people who would be touched by sadness, but they would be people who were fulfilling their share of Pen's bargain with the world. Who that knew Pen would feel his death deeply? A bleary-eyed butler who stole his wine? Wilma, Pen's wife? Had she not revealed herself with her remark that it was "somehow worse for a woman"? She could have pity for another woman; she had none for Pen. The surprise, the fuss, the excitement, the confusion, the threatening notoriety had produced an emotional disturbance to which she was ready to give sexual release, but in Wilma's case the same effect might easily be produced by a frustrating meeting with her young lover.

The honest and sensible thing to do now was to get through the next few days with dignity and efficiency. Ironically, the scandalous circumstances of the night's bloody business demanded just such a performance and made it easy. The world would see as stiff an upper lip as ever betrayed controlled emotion. "I'll show them," he muttered, and so saying he was able to sleep.

Four hours later he was awake and refreshed. It was too early for a proper breakfast, but he rang for coffee and it was brought to his room and it was fresh. "The first thing the day side do when they come on is make fresh coffee," the bellboy explained. "All the way down on the 'L' every morning I keep thinking to myself, I'll be getting a good cuppa coffee once I get there. The next fresh coffee they don't make till ha' past eight or nine."

"A good thing to remember," said George Lockwood. He also noticed that the bellboy refrained from offering sympathy or otherwise commenting on the morning scandal. DeBorio had obviously issued instructions to the staff. This became evident when the head bellboy unlocked the door of the adjoining room. "Your extra room, sir," he said, and left. George busied himself with a list and then a schedule of telephone calls to be made. It was the kind of thing he *liked* to do. He was thorough. He estimated the length of time he required for each call, and allowed for time in which to have conversations that he could not now anticipate. His first outside call, to his astonishment, was at one minute past eight, from Wilma.

"I've just had a wonderful, long telegram from George, your son. Shall I read it to you?" she said.

"Not if it's too long," he said. "I'd rather read it later."

"It's a whole page," she said. "But I thought you ought to know that he's coming East."

"When?"

"I think he must be on his way. There's a difference in time there. What is it?"

"They're three hours earlier. When it's eight o'clock here, it's five o'clock there. Is he coming to New York or where? He could take a train from Chicago to Philadelphia and go from there to Swedish Haven, by train or by motor."

"He doesn't say. He just says, 'Taking first train East.' "

"Well, I suppose we'll hear more. Meanwhile, Wilma, I'll be here all morning, and remember James Sherwood. That's the phone in the next room."

"I forgot this time, but I'll remember," she said.

All day he followed and rearranged his schedule, talking to lawyers, undertakers, public officials, friends of DeBorio's, and Daisy Thorpe at the office. All the office staff showed up for work, and all but Daisy were sent home. Whenever it appeared that he might have an idle minute, George created a task for himself: he did not wish to be idle, for idleness would mean that he could not postpone the moment when he would have to think of his son.

Throughout the entire business of the previous night, beginning with Geraldine's telephone call, he had not once given a thought to George. Not once had he considered notifying him, of communicating with him directly or indirectly. It was as though George did not exist. Now and then a name had come to mind, names of Pen's school friends and business acquaintances, men and women of varying degrees of intimacy and importance in Pen's life. But it had never occurred to George that he had a son of his own whose uncle had murdered a woman and committed suicide and who was entitled to some information. Presumably his son had read about the scandal in the California newspapers. The boy was fond of his uncle. They had seen little of each other, but their relationship was banteringly warm and affectionately easy. They were uncle and nephew, formally, but often they seemed more like younger brothers of older brother George Lockwood Senior. Pen's death and the manner of it, would be shocking to young George; and now his father had discovered someone whose sadness would be deep and genuine and all the things that the sadness of the others was not.

George Lockwood could not blame himself for overlooking his son; it had not been a deliberate snub, an act of meanness or vindictiveness. It had been the negative act of forgetting, and yet it was not yet forty-eight hours since his son had been very much on his mind. The situation was embarrassing because it could never be explained away. Explain to whom? To his son? Explain to him that he had forgotten all about him? It was embarrassing because he was confused by the hidden, underlying reason for his forgetfulness, and any sort of confusion was embarrassing to a man who was so seldom confused. He began to dread the return to Swedish Haven and the meeting with his son. Now there would be no little game between him and the world, the masquerade of the stiff upper lip. He could begin to feel his son's eyes on him, for although he had not seen the boy since his expulsion from Princeton, he could imagine a great deal about him. Hibbard's snapshots had shown the physical growth. The boy was a husky man, a manly man, who had done hard work and earned his success and along the way had learned to give orders. Fortunes in oil were not made by the gutless; the competition was largely among men who had come up from their beginnings as roustabouts, with a background of hard labor, hard fighting, hard drinking, and the instinct to gamble. Oil men belonged in the same category of toughness as steel men, cattle ranchers, men who survived and prevailed through a combination of muscle and mind.

And now George Lockwood was beginning to discover the cause of his forgetfulness. It was not forgetfulness at all. It was hatred, and it had been started with Preston Hibbard's visit, his report on Bing and Bing's wife and Bing's children and Bing's Rolls-Royce and Bing's standing in the Far West. The boy was self-sufficient and had made himself so with no help from the father; and he had made his mark in a kind of existence in which the father could not have survived. George Lockwood had not forgotten his son, but had banished him from his mind, and the son had made him lie to himself. He had not been overcome with desire for Marian Stademyer but by the urgent need to dominate a human being who, being a woman, could give him pleasure in the process. Yet even that was a form of postponement. He now knew that even without the violent consequences of his rendezvous with Marian Strademyer, a meeting with his son was unavoidable—because he would not have avoided it. The Hibbard snapshots had made the meeting necessary. George Lockwood had been compelled to have one more try at dominating his son even though the attempt would end in disastrous failure.

The only thing left to save was his position. He had always been a sonofabitch in the eyes of his son. He would maintain that position. His son must be kept from knowing that his triumph in life was also a triumph over his father.

George Lockwood wondered why he had not heard from Ernestine.

Schissler was not going to make much money out of this one. The embalming had been performed in New York City and the casket purchased from the New York firm. The remains was coming by train, to be lifted off the baggage car and put in Schissler's hearse, and then on to the cemetery. When George Lockwood said strictly private he meant strictly private. The hearse and two automobiles formed the entire cortege, and both automobiles belonged to Lockwood, so there would be nothing on the bill for cars. No pallbearers. No flowers. The fellows at the Legion had offered to supply a guard of honor, because Penrose Lockwood was a veteran, but George Lockwood had turned them down. The whole thing wouldn't come to a thousand dollars; it was not going to be easy to get it up to five hundred.

Shortly before ten-thirty the Lockwood Pierce-Arrow and the Lockwood Lincoln drew up to the Reading station. The occupants remained in the cars. George Lockwood and his wife and another woman in the Lincoln, and the other people in the Pierce-Arrow, which was a touring car but had the side curtains up, so you could not see who was inside. Andrew was at the wheel of the Lincoln; Schissler did not recognize the driver of the Pierce-Arrow. He looked something like Deegan, the fellow from the detective agency who had once worked for Lockwood as night watchman. Yes, that's who it was. He looked different in a chauffeur's cap. That's who it was; Deegan, from Gibbsville. Not even a Swedish Haven man.

Schissler went over to the Lincoln, took off his high silk hat, and opened the rear door. "Good morning, George. Mrs. Lockwood. Number 8 is on time. She was a little late leaving Reading, but she'll make that up. You got about five or six minutes' wait."

"Thank you, Karl," said George Lockwood.

"Will I tell the folks in the Pierce?" said Schissler.

"You might as well," said George.

There were two middle-aged couples in the Pierce-Arrow. He opened the rear door and saw that they were all strangers. "I just thought you folks would wish to know, the train is on time. I'm the funeral director, Schissler's my name."

The men mumbled their thanks, and Schissler, after a momentary hesitation, slowly closed the door. They were a stuck-up bunch, especially considering Pen Lockwood and the disgrace he had brought on himself and the town. Swedish

Haven had been mentioned in all the papers, New York and Philadelphia.

Schissler returned to the north end of the platform, where the baggage car on Number 8 always stopped. He was joined by Ike Wehner, the baggagemaster, wearing his uniform cap and striped overalls.

"She on time?" said Schissler.

"She had two minutes to make up leaving Port Clinton," said Ike Wehner. "But that's no trouble for Ed Duncan. Ed could make up two minutes between here and Gibbsville if he felt like it."

"Be retired in another year," said Schissler.

"Ed? No, Ed got closer to two years yet. Well, there he is, whistling for Schmeltzer's Crossing." Ike Wehner took out his watch. "He made it up. I wouldn't like to be firing for Ed when he's real late."

The door of the baggage car was already open as Number 8 pulled in. The conductor and two members of his crew pushed the casket, which rested on a dolly, on to the station hand-truck. "Careful, now, careful," said the conductor, his crew, Schissler, and Wehner. One of the trainmen, younger and fresh, said to Wehner, "I guess they left the woman back in New York, huh, Wehner?"

"Ah, shut your face," said Ike Wehner.

The trainman laughed.

Wehner signed for the casket, handed the slip of paper to the conductor, and pulled the hand-truck down the platform to the hearse. Schissler, his assistant, and Wehner transferred the casket to the hearse. "Thanks, Ike," said Schissler. "So long."

"So long," said Ike Wehner.

Schissler bowed deeply to Andrew, George Lockwood's chauffeur, to signal him to follow, and the cortege was on its way.

Already waiting at the grave was young Faust, assistant pastor of the Lutheran Church, wearing an ordinary suit. He had got there under his own power—walked, more than likely. Schissler wondered whether to offer him a ride back to town. It was a small item, but it would bring the total closer to $500. The service took less than ten minutes, and there was no sign of emotion by any of the seven mourners, Schissler watched the widow particularly, but she showed nothing. Considering how Penrose Lockwood died she could not be expected to show much grief, but she showed nothing else, either. She might as well have been witnessing the burial of a dead cat.

Young Faust nodded to George Lockwood, indicating that the service was at an end. George and the widow thanked him, and they all headed for their cars. At that moment two strangers with cameras took flashlight photographs of the group. Where they had come from Schissler did not know. He had not seen them before, and they hurried away when they had taken their pictures. He wondered if he had got in the picture. He followed George Lockwood to his car.

"Everything satisfactory, George?" he said.

"Everything but those photographers, but I can't blame you for that. I thought we were going to have a policeman here."

"Well, we're not in the Borough, George. We're just outside the Borough limits here."

"Oh, well," said George.

"Straight home, sir?" said Andrew.

"Straight home," said George Lockwood. "Deegan knows the way from here, doesn't he?"

"Yes sir. He knows all these roads, better than I do," said Andrew.

"All right, let's go," said George. He got in the Lincoln and sat between Wilma and Geraldine. "I'm sorry about those photographers," he said.

"They didn't get much for their trouble, a woman with a veil," said Wilma. "Do you think they came all the way from New York just for that?"

"I don't know, but they'd better not try anything at the house. Deegan, the man that's driving the other car, is a private detective. Actually a watchman, who works for a detective agency. One word to him, and there'll be some cameras smashed. Maybe even a nose or two."

"Oh, dear, are we going to have trouble?" said Geraldine. "Let's not have anything like that."

"Seems to me you've had the least trouble of anybody, this past week," said George.

"I was thinking as much of Wilma as of us," said Geraldine.

"Oh, sure," said George.

"This is really very pretty country," said Wilma. "I love those great big red barns. They build them right into the side of the hill, don't they?"

"For a reason," said George. "For several reasons, as a matter of fact. On the lower level they keep the livestock. The cattle, the horses. On the upper level they store the grain, the hay and straw. The corn cribs of course are separate. But the hay and straw and grain are kept dry, on the upper story of the barns."

"Not the animals?"

"Oh, they bed them with straw, but the farmers believe that animals are healthier standing on the ground than on wooden planking."

"George will embark on a lecture at the drop of a hat," said Geraldine. "I never knew any of this."

"You never asked the right questions," said George. "I have resources of information that you haven't tapped, Geraldine."

"I'm sure you have," said Geraldine. "Some of them I'd hesitate to ask about."

"Then they wouldn't be considered the right questions, would they? Wilma was only interested in the Pennsylvania Dutch barn, and since I was born and raised here, it's a subject I know something about."

"But you tore down one of those barns to build your own house."

"I had no intention of becoming a farmer. I was building a country place for you and me, dear. Just you and me."

"Fiddlesticks. You were building a manor house for future generations of Lockwoods," said Geraldine.

"If I was, I made a big mistake, didn't I?"

"Speaking of which, I wonder what happened to Bing? He was going to be here today," said Wilma.

"He could have missed connections in Chicago, or he may have changed his mind without letting you know. Or whose car is that going up our road? If it's those damned photographers, I'll have them out of there in a hurry." He spoke to Andrew through the tube. "Andrew, do you recognize that car, going up our driveway?"

"No sir. It's a last year's Cadillac but I don't recognize it. One of them four-door coops. There's two of them like it in Gibbsville, but I know both of them."

"He's going right in our driveway, too," said George. "You don't recognize the car, do you, Wilma?"

"No."

"Now he's getting out. He's alone," said George. "And do you know who it is? It's my son!"

"Oh, I'm dying to meet him!" said Geraldine.

"Well, don't wet your pants. You're about to meet him," said George.

"It is he, isn't it?" said Wilma. "Oh, I'm really glad he got here."

Bing Lockwood was standing at the front door, waiting to be admitted, when the Lincoln pulled up. He was wearing a blue serge suit, white button-down shirt, and black knit tie. He was deeply tanned, almost of another race among the white faces that now got out of the Lincoln.

"Hello, Father," he said. "I went to the wrong house."

"Hello, son. The wrong house? What wrong house?" They shook hands.

"The old house. Homè. Hello, Aunt Wilma." He put his arms around her and kissed her cheek.

"Your stepmother," said George.

"Hello, stepson," said Geraldine. "I'm so glad to meet you at last."

"Of course, you've never seen this place," said George. "Well, shall we wait for the others? Here they are, so let's get the introductions over with. Mr. and Mrs. Sherwood James, cousins of your Aunt Wilma."

"We met a long time ago," said Bing, shaking hands with Dorothy and Sherwood James.

"And Mr. and Mrs. Desmond Farley, also cousins of your Aunt Wilma's."

Bing Lockwood shook hands with the Farleys.

"Geraldine, will you take them in, please. I have to have a word with Deegan. Andrew, will you take my son's bag? Where did you come from, son?"

"Philadelphia. I got in early this morning and a friend of mine lent me this car, but I got lost on Stenton Avenue, and then when I got here—"

"Stenton Avenue? What were you doing on Stenton Avenue? We haven't gone that way in years," said George.

"Well, I won't go that way again," said Bing. He put his arm about Wilma's shoulders, and a shy sadness came into her eyes. George saw it, and at first was shocked by the hypocrisy of it, but she was not being hypocritical, he saw: she was simply being affected by the magnetism of his son, whose sorrow was genuine and infectious.

George spoke to Deegan about the newspaper photographers. "Andrew will see to it that they don't come through the main gate, but you might keep an eye back gate," said George.

"They won't be coming over the wall, that's sure and certain," said Deegan.

George did not feel that it was quite necessary for Deegan to remind him of the spikes in the wall, but he made no comment on that. "I'll rely on you to keep them out," he said, and returned to the house.

The mourners had dispersed to various lavatories. Luncheon was to be served whenever Geraldine gave the order, a time unfixed because of the unpredictability of the length of the funeral service. For the moment George was alone in his study. The Farleys and Sherwood James were returning to New York on an early afternoon train. Dorothy James and Wilma were staying overnight. Wilma had the inevitable papers to sign, and was seeing Arthur McHenry in the morning. All plans were known to George except his son's.

Geraldine appeared. "What do you think? Serve cocktails here, or in the front room?" she said.

"Be a little crowded in here," he said. "Did you find out anything about George's plans?"

"Yes. He's going to wait over and take Wilma and Dorothy as far as Philadelphia in his car, tomorrow. Then they'll go from there by train."

"He *is* spending the night, then," said George.

"Yes, he seemed to take for granted that we expected him to. He's very attractive. He asked me to call him Bing, by the way. He said nobody in California calls him George."

"I'm sure they don't," said George.

The luncheon proceeded according to the improvised rules of the particular occasion: no mention of the dead, some sketchy local history by George Lockwood, some discussion of the petroleum industry between Desmond Farley and Bing Lockwood, and finally a half-apologetic reminder by the hostess that if the Farleys and Sherwood James had any packing to do, they should allow fifteen or twenty minutes for the ride to the railroad station.

Soon the Farleys and Sherwood James were gone, and Geraldine, Wilma, and Dorothy James retired to Geraldine's upstairs sitting room. George Lockwood and his son were alone for the first time in six years.

"Have a cigar, son?"

"Believe I will, thanks. I've taken to cigars. A lot of times we're not supposed to smoke on the job. One careless match could raise hell with us, so I always carry a few cigars to chew on. Don't light them, just chew on them. A habit I picked up."

"I'm told you're doing extremely well. Preston Hibbard was here and gave me a full report. He even brought along some pictures of your wife and children."

"Yes, we had a nice visit from Hib. Quite a guy. I never thought much of him in school, but Harvard must have made a man out of him. I *guess* it was Harvard. Anyway, he found out what he wanted to do, and he's doing it. That's what's wrong with a lot of guys our age. They don't know what the hell they want to do, and if they have no financial problem, they just sit on their asses till it's too late."

"I gather you have no financial problem," said George.

"Personally, no. By that I mean, with the first big money I made, I socked it right into a trust fund for my wife and children. Nobody can touch it. I can't, they can't. Once that was taken care of, I could take some chances, and I have, and they've been paying off."

"Fifty thousand to St. Bartholomew's and fifty thousand to Princeton," said George. "I was interested in the Princeton donation."

"Yes. Well, I said to myself, God damn it, I did learn a few things there. The kind of stuff you go there to learn. But I learned something else when they kicked me out. Not about cheating. I didn't have to go to Princeton to learn that that was wrong. Mother was always strict about that, and so were you. But a couple of men at Princeton taught me to take my medicine."

"How?"

"Well, by being tough. Firm. There was never any question about my being kicked out. But they could have made my offense seem like some paltry misdemeanor, and it wasn't. In that world, it was a major crime, and deserved major punishment. On the other hand, they assured me that I'd get full credit for any good things I'd done, and I don't only mean academic credit. If anybody wanted to find out why I'd left Princeton, they would be the judge of how much to tell them. Fortunately, the only man I ever worked for knew exactly why I'd been kicked out, and he gave a lot of men their second chance."

"Do you think I was too tough?" said George.

"I did, but I don't any more," said Bing.

"What made you change your mind?"

"Oh—distance, I suppose. And meeting the right girl and marrying her. Making a home of my own. And financial success."

"All adding up to independence," said George.

"Yes. When I heard about Mother dying, I was completely on my own. Ernestine, of course. But what is a sister going to be in a man's life except a sister?"

"What about a father?"

"Well, I have two of my own, now, and I wonder about that. I may be as tough as you were, but not in the same ways. As I look back on our relationship, you had your own ideas of what you wanted me to be, but they weren't necessarily mine."

"You didn't know what you wanted to be. As a matter of fact, you were well on the way to being what I wanted you to be."

"That's true. I know that. But that may be why I cheated. Underneath it all, I didn't want to be a carbon copy of you or of Grandfather Lockwood. I'd had six years of that at St. Bartholomew's and nearly four years at Princeton, and began to think it was so much shit. What are we, anyway? Your grandfather was a murderer, and what his father was, nobody knows. Mother's father wasn't much, and as far as the Richterville branch of our family's concerned, we probably have cousins up in the hills that are screwing their own sisters. No. I never thought we were so God damn elegant."

"Elegant is a housemaid's word, like swell," said George Lockwood. "I noticed you used that word at lunch. In any event, it never seemed to occur to you that there was anything worthwhile in what my father was trying to do, and I've tried to do, and was hoping you would do, and your children would do."

"What's that?"

"Make this family, that started with a murderer, mean something. You're a snob. In your mind you've probably compared us to the old families in England, with inherited titles and the rest of it, going back three or four hundred years. But little do you know how many murderers and rapists and thieves there were in those families. Or the American aristocrats that brought niggers from Africa and sold them as slaves. I give you some of the great fortunes that were made in this country in the last century, big contributors to Princeton and Harvard. The dirtiest kind of money."

"Yes, but they're the people you most admire."

"No, they're not. I wanted us to be better than they are," said George Lockwood.

"All right. I will be. But starting with me, not with you or your father or his father."

"Why, you impudent ignoramus, you must think the doctor brought you here in a satchel. You came from your father's balls, just like anyone else. There isn't the slightest doubt about that, either. You even look like your great-grandfather. The murderer, by the way."

"Well, he had balls. I'll say that for him. I'd rather be like him than some of those that came later."

"Meaning me?"

"Well, since we're being so frank with each other—yes," said Bing.

"To change the subject slightly, I wonder what ever made you come here. Were you really that fond of your Uncle Pen?"

"Yes, I was. But you're right. There were other reasons. I

wanted to take a look at Mother's grave, because I never expect to see it again. And I was curious about this house."

"You said you went to the old house."

"I did. I was already late for the funeral, so I went and had a look at the old house. I thought it was going to be turned into a hospital. It's a shoe factory!"

"I sold it to the shoe company and gave the money toward a hospital. They haven't started building the hospital, but if you're feeling generous I'm sure they'd be glad to have a donation."

"Sorry. I've severed my ties with Swedish Haven," said Bing.

"Then what were the other reasons for your coming here?" said George. "You wanted to see this house? Why?"

"Well, naturally I'd heard about it from Ernestine, but I wanted to see for myself."

"If it meets with your approval, I'll consider it a failure," said George.

"For you, it's just right. Your wife seems like a nice woman, and I guess she must have had a hand in it."

"Feel free to criticize. She had nothing to do with the house, except the interior. The rest was all mine."

"I could almost tell that," said Bing. "All that's missing is a moat and a portcullis."

"What *is* a portcullis? Do you know?" said George.

"The bridge you let down over a moat, isn't it?"

"No, it isn't. When you get home, look it up," said George. "You may want to install one sometime. Now a moat might be a good idea. I understand you're troubled with rattlesnakes, and go shooting them every afternoon. Considering what's just happened in this family, I hope that doesn't make your wife uneasy."

"That's a hell of a thing to say," said Bing.

"I just want to remind you, son. Moving to California hasn't changed your blood. You have a fine, healthy sunburn, but you are what you are, inside."

"I discussed that with my wife. She's not worried."

"Nobody worried about your Uncle Pen, either," said George.

"What the hell are you trying to say?"

"I've already said it. You are what you are. Shit is what you called the kind of life I prefer to lead. But what kind of a car did you buy for yourself? A Rolls-Royce. A Ford or a Dodge would have done just as well, but you bought a Rolls and then invented an excuse for buying it. I have a Lincoln, a Pierce, and a Packard. *And* a Ford, half-ton. I could manage a

Rolls, but I didn't need it to express my individuality. And if I had, I wouldn't make excuses for it. I've never made excuses to anyone for anything I've ever done."

"No, not even when you should have," said Bing. "Well, Father, this isn't as bad as I thought it might be, but it isn't very good, either. So if you'll excuse me, I'm going to take a ride out to the cemetery."

"Your mother's grave is two away from your uncle's. I imagine there'll be some workmen around there," said George. "And judging from this conversation, you don't wish to have me go on holding a plot for you."

"No thanks. In fact, I'm surprised you'd saved a space for me."

"I hadn't exactly saved it. I just hadn't given it up," said George Lockwood.

"What time is dinner? I may ride around for a while."

"Seven, as a rule. Ask your stepmother. This phone connects with her sitting-room. Just push the button that says 2F-SR. Second-floor sitting-room."

"I'll be back before that," said Bing. "There isn't much I want to see."

The women went for a drive, making a clockwise circle that enabled Dorothy James to see the farming country, the forests, the coal mining patches, the county seat, Gibbsville, and back to the Lockwood house. They were gone a couple of hours, but they were back ahead of Bing.

"Well, what's your verdict?" said George Lockwood.

"Beautiful, and horrid," said Dorothy James. "Therefore fascinating. To see what care the farmers have taken of their land, how hard they must work to keep everything looking so neat and orderly. Then a few miles later, the forest primeval. I could almost see Indians hiding behind the trees. Then those hideous coal mines. Those mountains of coal dust and those shabby little villages, and the gouges in the land. I really shouldn't say that, of course. Sherry's uncle is a director in one of the coal companies. And then we drove down that street in Gibbsville, the one with the lovely chestnut trees."

"Lantenengo Street," said George Lockwood.

"Some ladies were coming out of one of the big houses. An afternoon of bridge, I suppose. Limousines lined up on both sides of the street. Precisely the same ladies that come out of the Plaza after one of Mr. Bagby's Musical Mornings. I couldn't help but wonder how long it'd been since any of them had *seen* one of those mining villages."

"Well, not lately. There's been a strike, and the limousines try to avoid the mining villages. They're known here as patches, by the way."

"I think one or two of them recognized our car," said Geraldine.

"What if they did?" said George. "What time are we having dinner?"

"Wilma would like to lie down for a half an hour, and I thought we'd have dinner at seven-thirty," said Geraldine."

"Bing hasn't gone, I hope," said Wilma.

"No, he went for a drive, too," said George.

"Such an attractive boy—*man,* he's turned out to be," said Dorothy James. "It's so encouraging to see them after a long period of years, *if* they turn out well. The others—well, there are enough of those. But your young man is the sort we can count on. The country, I mean. I wish we had many more of them instead of those tiresome polo-players and their chorus girls."

"Dorothy, I'm beginning to think you must be a reader of Heywood Broun," said George.

"Oh, I'm afraid I don't think so very much of him, either," said Dorothy James. "Sherry tells me he comes into the Racquet Club every day, and I'd like to know what Heywood Broun is doing in the Racquet Club in the first place? Why would he want to belong to the Racquet Club? No, I never see the New York *World*. I *love* Don Marquis, though, and I miss Christopher Morley in the *Post*. The *Post* isn't the same without him, really. Didn't he come from this part of the world?"

"Oh, I don't think so," said George. "As far as I know, there's never been anyone literary in these parts."

"Do you know who I thought of today? D. H. Lawrence," said Dorothy James. "Have you ever read anything by him? He's one of the younger English writers, and I wouldn't recommend him to everybody. But those coal mines made me think of him. *Wilma!* I'm keeping you from your nap. You go right upstairs and I'll sit here and have a cigarette with George."

Wilma and Geraldine left.

"I drove her away," said Dorothy. "On purpose. I wanted to talk to you about Wilma. I know that she's going to be comfortably fixed, financially. But we're all going to have to do something to keep her occupied, or Wilma's going to make a mess of things. She's been perfectly splendid these past few days, but she's said certain things to me that I don't like. She has a lover. You knew that."

"Yes, I did," said George.

"*And,* he could be a godsend for her, to get her through the first few months. But she's said things to me that—well, I wish I knew you better, George."

"Pretend you do," said George.

"I guess I'll have to, because I know I'll get no help from Sherry. You know Sherry. Everything is black or white to him. No middle ground in between. I couldn't tell Sherry that Wilma has a lover. He wouldn't have her in the house. And goodness knows, some of the things she's confided in me, he wouldn't let me see her again. To put our cards right on the table, Wilma has practically told me in so many words that the sky's the limit."

"The sky's the limit, eh?"

Dorothy nodded. "She spent most of her life looking after Pen, but she accuses herself of having failed there. *I* don't agree with her, on that. Everything was all right until Pen fell into the hands of a designing woman. It's exactly like the case of that Judd man. The corset salesman, and Ruth Snyder."

"The outcome was different," said George.

"Not *really,* you know. Everybody says they're going to get the chair, both of them. So it's going to be just the same as if the Judd man had murdered her and committed suicide."

"Well, if you look at it that way," said George.

"They've never solved that other case. The minister, Hall, and Mrs. Mills. Do you remember that? That was hushed up, if anything ever was."

"It seemed that way," said George. "Go on, Dorothy."

"The corset salesman, of course he shouldn't be mentioned in the same breath with Pen. But the Hall and Mills case involved some very prominent people. *I* don't know them, but I know people who do. I'm trying to explain to you that regardless of your station in life, or how carefully you were brought up, there comes a time in some people's lives when they forget all about their upbringing and so on. Unfortunately that happened to Pen, and what worries me is that it may happen to Wilma."

"Ah, now I see," said George.

"Not that I foresee anything like what's just happened to Pen and Marian What's-Her-Name."

"Marian Strademyer."

"Incidentally, I didn't say anything, but we passed a farm this afternoon with that name on the mailbox. Fortunately, Wilma didn't notice it."

"No relation. She came from the Middle West, I believe," said George. "But a remarkable coincidence."

"As you say, a remarkable coincidence. I'm so glad she

didn't see it, because Geraldine and I have been at our wits' end to keep her mind off the subject."

"Good for you, Dorothy," said George. "But you think she is facing some sort of a crisis?"

"A nervous, or moral, collapse. Or both."

"You feel that strongly?"

"I do, George. I can't repeat some of the things she said, because they were one woman to another, under stress and strain. But the sky's the limit, George. And a girl that was gently brought up, as Wilma was, hasn't much to fall back on. I mean she can't take such things lightly."

"You haven't said this, but what you're afraid of is that Wilma isn't going to care who she sleeps with from now on," said George.

"The sky's the limit. Those were her own words."

"Well, I certainly agree with you that it could be a very serious problem," said George. "But let's wait and see if it becomes a problem, and if it does, then we'll have to see if there's anything we can do about it. Wilma's in her middle forties, still a rather attractive woman. She may find someone she'd like to marry. I don't wish to seem cold-blooded about this, Dorothy, but she's not going to marry a man unless she sleeps with him first, is she?"

"Probably not."

"Then what harm is it going to do her if she has one or two affairs, with the possibility that one of them will end in marriage?"

Dorothy nodded slowly five or six times. "I knew you'd see it more clearly than I have. I don't approve of that—that course of action. But you're a man of the world, and there are no children to have to think about. I only wish that I could be more outspoken, but I can't."

"Something she said?"

"Yes," said Dorothy James.

"Well, she said the sky's the limit. I can infer from that that that's what she means."

"There was some nastiness to it. I believe that the relationship between a man and a woman can be tender and beautiful. I've found it so. Wilma isn't approaching it that way. That's really as much as I can say, George. But thank you for your patience."

She rose, and it was obvious that she was depressed. She was an odd little woman, and at the moment she reminded George of a sparrow pecking at horse-droppings; but that was natural to sparrows.

In a few minutes Bing Lockwood returned from his drive.

"There was more to see than you expected," said his father.

"No, but I had the extra time on my hands so I went and had a beer with my old Princeton classmate Ken Stokes," said Bing.

"And distant cousin. What is he doing these days?"

"What is *he* doing? You know he's a distant cousin, but didn't you know he was blind?"

"I knew that one of them had lost his eyesight. They're all cousins of ours, but I've never tried to keep track of them all. He was blinded in an explosion, wasn't he?"

"His first year out of college. The Reading Company chemical lab."

"Why did you pick him?"

"Because I suddenly remembered that he wrote me a hell of a nice letter when Mother died. It must have been one of the last letters he ever wrote."

"Has he a job?"

"He has a music store, way out West Market Street. He wrote some songs for the Triangle shows. Played a very hot piano, in those days. Now he makes his living selling records, Victrolas, sheet music, musical instruments. Recognized my voice almost instantly. 'Wait a minute, I know that voice,' he said. 'Someone I haven't seen for a long time.' Strange how they go on talking about *seeing* people. He hasn't been able to see anyone for six years. 'I know,' he said. 'It's Bing Lockwood.' "

"The Lockwood name has been in the papers lately," said George. "I imagine he has someone read to him."

"His wife. He married out of the country club set. A very pretty little Irish girl. They have four children and a fifth on the way. Maybe a fifth and sixth. They already have one set of twins. Do you ever listen to records?"

"Geraldine does, your stepmother."

"Well, I bought you a house present. Some Blue Seal, some Red Seal, and a whole batch of Whiteman and George Olsen and so on. Ernestine might like them, if you don't. And you can exchange any you already have."

"Thank you very much. Dinner is at seven-thirty, if you want to take a shower."

"I'll do just that. Can I have a drink sent up to my room?"

"I'll send it up. What would you like?"

"An Orange Blossom. We raise oranges in California, you know. The Sunkist State."

"You're feeling pretty good."

"What the hell, why not?"

"Well, I didn't think of it as an occasion for rejoicing, but you seem to."

"Father, I have some things to do in New York the day after tomorrow, and then I'm taking the Twentieth Century Limited to Chicago, and I hope that's the last the East will see of me for ten years. In other words, I'm on my way home. That's the occasion for rejoicing. As soon as I came out of that cemetery I was on my way home. That was the turning-point."

"Perfectly clear, my boy. Go take your shower, and remember to wash behind your ears."

"You can't make me sore. I'm in too good a mood."

"I hope it lasts through dinner. I've seen people like you turn very ugly."

"Well, send up those Orange Blossoms, please. Not too much powdered sugar."

As the four Lockwoods and Dorothy James met for cocktails the spirit of the gathering was established by Bing. Earlier, at the luncheon, his father had seen how Bing conducted himself when a certain solemnity was called for and the company were all older than he: then the boy, the son, was a well-brought-up young man whose vitality and healthy good looks made him a welcome addition to the party. They had said he was attractive, and he was. Now the tone of the gathering was different: the absence of the Desmond Farleys and Sherwood James, all three extremely conventional individuals in word and deed and appearance, had a relaxing effect on the survivors of the luncheon group. The other principal relaxing factor was alcohol. George Lockwood was spacing out his own drinks, as he always did, and Dorothy James was having only a strange concoction of gin and bitters diluted with ice water, which was all she ever took as a cocktail. There was hardly more gin than bitters in the drink, but it was an expression of her political opposition to Prohibition. (During her suffragette days she had been in favor of Prohibition.) But Wilma and Geraldine had had something to drink before coming downstairs, and Bing Lockwood had had enough of the Orange Blossoms to have a noticeable effect. He was not drunk, but he had reached a state of euphoria that was prevented from becoming silliness by an air of masculinity to which the women responded and which his father saw as a first sign of ugliness.

At half-past seven the maid announced dinner, and Geraldine said, "We'll be another ten minutes, May."

"Why?" said George.

"Because I for one would like another cocktail," said Geraldine.

"And so would I," said Wilma.

"That's the way to talk," said Bing. "I'll be happy to tend bar, Father."

"Go right ahead," said George. "But if we're going to turn this into a drinking party, don't say *ten* minutes, Geraldine. Call May back and tell her we'll be a half an hour or an hour, or *two* hours. But let's not have dinner ruined."

"Ten minutes isn't going to ruin dinner," said Geraldine. Now that she had the support of Wilma and Bing she was not to be intimidated. She was rather enjoying her own performance as chatelaine.

All the leaves had been taken out of the dining-room table, but five was a difficult number to seat, and the table was still large. "Have you decided where to put everybody, Geraldine? If not, I suggest I have Dorothy on my right, Wilma on my left. Son, you will be on your aunt's left, and Geraldine, to the right of Dorothy," said George.

"It reminds me of the open end of Palmer Stadium," said Bing.

"Palmer Stadium," said Dorothy. "Do you know that I have never been to Princeton? Sherry went to Columbia. Almost nobody goes there now, but in his day it was well thought of."

"It still has a very high standing scholastically," said George.

"Yes, I believe it has, but I wish Sherry's father had sent him to Harvard."

"Why?" said George.

"Because nearly all his friends went to Harvard. My two brothers, and so many of his close friends. And it would have done him good to get out of New York. He went to Cutler School, then to Columbia, and an extra year at Columbia Law School. All in New York City."

"But if he'd gone to Harvard with all his friends, it would have amounted to the same thing," said Bing.

"That's the kind of thinking I'd have expected from your father," said Wilma.

"Now, Aunt Wilma, give me credit for some thinking of my own," said Bing.

"I will if you stop calling me Aunt Wilma. You're old enough and I'm young enough to be Bing and Wilma. And actually, I'd have been too young to be your mother, so I don't consider myself a genuine aunt. As far as that goes, Geraldine wouldn't have been old enough to be your mother."

"I unfortunately would have been," said Dorothy. "Not that I'd object to having you as my son, but I—"

"Age, age, let's stop talking about age," said Wilma. "It's not a very pleasant thing to think about, and I'm sorry I brought it up."

"As much the oldest member of this party. I agree," said George. "Having ruled out that topic, we're left with all the other topics. What shall it be, Dorothy?"

"Well—I'd like to hear more about California," said Dorothy James. "We visited there ever so many years ago, but we didn't meet many Californians."

"There aren't many, are there? Didn't most of them move there from somewhere else?" said Geraldine.

"That's one of the best things about it," said Bing. "I'm there because I want to be, and I'm staying there because I never want to live anywhere else."

"That's exactly the same answer *I* got from Francis Davis when we were there," said Dorothy. "Do you all know Francis Davis? You do, Wilma. Do you, George?"

"I know of him," said George.

"No, Father doesn't know him, but I do. I see him once in a while in San Francisco," said Bing.

"Who is he?" said Geraldine. "Is he somebody important?"

"Only two ways. Financially, and socially," said Bing. "He has all those social connections back East, and I wouldn't be a bit surprised if he could raise forty or fifty million by Friday, if he had to. He's an old Beacon Hill Bostonian. He's in shipping and real estate, banking, insurance, God knows what all. And one of the worst poker players I've ever met."

"You've played poker with him?" said George.

"Once a month," said Bing. "If we played oftener I wouldn't have to work for a living. But we only play once a month, and never for high stakes. The most anybody ever loses in that game is three or four hundred bucks. But we have fun."

"Where do these games take place? At the Pacific Union Club?"

"No, God, I'm not a member there. I'll be lucky to get in by the time I'm forty. No, we take turns playing at each other's houses."

"But aren't you pretty far from San Francisco?" said George.

"Yes, but Francis has property near us, and he combines business with pleasure. We all do, as a matter of fact. I have to go to San Francisco and Los Angeles. Out there we think nothing of driving three or four hundred miles. On a normal day I'll drive at least seventy-five or a hundred. My office is as far as from here to Reading and I go there five or six days a week. Fortunately I love to drive."

"And you *have* got that Rolls-Royce," said Geraldine.

"Oh, have you got a Rolls? If I come out and visit you, will you take me for a long ride in it? Pen would never buy one. I asked him to, over and over again, but no," said Wilma.

The first mention of Pen Lockwood's name, so casual and so curt, acted on the others like an unfair trick, but the sorriest victim of it was Wilma herself. "Oh, Christ," she said, barely audibly, and looked down at her plate.

Bing put his arm around her shoulder. "You come out to California, and I'll show you places the natives don't know about."

"Thank you," she said, and let her head rest on his arm. She was quite drunk.

"I always wanted to tour New England on horseback," said Dorothy James. "You can, you know. You start at Fort Ethan Allen, I believe, and there are maps that show you how to avoid all the main highways. Stay at little country hotels." By changing the scene she changed the subject, and no more was said of Pen Lockwood. They finished dinner in a condition of disorganization and not as the unit that had been formed when they sat down.

"Will you have a cigar?" said George Lockwood to his son.

"Oh, now don't you two go off by yourselves," said Geraldine.

"I don't think I'll have a cigar, thanks," said Bing.

"No, and let's have our coffee in the little room," said Geraldine. "You haven't seen the little room, Dorothy, or you either, Bing."

"You mean Father's little room?" said Bing.

"No, the little sitting-room. We never got in the habit of calling it the library, but that's what we intended it to be. The library," said Geraldine. "We've never called it the library because most of my books are upstairs, and your father keeps his in his study."

"Didn't I hear of some movie actress that bought her books by the yard," said Dorothy to Bing.

"Search me. I've never met any of those people," said Bing.

"Oh, we did! We met Douglas Fairbanks and Mary Pickford, and they invited us to lunch, but we were leaving the next day," said Dorothy. "I thought he was charming. I didn't get to talk to her."

"Does she still wear those curls?" said Wilma.

"Yes, but I suppose she has to," said Dorothy. "She must

have been very close to thirty when we met her. It was soon after they were married."

"There we are, back on the subject of age again," said Wilma.

"It keeps cropping up, but at our age it somehow does," said George Lockwood. "Who will have cognac? Dorothy?"

"Not for me, thank you," said Dorothy.

"Wilma?"

"Of course," said Wilma.

"None for me, thanks," said Geraldine.

"Me either, but I'll help myself to some of that whiskey," said Bing.

"This is a comfortable room," said Dorothy.

"It will be, I think," said Geraldine.

"I like what you did with the big room," said Dorothy.

"Thank you, I like it too," said Geraldine. "But we don't use it much. If we entertained more, but George spends most of his time in his study, and I come in here or else I have my upstairs sitting-room. I've become a radio fan, and that's where I have my big set. George thinks it's a waste of time, but I enjoy it."

"Oh, you and Sherry should have compared notes," said Dorothy.

And so on. But when the grandfather's clock in the hall boomed out the hour and they all realized that it was ten, not nine, Dorothy got to her feet. "I had no idea it was so late, and we have a big day tomorrow, Wilma," said Dorothy.

"I'll go upstairs with you," said Geraldine.

"I'll be up after a while," said Wilma. "Bing is going to fix me a highball, aren't you, Bing?"

"If you say so," said Bing.

"Well, then I'll say goodnight to you two," said George. "But don't keep your Aunt Wilma up too late. We're all rather tired, you know. Goodnight, Wilma." He kissed her cheek. "Goodnight, son. I think we'll all want to have breakfast at eight-thirty. In your rooms, if you like, but Arthur McHenry is coming here at ten, Wilma."

He went upstairs with Dorothy and Geraldine, and said goodnight to them on the second-story landing. He went to his dressing-room, closed the door, and undressed. He was tired, but not sleepy. With the exception of Dorothy James, they were a disquieting lot, and he had seen enough of them for one day. More than enough, in the case of his cocky son and his drunken sister-in-law. For the moment he had seen enough of Geraldine, too, but he was accustomed to her, and whenever he wanted to, he could get away from her for a few days. Unprepared by the immediate train of thought, he found that he was thinking of his brother; now, for the first time, came a full realization of the death of Pen. Until now, until he could think of Pen as a lifeless body deep in a grave and covered with patted-down earth, the fact of Pen's death had been incomplete. The murder and suicide, the events succeeding them, carried with them a vitality of their own; but Pen in a grave was flesh and blood that was his flesh and blood and a cold reminder of the unacceptable inevitable. For the very first time in his life, George Lockwood believed that he could die, too. As he considered his life at the moment, he very nearly wanted to—and then he thought of Ernestine. He had always loved her, in a formal way, but now she meant something else to him. He wondered if he would be making a mistake to send for her. It would be a great mistake if she were to offer some plausible reason for not coming.

Through the closed door he could hear the tiny strain of music from Geraldine's radio, just enough to make him aware of her futile presence. All she was now was the thin sound of a saxophone, playing an unrecognizable tune in a dance-hall in Detroit, Michigan. In other times she would be other things, but she was only that now. He had a book in his lap, a copy of *Life on the Mississippi,* which he knew well enough to open anywhere and close any time. It was one of a dozen such books that he kept in his dressing-room; they did not make demands to interfere with cogitation, and they did not keep him awake. The thin sound of Geraldine's radio had faded away, and the hall clock struck eleven. It was possible that he had dozed off, and he was not sure. He went out into the hallway; all the lights that had been on were still on, on the second story and on the first. He listened outside Geraldine's door, and heard nothing.

He returned to his dressing-room and locked the door from the inside. He kicked off his bedroom slippers and slid open the panel that guarded the hidden stairway. He went down to his study and let himself in, so far unobserved and unobservable to anyone in the hall. He opened the study door cautiously, and now he heard Wilma's voice. He could not make out what she was saying, and then as he continued to listen he realized that she was not saying anything. The sounds she was making were murmurs of pleasure. He moved closer to the doorway of the little room and looked in. There on the deep sofa was Wilma, and his son was sucking her breast. She was stroking the top of his head. "Now me you," she said. Quickly George Lockwood returned to his study and made his way back to his dressing room.

They had been leading up to it all evening, but George Lockwood had never been sure that they themselves knew it. He was now sure that Dorothy James had known it. Funny little Dorothy James had probably known it from the moment Bing arrived at his father's house, and known it with such conviction that she had abandoned hope of frustrating it. George Lockwood put on his slippers and went to Geraldine's room. She was asleep, but he stayed.

In the morning they all breakfasted at their various times and occupied themselves until Arthur McHenry completed his business and the others were ready to leave. Bing's borrowed Cadillac was at the front door, and Dorothy James and Wilma Lockwood were settling in the back seat. Geraldine was standing at the rear door of the automobile, engaging in the last-minute conversation between hostess and parting guests. George Lockwood was standing in the driveway, on the other side of the car.

His son went to him, hand outstretched. "Well, Father, I don't know when we'll be seeing each other again," he said.

George Lockwood did not immediately speak. He looked at his son steadily. "You must be very proud of yourself," he said.

Bing frowned. "What?"

"I said, you must be very proud of yourself."

Bing looked away. "I could cut my throat," said Bing.

"But you won't," said his father.

"No, I won't," said Bing. He got in the car and closed the door.

Geraldine linked her arm with her husband's and they waved at the car until it had passed through the gate. "Well, that's over," said Geraldine.

BOOK 3

■

GEORGE LOCKWOOD was now ready to devote more time and thought to his daughter Ernestine, and in this he was assisted by Pen Lockwood's last will and testament. It was a simple document, as simple as Pen had always appeared to be, and yet it contained two bequests that were as puzzling to George as any departure from routine on Pen's part was apt to be. In a man as simple as Pen, the slightest deviation became an eccentricity.

In his will Pen established an iron-bound trust fund for Wilma. The income was to go to her throughout her lifetime, and upon her death two-thirds of the principal was to go to Princeton, and one-third to St. Bartholomew's. So far, a conventional, Pen-like document. But the surprises were in two bequests of $50,000 each to be paid to his nephew, George B. Lockwood Junior, and his niece, Ernestine Lockwood. These were to be paid in cash as soon as practicable after his death.

Pen's gross estate was estimated to be in the neighborhood of $1,800,000, and the bequests to his nephew and niece were therefore not likely to make a conspicuous dent in the bulk of his fortune. Nevertheless the thinking behind the bequests was puzzling to George. Pen had been fond of his nephew and niece, and they of him, and a polite token of their mutual affection was more or less to be expected. Ten thousand apiece would have served that purpose; fifty thousand, to be paid in cash before the establishment of Wilma's trust fund, was quite another matter; especially since Pen had known that his nephew and niece had inherited about $400,000 apiece from their Lockwood grandfather, and in all probability would some day inherit from George. Why did Pen Lockwood feel impelled to supply his brother's children with so much ready cash?

The date of the will did not make the puzzle easier. It had been signed eight months before Pen's death, or at a time in which Pen could have had knowledge of Bing's prosperity and was quite definitely aware that Ernestine preferred New York and Europe to Swedish Haven. Certainly she had made no secret of her intention to live what she called her own life, and her attitude toward Geraldine was one of hostility that remained quiescent so long as they did not have to be in the same house for more than a week at a time. Ernestine had a room of her own in the Swedish Haven house, and Geraldine was careful not to disturb its contents, but it had seldom been occupied. Presumably Pen had been told of Ernestine's distaste for her stepmother, and even if he had only guessed it, the guess was not extraordinarily shrewd.

Actually these terms of the will were not so much a puzzler to George as an irritating reminder of the degree to which he had misjudged his brother. Pen Lockwood had been the kind of man to whom you said, "Don't do anything rash," and evoke laughter from the man himself; and yet the newspapers had specifically used the phrase "rash act" in their accounts of Pen's death. Now there was this will, with its substantial gestures toward Ernestine and Bing, to create the inference that Pen Lockwood had been less dazzled by his brother than had appeared to be the case. George wondered whether he had been given the real reason for Pen's staying out of the candy company deal, for instance. He made a mental note to reexamine other instances in which Pen had opposed him. One instance worth reexamination was Pen's extreme diffidence when George was expecting automatic approval of his decision to marry Geraldine. In the long run it might turn out to be a compensative exercise if he could rid himself entirely of all sentimental feeling for Pen. Present indications were that Pen had been, in his quiet way, a tricky bastard. Why else had he provided Ernestine and Bing with so much cash?

Because of the various delays of communication and travel, Ernestine had not returned from Europe, and was not present for the reading of Pen's will, which took place in the library of Wilma's house. Those present were Wilma, George, and two lawyers, and the meeting lasted less than an hour.

When the lawyers had departed Wilma said, "Well, what did you think of it?"

"He was rather generous to my children," said George.

"And made sure I didn't make any foolish mistakes," said Wilma.

"Well—don't you ever make mistakes, Wilma?"

"What do you mean by that, George?"

"A rhetorical question. We all do make mistakes," said George.

"You probably meant a great deal more than that, but I'm not going to try to worm it out of you. I'm not up to it," she said. "I thought Bing and Ernestine had to be here."

"No. Nobody has to be here."

"When my grandfather's will was read, it was up in the country. House near Rhinebeck. The diningroom, I guess because it had so many chairs. Every stable-boy that was getting five hundred dollars. All the maids. Two men from Harvard. And family. A mild punch was served, I remember. Everybody was quite embarrassed because my grandmother, who was quite fat, and also quite deaf, let go with one of those high-pitched farts that she was famous for. She always looked around to see if anyone had heard her. They had. And she was furious. Nobody was supposed to hear her. Like the king that didn't have any clothes on. But one of the maids and one of the stableboys giggled. The maid was fired the next day."

"But not the stable-boy?" said George.

"I don't know why she didn't fire him. I guess because good maids were easier to get than good stable-boys. In *those* days."

"Have you made any plans?" said George.

"Tentatively. I'm going to sell this house and rent a small apartment. I hope to travel."

"That seems sensible. Get Dorothy to go with you?" said George.

"Oh, she'd never leave Sherry for any length of time. No, I'll have to find someone else. Where is Ernestine now?"

"She's in London, but I want her to come home."

"Why?"

"Because she ought to. She should have been here long before this. When there's a family crisis, you ought not to be allowed to pretend that nothing's happened. And that seems to be her attitude. She had some excuse for not getting here for Pen's funeral, but she should have come home as soon as she could."

"I'm on her side. What earthly use is there to come home now?"

"Wilma, I don't want to have to be unpleasant, but I can be and I will be. I don't want you interfering in my children's lives."

"Now just a minute, George. That's twice you've said things that sound to me like innuendo. Just what are you driving at?"

"If I were *driving* at something, I'd hit harder and you'd be in tears."

"For somebody that doesn't want to be unpleasant, you're getting awfully close to it."

"I hope I don't have to get any closer. And so saying, I shall now make my departure. I'll be at the office all day tomorrow, and the next day I'll send up some papers for you to sign. You're going to have to sign a lot of papers, and I suggest you find a good lawyer especially if you plan to travel. You may want to sign a limited power of attorney. But don't give it to Mr. Hyme. Legally, you can, but if you do you'll be making a great mistake. Not your only mistake in that line."

"I've lost interest in Mr. Hyme."

"Yes, I suppose you have. But this time get an *older* adviser."

"I think I hate you, George. I really think I do."

"But not enough," he said.

"Not enough for what?"

"To make it interesting," he said.

"But I'll bet I could," said Wilma.

He nodded. "You almost did, a few weeks ago. But things may have changed since then. I have to go now, Wilma. Thanks for the story about your grandmother."

"Don't make too much of it, George. She was also a very great lady," said Wilma.

At the office George wrote a stern letter to Ernestine, insisting on her return to the United States without further delay. She could, of course, refuse. She had her own money, she was twenty-six years old. He therefore was obliged to make his demands on ethical grounds, and to exercise some restraint.

> It is simply a matter of family loyalty (he wrote). Your brother came all the way from California despite the fact that he and I have had our differences. He returned to California without our relations having been improved, but at least I shall always respect him for the respect he showed your Uncle Pen. You will shortly be notified that Uncle Pen left you a large sum of money . . .

Ernestine came home two weeks later. George and Geraldine were at the train to meet her in the Packard instead of in the chauffeur-driven Lincoln or Pierce-Arrow. The gesture was not lost on Ernestine. "No Andrew?" she said.

"We wanted to meet you ourselves," said George.

"You didn't have to go to that trouble," said Ernestine.

"We wanted to," said George.

After dinner Geraldine retired. "You two will want to talk," she said. "I'll be in my sitting-room."

Talk did not commence the moment the father and daughter were alone together. They made several false starts with trivialities, then Ernestine changed chairs, lit a new cigarette, and opened up. "You didn't make me come back here without some reason, Father, and I've been trying to figure out what it was. By the way, I hope you're going to reimburse me for this trip, because I was planning to stay abroad."

"Were you? I was under the impression that you were only going to be gone a couple of months. I'm not trying to get out of reimbursing you. But when you left you had no intention of staying very long."

"Then you are reimbursing me?"

"I said I would, or implied it."

"Good. Well, while I was there I changed my mind. I would like to live abroad for at least a year, maybe longer. Maybe much longer. Right now I'm tempted to say I'd like to live abroad permanently."

"In heaven's name, why? The obvious inference is that there's a young man."

She shook her head. "There was a man, not so young. Thirty-five or so."

"The usual charming Frenchman?"

"The usual charming American, but married and with no intention of marrying me. All the usual objections to the charming foreigner except he happened to be an American."

"Did you fall in love with him?"

"Yes."

"But he didn't fall in love with you?"

"No. Or even pretend to. Love wasn't mentioned very often in that crowd. If you talked about love it was the next thing to talking in legal terms, and they were all trying to avoid that. Some of the people *were* in love, but they were very old-fashioned about the word. They were afraid to say it because of the implications. In that respect they were the most old-fashioned people I ever met. Do I make any sense to you?"

"Yes, I think so," said George.

"College boys will tell you they're in love with you the first time you go out with them, but those people wouldn't even say it when they meant it. Of course most of them were married."

"What sort of crowd was it?"

"Mostly Americans, most of them had money. The women had husbands in London or Paris. The men had wives back in the States or working somewhere. Actresses' husbands. One opera singer, whose husband was plastered most of the time. Two of the men were writers. Oh, they weren't like the Lantenengo Country Club crowd, but they weren't the Left Bank, either. They weren't literary or artistic as a crowd. Mostly they seemed to have gotten together after the war, formed their own group, and when one dropped out, someone new came along to take his or her place. Money. They all had money, but nobody was very rich."

"Your man, what did he do?"

"Something to do with the electrification of the railroads. Not as an engineer, but the financial part. He worked for a Wall Street firm, actually. I never quite knew exactly what he did. He called himself a trackwalker, but isn't that one of those men that go around with hammers and repair the tracks? Obviously he wasn't that."

"What was his name?"

She shook her head. "It no longer makes the slightest difference, to him or to me. It's a dead issue."

"Not to you it isn't," said her father.

"That's how little you know me, Father. When it's over, it's over."

"No bitterness?" he said.

"Some bitterness, sourness, yes, but I'll get over that, too."

"You had an actual affair with him, of course?" he said.

"Do you think I'd make so much of it if I hadn't? I'm past the hugging and kissing stage." She had acquired a new mannerism: she would gaze at the floor as though she were on the top of a mountain and looking down into the activity in the valley. It was a disconcerting mannerism that excluded her listener from participation in her thoughts, and was intended to do so. "What do you *want,* Father?" she said, turning and facing him.

"I doubt if I'd get anything I want, from you. In your present state of mind," he said.

"But you got me back here, so you might as well tell me what it is," she said.

"Well, I've found out that you're miserably unhappy."
"Yes, I won't deny that."
"And I'd like to do something to rectify that, if I can."
"Thanks, but how can you if you don't know why I'm unhappy—"
"And you're not going to tell me," he said.
"No. Because I don't know. A few years ago I would have worried about having halitosis. But I'm quite sure it isn't that. I'm just not getting very much out of life, and this is when I ought to be getting the most."
"Who said so? Just because you're young? Youth isn't everybody's time for happiness. For some people it is, but by no means for everybody."
"What was *your* best time?"
He nodded. "Yes, I knew you'd ask me that."
"Well, when were you happiest?"
"I have to give you the answer you gave me. I don't know."
"You *must* know *that,*" she said. "Was it when you were in college? When you were first married to Mother? Now?"
He pondered her questions. "Now. This minute," he said.
"You don't seem particularly happy," she said.
"I'm sure I don't," he said. "But at this moment, sitting here with you, I'm closer to happiness than I've ever been in my entire life."
"Happier than when I was born? Happier than when Bing was born?"
He nodded. "Yes. Those were times for celebration, but I'm closer to happiness with you now than I ever was before. I've never stopped to consider happiness before. And now that you've made me consider it, I don't believe I ever have been happy. No, I haven't. I've had some good times, of one kind or another, but happiness—no."
"Why are you happy now? Or close to it?"
"Will this embarrass you? Yes, it will. But I'll say it anyhow. This is the first time I've ever loved anyone."
"Me? Now?"
"Yes."
"You never loved any of those women?"
He hesitated. "Yes, I loved one."
"Not Mother, I know that."
"No, not your mother."
"And obviously not Geraldine," she said.
"No, not Geraldine. It was a girl who had no brains at all, no particular distinction of any kind. But I loved her in a way that I never loved anyone else or even wanted to love anyone

else. A passionate dumb-Dutch girl that was the only woman ever to take me outside myself."

"It was sex, then?"

"Oh, my, yes. It was sex."

"Is there sex in what you feel for me?"

"Well, your generation believes that there's sex in everything. No, what *you've* done, that *she* did, was to take me outside myself. Why? How? Because in her case, she loved me, passionately. In your case, I feel needed. You are miserably unhappy, and you've turned to me. Maybe that's why you came home against your will. We can't know that. We may never know. Too many subtle things we don't know about ourselves, Tina. Subtleties we can't be truthful about. Hundreds of tiny changes that occur before we grasp a recognizable thought. And it has to be a recognizable thought or we don't grasp it. And now I'm back inside myself again, trying to rationalize, to analyze, to *think*—and doing the thing that everybody hates me for. I don't know why I sent for you. How can I go back through a million half-thoughts I had before I recognized one, which turned out to be the thought that I wanted you to come home? The reasons are somewhere in the half thoughts, and they remain half thoughts because we don't like the reasons."

"Father?"

"Yes?"

"I think you've cut yourself," she said. "Isn't that blood on your hand?"

He looked at the palm on his left hand. "Why, yes, it seems to be," he said. "I seem to have scratched myself. On what, I wonder? There must be a nail loose on this chair. But there aren't any nails on this chair."

"I'll get some iodine," she said.

"No," he said. "You know what I've done, don't you?"

"No," she said.

"I scratched myself with my own fingernail."

"That's an odd thing to do," she said.

"It's worse than that," he said. "I got so intense in that last speech of mine that I cut myself open with my own fingernail. I've never known that to happen before."

"Let me put some iodine on it," she said.

"All right. But I don't want you to tell Geraldine how I scratched myself. Just look at that, that's quite a gouge. There's a small bottle of tincture of iodine in the lavatory. Tiny bottle, not more than three ounces. And a roll of absorbent cotton. Will you administer to your embarrassed father's wound? Is it administer to, or minister to? The ministering angel. Well, in future I must learn not to become so intense."

"Better than biting your lip, which is what I do sometimes," she said.

He tried to make light of his self-inflicted wound, but by her over-casual manner and her avoidance of his look he knew that she did not consider the scratch a trivial matter. Nor did he. She daubed the wound with iodine—which gave them something to do, her to daub, him to pretend to exaggerate the twinge of pain. He waited to see if she would invent an excuse to leave him. She did not.

"Shall we talk about this?" he said, holding up his stained hand.

"If you like," she said.

"I think we ought to," he said. "I owe you something for coming home."

"Eight hundred and some dollars," she said.

"You'll never have to worry about money, Tina. You must know that. I would never use money as a bludgeon. Not on you."

"On Bing?"

"Not on him, either, and anyway it's too late for that. I have reason to believe he's worth more than I am, at this moment. Good for him! And I mean that. His financial independence is good for me, too, you know. He's wanted to be free of me, and now he is. But anybody who wants to be free of me makes me want to be free of them."

"So you two are free of each other. Yes, I knew Bing'd gotten rich. He writes to me, always has. The past few years he's been telling me how successful he is, financially. He bought a Rolls-Royce."

"I know," said George Lockwood.

"And he knows all the big shots."

"The big shots? What are they?"

"That's slang, Father. Important people. You don't keep up with slang, I can see that."

"I thought I did, but big shot is a new one on me. But I knew your brother was on good terms with them. Oh, he's doing very well indeed. In oil. Oil has always seemed to me a very risky proposition, but he hasn't lost his head. So far. He's provided for his wife and children, and now there'll be no stopping him. The money you and he were left by your Uncle Pen is going to seem like small change to him."

"Not to me, though," she said.

"No, if you wanted to, you could live abroad for the rest of your life on the income from it. Not at the Paris Ritz, or Claridge's, but comfortably. As it is, you're a rich American, with your present income."

"Yes," she said, and she was again looking at her private valley on the floor.

He examined his hand. "I wasn't trying to change the subject," he said.

"You didn't," she said. "We digressed to Bing, but that's part of the subject, isn't it?"

"Yes," he said. "So is your Uncle Pen. His legacies. Your income. And me cutting myself open with my fingernail."

She nodded. "And me the rich American in Europe," she said.

"Do you know very much about this family?"

"Our family?" she said. "Not as much as I ought to, I guess. I didn't realize there was very much to know. Is there? I've always had the feeling that the Lockwoods had a knack for making money, but were never quite respectable. That's strange, because after a hundred years we ought to be very respectable. Some families get there in one generation, and we've had three. Is that right? Yes. I'm the fourth generation—and look at Bing. He's going to be so rich that the others will seem poor by comparison."

"You put your finger on it. We never have seemed quite respectable. Do you know why?"

"My great-grandfather killed some people, I knew that. But the rest of you've been pretty well behaved—until poor Uncle Pen—"

"Excuse me. Did your trackwalker friend desert you on account of Uncle Pen?"

"It may have been coincidence," she said.

"But you don't really think it was?"

"No, I don't really think so. His manner toward me changed. It was mostly the way he looked at me, as if I'd been masquerading as a fairly nice girl but was really a strumpet. And he's very ambitious, very cagy."

"You're going to encounter that for the rest of your life, or at least until you marry and change your name. Is that why you want to live abroad?"

"Not the original reason, but when all that happened to Uncle Pen, I had a hunch what it was going to be like at home. My cagy gentleman friend was a clue. And then I thought, good heavens, what must it be like in Swedish Haven and Gibbsville? It was the older women in Gibbsville that first made me feel that my petticoat was showing. At dancing school, at children's parties. *They'd* look at me."

"Yes," said her father. "And I can see them. Hands folded in their laps. Unable to find anything wrong with you, or the way your mother dressed you. And not saying anything, because your mother was a Wynne, and the Wynnes were coal money. And we had some Stokes connections. But *your* name wasn't Wynne, *or* Stokes. It was Lockwood. How well I know that Gibbsville look, and I could have erased it in a twinkling if I'd married a Gibbsville girl and moved to Lantenengo Street. If my father had married a Gibbsville girl. Or even if your Uncle Pen had married one of their virgins and settled down there. So we never became quite respectable in their eyes, and I daresay we never felt quite respectable on account of that. The Lockwoods took Swedish Haven by brute force. The brute force otherwise known as the almighty dollar. And there was never anyone here that dared to oppose us. After all, your great-grandfather killed two men, right here in this town, and we don't know how many others he may have killed in the Civil War. He was never without a pistol, and half the town owed him money. If one of your ancestors could have been an honest judge, you might never have seen that Gibbsville look. But even your most respectable relative murdered his mistress and killed himself."

"You've been under a strain, Father," said the girl.

He looked quickly at his hand, then at her. He smiled. "I half expected to see I'd scratched myself again," he said. "Yes, I have been under a strain, and this is the first time I've admitted it."

"Let's not talk any more," she said.

"Do you think I get myself all worked up, as your grandmother used to say?"

"You never used to at all," she said. "Let's go for a walk?"

"A walk? Where to?"

"Nowhere. This past week I've been doing twenty times around the deck every day, and I always ended up just where I started. The saloon bar."

"All right, let's walk," said George Lockwood.

"Can I borrow a coat from you?" she said. "I'd rather not go upstairs."

"Certainly," he said. "There's a nip in the air."

"She chose his army trench coat, which he kept in the hall closet. He put on a camel's-hair polo coat, long and belted, and a cap.

"You have style, Father," she said.

"Have I? Thanks, I've always spent too much money on

my clothes, and encouraged your brother to. It isn't only how you look in good clothes. It's how you feel. But I couldn't help noticing that your brother is economizing in that respect. Perhaps that's part of getting free of me. Care to have a walking stick?"

"Yes," she said. She smiled. "Boys have started carrying canes again."

"I've seen them. Malaccas. But I'm taking something heavier. When I was building this house I killed two copperheads in one day. I've never seen one since, but if you ever walk to the top of the mountain, look out for them. And there are rattlesnakes up there in the rocky part."

"I thought they stayed in their holes at night."

"Don't count on that," he said. They left the house and went through the gate, down the hill toward the county road. "I think you'll find a pair of gloves in that coat."

"It *is* nippy," she said.

"If you get tired, tell me," he said. "You're not wearing the best possible shoes for hiking."

Halfway down the hill he stopped. "Your grandfather had a plan to buy up all the land from here to Richterville."

"All the way to Richterville?" she said.

"I used to wish he'd gone through with it, but as things have turned out I'm just as well pleased he didn't."

"What things?"

"Well, obviously your brother never intends to live here. And neither do you. That would only be a lot of land for me to dispose of."

"You would have been the squire," said Tina. "You'd have enjoyed that."

"Yes," he said.

"It's very pretty in the moonlight," she said. "All the farmers seem to have gone to bed."

"They have to. They'll be up at four in the morning. Feed the stock, get the milking done. And those enormous breakfasts. They need them. They'll do a day's work before noontime, and another day's work before they go back to bed. Yes, I'd have enjoyed being the squire. I have a feeling for this valley that I don't altogether understand. None of us were born here, although your Grandmother Lockwood was born at one end of the valley—Richterville—and your grandfather was born at the other end—Swedish Haven. And you have many cousins that you never heard of that live not far from here."

"Who are they?"

He smiled. "I don't know them either," he said. "Hoffners and Hoffner connections."

"That was Grandmother Lockwood," she said.

"Yes, they were pioneers. They cleared the land, cultivated it, brought in the livestock. The Lockwoods, as far as we know, were a different sort altogether. They were opportunists. But I will say for them that they stood off their opposition for a whole century. They made no friends, but they did the next best thing, which was to repel their enemies. Where would you like to live when you settle down?"

"You don't believe I could settle down in Europe?"

"No. This is too much a part of you, whether you know it or not. Your brother is starting all over again in California, but he's really only repeating what Moses Lockwood did a hundred years ago."

"I don't think *place* makes that much difference to me," she said.

"I do. In over a hundred years we've had no connection with the Europeans or the European ways of life. It's probably closer to two hundred years, if we belong to the New England Lockwoods. I don't know that we do, but I don't know that we don't. But no matter where you lived in Europe, you'd always be a foreigner, to them. Always. And as you got older that would make a bigger difference to you. You're nothing if not American."

"I could live in China, if I married a man who lived in China."

"Well, I've never been to China, but it might be easier for you to live there than in—Spain, or France, or Italy. Occidentals form their own little communities in China, much more so than they do in the European countries. Americans are never absorbed into Chinese life, and they're never absorbed into French life either. But in France and the other European countries they'd like to be, and it's impossible."

"What are your plans for me, Father?"

"Plans, none. Hopes, many. I would hope that you fall in love with an American, marry him, and live somewhere in the United States. Preferably on the Eastern Seaboard, but the Middle West is only a sleeper jump away."

"Have you got someone picked out for me?"

He hesitated. "Oh, yes. Likely young men that I see at the Racquet Club and downtown New York. But you'd never consider anyone I recommended—and you shouldn't."

"I owe you an apology. I'd somehow suspected that you had

picked out someone closer to home. And hence the sales talk about this part of Pennsylvania."

"No, I'm afraid I don't know any of the young men around here. Friends of your brothers, but I never see them. I never go to the country club, and when I go to Gibbsville I see Mr. Chapin and Mr. McHenry, but not any of the younger fellows. The Walker girl married Julian English, and I'm glad to see he's out of the way. You always liked him."

"When we were younger I did. Every girl I knew had a crush on Julian at some time or other, except Caroline. So she turned out to be the one that married him."

"Lord help her. We're in no position to criticize anyone, but I don't like to see a girl like Caroline wasted on him."

"Charm, Father. You had it too," she said.

"Your choice of tenses isn't very complimentary."

"All right—you still have it. But you have something else now."

"What?"

"That scratch on your hand," she said. "I like that better than charm. I've had enough of charm to do me for a long time."

They stood in silence for a little while. Presently he spoke. "I do own as far as the eye can see—in this light," he said. "In this light, and from this angle. I suppose that ought to be enough."

"Isn't it?" she said.

"Oh, I suppose it is," he said. "But if I'm content with that much, or that *little,* it proves I haven't got the vision that your grandfather had. Literally, I'm not as far-seeing as he was. He and your great-grandfather could see miles farther than I can. My world is very small, isn't it?"

"I don't know. Is it?" she said.

"I'm beginning to think it is. Myself. You. My wife. My house. And from here to that stand of timber in back of the Schweibacher farm. The Schweibacher farm that I own. All told, it isn't exactly a dream of empire, is it?"

"No, thank goodness," she said.

"Wait a minute before you start thanking goodness. Your Grandfather Wynne wanted to be a missionary. He never was, but that was his dream. And if you stop to consider, missionary work is a form of conquest."

"A form, yes," she said.

"And his cousin, Tom Wynne, he was master of all he surveyed, if you'll pardon a small joke. In Africa or South America he would have owned millions of acres, just using the same energy he expended in Eastern Pennsylvania. Your brother has that energy and look what he's doing in California. And Mexico. In other words, Tina, it's in your blood. You get it from both sides of the family."

"Get what?"

"The thing that I lack and that your Uncle Pen lacked. A large-scale ambition. It skipped our generation, but I can see it in your brother, and even though you may not have it for yourself, you may pass it on to your children."

"You've made money," she said.

"I've made a lot of money, but do you know how I'm going to make the most I ever made? In a five-cent candy bar. I don't consider that conquest, or large-scale ambition. I consider it a five-cent candy bar accomplishment. Your brother in his short life has already eclipsed me. He digs oil wells in the ocean. He plays poker with the big shots. I'm a small man, with small dreams, and I never knew it till just lately. I'm very glad you broke off with your trackwalker."

"But he had great ambitions," she said.

"He thinks he has. But from what little you've told me about him, he sounds too much like me."

"Why, Father, you're positively occult. He was a *lot* like you. How did you know that?"

"I'd have to tell you a lot more about myself than I'm ready to tell you," he said. "Suffice it to say, I recognized him. He was me. Not even a first-rate scoundrel."

"He could still be a first-rate scoundrel. So could you, I guess."

"No. Your fellow and I will never be first-rate scoundrels. The genuine, first-rate scoundrel doesn't care what people think. He does, and so do I. We can do wicked things, but we don't want to be found out. My father was closer to the real thing than I am."

"Is Bing a scoundrel?"

"Oh, you caught me off my guard," he said. "I wasn't ready or that one."

"Is he?"

"The fact that you're putting it in the form of a question, instead of stoutly declaring that your *brother* isn't a scoundrel —that's interesting. Are you a little worried about him?"

"His letters are more revealing than he must realize," she said.

"I write postcards. They come in envelopes, but I do my best to say as little as possible. What worries you about him?"

"I guess it's the same things you've been saying. Expressed differently, of course. But things about ambition. And you, and Uncle Pen. The Lockwood family history."

"What does he say about *himself?*"

"Intentionally, or unintentionally?"

"Either. What does he say that has you worried?"

"It isn't exactly worried, Father," she said. "There's nothing to worry about so far. At least I don't think there is. Oh, what am I talking about? I am worried. He's gotten *tough.*"

"Well, that's understandable. They rather pride themselves on their toughness, oil men. I went to school with a boy whose family made their money in lace. Cheap, machine-made lace. But it was still lace. He was the dirtiest, most vulgar, toughest boy in school. I wonder what happened to him when he went into the family business."

"You think Bing's toughness may be due to the kind of work he's in? I don't. I don't think you do, either."

"No, I guess I don't," he said. "The only other explanation is that I made him tough, and of course I don't like to admit that."

"I'm glad you did, though. You had something to do with it."

"Of course I did," he said. "But if all you're worried about is his toughness, stop worrying. He's going to need it. Without it he'd get nowhere, and then you'd really have something to worry about. Your brother isn't so tough that he could stand failure. In fact, you might as well know this, Tina. Your brother is a weakling."

"Have you got any particular reason for saying that?" she said. "Or is that just a general observation?"

"Both," said her father.

"You wouldn't care to tell me what the particular reason was?"

"No, I would not."

"Is he crooked?" she said.

"I doubt it. I'm sure he's not. The kind of men—the kind of big shots he plays poker with—wouldn't play poker with him if he was crooked. They might do business with him, but they wouldn't play poker with him. They wouldn't go to his house, or have him at theirs. No, he's not crooked."

"Then I know the other weakness," she said. "Women."

"You seem positive of that."

"I am. I just wondered how you found out. It only started after he got married, and you haven't seen him since then."

"How did *you* become so positive?" he said. "You've seen very little of him."

"Yes, but he talks to me. And writes to me. What happens to men, Father? Rita's a nice girl, an attractive girl. Actually a superior person to Bing. But almost as soon as they got married he went on the make."

"I suppose that means what I think it means," he said.

"It does. He has affairs."

"Does his wife know about them?"

"I don't know. I've only seen her twice, and she isn't the kind of girl you get close to right away. She's very much in love with him, and he could probably fool her for a while. He has so much vitality, always on the go. She could be deceived by that."

"And doesn't see what she doesn't want to see, as is often the case," he said.

"Yes. But I'm not at all sure that he'd be as tolerant. And Rita is some dish, don't make any mistake about that."

"I don't. I've seen pictures of her."

"Of course I may be all wrong about her, now. It's nearly two years since I've seen her. Her patience may have been exhausted."

"No, I'm sure it hasn't been. And another thing I'm sure of, is that your brother is still in love with her."

"I hope so," she said. "You're not telling all you know."

"No," he said. "But then I never have. I'm secretive by nature."

"I'll say you are," she said. "You've opened up more tonight than ever before in my whole, entire life."

"Beginning with the skin of my hand. Shall we go back? I think we've had enough fresh air."

"But I'm glad we can talk this way," she said. "Why can we, when we never have before?"

"I guess we can thank you trackwalker for that," he said. "And your Uncle Pen. And whatever's been happening inside me lately."

They were headed toward the house and the driveway at this point was at its steepest. They consequently walked slowly. "I'm glad I brought an alpenstock," she said.

"We ought to walk more. We're losing the use of our legs," he said.

"We ought to walk more and talk more," she said.

"I wish you'd stay around a while," he said. "You don't *have* to. The money can be deposited to your account at Morgan, Harjes. A few papers to sign."

"What money? Oh—Uncle Pen's," she said. "I'll stay on for a while, and when Geraldine and I get on each other's nerves I can always go to New York."

She had no car of her own, and he let her use his Packard.

She could come and go as she pleased, and George was surprised to see that she invited Geraldine to accompany her on shopping trips to Philadelphia, to the hairdresser in Gibbsville. He attributed this change in their relationship to the major change in Tina herself: his daughter was a woman now, and his wife treated her as one. It was very perceptive of Geraldine—or not perceptive at all but a woman-to-woman instinct. He made no comment and asked no questions, and he could not guess what they talked about; but obviously they enjoyed the improvement in their relationship. Temporarily, Geraldine had a companion for whose companionship she was grateful; and Tina at this stage of her life found at least a limited compatibility with an older woman that no young woman could supply. Tina had jumped into womanhood, as it were, and she was seeing what it was like.

On these terms Tina's visit was prolonged indefinitely. No understanding was reached as to the permanence of her stay; rather it continued to be regarded as a visit. She declined, for instance, her father's offer to buy her a car. "If I can't use yours, I can always drive the Pierce."

"Pretty heavy for a girl," said George.

"Oho, you should have seen the Renault we had in France. As big as a Mack truck and looked like one, with that radiator," she said. "No, thanks, Father. If you bought me a car you might be stuck with it. I might take a sudden notion to leave the day it arrived."

"And you don't want to feel tied down," he said.

"A car wouldn't be enough to tie me down," she said.

Thus a month passed. The weather became a factor in her stay. The word had got around that she was remaining at home, and she was sought after by girls and young men who respected her tennis game. When on her game she could beat any of her Gibbsville contemporaries; she had played a lot with her brother, who had twice won the county singles championship. She had no intimates among the girls she grew up with, but now they reentered her life by way of the country club tennis courts. It was a warm spring, and she could have played every day if she had been willing to engage herself with the tennis-playing set. But she kept them at a certain distance, and she thereby inadvertently revealed to her father that her prolonged visit was something of a rest cure.

She came home from the country club one day while he was having lunch alone on the terrace. "I think I'll have exactly what you're having," she said.

"You always play in the morning, and never stay there for lunch," he said.

"I don't always play in the morning, but I make sure that I'm not around there when the drinking starts. I want to play tennis, and not get mixed up in the social side. The social side is cocktails and gossip. To hell with that. If I rush to the defense of Julian English, they think I never got over my crush on him. And good heavens, those same people must have had a field day with Uncle Pen. Think what they'd say if they knew I'd been jilted by a married man."

"I didn't realize you were jilted," said her father.

"That's how it would seem to them. No, I enjoy the exercise, but otherwise I prefer to vegetate. You aren't the only one that's been under a strain, Father. Funnily enough, I thought being here would be a strain, but it hasn't turned out that way. I'm down to ten cigarettes a day, and I sleep like an innocent babe. Of which I'm neither. I'll soon be sufficiently recovered to try my luck again."

"Try your luck at what?"

"That *was* an odd thing to say, wasn't it?"

"It may have been very revealing," he said.

"To me, as well as to you," she said, and lit a cigarette. "Fourth today."

"Geraldine and I hadn't decided what to do this summer, and then when your Uncle Pen died we never seemed to get around to it again. Have you any ideas on the subject?"

"No," she said.

"I don't want to be too far away from New York," he said. "This is going to be a busy summer for me. Uncle Pen's estate, and my candy company, in addition to my usual dabblings and so on. In other words, we can't go abroad. Also, we have to face the fact that we've been touched by scandal, and therefore we'll do well to stay away from the so-called fashionable resorts. There's a place on Cape Cod—"

"Why don't you stay here? This house is cool, quite high up. Plenty of trees. Swimming pool. Tennis court. What more do you want?"

"Geraldine would really like to get away for a while. And she's entitled to that. Pen was my brother, not hers, but she fell heir to some of the unpleasantness. As a matter of fact, Tina, I've all but signed up for a cottage on the Cape. Nothing very elaborate, and not in any town."

"Have you seen it?" she said.

"Photographs of it. The house is fairly old. Grey shingles. A small boat goes with it. A clay tennis court. A putting green for anyone who may be addicted to clock golf. And a small stretch of beach for ocean bathing. Very expensive, I might add. But we wouldn't have to join a club."

"It sounds ideal. What's the hitch? Why hasn't it been rented?"

"It's owned by a Boston couple, who'd rather not lease it at all then have it rented by a family with children. Small children, of course. They don't object to daughters of advanced years. I'd be delighted if you'd say you'll come. It would make all the difference in the world to Geraldine."

"How did you hear about this place?"

"Through an agency," he said. "It's always wise to do things like that through an agency. Our law firm gets in touch with their correspondent law firm in Boston, and the Boston people recommend a real estate agency. All done in very orderly fashion. Everybody knows who everybody else is, but the principals—in this case, me and the owner—never have to meet, unless there's some reason to. The owner, for instance, knows all he needs to know about me. My credit. My social standing, such as it is. Clubs I belong to. I had an interesting correspondence with the real estate agency. Would you like to take a look at it?"

"Not particularly," she said.

"Well, it *is* on the dull side, except as an example of the negotiations I just described. What I care about now is, *will* you come? Would you try it for the month of July? If you get bored, you can pack up and leave. My offer of a car still stands, by the way. As a matter of fact, if and when we get there I'm going to buy one of those Ford station wagons."

"Oh, I love them. With the curtains on the side, and those tiny little doors in the back?"

"I'll buy it there so that the local dealer will make a little profit. Good will, of the sort those Yankees understand."

"You've thought this out pretty thoroughly," she said.

"I always do, don't I?"

"Yes, but I never cease to wonder at how thoroughly," she said. "It'll be quiet, just like this?"

"That's the whole point," he said.

"Then I'll come for July. As for staying all summer, I can't say now," she said.

"Done and done. I'll sign the lease and mail them a cheque today," said her father. "Geraldine will be terribly pleased."

It had worked out beautifully, as things were likely to do with careful planning. His offer to show Tina the real estate correspondence was intended to allay any remote suspicion she might have as to—any remote suspicion she might have. She was sharp. But then she could not have known—only guessed wildly—how very carefully he had been planning, or why.

Basically, he had decided that he wanted her to marry Preston Hibbard. His plans and his planning proceeded from there. He recalled that Hibbard had made a passing reference to Maine as the place where he spent his summers. Cape Cod therefore fitted in perfectly; far enough away from Maine to allay any suspicion Hibbard might have that he was being pursued (and Hibbard would have such suspicions), and yet only a brief motor trip from Boston. Sometime in July, and perferably not on a weekend, Hibbard would be invited to come to the Cape for an informal discussion of the terms of Pen Lockwood's bequests to St. Bartholomew's and Princeton. George Lockwood was not an executor of Pen's estate, but he was better acquainted than anyone else with the details of Pen's securities and other investments. He anticipated several, if not many, such discussions with St. Bartholomew's and Princeton.

Partly because of her disillusioning experience with the trackwalker, Tina had graduated from youthfulness to a maturity that a Preston Hibbard apparently was accustomed to in his Boston girls. At the same time she was uniquely attractive—and George had subjected her to the severe scrutiny of a father who had known more than his share of women of all ages. She was tall for a girl (girls seemed to be getting taller in the Twentieth Century), leggy rather than bosomy, but her ankles were slim and her breasts were high and firm. She had fortunately not inherited her mother's bust. In the prevailing fashion she wore her hair bobbed to the shortness of a man's haircut in back and at the sides, with a large wave left in front. The fashion was becoming to the shape of her head and the color of her hair, which was the lightest shade of brown next to blond. She breathed through her nose, a not unexceptional characteristic among her contemporaries who had undergone unsuccessful tonsillectomy, and in repose her mouth formed a thin line, placid if not severe. Consequently when she smiled her nearly perfect teeth were a surprise and a reward for people who suspended judgment on the severity of her expression. Preston Hibbard would be getting more than he deserved, but there had to be some inducements to divert him from a Boston marriage. Tina, or her father, would be likely to encounter resistance on the part of Preston Hibbard's female cousins, since local custom was tolerant of intermarriage between parties of close degrees of kindred. As an out-of-town girl Tina needed all her attributes, and as the niece of Penrose

Lockwood she needed something extra. Preston Hibbard's eccentric brother might be relied upon to provide a scandal of major proportions, but thus far his unconventionality had not brought him to the notice of the police and the press. Indeed, there were in Boston men of middle age who in their youth had behaved with more abandon than Henry Hibbard, and who had so outgrown their wildness that they were immune to the hazards of *l'age dangereux*.

George Lockwood considered it his duty to take a hand in the fashioning of his daughter's future, for in spite of her recent maturing experience, she was not capable of originating forthright action in her own interest. And time was a-wasting. Without her father's delicate intercession she could be overlooked, left unmarried and childless at thirty, and hardening into the kind of woman who attended symphony concerts by herself and had lovers who turned out to be repetitions of her trackwalker. There was in her enough of her mother to make just such undramatic tragedy possible; Agnes had had the makings of an old maid, and might well have been happier, or less unhappy, if she had remained a virgin. Tina, half Lockwood, had by nature an equipment of passion that had already given her some trouble and could continue to give her more. With a slight shock George Lockwood discovered that he had been unconsciously finding resemblances between Tina and Marian Strademyer. They were, of course, completely unalike, he reassured himself. Completely. And he proceeded to stack up all the evidence to prove how different Tina was from Marian. But having done so, he returned to his original discovery, and the rediscovery was not shocking; it was alarming. He loved Tina, now more than ever before, and the potential danger of her destruction by a man like Pen Lockwood became the cause for action that was all he needed. If a Pen Lockwood could murder a Marian Strademyer, a successor to Tina's trackwalker could murder Tina. And even if her destruction were not accomplished by a bullet, it could be done with the same finality by rejection and neglect. He wanted, by God, more out of life for her than that.

He signed the Cape Cod lease, had his signature witnessed by one of the maids, and put it in the mail pouch that Andrew took to the Swedish Haven postoffice every afternoon. For the first time in months he felt *good*.

■

HE had never thought of Tina as beautiful. Perhaps the women who held those uncomfortable poses for Charles Dana Gibson were beautiful. Elsie Ferguson was beautiful. One of the English duchesses was probably beautiful. One evening Marian Strademyer, standing perfectly still and nude and watching the water filling a bathtub, was very nearly beautiful. But beautiful women generally were fragile and remote and unexciting. They were, in a word, dull. In another word, inanimate. After a week at the Cape Cod house Tina was not beautiful, but she was lovely. The seaside sun had bleached her hair, her skin was brown. She was lovely, she was handsome, and if he had not retained his prejudice against the word he would have called her beautiful because it signified the superlative degree.

The moment had come for summoning Preston Hibbard, and a great deal depended on how it was done, but this was the sort of maneuvering at which George Lockwood excelled. He had respect for the mind of Preston Hibbard, which made the task of outwitting him more pleasurable. "If it would be convenient for you to come down next Wednesday," he wrote Hibbard, "we could have a swim and lunch. That would leave us the afternoon for our business. You would then have ample time for the drive back to Boston before dark. I promise you we will not be interrupted as my wife and daughter plan to spend the day in Edgartown."

He had, of course, arranged the absence of Geraldine and

Tina. "I would appreciate it if you ladies would make yourselves scarce next Wednesday," he told them. "There's a young fellow coming down from Boston to talk about Pen's estate. It's going to take all day, going over Pen's stocks and bonds and all the rest of it. He'll be here for lunch, and I think I can probably get rid of him by four o'clock."

"We might go up to Boston for the day," said Geraldine.

"You might do that, or you could run over to the Vineyard," said George. "The Vineyard's much closer, and it's a pleasant boatride. All I care about is getting through with this chore."

"Who is this horror that you don't want us to see?" said Tina.

"He isn't a horror. His name is Preston Hibbard and he's the acting bursar at St. Bartholomew's. But this won't be a social visit."

"I know Preston Hibbard. He went to school with Bing," said Tina. "I say I know him. Actually I've only met him."

"I met him too. He came to Swedish Haven," said Geraldine. "Don't you think it'd be nice to ask him to spend the night?"

"No," said George. "I want to keep this on a businesslike basis, and I'm sure he does too."

"Let's go to Nantucket," said Tina. "I've never been there."

"All right. I know some people there," said Geraldine. "I'll look up boats, and we can plan to be back late in the afternoon."

Preston Hibbard arrived in his Dodge coupe half an hour after Tina and Geraldine departed for Woods Hole and the Vineyard-Nantucket boat. "My wife was sorry to've missed seeing you again," said George. "But I explained to her that you're a very busy man."

"Sorry to've missed her, and your daughter," said Hibbard.

"How was your ride down? You've probably taken it many times."

"Quite a few times. I know every foot of the way."

"Then you must be ready for a dip," said George. "Did you bring your bathing suit?"

"Yes I did," said Hibbard. "And I know where to change."

"You've been to this house before?"

"I have. Elias White is a friend of my father's, but not of mine particularly. We came down here one time when we were small boys, my brother and I. Henry, my brother, accidentally set fire to the tool shed, and we were never asked back again."

"So that's why Mr. White won't rent to families with small children," said George.

"That was nearly twenty years ago, but Elias still barely nods to Henry and me. I'm sure he wasn't a bit surprised when Henry turned out to be a bohemian. Coming events cast their shadow, and so forth."

"Well, let's get into our bathing togs," said George.

There was more muscle to Preston Hibbard than George Lockwood had been aware of. He had good shoulders and chest and biceps, and well-developed thighs and calves. "You're in good condition for a man in a sedentary occupation," said George.

"I do setting-up exercises," said Hibbard. "Fifteen minutes a day. I've always liked gym work. The horizontal bar. The rings. The horse. Trapeze."

"Oh, really? That's interesting."

"Oh, it's very dull unless you care about it, but it's good discipline. Occasionally I work out with the gym teacher at St. Bartholomew's. He's really good. A German."

"They had no such thing when I was there," said George. "We didn't even have a gymnasium."

"No, the gym was built in 1908, I think. In plenty of time for your son Bing. He was pretty strong, but he didn't like gym. But that was before Hans Richtenwald was there. Very inspiring man. An absolute nut on physical fitness. He came over here after the war and was recommended by the Y.M.C.A. College in Springfield. He's responsible for the high average of physical fitness at St. Bartholomew's, no question about it."

"It *is* high? I didn't realize that."

"Very high. And another thing he does, he keeps the boys from playing with themselves."

"How does he do that?"

"By talking to them. He can look at a boy and know right away that he's jerking off. So he has him in for a talk, and believe me he puts the fear of God into them."

"So you have sex education at St. Bartholomew's? I didn't know that, either."

"They don't call it that, but that's what it is. Quite a frightening lecture on venereal disease. If a boy catches gonorrhea or syphilis, it's his own fault, after one of Hans's lectures."

"Well, I do declare," said George. "I was a senior in college before I really knew the difference between one and the other."

"That's the way it used to be but not any more. Hans works very closely with the chaplain, and the record shows that the system is worthwhile. In the last five years there hasn't been a single case of a boy who had to be sent home because of a venereal disease."

"I can't recall any in my time," said George.

"In your time they were sent home, but they gave other reasons. The real reason is in the confidential records."

"You have access to the confidential records? You must know a great deal about me. That's very disconcerting."

"No. In your case it's mostly complimentary. I shouldn't even be telling you that much, so please don't ask me any more."

"Of course not," said George. "Were you allowed to see your own record?"

"I saw it. It wasn't as complimentary as yours, but I'm not going to divulge any of my own secrets."

"Well, let's wash away our past sins in the cold salt water," said George.

The water was indeed cold, too cold for George Lockwood. He stayed in it three or four minutes and came out and sat in the sun, watching Hibbard disport himself in the surf.

"After the temperatures in Maine, this is practically tepid," said Hibbard.

"I think you're boasting," said George.

"Well, perhaps I am."

"Of course you are," said George. "Have you had enough?"

"Enough to give me an appetite," said Hibbard.

"Then let's have lunch," said George.

They had lunch on the screened porch; lobster Newburg, rice, string beans, strawberries, and coffee. "I knew I could count on a good meal at the Lockwoods', and I seem to've done justice to it," said Hibbard.

"One thing about Pennsylvanians, we like to eat," said George. "My grandfather used to say, nobody goes away hungry from our table."

"I'm glad to see you've carried on that tradition," said Hibbard.

"Well, we haven't got so many," said George. "Now if you're ready, we can have the table cleared and get down to business out here. I think we'll be more comfortable than inside. If you'll excuse me while I get my brother's folder."

It was now two o'clock and George knew that by judiciously explaining Pen's various holdings, it would be well past four o'clock before he got through. Tina and Geraldine should be returning no later than four-thirty. And so for the next two hours Preston Hibbard was given a history of Penrose Lockwood's investments which was still incomplete when the Packard drove up to the front door.

"How nice, you're still here," said Geraldine. "I believe you have met our daughter."

"A long time ago," said Tina. "Don't pretend to remember."

"I remember the occasion, but the lady herself has changed considerably," said Hibbard.

"Well, we won't disturb you," said Geraldine. "Go on with your work."

"I think I'll go for a swim. Anyone else?" said Tina.

"You couldn't pay me to go in that ice water again today," said George. "However, if Mr. Hibbard wants to show off again he can. We won't be able to finish up today, Hibbard. I'm afraid you'll have to come back some other time."

"Why not spend the night?" said Geraldine.

"Because he has other things to do," said George.

"That's not very hospitable," said Geraldine.

"I asked Mr. Hibbard to come down as a favor to me. I can't impose on him any more. I'm sure he has a full day tomorrow."

"I have got a full day tomorrow, but that's not saying I can't spend the night," said Hibbard. "I'd *like* to spend the night, if that's all right with you."

"Of course it is. You mean we could work after dinner?" said George.

"Yes, or I could come down again. I'd like to go for another swim. The water'll be warmer now, Mr. Lockwood."

"Not warm enough for me. I'll get you a bathing suit. I don't imagine yours is dry."

It was Tina who had done it; there could be no mistaking Hibbard's instantaneous attraction to her, and when she reappeared in her bathing suit, swinging a white rubber cap and slightly impatient to get to the ocean, Hibbard was obedient. It was not like Hibbard to be obedient.

They were gone nearly two hours. What they had found to talk about did not much matter, but when they came back to the house it seemed to George that Tina was indifferent and Hibbard anxious to please.

"What size shirt do you wear?" said George.

"Fifteen-and-a-half. Thirty-three-and-a-half sleeve," said Hibbard.

"We wear the same size collar," said George. "I'll lend you a couple of shirts. One for tonight, and one for the morning. My pajamas and underwear will fit you. Dinner's at seven-thirty. I'll show you your room."

"I hope I'm not inconveniencing you, Mr. Lockwood," said Hibbard.

"Not a bit. Why?"

"Well, frankly, your daughter said you were working too

hard and you were here for a rest," said Hibbard. "She made me promise not to do any work tonight."

"I suppose she told you I was under a strain," said George.

"Yes, she did, and I can very well understand that."

"Tina's a very perceptive young woman. She's been very helpful. We'll be having cocktails about seven. On the same porch. Come down whenever you feel like it."

Preston Hibbard's efforts, before and during dinner, to ingratiate himself with Geraldine were indicative of a desire to have her on his side. More subtly, Hibbard's wish to have Geraldine on his side was taken by George to indicate Hibbard's intention to see more of Tina. He told amusing stories of his previous visits to the house, and they were directed at Geraldine; he was alert with matches when she needed a light for her cigarette. The small attentions were appreciated by Geraldine, and she all but purred. "We have some tickets to the summer theater at East Sandwich," said Geraldine. "If you two'd like to use them. I don't know what's playing, but you could call up and find out."

"*I* know," said Tina. "It's *The Bat.*"

"Oh, yes," said Hibbard. "The play based on *The Circular Staircase,* by Mary Roberts Rinehart. Would you like to see it?"

"All right," said Tina. "If we don't like it we can always leave."

"Then I think you'd better quickly drink your coffee. These things start early," said Geraldine. "I'll probably have gone to bed when you get home, so I'll say goodnight to you now."

"Will I see you in the morning, Mrs. Lockwood?" said Hibbard.

"Probably not, so this is goodbye, too. But come again soon. Don't wait for some business to come up. Just come, any time," said Geraldine.

When they had gone Geraldine said, "You ought to encourage that, George."

"May I ask why?" said George.

"Because Tina needs someone like him. He may seem rather dull, but he has good manners, and he's *safe,* if you know what I mean. Also, I think he's fallen for Tina."

"*Fallen* for her? That's jumping to conclusions, I must say."

"Not impossible, though. You always knew right away when you were attracted to a girl."

"Don't compare me to young Hibbard."

"Oh, I don't know. You have things in common," she said.

"Very little. However, if you think he'd be good for Tina, as a sort of stopgap, we can have him down again."

"Yes, and don't let too much grass grow under your feet," said Geraldine. "She needs someone now, or she's liable to take up with the wrong kind."

"She's been confiding in you?" said George.

"Much more than she meant to," said Geraldine.

"You being a woman of the world, of course you can read between the lines."

"That just happens to be the truth," said Geraldine. "Well, almost time for my French lesson."

"Your French lesson?"

"I get Montreal on the radio, and it's fun to see how good my French is."

"Au 'voir, chérie," he said.

"Au 'voir," she said. "Don't stay up too late. At least don't be downstairs when they come home. Give them a *chance*, George."

He was not downstairs, but he was wide awake when they got home. He heard the car—Hibbard's Dodge—and then he saw them walk toward the beach. It was ten minutes to twelve. Two hours later he heard them again, moving about in the kitchen, closing the door of the refrigerator, chair legs moving on the linoleum, the footsteps on the stairs. He wondered how "safe" Hibbard was. He wondered about Hibbard and that gym teacher at St. Bartholomew's. He slept badly that night. The silent house seemed to be full of people lying awake with their thoughts. So it seemed to him, at least.

At breakfast George Lockwood was the only member of the family who came down to speed the parting guest. "You're going to see me again this weekend, Mr. Lockwood," said Hibbard.

"I am? Here?"

Hibbard nodded. "I'm sailing down from Marblehead, some friends of mine. And Tina's joining us. Spend Saturday night in Nantucket. Sunday we'll be at West Chop for lunch, and then I'm coming here to spend Sunday night."

"That ought to be nice," said George.

"I'm hoping to persuade her to come to Maine two weeks from now. Will you put in a good word for Maine?"

"No, but I won't put in a bad word. Tina does as she pleases, and I encourage that."

"She has great, great admiration for you. She thinks her father is quite a fellow."

"I think she's quite a girl," said George Lockwood. It was

the moment, and George Lockwood sensed it, for a restrained demonstration of paternal love.

"If I may say so, so do I," said Hibbard.

"Glad to hear it. I want her to have more friends on this side of the ocean. Europe is no place for her, not as a permanent thing."

"She wants to live abroad?" said Hibbard.

"Oh, she's made up her mind to. She's only here now because of me. You know how things are between my son and me."

"Yes," said Hibbard.

"And my brother's death took it out of me, more than I knew at the time. But as I said yesterday, Tina's a very perceptive girl. Have some more coffee."

"No more, thanks. I'll return your shirt on Sunday," said Hibbard.

"Don't you dare forget," said George Lockwood, and smiled.

Tina saw Hibbard at least once a week throughout the summer. There were so many gaps in her unsought explanations of her comings and goings that George Lockwood recognized the signs of an affair. She paid him the courtesy of her explanations, but she grew uncommunicative during their moments together. He did not press her, a strategy that was less inspired by delicacy than by a growing conviction that she had not yet committed herself to love and was mystified by her self-repression. The girl had discovered on her own the complexities in Hibbard that he had unconsciously revealed to her father. George Lockwood wanted to tell her that bisexuality was neither monstrous nor rare; but in return for the information she might laugh in his face. What did he really know of what went on in that well-shaped head or between those now sunburned thighs? Who had kissed her, where and when? Whom had she kissed? These were things he would never know, because only she could tell him.

Nevertheless he was content for her, in spite of her retreat from their previous tentative rapport. This much she was alive, engaged with the life of another human being. Superficially she bloomed, when she might instead have been wilting. She was, moreover, present instead of absent, and if she was questioning the degree of her commitment to love, her turmoil was observable and not taking place in some foreign surroundings. Whichever way her decision went, it would be made here, where her father would not have long to wait to see it, to hear it.

She came down to breakfast one morning late in August, and on her plate, on top of some letters, was a small package, insured parcel post with the return address of a Boston jeweler-silversmith.

"I hope your mail is more interesting than mine," said George Lockwood.

"I think it will be," she said. She got a fruit scissors off the sideboard and opened the parcel. Out of a long, slender blue imitation-leather box she lifted a gold wristwatch and dangled it before him.

"I've never seen that before," he said.

"I've only seen it once before myself," she said. "It was being engraved."

"Am I to be allowed to examine it?"

"Of course," she said.

He laid it flat on the palm of his hand. The bracelet was of fine gold mesh, the face of the watch was surrounded by diamonds, the top of the stem was a small ruby. "Exquisite," he said.

"You're dying of curiosity. Go ahead and read the inscription," she said.

He looked on the back and read aloud: " 'Tina—time is a-wasting—P. H.' " He handed the watch back to her. "He could have sent you the same message on a penny postcard. But that's no penny postcard."

"No," she said, looking at the watch.

"I'm not going to ask you anything, Tina. I'll be damned if I will," said her father.

"Do you have to?" she said.

"Yes, I have to, but I'm not going to."

"He wants me to marry him before school opens," she said.

"Are you going to?" said her father.

"I think I will," she said.

He laughed. "You think you will. School probably opens in two or three weeks."

"Three weeks from next Tuesday, to be exact," she said.

"Where would you be married, if you decide to be?"

"At a justice of the peace. Obviously we couldn't have a big wedding this year, and I never wanted one anyhow."

"You could have a small wedding in Swedish Haven. Just the two families."

She shook her head. "The two families aren't getting married, Father. Only Pres and I."

"I'm not going to be there to give you away?"

"I'm afraid not. I'm not being secretive. I really haven't quite made up my mind. But when it happens, if it happens, I'm going away, and the next time you see me I'll be married."

"Is that what Preston wants, too?" said her father.

"It's very much what he wants," she said.

"Is it what his family want?"

"They haven't been told. I've met them all, except the brother in Mexico. They've had a look at me, so when they get the news they'll be able to say they've met me. That I'm white, young, and not hideously ugly."

"I said I wouldn't ask you anything, but I seem to be doing nothing else," he said. "This is the only question of any real importance. Why are you unable to make up your mind?"

"So many answers to that, Father, and I don't know which is the right one. The real one."

"Then I guess I didn't ask you the right question. Do you love him?"

"No," she said.

"Is it because you're afraid to love him?"

"Possibly," she said. "You mean afraid because of what happened abroad?"

"I didn't say that, Tina. I asked if you were afraid to *love* him."

"I'm not afraid to love him, Father. I just don't."

"Then what is this marriage based on?" he said.

She thought a moment. "Compatibility. Friendship. Companionship. Sex. Mutual protectiveness."

"I thought so! And fear," he said.

"Fear of what?"

"You know what, Tina. Let's be honest with each other. No one's listening. I'm all for this marriage if it's what you want. But be sure you know what you may be getting in for."

She smiled, a pleased smile that was the last thing he expected of her. "Good for you, Father!" she said.

"Good for *me?*"

She fondled the watch in the fingers of her right hand. "He wondered if you would remember, and you did. He thought you would, but he wasn't quite sure. I said you *would,* that you never forgot anything."

"Make sense, girl. Make sense."

"The first day Pres came here, he told you about his friendship with the gymnasium teacher at school."

"He certainly did," said George Lockwood. "I wasn't likely to forget that."

"Naturally you concluded that the friendship was more than just a friendship."

"I did," said her father.

"Well, you were right. Pres has had relations with both sexes. He has had since he was a boy. And he doesn't know whether marriage will cure him or not."

"I can tell you, Tina. It won't, if you mean curing him of homosexuality. Is that why you're afraid to marry him? Or so hesitant?"

"No. The homosexuality is what the friendship was based on. The problem. He had his problem. I had mine. I *have* mine."

"What is yours? You're not a Lesbian," he said.

"No. My problem—the polite word for it is promiscuity," she said.

"One of two affairs in Europe," said her father.

"Hah!"

"Well, you're twenty-six. It depends on your definition of promiscuous," he said.

"An odd subject for the breakfast table," she said. "Father, I've only had one *real* affair in my life. With the trackwalker. That was the only affair that lasted long enough to be called an affair, and that's why I was so upset when it broke up. I thought I'd found a man who could keep me from being a whore. But the whore came out, and he dropped me. I told you about an opera singer whose husband was drunk half the time. I was caught in bed with him. And I was almost sure I would be, but I went to bed with him anyhow. If I lived abroad, Father, with those people, I'd be only one of many. Here—in the United States, I mean—and among the people I'm most likely to see, I'm a marked woman."

"A marked woman," said her father. "I should think you'd be marked in more ways than one."

"I am," she said.

"I wasn't only referring to your character."

"Neither was I," she said. "Don't expect any grandchildren from me, Father. Three years ago I had an operation that took care of *that.*"

"You had an abortion?"

"Oh, nothing as mild as that," she said. "I caught a disease, and that's why I had the operation. Uncle Pen knew all about it, and Aunt Wilma. Uncle Pen paid for everything. And I think that's why he left me that money, in cash. You're *stunned*. You *look* stunned." She put her hand across the table and rested it on his arm. "Tell me to go abroad, Father."

He shook his head. "No," he said.

"I'd go if you told me to," she said. "Otherwise, I think I'll marry Pres."

"Does he know all this?"

"Most of it. The worst of it. He had a few things to tell, too," she said.

"Yes, I guess he did," said her father.

"Most people start their marriage with high hopes. We'd start with hardly any at all."

He patted the back of her hand. "Don't be deceived by that. Don't think things couldn't get worse."

"You're not as much for this marriage as you were a few minutes ago?"

"I don't know," he said. "I haven't had time to think. But I'm not going to *tell* you to go abroad. Don't try to shift that over on me, Tina. If your Uncle Pen were still alive, he'd know what to say. But I don't."

"Don't be hurt because I went to Uncle Pen. I didn't dare go to you. I wouldn't have gone to you six months ago. But here I am now, asking you what to do."

"Whatever I tell you, Tina, is going to be wrong unless you really want to change your ways. And I don't know whether you *can* change your ways. They have these psychologists, psychoanalysts, but I don't know how much help they are."

"I slept with one in Paris. A hideous little man. A gnome. He was a Russian Jew with a long moustache, and I towered over him. He's the only psychoanalyst I ever knew, but he wasn't helping me. I was helping him, and he said so quite frankly."

"You see, Tina? I couldn't possibly be the one to advise you, to tell you what to do. You have another personality that I'm just hearing about for the first time." He looked out at the gardener who had begun to mow the lawn. "And yet, I know where it all came from. All of it." He cupped his hand under her chin. "I know where the eyes came from. The cheekbones. The shape of your head." He dropped his hand. "And most assuredly I know where the rest of it came from, good and bad. I doubt if any Jew with a long moustache, or for that matter any Gentile with no moustache could make you different from the way you are. And I wouldn't want them to."

Instantly she broke into tears, got up and left the table. They had had all they could stand, and she had the privilege of yielding to a more complex emotion than she was used to yielding to.

The basic routine intervened before he could lose himself in retrospection. The maid swung open the kitchen door. "Isn't Miss Tina ordering her breakfast?" she said.

"Not just yet," said George Lockwood.

"I heard her go upstairs, and she likes her bacon crisp. I could have it ready by the time she came down again. You don't know what kind of eggs she wants?"

"Golden eggs," said George Lockwood.

"Golden eggs? Is that your way of saying sunny side up? You know, Mr. Lockwood, you don't always talk very plain. Sometimes I can't hardly understand what you're saying. It runs in this family."

"Sometimes I don't hardly understand what you're saying, either, May," he said. "Miss Tina will be having her breakfast when she has it. When that will be I don't know."

"Only a cup of coffee is no breakfast for a healthy young girl. And she didn't even drink all of that. People shouldn't fight at breakfast. It ruins the whole day." May let the door swing shut behind her to neutralize any reply he might be making.

He was not about to make one. May was the kind of servant that could be easily forgotten when she was not actually present, the nearest human thing to a kitchen utensil. Upstairs Tina was in extreme misery, and he could not help her. The sense of his ineffectuality was worsened by his inability to plan her way out of her unhappiness. For the first and only time in his life he thought of taking her away with him to some strange land where he and she could get a new start. There was no such land; he knew it; but he recognized the thought as a symptom of his ineffectuality.

He left the porch, taking the Boston and New York papers with him, and sat on the sofa in what the Elias Whites called the drawingroom. The term invariably conjured up a picture of ladies and gentlemen in formal evening dress, on their very best behavior, while a string quartette played softly behind a bank of potted palms. The Elias Whites surely had never had so much as a single violinist to play in their cottage, but in all descriptions of the house, in letters and on the floor plans, this was designated the drawing-room. Very well; in the drawing-room George Lockwood would pretend to read the morning papers while suffering retrocessively with his daughter's contraction of a venereal disease. How had she discovered it? In all probability by being told she had passed it on to someone else. If that were the case, a man lived who despised her, and she would go through life knowing a man despised her. Sooner or later he had surely said, "I got a dose of clap from Tina Lockwood," and even if he whispered it Tina would know he was saying it and could always say it. For her, too, there would be the moment when a man asked her to marry him and she would have to say, "I can't have children." And being Tina, she would have to tell him why.

And yet it apparently had made no difference to Preston Hibbard . . .

George Lockwood tossed the papers aside and went upstairs to Tina's room. He knocked on the door. "It's me. Father," he said.

"No," she said, and even in the tiny word her voice was weak and tragic.

The door was not locked, and he entered the room. She was bent over in a rocking-chair. He closed the door behind him and went to her and put his hand on top of her head. "I've been thinking, Tina," he said.

"Oh, don't think, Father. I've done all of that that's necessary. I'm going away."

"I wouldn't if I were you," he said. " 'Time is a-wasting.' "

She looked up at him and then compulsively at the wristwatch that lay on her dressing-table. He nodded. "Yes, I mean him. I want you to go to him now. Today."

"And what?"

"And marry him."

She straightened up. "You couldn't have been listening very carefully."

"I heard every syllable, and more to the point, *he* did when you were telling *him* the same things. What I think doesn't matter, but that watch does. The watch, and what he says on it. Do you know where he is today?"

"Today? Yes, he's at school," she said.

"Go there. Don't tell him you're coming. Just go. Even if it only lasts a few years, Tina, it'll be good for both of you."

"Why will it?"

"Because it's what you both want to do, and that's reason enough. Do you want a high-minded reason? I can give you that, too."

"I can't think of any," she said.

"There is one, though. Actually there are two. He needs you, and you need him."

"High-minded? That's selfish."

"Think about it on your way to St. Bartholomew's," he said.

"You know, I've been to a lot of weddings, but this is the first time I ever really felt that the father was giving the bride away."

"I feel the same way," he said.

"I'm not going to tell Geraldine."

"Send us a telegram," he said.

Then, as if uttering a black prayer, she said, "And he can't ever say he didn't know what he was getting, can he, Father?"

They were married the next morning in Central Falls, Rhode Island, because the state law did not require a waiting period. Their telegram read:

TIME IS NO LONGER A-WASTING. WE WERE MARRIED AT TEN O'CLOCK THIS MORNING. MUCH LOVE.

It was signed "Pres and Tina Hibbard." The telegram was delivered while George and Geraldine were at lunch.

"You of course knew about this," said Geraldine.

"I was about to say the same thing to you," said George.

"Yes, but I said it first. You did know about it, didn't you?"

"I knew it was in the air," he said.

"Are you pleased? You are, aren't you?" she said.

"I can't imagine anything that would please me more," he said.

"Well, of course I was for it from the very beginning," said Geraldine.

"That's right, you were," he said.

"I wonder where they'll live. Do you think he'll stay at St. Bartholomew's? I can't imagine what it would be like to be surrounded by hundreds of boys just finding out about sex."

"When I was there nobody ever thought about sex."

"When you were there there was at least one person thinking about it. You were probably screwing a chambermaid."

"Didn't have any. We made our own beds."

"Well, the wife of the headmaster or somebody."

"The headmaster's wife was probably the reason why we gave so little thought to sex. As a matter of fact there weren't any females worth lusting for. There was a certain amount of buggering among the boys themselves, and if you got really hard up you could usually find someone to relieve you in one way or another. But no female while I was there. I'm sure Tina will be able to cope with the problem."

"I'm sure. It's just that whenever I've visited a boys' school, they *look* at you, and Tina's worth looking at. And of course she being a brand-new bride, they'll all be thinking the same thing."

"Those thoughts won't be confined to St. Bartholomew's."

"I think it'd be a good idea if Tina had a child right away," said Geraldine.

He did not dare look at her. "Do you indeed? Why do you think so?"

"Well, you know as well as I do that she's not a virgin, not by any stretch of the imagination. If I'd had children, my life would have been a great deal different."

"No doubt it would have."

"I might have made a very good mother."

"Well, I don't think you'd have made a bad one. But you

must admit there are some women who lead a perfectly satisfactory life without adding to the population."

"Satisfactory to whom?"

"To themselves and to the men they sleep with. Wilma, for instance, is better off without children. And so is the world. Not to mention the children she might have had."

"Wilma, for your information, is anything but a nice woman. I've had to change my opinion of her."

"It was never very high," he said.

"No, and it's lower than ever. Don't ask me why."

"Why?"

"I won't tell you. But with all your thinking and all your analyzing people, there's a lot you miss," she said.

"I never miss a thing," he said. "Not a thing."

"You're feeling pretty good. You *are* pleased about Tina."

"Of course I am. I planned it all."

"You're insufferable, positively insufferable. If anybody planned this, I did."

"Sorry. It was me."

"In a minute you'll have yourself believing that," she said.

"However, I do thank you for the small part you played in it. You were very helpful. I shall reward you with a suitable present."

"You don't have to give me any more presents. The only present I want from you is seeing you this way. In really good spirits for the first time in I don't know how long."

"Nevertheless I'm going to give you a present. I'll find something in New York tomorrow that'll knock your eye out."

"You're going to New York tomorrow?"

"A meeting of the candy bar company. Like to come along?"

"No thanks. The thought of leaving this beautiful weather for hot stuffy New York—no thanks. I'd almost like to stay here till the first of October."

"Through the hurricane season?"

"There may not be any hurricane."

"True," he said. "Well, I'm sure Elias White will be pleased to accept an extra three weeks' rent. Our lease is up the tenth. I'll speak to the agency. However, if we're staying till the first of October, one of us ought to go to Swedish Haven just to have a look."

"A look at what?" she said.

"A look around, actually. We planned to reopen the house on the eleventh of September, but it'll be three weeks later now. So I think I'll run over and see how the place came through the summer, and arrange for the watchman and the gardener to keep coming. I'd like to get the place in good shape for Tina's first visit with Hibbard, whenever that will be. Later on, of course, there'll be the usual exchange of visits with his family. We ought to do some entertaining for them. They won't expect much, but a fairly good-sized dinner party in November, don't you think?"

"Or a dance. We've never had a dance in that house, and we can't go on forever reminding people of Pen and Marian Strademyer. We ought to have a dance at Christmas. Have the Boston people as our house guests, and Emil Coleman's orchestra."

"I'd be more inclined to have Markel."

"No, not for this kind of a party. Emil Coleman is all the rage now," she said.

"Whatever you say. A dance is your idea. Don't tell me you've been wanting to have a dance all along?"

"No, but I do now, and we'll never have a better excuse to have one. We'll invite everybody. Tina's friends. Your old friends. My old friends. Preston's friends. The whole membership of the country club."

"I'll have to make arrangements with the bootlegger. A party that size, we'll have to order the liquor well in advance, if we want good stuff. Wimley used to be the caterer. Philadelphia."

"You're as enthusiastic about this party as I am," she said.

"Well, if we're going to have this kind of party, we have to do it up brown, whatever that means. I remember a party in Fort Penn, when Grace Caldwell married Sidney Tate. Agnes couldn't go, but I went anyway. I wouldn't have missed it for anything. Handsome girl. Still is, I should imagine. They had everybody from the governor to a trainload of people from New York, mostly Yale. Sidney Tate was an Eli. He died several years ago. They weren't getting along so well. I used to run into her brother, Brock Caldwell. It's really not too early to start getting to work on an invitation list. A good party is either impromptu, on the spur of the moment, or everything planned well ahead, I, of course, would rather plan ahead. I'll come back from Swedish Haven full of ideas."

"And when will that be?" said Geraldine.

"Let's see. Tomorrow night I'll be in New York, at the Carstairs. Take the early morning train to Philadelphia. Change trains there and get to Gibbsville in time for lunch with Arthur McHenry, and he can drive me to Swedish Haven. I'll have all afternoon at the house. Order a taxi to pick me up at the house and drive me back to Gibbsville. There I can have dinner at the club or the hotel. That will give me plenty of time to take the sleeper from Gibbsville. Be in New York early the next morning and get a train to Providence. Andrew can meet me there. I'll be home in time for dinner the day after the day after tomorrow. Not bad, considering what I'll have accomplished, and the distance covered. Planning will do it."

"You'll be awfully tired of trains when you get home," she said.

"But I don't just sit there, you know. I'll be busy every minute. I like to work on a train. The porter puts one of those little tables in front of you, and if nothing else, it keeps the bores away. What will you be doing while I'm gone?"

"Well, I've come to depend so much on Tina for company that I expect to be bored to death. So do come back as soon as you can."

"If you have any messages for me, the Carstairs tomorrow. After tomorrow, either the Gibbsville Club or Arthur's office. You have both numbers in your book. Of course you could reach me at the house, the day after tomorrow, between three o'clock in the afternoon and six o'clock in the evening. But I may be outside and not hear the ring."

"I doubt if there'll be anything. Tina won't call us this week."

"No, they have to get used to each other," he said.

"Yes, that applies to every married couple, whether they're young or not so young."

"I agree with you," he said. "And when I come back you can tell me what's on your mind. We have to plan for *our* future. If anything, more carefully than the young do theirs. I hope yours is going to be with me, but you'd have damn good reason for making other plans."

"As you said, we can discuss all that when you get back," she said.

"One of the fascinating things about life is the different levels we can think on at the same time. You and I can plan a big party, to take place four months from now. That's one level. On another level, a conversation we have three days from now could very well put a quick end to our marriage. It will largely depend on the degree of your discontent."

"And, since you're such a great planner, what you plan to do about it," she said.

"Precisely. But don't, *please* don't spend the next couple of days in building up righteous indignation. If you were to do that, there wouldn't be much use in my coming back. I might just as well stay in Swedish Haven."

"I want you to come back," she said.

"That's good. I want to," he said. "And I have to deliver your present. That's what might be called thinking on three levels."

"The way your mind jumps around, you don't stay on any one level for long," she said.

"Hmm. My mind jumps back to a few years ago when there used to be a slang expression, 'he isn't on the level.' You remember?"

"There was a song. Devil on the level. She's a devil, on the level. Something like that rhymed devil and level."

"I'm not very good at songs," he said. He put down his napkin. "A lot of work to do this afternoon." Anger had come over him and he did not wish to show it. Their conversation had taken a turn that put their relationship on a tentative basis. He had intended to go to bed with her that night, but he could anticipate their self-consciousness and its enervating effect; the limp man and the dry woman, benumbed and hostile. For at least three nights he was to be deprived of the pleasure of her body, and if the conversation on his return revived her resentment, it might be a week or even longer before she wanted him. It was not always necessary for her to want him; he knew that. There had been times when anyone else would have done just as well, and on several occasions their love-making had the character of adultery, for him and for her. ("You were thinking of someone else," he once said. "So were you," she said.) But until they settled the problem of her discontent they would be kept apart by surly mental activity, and he had not married her for her mental activity. More's the pity, he had allowed her to discover that fact.

They were polite enough to each other when he left to take the train. He kissed her, and she smiled. He got into the little station-wagon beside Andrew, raised his hat and shook it in amiable farewell, and left her standing in the doorway in her negligee. She had at least come downstairs to see him off. The thought occurred to him that if he never saw her again—a not unusual thought at some of their partings—he would remember her as the source and repository of numerous hours of various pleasures. For that he *had* married her.

Daisy Thorpe, successor to Marian Strademyer at the Lockwood office, stood in front of George's desk, ticking off with her pencil the items on her notepad. ". . . And last but not least, Mr. Edmund O'Byrne. Phoned twice yesterday and twice the day before. He was going to phone this morning, but he hasn't. You can reach him at Watkins 2044 if you wish to, but if he's in the same condition he was when I talked to him, you won't get much sense out of him."

"The condition being a state of intoxication?" said George.

"To put it mildly. I refused to give him your number on the Cape," said Daisy Thorpe.

"Thank you. If he calls again, I'm not here. *No!* Wait a second. Call our broker and find out the latest price on a stock called Magico. It's not listed on the Big Board."

"Right away?"

"Please," said George.

He waited while she had the conversation with the broker. She hung up. "It *is* on the Big Board. It closed yesterday at 92½ and opened this morning at 93," she said.

"Hmm," he muttered. He remembered his last conversation with Ned O'Byrne. The name of the stock was easy to recall: Magico. A radio company. His memory of the figures O'Byrne had mentioned was somewhat vague, but it came back to him that O'Byrne planned to get out when the price reached 40 or 50. "Get me Mr. O'Byrne," he said.

"I happen to know the Watkins number is a speakeasy, Mr. Lockwood."

"I happen to know it, too. Do you go there?"

"Every Sunday evening."

"Odd we've never run into each other there."

"Oh, I've only been going there lately, since I moved," she said. She called the number and got O'Byrne on the telephone.

"Ned? George Lockwood. I just got your message. How've you been?"

"Are you on the Cape, or in town?"

"I'm at my office. What can I do for you?" said George.

"Can you have dinner with me tonight?"

"Yes, as it happens, I can. Where and when?"

"I'll meet you at 42 West Forty-nine, seven o'clock. Is your wife with you? We want to be sure of a table."

"I'm alone. How about you?"

"I'm alone too," said O'Byrne. "However, that can be rectified, after I've talked to you."

"Well, we'll see," said George.

Throughout the rest of the day he wondered what O'Byrne had on his mind. There was an unmistakable ring of confidence in O'Byrne's voice which probably was related to the price of the Magico stock. But at seven o'clock, when they met at the 49th Street address, O'Byrne was showing the effects of a day's hard drinking.

"I never wrote to you about your brother because I didn't know him. Also, because you didn't write to me about *my* brother."

"I didn't know about your brother," said George. "What happened to him?"

"I didn't think you did. He fell in front of a subway train, a few weeks before your brother died. There wasn't much in the papers about it. Princeton football star killed in subway. Two or three inches of type and that was all."

"I'm sorry, Ned. It was probably one of those days that the New York papers missed the train. Although you might have thought I'd have heard about it later."

"Well, you didn't, so you're forgiven. Kevin never amounted to anything much. A wife and two children in East Orange, and a job in an insurance agency. Not even a partnership. Just a job. That isn't what I've been calling you about. Our unfortunate brothers. And I don't want to borrow any money from you. I'm doing pretty well in that respect, I'm happy to say. You won't remember, but I told you the last time I saw you, that night we had dinner together, I had a stock tip. Well, it turned out to be a good one."

"Vaguely. General Electric, or something, wasn't it?"

"Hell, no. Mine was a real speculation, but it's on the Big Board now and I'm sitting pretty. Let's sit down. Georgetti, can we have this table? And two more Planter's Punches, please."

They sat down. "George, I'm going to put it right on this tablecloth for you. I've debated with myself, what was the right thing to do. I gave the subject a lot of thought, and I finally came to the conclusion that by and large, you and I were pretty good friends. We *were* good friends in college, and while I haven't seen so much of you since those days, I still consider you a friend of mine."

"And rightly so," said George.

"You have to be patient a minute, because what I have to tell you isn't something you blurt out without any preamble."

"We have all evening," said George.

"It won't take that long, I can assure you," said O'Byrne. "First I have to ask you, did that mess your brother got into have a very bad effect on you?"

"More than I realized at the time. Why?"

"The same with me. It wasn't so much the initial shock as the slow realization that this is a son of a bitch of a life. Kevin was a nice, decent guy. Married to a dull woman and had two uninteresting kids. Never made any money to speak of. Then one day he fell in front of a train on the Lexington Avenue subway. Heart attack. Much, much later I found out that for about twenty years he'd been in love with a woman that he couldn't marry or that wouldn't marry him because they were both Catholics. She came to see me after he was killed, to ask me if I'd do her a favor. The favor was to get something personal of Kevin's, like a ring or a stickpin or any small thing that he wore or carried around with him. It finally came out that what she wanted was a pair of rosary beads that he always carried. You know what they are, rosary beads?"

"Oh, sure."

"These were silver beads on a silver chain, very small, in a little silver box the size of a pillbox. She had nothing of Kevin's. They'd never been able to exchange presents, because her husband or Kevin's wife would have noticed it. For twenty years this woman and my brother had been in love. Maybe a couple of times a year they could manage to go to bed together. Not often, though, and she told me that they gave each other up several times and then they'd go back together again. Walks in the park. Rides on the Fifth Avenue bus. Trying to keep it platonic, which was just as hard for them as it was to have an assignation. Her husband was the exact counterpart of Kevin's wife. Unsuspecting and dull. A lawyer. Quite prominent in Catholic circles. The son of a friend of my father's. The nearest thing to a priest that a married layman can be. More money than Kevin ever had, and the two couples never saw each other." He sipped his drink.

"Sad," said George. "Very sad."

"The day Kevin fell in front of the train he was on his way to meet her. Probably the excitement of going to see her had something to do with the heart attack. In any case, he had it and was badly ground up. The poor son of a bitch. She waited for him, and she didn't know anything about what had happened to him till the next morning when she saw it in the papers."

"And they can be pretty bad," said George.

"She couldn't even go to Kevin's funeral. She was left with nothing, *except one thing*. The terrifying thought that he *could* have had the heart attack while he was in bed with her. Can you imagine what that kind of guilty feeling can do to a Catholic? No, I guess you can't. You'd have to be that kind of Catholic to know. I was brought up a Catholic, but I had a hard time putting myself in her place. She told me. First, the guilty feeling because he was on his way to meet her, the narrow escape. Then to add to it, the feeling that she must do penance. But worst of all, the knowledge that she was still in love and that that part of her life was finished. It is, too. She told me she felt sinful about asking me to get Kevin's rosary beads, but that if she didn't have something of his she would go out of her mind."

"I hope you got them for her," said George.

"I did. His wife was only too glad to see any sign that I was getting religion. And of course when I pretended that I lost the beads, she thought it was typical of me. Fuck her. I didn't care what she thought. It was Kevin's girl I was thinking of. The one he loved, and that really loved him. She goes to Mass every morning, and if you think it's a comfort to her, it isn't. She's only about fifty, but I'll bet she doesn't live another year."

"I'm really sorry about Kevin. He was a nice guy," said George.

"And this is a son of a bitch of a life, George. And now comes your turn."

"My turn?" said George.

"As if you hadn't had enough with your brother," said O'Byrne. "How much do you know about that kid of yours?"

"Which one? My daughter, or my son?"

"Your son. Bing? Isn't that what they call him?"

"Yes," said George. "We're not very close. He lives in California, and the only time I've seen him since college was when he came to my brother's funeral. He's making a lot of money, I know that much."

O'Byrne nodded. "And headed for trouble."

"Which kind?"

"I was out there last winter. I spent a month in California, getting to know people in the oil business. Do you remember a fellow at Princeton named Jack Murphy?"

"No, I don't believe I do. Jack Murphy? It's a fairly common name."

"A class behind us. He was never any particular friend of mine, but he was Irish and we had the same feeling at Princeton that you and Harbord would have had if you'd been at Fordham. But I looked him up last winter and he was exceedingly cordial. Hospitable. He asked about you and of course wanted to know about your brother and what happened there. I wasn't able to give him any inside dope, which caused him to infer that you and I weren't very great buddies, and therefore he spoke freely. He said you had a son out there—which I didn't know—and that the son was going to be the next Lockwood that got in the papers. Don't you know *any* of this, George?"

"Nothing about any trouble," said George. "What *kind* of trouble?"

"Well, Murph told me that if your son doesn't get a bullet in his head from some jealous husband, he's liable to get one from somebody in the oil business."

"The jealous husband part doesn't surprise me. The other part does. I had the impression that he was making quite a name for himself in the oil business."

"Quite a name is right," said O'Byrne. "According to Murph—and some other fellows I met—there are lots of dirty tricks in the oil business, and your kid knows every one of them. Apparently he made a nice pile of money legitimately, through some friend of his."

"The father of a friend of his," said George.

"But he wasn't satisfied with that," said O'Byrne. "Who ever is? And when you're that young—"

"Don't start making excuses for him, Ned. You'll only confuse the story. Go on."

"I may have been making excuses for myself, too," said O'Byrne. "At all events, he pulled a real fast one. This is the way I got it from Murph. Your kid went into business for himself, as a wildcatter. He bought or leased a lot of equipment and went around to people who had land leases but couldn't raise the money to dig wells. He dug a well for a man named Smith. Not Smith, but that's a good enough name. After a month or two he went to Smith and said he had no more money, knowing that Smith had none, either. He told Smith that unless they got more money, he was going to have to abandon the well, and that it didn't seem to him that there was much hope anyway. Smith of course wasn't very happy about that, and he wasn't going to make any effort to try and raise more money. So they agreed to forget the whole thing, and your kid began to remove his equipment."

"He actually moved the equipment away?"

"Dismantled the derrick and so on and put the stuff on trucks. Just one more dry well. Charge it off to experience. Better luck next time. Your kid said he heard about some property in Mexico that he thought he'd try next, but he was convinced there was nothing on Smith's property. Then some guy came along and offered Smith a few dollars an acre for grazing land. And Smith, short of cash, sold his lease to the stranger. A week later the derrick was back in place, all the equipment in working order, and digging was resumed *Two* weeks later they had a gusher."

"And my son was the owner of the oil leases? How clever of him."

"Well, it was clever if you don't mind living under a sentence of death. Smith has threatened to get even with him, and your kid takes the threat seriously enough to carry a gun. Never goes anywhere without one. Comes home at night and makes sure no one is hiding in the bushes around his house."

"It doesn't seem to me that Smith was very smart. Why did he believe my son when he said it was a dry well?"

"I guess because your son really knows the oil business. And until then he had a good reputation."

"That probably would explain how my son knew there really was oil there," said George. "If Smith got a good lawyer, he could probably sue my son for misrepresentation. The man who bought the lease from Smith—"

"A small ranch-owner. Nobody."

"But a man who might be subpoenaed to testify against my son. Therefore a potential blackmailer. Otherwise it was a good scheme, wasn't it? Not admirable from the standpoint of ethics, but I believe they have a different set of ethics in the oil business."

"You don't seem very shocked by this," said O'Byrne.

"Why pretend? I'm *not* shocked. It would be nice if our children grew up to be respectable and successful. But if they can't be both, it's some comfort to know that they're successful. You have no children, so you wouldn't understand that."

"Then I didn't have to worry about telling you all this?"

"Thank you for worrying, Ned. But I'm certainly not going to worry much about my son," said George. "Looking at it another way, with complete selfishness, if he'd turned out differently, I would be the scoundrel. I practically banished him, you know. He was expelled from Princeton for cheating, and I was very unsympathetic. So he went out to California and got in the oil business. Made a fortune legitimately, made a second fortune crookedly, and thereby confirmed my harsh opinion of him. Frankly, Ned, what you've told me here makes me sigh with relief."

"You always *were* rather peculiar," said Ned O'Byrne.

"So were you. You used to have ideas of living in Ireland, fishing for salmon and filling yourself with Irish whiskey. You had a lot of odd ideas. Something about Africa, long ago. What's happened to you, Ned? Money?"

"Probably. For the first time in my life I have enough of it to do what I wanted to, like living in Ireland. But instead of one million, I now want two million. And I don't think I'd be very contented fishing for salmon. It wouldn't be as exciting as matching wits against the stock market. The way I trade, George, I could lose it all in a couple of bad days. I may yet end up in Ireland, but I'm beginning to doubt it."

"How does your wife feel about all this?"

"You've met Kathleen," said O'Byrne. "Did she strike you as the sort of woman who wanted to live thirty-five miles from the nearest hairdresser?"

"You have a point. In other words, she wouldn't care to join you in the salmon fishing."

"She wouldn't mind living in Dublin, especially if I became a papal count and all that. But she's a city girl, and she'll never be anything else."

"You're a city boy," said George.

"Against my will. I would like to have a small house within walking distance of an Irish village and not too far from a well-stocked stream. When I wanted conversation I'd have the local doctor, the solicitor, and the parish priest in for a meal. But that wouldn't be often. I'd be content with my books, hundreds of books that I've put off reading, and some to reread. At intervals I'd go to Dublin or Belfast for a piece of tail. I'd have a Baby Austin but no telephone, and a deaf old woman to cook for me and do the housework."

"Why deaf?"

"Because I'd prefer to keep our conversation at a minimum. Once I got her well trained there'd be weeks at a time when we wouldn't have to exchange two words. She, of course, would live out, but would bring me my tea in the morning."

"There is no wife in this picture," said George.

"No, there isn't, is there. The only reason I have a wife in New York is for protection. Protection from all the women who are looking for a husband. To me, having a wife is like having a lawyer. If you have a lawyer, the other lawyers don't look for your business. I may say they're slightly more ethical about it than women. Slightly. No, there's no wife in the picture I've drawn. Only whores. I've never had the kind of vitality that a husband ought to have. As far as I know, I'm perfectly normal. Heterosexual, that is. But I seem to be able to get along without a screw longer than most of my friends. When I want it, I want it just as much as anybody, but not as often. For that reason I'd have done better to stay a bachelor. I don't wish to imply that Kathleen is insatiable, but she's never believed that I haven't had a lot of women on the side."

"Haven't you?"

"Not very many."

"How many?" said George.

"Oh, that'd be impossible to say at my age. In the hundreds. But that's because there have been so many women that I only slept with once. Variety. A madam will call me up and say she has a new girl she thinks I'll like. So I obligingly present myself, and that's it. The number of women wouldn't matter except that every time I go to bed with one of those girls, I'm being unfaithful to my wife. Statistically, Kathleen is right. I've been unfaithful to her hundreds of times. But if I weren't married to her, I'd be considered just a guy that gets laid once or twice a month. Not many normal men can get along on as little as that."

"A very interesting point of view. I've never thought of it that way. I always considered you a bit of a whoremaster."

"When in fact I'm comparatively ascetic. Would you be interested in having your ashes hauled this evening?"

"I might be. I couldn't be sure until I saw the woman," said George.

"They're whores. That is, they do it for money. But they're not cheap, and they don't look cheap. We could have dinner with them right here and you wouldn't be ashamed to be seen with them."

"I'd rather go some place else for dinner. I've already seen two Racquet Club fellows come in and out of here. One with his wife. And thanks to my brother, I'm semi-notorious."

"Why semi?"

"Semi, because not many people recognize me, but they recognize the name. We'll take the ladies some place else."

An hour or so later the foursome was formed in another speakeasy in Fifty-fifth Street. The women were strikingly handsome. The blonde, who was for O'Byrne, had a fixed grin. Her name was Elaine, and her manner revealed that she was not one of the girls whom O'Byrne had seen only once before. The other girl—neither woman was yet thirty—was rather dramatically turned out in a shiny black silk suit with a white piqué dickey below a bare chest, sheer black silk stockings and black patent-leather pumps. She wore no hat, and her black hair was slicked down, parted in the middle, with buns over her ears.

"And what did you say your name was?" said George.

"Angela. And no cracks," she said.

"Angela what?"

"Angela Schuyler."

"But you can call her Schultzie," said the blonde.

"If you do I'll hit you right over the head with this," said Angela, raising a patent-leather handbag. She turned to George. "What name do you go by?"

"George Lockwood."

"I know that name from somewhere. Are you from the Coast?"

"No, I'm from Pennsylvania. Why? Do you know some Lockwoods on the Coast?"

"I know one named George Lockwood, the same as you. But a lot younger," said Angela.

"It's a fairly common name," said George.

"Yeah, and maybe you just took it," she said.

"No, it's really my name," said George.

They ordered dinner, and the girls displayed their knowledge of the most expensive foods without studying the menu. The blonde also contributed suggestions for the wines. "This Ginzo has as good a wine list as you'll find anywhere," she said. "He bought some rich guy's cellar when he died."

"How do you know so much about wine?" said George.

"How do I know so much about wine? I'm a Ginzo myself. Don't let the blond hair fool you."

"It doesn't fool anybody," said Angela. "And if it does, they soon find out."

"Yeah, but it costs them plenty to find out, doesn't it, Ned? He can speak from experience."

"Do we have to talk about money?" said Angela. "George, you give me a hundred dollars now and we don't have to talk about it any more."

George opened his notecase and took out several new never-folded bills. "Will two fifties do?"

"Uh-huh. That makes it easier to count," said Angela. "Now we can all relax." She put the money in her purse and became gracious. All through the meal George caught her minute studies of him, of his clothes, of his hands, of his hair, of his teeth, and of his interest in her bare chest. She could not have been more thorough if she had been planning to buy him. "This Lockwood on the Coast, he reminded me a little of you. Or the other way around, I guess. What business are you in?"

"I'm in the investment business."

"Investment. Do you ever invest in any oil wells?"

"Never have, but I'm told it can be very profitable," said George.

"Yes, I know some chaps in the oil business and I never met a stingy one yet," she said. Her study of him continued to be intensive.

After dinner they went to two other speakeasies, and O'Byrne wanted to go to Harlem. "I'm afraid you'll have to count me out on that," said George. "I have to get up early."

"No Harlem for me, either," said Angela.

"Come on, a good dirty show," said the blonde.

"I've seen them," said Angela.

"*Seen* them? I'll say you have," said the blonde.

"So if you'll excuse us," said George hastily.

"Yes, and don't talk so much, Elaine. You only have one thing bigger than your mouth and you know what that is," said Angela.

"So do you," said Elaine.

The men shook hands, the women did not even say good-night. In the taxi Angela told George her address, an apartment house on Central Park West. "I just took it for granted you didn't want to go to your hotel," she said. "Anyway, I don't like going to hotels. The bellhops get to know you. I knew a friend of mine was up in the Casino the other night and who should keep pestering her but some bellhop from some hotel. A fag, at that. She couldn't place him, in his Tux, but he kept trying to sit at her table. She was out with some movie producer and I guess the fag wanted to meet him. If there's anything I can't stand it's a fag. They cause more trouble than they're worth. You got a couple at that club of yours."

"What club?"

"Isn't that the Tennis and Racquet tie you're wearing?"

"Racquet and Tennis, but very observing. The Tennis and Racquet is a Boston organization."

"I would of known you were a member without the tie," she said. "Say, that rings a bell. The Lockwood from the Coast, *he's* a member, too. He was wearing the self-same tie. Come on, give."

"He's my son," said George.

"Well can you imagine that! What a small world. But not small enough, huh?"

"You mean not big enough."

"That's what I mean. Not big enough. You don't mind, do you?"

"Mind what?"

"Well, me and your son, and now you. *I* don't mind, but with you it might be mental. We'll try it and see, huh? When I get my clothes off maybe you won't care. And don't forget, I don't get a hundred dollars a night for just having a good shape. I had a friend of mine last year, he sent for me all the way from London, England. Two nights in London, and then back to New York. That must of set him back plenty. And he gave *me* a thousand. I told him, I said I wouldn't go over for less. I didn't tell him I made some on the boat coming back. I just told him, I said two weeks the minimum I'll be away from New York. You could figure that for fourteen hundred. I like to *average* a hundred dollars a night. It won't be long before I'm not as pretty as I am now, so I'm getting it while I can."

"And then what?" said George.

"Well, I was thinking of getting married. Or else I was thinking of opening a beauty parlor. Get some john to set me up in business. The prices these hairdressers get. You know, seven dollars a curl for a permanent. You notice I don't have a permanent, not because I'm afraid to spend the money. But with my particular looks—here we are."

It was a small apartment. The livingroom was astonishingly tasteful, as though furnished and decorated by a professional from W. & J. Sloane. The period was Colonial American, and in the entire room the only item of identification with Angela Schuyler was a cabinet-size photograph of herself in a silver frame. The photograph was from the White Studio, and in it Angela was wearing a black satin evening dress with two panels that covered the nipples of her breasts but left the rest of her torso bare. "You go in for black and white," said George.

"The hell I do, that's why I wouldn't go to Harlem," she said.

"I was referring to your clothes."

"Oh, that's different," said Angela. "You want to take a bath? I'll take one with you if you want to."

"That'd be fine."

"Unless you'd rather I didn't."

"I'd rather you did. I've never done that."

"You never took a bath with a girl? Not even your wife?"

"Not even my wife," he said.

Her bedroom was not done by a professional from W. & J. Sloane. The bed was large enough for four adults. The chairs, dressing table, chaise longue and framework of three sets of triplicate mirrors were done in matching ivory, touched with gilt. "I've been trying to get up enough nerve to put a meer up in the ceiling, but that'd be the tip-off. When I signed the lease I was working for Carroll. Earl Carroll. And I put down show girl for my occupation. But if the owner ever came in here and saw a meer up in the ceiling, that'd be the tip-off. The building is full of married couples, middle-aged if not past it. Care for a drink?"

"No thanks," he said.

She opened a dresser drawer and took out a white leather-bound photograph album. She tossed it to him. "Have a look at these. They'll put you in the mood," she said.

"Pictures of you?" he said.

"Christ, no! Take a look."

The photographs were glossy prints of men and women engaged in various forms of sexual activity. She stood behind him as he turned the pages, and he became conscious of her hand on the back of his neck, rubbing his skin when he lingered over a photograph, holding her hand still between pictures. "I wanted to see which ones you liked best," she said.

"Which do you?" he said.

"I'm not saying."

"Let me guess," he said.

"Go ahead," she said.

"You liked the one of the young boy," he said.

"The kid with the big dingus. How did you know?"

"Pure guesswork," he said. It had not been guesswork at all; her hand on his neck had revealed her agitation.

"Imagine a young kid with a thing like that? Elaine told me she saw the boy, putting on a dirty show in Cuba. The picture's not a fake. I thought it was a fake, but Elaine saw him. That thing must be a yard long."

"Oh, not a yard. Not even a foot."

"But on a kid fourteen years old. Maybe fifteen. What a future he has!"

"That picture puts *you* in the mood, doesn't it?"

"You want to know the truth? Yes, it does. Sometimes I dream about that kid. He could make a fortune if he came to New York. A fortune." She stood up and stretched her arms back as far as they would go, then suddenly she took off her jacket and the dickey and put her hands over her bare breasts, and looked down as she gently squeezed them. "The best in New York City," she said. "Aren't they something?"

"Yes they are," he said.

He was not equal to the demands created in her by the picture of the Cuban boy, but as a professional she was there to entertain him and she did. When it was over she washed him and lit a cigarette for him. "How often do you come to New York?" she said.

"Fairly frequently," he said.

"But with your wife."

"Not always."

"When'll you be here again?"

"The day after tomorrow, passing through. Changing trains. Then I'm not sure when I'll be back again. Why?"

"Do you want to make a date for between trains? I'll be here. Or is that rushing you?"

"It might be."

"And you have to give your wife a screw when you get home. Is that it?"

"Well, I'll have to be ready to."

"That's where your kid had the advantage."

"My kid? God, I forgot all about him."

"Sure you did. I fixed that. That's where I'm good, see? Any common ordinary hooker can give you a quick lay, but I sized you up all evening."

"You're absolutely wonderful," he said. "That's the kind of thinking I admire. If you knew me better you'd know that."

"Oh, sure," she said. "If you had that kid on your mind all night you'd of blamed me for it."

"What did you mean about his having an advantage?"

"You have to go home the day after tomorrow and be ready to give your wife a screw. But your kid had five days' train-ride before he saw his wife."

"I see," said George.

"Five days on a train, he'd be as horny as a guy just out of prison. He is anyway. I'll bet you were the same way when you were younger. Did you used to go around with a hard on when you were young?"

"Yes, I guess I did."

"A few hours' sleep and you'd be all set again, but I don't allow anybody to stay here all night. Not anybody. It's against my rules. So I guess if you're gonna get any sleep you better go back to your hotel. Take down my number, but be sure and don't write down my name. There's not many people have this number, and I change it every so often."

"Angela, I'd like to ask you something."

"Anything. You're entitled," she said.

"Then I'll ask you two things. First, did you really deliberately go about taking my mind off my son tonight? Or was that an afterthought?"

"I can prove it to you. O'Byrne and Elaine would have stayed in that Ginzo's place all night, but who was it said let's go some place else? Me. So we went to the Aquarium. Then who was it said let's get out of the Aquarium and go to the Ball and Chain? Me. And when we got here, who showed you the dirty pictures? This could of been a lousy evening for the both of us if you kept thinking about that kid, but it didn't turn out that way, did it? You gave me a pretty good time, I gave you a pretty good time. What's the other question?"

"You've more or less answered it. I was going to ask you if you really got pleasure out of this work."

"Most of the time. You know the old gag. She gave away a million dollars' worth before she found out she could sell it. I take on some fellows that almost turn my stomach, what they like to do. But we're all human, and the money is good. I bank an average of five hundred dollars a week, clear profit. And I got a promise of backing for my beauty parlor. A hustler has three worries. The Vice Squad. The mob. And getting a dose. Well, I never let a week go by without my doctor checking up on me. And I have a politician that takes care of the Vice Squad and the mob boys. You have to have a politician in this business, otherwise the mob moves in and you do what they say. Which usually means you're only good for two or three years of the good money."

"Do you pay the politician?"

"Oh, he's too big to keep it himself, if that's what you mean. The money I give him goes to the party. Small change to him. That's not saying I don't do him other favors."

"Such as?"

"Like spying on other politicians. Like spying on men that aren't politicians, too."

"You could be spying on me, for that matter."

She shook her head. "I never *heard* of you till tonight."

"I see. I'm not important enough," said George.

"Maybe you're important, but I never heard of you. The ones they use me for are the big shots, that everybody heard of. Like the fellow I went to London for two days. In June I was in Saratoga for a Democratic convention. I only got my expenses, but since then *they* owe *me* a favor. A contract. In politics they say a contract. Any cop or any mobster that gives me the least bit of trouble. I just make one little phone call. A certain Bogardus number, that's all."

"Do you ever accept these contracts for people that aren't in politics?"

"You mean getting something on somebody?"

"I was thinking more of getting information."

"You want me to spy on somebody? Who? Some friend of yours?"

"Not exactly," said George. "A young man who just married my daughter."

"What the hell do you want to spy on *him* for? If your daughter married him my advice to you is stay out of it. Maybe I'd find out something about her that you wouldn't like. Politicians and big shots I don't mind. But a young married couple, give them a chance. I had a mother-in-law that was always interfering. No, no contract. I'd feel like a shit-heel. Your daughter won't end up a hustler, but my advice to you is stay out of it. Maybe she's like me. I wouldn't of stayed married to Frank as long as I did if it wasn't for his mother interfering."

"She is like you, my daughter. Very much so, if the truth be told," he said. "Well, Angela, it's been a very interesting evening, and I never thought it was going to be. Dinner with an old college friend doesn't usually turn out so well."

"Do you have a yacht?"

"Afraid I'm not in that class," said George. "Why?"

"Oh, I was looking for a ride on a yacht over the weekend. The summer's almost over and I only went cruising twice since June. I like to get out of town over the weekend. There's never anybody in town Saturday except actors. Anyway, how about giving me a ring on your way through town? I gave you the number."

"I'll call you at half past ten the day after tomorrow. If that isn't too early for you."

"You couldn't make it half past eleven?"

"Very well. Half past eleven."

"How did you like Elaine?" said Angela.

"Elaine? She was all right, I guess. Very pretty. Why?"

"Well, if you took a later train, I could have Elaine here. You wouldn't be any good for your wife, but I guarantee you, you'd have some fun."

"It wouldn't be the day after tomorrow, now. It'd be tomorrow. I'm going to my hotel to get a few hours' sleep, then a train to Pennsylvania, and tonight I'll be on a sleeper. So it'd be tomorrow, in point of fact. I think I'll need a little more rest, but I will telephone you at eleven-thirty. *Tomorrow*."

"Now don't forget. I *like* you."

"I'm glad to hear it. I like *you*," said George.

"I wouldn't trust you for a minute, and I'll bet you can be a real son of a bitch. But all the same I like you, and I don't say that to everybody. And I'll tell you frankly, I *didn't* like your kid."

"Well, I don't like him much myself, Angela."

"That I could tell. Now you better take a run-out powder or I'll start working on you and you'll *never* get any sleep."

"You're a very sweet girl, Angela. I hope we see a lot of each other."

"We will. I don't want you to go, but it's ten minutes of four. Soon it'll be daylight." She put her arms around him and kissed him, then handed him his hat. "Out. Scram," she said. She took his arm, led him to the door, and nudged him into the hall and closed the door.

In the taxi, all the way to the Carstairs, he was in a state of euphoria for which the right explanation eluded him. Then he remembered Eulalie Fenstermacher, the prim voluptuary, who had once produced in him the same happiness. Thirty years later he was falling in love with a genuine whore, and in what way could a whore fail him?

In Swedish Haven and in Gibbsville he attended to his business according to plan. Arthur McHenry, salt of the earth as usual and as usual considerate of the other man's time, had mercifully concise explanations of all the papers that were to be signed on this trip. He avoided small talk and discouraged the few casual visitors to their table at the Gibbsville Club. Their business and their lunch were completed before two-thirty. "I've taken the liberty of hiring a car for you," said Arthur. "It's a nice little Buick coupe. Rented it from Julian English. He just took it in trade on a Cadillac and he didn't want to charge you anything, but I insisted. Five dollars for the day. You can leave it here this evening when you're finished with it. Give the key to whoever's at the desk."

"I'm glad you insisted on payment. I don't like to accept favors from Julian English."

"Well, that's your business, George. He's not a bad fellow, but he does rub people the wrong way," said Arthur. "Once he settles down he'll probably become as stodgy as his father. Or me, for that matter. Now if there's anything else you want me to do, I'll be at my office. If you want to talk to Joe Chapin, he'll be in court till four, but he should be in the office around five."

"I can't think of anything that's likely to come up," said George. "You've taken care of everything in your usual masterly fashion."

"Well, most of it could have been done by a law clerk, but I like to go over everything so that your New York lawyers can't find any fault with what we do. Joe and I may be a couple of hayseeds, but we don't want the New York fellows to find that out. You understand that stuff about posting the bond, and those disbursements that we're charging against Pen's widow's share."

"All clear."

"Fine. Then I think I'll run along, George. Nice to've seen you. Please remember me to Geraldine and our best wishes to Tina."

"Thank you, Arthur. See you in a few weeks," said George. He would see no one in a few weeks.

HE parked the borrowed Buick in front of the garage, which was locked. He peered inside the garage, where the Lincoln was jacked up and covered for the summer. Thus shrouded and given the extra height of the blocks under the axles, the car seemed enormous. He made a mental note to give some future consideration to a trade-in on a new limousine. Brewster was putting out a town car on a Ford chassis that was just the kind of swank that Geraldine would enjoy. Geraldine was going to benefit in such ways from her altered position in his life. He wondered how long it would be —not long, surely—before she became fully aware that her position had been altered. He would stay married to her, continue to be courteous and generous to her, and he probably would sleep with her, since marriage to Angela was out of the question. On the other hand, if Geraldine decided to make trouble, even a little trouble, he would deal with that at the proper time. At the moment he was working on a schedule that went only as far ahead as the Christmas dance for Tina and her husband. At the moment Angela Schultz-Schuyler was in ignorance of the coming alteration of her position in life. Inevitably she, a retiring whore, would give him trouble; he was not deceiving himself on that. In a year, possibly sooner, she would have a tantrum and say, "Where am I better off than I used to be?" He would be prepared for such outbursts, and the most solid preparation would be to have Angela convince herself that she wanted to be his mistress, solely his mistress, and to let the idea seem to originate with her. It was an important point and would take some doing, but if he could not out-general a whore, he did not deserve to dominate her.

He was pleased with the way things were turning out for him. Another man—yes, a *lesser* man—would be crushed by the disasters of the past year. A lesser man *was* crushed and had created the principal disaster by murdering his mistress and killing himself. A lesser man, listening to the sordid confession of his daughter, would have succumbed to anger and self-pity. And a lesser man, informed that his youngish son was an outstanding crook among crooks, would surrender to shame, a shame that he might not feel so deeply as he felt that he *ought* to feel shame. Each disaster would have been crushing to an inferior individual; and when all three had made impossible a man's lifelong ambition of an enduring place in the history of his homeland, he had all the necessary excuses to plead for charity. An inferior man, getting closer to sixty, would allow himself to be subdued by charity and spend the rest of his days subsisting on compassion. But not George Lockwood.

In the whole country there was not—may never have been—a man who had come through such ordeals and vicissitudes with his spirit intact. No, not only spirit; integrity was better. Old Moses Lockwood, a man of vigor and violence, had survived and prevailed; Abraham Lockwood, the first of the line to learn manners, had behaved like a gentleman and misbehaved with the gentlemen's ladies; and George Lockwood's son, a scoundrel already, was almost predictably a man of national notoriety who would be immune to the tiny pinches of small morals. When the friendly biographer prepared the life story of Bing Lockwood—in 1960, at a guess—he would not fail to emphasize the integrity and independence that had been so characteristic of the family from generation to generation. George Lockwood now believed that the major triumph would belong to his son, but he was *his* son, just as he was the son of Abraham and the grandson of Moses. The previous postponements of major triumph were fateful; the Lockwood destiny, the Lockwood dynasty, either or both were awaiting a more suitable moment and a larger stage than the previous century and a small valley in Pennsylvania. J. P. Morgan's grandfather got rich in the hotel and stagecoach businesses before the family left Connecticut.

And why should he not be pleased with the way things were turning out? He was convinced by recent events (and his son's predictable future) that he belonged to a line of men who had proved and would prove that they were of harder stuff than the generations of conventional men who had rejected one Lockwood after another. There for the alert and friendly biographer to see was a record of struggle and conquest that in another day would have elevated the Lockwoods to the status of nobility—if, indeed, it stopped at nobility. The Lockwood women had contributed nothing much but the Lockwood sons, when they had contributed anything. The Lockwood daughters had gone insane or, in the case of Tina, been sterilized. Even Tina had not escaped the madness that had destroyed her great-aunts. George Lockwood would always love his daughter, but what was the use of denying that she was afflicted as her great-aunts had been afflicted, with an emotional disturbance that had left her a barren woman already and a bad risk for future stability? Among the Lockwood men only Pen had acknowledged defeat, yet even he in the final hour of his life had behaved with a kind of vigor and integrity that was not inconsistent with the acts of superior breeds. Self-destruction had never been contemplated by George Lockwood, but there may have been courage as well as desperation among the factors that dictated Pen's decision. In his own peculiar way Pen had met the requirements of the superior breed, as George Lockwood now saw them.

It was the right of the superior breed to do just what he was planning to do. History was crowded with cases of kings who had taken whores as their mistresses. It was almost the mark of the superior man to indulge himself with a female animal of low degree, to flaunt her publicly. The gesture would not be complete if he kept Angela hidden in a flat on Central Park West; in the weeks to come he would determine the extent to which he might conform to the royal precedent. He discovered now that secret liaisons with Marian Strademyers, supposedly exciting because of their secret nature, were actually paid for in a loss of dignity and self-respect. The superior man did as he pleased; the clandestine romance was for the Kevin O'-Byrnes. Were it not for the chance of spoiling Tina's party, he would have enjoyed having Angela make her debut as his mistress at the Christmas dance. Lantenengo County would never recover from that. But the party was for Tina . . .

He turned away from the garage window and saw a man in overalls and a yellow straw hat coming toward him. The man took off his hat and wiped his sweaty skull with a blue bandanna handkerchief.

"Good afternoon," said George.

"Hy, there, Mr. Lockwood. Don't rememper me, hey? Sam

Kitzmiller from the Haven. I work for Chester Stengler. I took care of your garden all summer."

"Uh-huh. Where is Chester?" said George. "I expected him to be here."

"He won't, though. He's down with a case of di'rea. The shits. They all got the shits from the Methodist picnic. Sauerkraut and pork, they say. I wouldn't eat no pork in the summertime if you paid me."

"Well, I am paying you, I guess. But not to eat pork. The garden looks pretty good, from here."

"We need rain. The son of a bitchin' dry spell, water from the hose line ain't the same as rainwater. It got chemicals in it."

"No it hasn't. Our water comes from two wells."

"I know that, but the ground has chemicals in it. Rain. Rain is what we need."

"I suppose you have a point. What else has been going on? Do you come every day?"

"You don't rememper me. I worked for you when you were building here. I was here one day the fellow got bit with a copperhead."

"I do remember you, now. Kitzmiller. Your people go to our church. You have a brother about my age."

"Lamarr."

"Lamarr, that's right. What's he doing now?"

"He moved to Gippsville. He's clerking in Stewart's store, the rug and carpet department."

"What the hell does *he* know about rugs?" said George.

"I guess he learned. He's there twenty-five years already."

"For Christ's sake. When I knew him he had trap-lines and spent all his time in the woods."

"He got married. She made him get a chob."

"And now he's selling rugs at Stewart's."

"He makes more than me, but I wouldn't trade him," said Kitzmiller.

"You must have married the right woman."

"Christ, they're all the same, but I don't take no bullshit. If she don't like how much I make, she can take in washing. But a son of a bitch if I let a woman tell me what work I do."

"A man after my own heart," said George. "Let's take a walk around. Have you got a pencil and paper? If not, I have."

"It'll be better if you write it. I don't get much practice."

"You can read, though, can't you?"

"Reading I don't have any trouble, but writing I don't do much of. What are we writing?"

"Taking notes on what I want done. I'll print the notes, but I'd like you to go along."

"Whatta you doing with such a Buick? Where is them other two nice cars?"

"In Massachusetts. The Buick doesn't belong to me. Why?"

"When yuz get ready to sell your Packard, let me know how much. If she's around four or five hundred I'll make you an offer."

"She won't be around four or five hundred. I expect at least fifteen hundred on a trade. So let's forget about cars and get down to the business at hand," said George. "What's that pile of lumber doing there? That was here when we left, two months ago."

"I guess maybe it was left over from some carpentring."

"It was, but they were supposed to come and get it. If Ed Muller thinks I'm going to pay him for those planks, he's in for a rude shock. If you see Muller, tell him I'm going to charge him storage. And if it's still here when I come back again, I'm going to burn it in my fireplace."

"I'll tell him," said Kitzmiller.

"God damn inefficient, and an eyesore," said George. "Smoke out that hornet's nest on the back porch."

"I'll do that tomorrow."

"And if you see any more, get rid of them. Did you leave that hose lying there overnight?"

"I guess I did," said Kitzmiller.

"How much is a foot of hose, do you know?"

"I guess it runs around ten cents a foot."

"There's a sixty-foot length of hose and a good nozzle. Half full of water and lying there to rot. No wonder you think I'd sell you my Packard for four hundred dollars. You must think I like to throw money away. Well, I don't."

"I'll blow the water out of the hose before I go home."

"You're damn right you will, or don't come back tomorrow. Say, the rhododendrons look nice and healthy."

"I water them with the sprinkling can. But take a look at the ground, how dry it is. The sprinkler's all right for the grass, but the plants and flowers all gotta be done by hand. I'm here till eight o'clock every night, watering. It don't do no good to water till the sun goes down."

"I'm glad to see you know that," said George. "Most people don't. Let's go over this way."

"I got the arbutuses looking nice," said Kitzmiller.

"So I see. My compliments." They were walking on a line parallel with the west wall. George Lockwood came to an abrupt halt, not knowing why. Then he looked at the wall and saw what had stopped him: all along the wall, from one end to the other, ivy had been planted so that in two years the growth fairly well covered the bricking. But there was a gap in the growth about three feet wide that left the wall blank from the ground to the top. "What happened here?"

"How do you mean?" said Kitzmiller.

"Can't you see, man? You're supposed to be a gardener. Look at this wall. A fine growth of ivy the whole length of it except for right here. How do you explain that?"

"Search me," said Kitzmiller. "It don't look like there was anyting planted there."

"Don't tell me this is the first time you noticed it," said George Lockwood.

"Well, it's the first time you noticed it," said Kitzmiller.

"But I've been away all summer. And as a matter of fact I haven't walked in this part of the garden—in quite a while." He involuntarily looked up at the top of the wall, and he saw that Kitzmiller was watching him with an expression of loutish cunning. "What do you know about this, Kitzmiller?"

"I don't know what yuz are talking about," said Kitzmiller.

"You're a stupid, lying bastard," said George Lockwood.

"You watch what you're calling me, Lockwood. I don't get paid for insults, and I'm a man."

"Was it you, or was it Stengler? You left this space blank deliberately."

"It was Stengler, but it would of been me."

"Because this is where the Zehner kid was killed."

"The Zehner kid was related to Stengler and I'm related to Stengler. You come any closer to me and I'll chop you with this sickle."

"Get off this land," said George. "Get—off—my—land!"

Kitzmiller backed away, keeping an eye on George Lockwood until he was at a safe distance. George Lockwood remained where he stood, quivering with the suppressed impulse to murder the man. He was unconscious of time until he heard Stengler's half-ton Ford leave the property, no more than five minutes later, but he felt sleepy. In another minute he would have had to lie on the ground and give in to sleep.

He walked to the house and let himself in through the front door and went to his study. He was too tired to turn on any lights, to do anything but slump down in a chair and yield to the desire to sleep. When he awoke he had again lost track of time, but oddly enough, in spite of the total darkness of the curtained room, he knew where he was and the deep sleep had restored his vitality. He sat in the dark silence and could very nearly feel the strength coming back as his heart pumped the blood through his veins. Eleven seconds, was it not, that it took for a single complete circuit of the cardiovascular system? About five times a minute, if that were true, he was getting new energy. The luminous dial of his wristwatch was so bright that it demanded his attention, although for the moment he was content to forget about time. It was eighteen minutes to six. It was seventeen minutes to six. It was sixteen minutes to six. Fifteen more times the blood had flowed through all those arteries and organs, and as it cleared his brain almost his first thoughts were of Angela Schultz-Schuyler. He knew that tomorrow in New York he was going to interrupt his journey to begin the conversion of her way of life to a way that would be more desirable to him and certainly an improvement for her. If she were with him now they would make love, but he appreciated the favorable aspect of the circumstance that prevented him from appearing over-eager. She must be made to feel that his company was increasingly indispensable to her happiness. He was dealing with a woman whose ugly life had made her a monster of selfishness, defensively and aggressively. She was aware of the cash value of every tooth in her head and every hair on her body, and it was essential to his relationship with her that she be made to believe in love.

He proceeded from the thoughts of her—to which he would later and frequently return—to more immediate realities. The odor of the darkened study was musty, heavy with the smell of leather and wood and the muslin coverings of the furniture in a room that apparently had not been aired all summer. (Inefficiency on the part of Geraldine, who should have seen to that.) The air was so unpleasant that a cigarette or a cigar would have made it worse. Then he had a happy inspiration: since he was dining at the Gibbsville Club, which had long since exhausted its supply of wine, he would treat himself to a bottle of champagne from his own cellar. He was not a connoisseur of champagnes, but almost any he owned would serve the purpose of getting rid of the mustiness of the study, which had lodged in his mouth and nostrils. He would take the bottle to the club with him and he might even share it with one of the dreary men who ate and slept there. If he drank half a bottle at dinner, he probably would sleep better on the train. He congratulated himself on his inspiration and reached out with a sure hand for the light switch. He pulled the chain switch on one lamp.

He got up and turned the gargoyle in the fireplace that opened the panel of the passageway. From force of habit he closed the panel behind him and was again in total darkness. Then something went wrong. Perhaps the transitions from darkness to light to darkness; perhaps the heavy sleep in the bad air; perhaps an incomplete recovery from the extreme provocation by Kitzmiller. Whatever the cause, he fell.

The stairway in the secret passageway wound around a central post and the steps were of uneven width, from zero to eight inches. He missed the first step completely, and he fell to the cellar, buffeted from side to side all the way down. Before even coming to a jolting stop on the cellar floor he knew that his leg was broken. The pain seemed to prolong the fall, and when at last it ended and he lay still, he wondered why he had not landed sooner. In the blackness he was wholly blind and strangely deaf until a silence entered his ears and he realized that he had created the silence by pausing in the midst of his screaming. The lower half of his left leg had twisted itself crazily and did not belong to the rest of him except as the source of his agony. He reached down, impelled by irresistible curiosity, and forced his fingers along his trouser-leg until he could touch the broken skin. Beyond that his fingers would not go, and for the first time he fainted. But consciousness returned immediately; the pain was too lively for quick relief, and he was trying to shout again. Now a previously unnoticed pain competed with the shrill agony of his leg. He put his fingers to the right side of his skull and touched a sticky substance that he knew was blood. The scalp was cut. The roaring sound he was hearing could have been his own voice in a cave, and this passageway was a sort of cave. In the blindness of the dark he could not tell whether he had actually lost his sight, a symptom he vaguely remembered as having to do with a skull fracture. He held up his left wrist; he could not see the dial of his watch. He was blind.

He did not need his sight to observe the next development. It came out of his nostrils without extra pain but with an urgency that was like a bursting dam. It cascaded over his mouth and sickened him, and now he knew that he was going to die. He lost consciousness once more and this time when he awoke he found that his body—not he—was fighting for breath. A compartment of his intellect contained the information that he could not last the night, and that it would be morning before anyone would help him. Who would miss him? He had made no engagement for dinner. A woman in New York (he could not think of her name) was expecting him to telephone her, tomorrow. The man whom he had last seen, Kitzmiller, would not be here tomorrow. And who knew of the existence of the secret passageway? One man, Hibbard, and no one else but the vanished craftsmen who had built it. And so this was the way it all ended, to die hoping to die because there was no hope of living. He screamed again, but the cry was muffled by the stuff that was strangling him. Then soon—always soon, no matter when—came the moment that no one has ever told anyone about. And no one will ever tell anyone about, because it is a secret that belongs to Them.

FINE WORKS OF FICTION AND NON-FICTION AVAILABLE FROM CARROLL & GRAF

☐	Brown, Harry/A WALK IN THE SUN	$3.95
☐	De Quincey, Thomas/CONFESSIONS OF AN ENGLISH OPIUM EATER AND OTHER WRITINGS	$4.95
☐	Farrell, J.G./THE SIEGE OF KRISHNAPUR	$4.95
☐	Friedman, Bruce Jay/LET'S HEAR IT FOR A BEAUTIFUL GUY	$3.95
☐	Gurney Jr., A.R./THE SNOW BALL	$4.50
☐	Hayes, Joseph/THE DESPERATE HOURS	$3.50
☐	Higgins, George V./A CHOICE OF ENEMIES	$3.50
☐	Higgins, George V./A CITY ON A HILL	$3.50
☐	Higgins, George V./COGAN'S TRADE	$3.50
☐	Hilton, James/RANDOM HARVEST	$4.50
☐	Huxley, Aldous/GREY EMINENCE	$4.95
☐	Innes, Hammond/ATLANTIC FURY	$3.50
☐	Innes, Hammond/THE LAND GOD GAVE TO CAIN	$3.50
☐	Innes, Hammond/SOLOMON'S SEAL	$3.50
☐	Innes, Hammond/THE WRECK OF THE MARY DEARE	$3.50
☐	Johnson, Josephine/NOW IN NOVEMBER	$4.50
☐	Kuppig, Chris (ed.)/NINETEEN EIGHTY FOUR TO 1984	$3.95
☐	L'Amour, Louis/LAW OF THE DESERT BORN	$2.95